PRINCESS OF

gossip

PRINCE

POCKET BOOKS

New York   London   Toronto   Sydney

SS OF

gossip

Sabrina Bryan and
Julia DeVillers

Pocket Books
A Division of Simon & Schuster, Inc.
1230 Avenue of the Americas
New York, NY 10020

First MTV Books/Pocket Books trade paperback edition October 2008

Designed by Jamie Kerner

Manufactured in the United States of America

10 9 8 7 6 5 4 3 2 1

Library of Congress Cataloging-in-Publication Data
Bryan, Sabrina
   Princess of gossip / by Sabrina Bryan and Julia DeVillers—1st MTV Books/Pocket Books trade
paperback ed.
       p.   cm.
   Summary: After moving to Los Angeles from Ohio, a celebrity-obsessed high school student's
life changes drastically when she inadvertently becomes a popular internet gossip columnist.
   [1. Gossip—Fiction.   2. Internet—Fiction.   3. Dating (Social customs)—
Fiction.   4. Celebrities—Fiction.   5. High schools—Fiction.   6. Schools—Fiction.   7. Los
Angeles (Calif.)—Fiction.]   I. DeVillers, Julia.   II. Title.
   PZ7.B8295Pr2008
   [Fic]—dc22   2008021142

ISBN-13: 978-1-4165-7065-3
ISBN-10:   1-4165-7065-9

To Team Sabrina, who inspires us every day

ACKNOWLEDGMENTS

I have to thank God for all of the people and opportunities he has put in my life to help make all my dreams come true. Mom and Dad, you are the most important people in my life and your unconditional love has always been the rock that gives me the courage to reach for the stars. Having our family as a foundation, I know that anything is possible and I can conquer any obstacle. Thank you for everything, I love you so much! Starr, my amazing sister! I love you so much, thank you for always being there to support me in every way possible. I'm so blessed to have you to experience every emotion that sisters get to share together. My family for being my biggest fans who show their love with every new and exciting project. You mean so much to me and I love you with all my heart.

My Cheetah family!!! Kiely, I don't know what my life would be like without my Kiki! Every day is an adventure with us together (even if it's just going to Robos) and I love every minute of it. You inspire me to be a better person and to reach far and beyond my dreams. We have a friendship that will last a lifetime and I can't wait to see what kind of adventures we have in the future. Adrienne, your drive is so incredible and I've learned so much just watching you charge toward your dreams without holding back. You always keep me laughing and enjoying each second of the amazing experiences we share. I love you Cheetahs! Shi Shi . . . the car rides, the couch days, and the lunch dates . . . all my fav activities we share. I love that we rely on each other through the ups and downs. I love you!! Wen, Tiff, and Ricky thank you for being the people I can always turn to when I'm away from home. Muah!!! Taffy my baby. Over the years you have been more than a best friend. You've been a sister that has always been there, and I can't thank you enough. You've been through it all and I couldn't have gotten through some of those times without you. I love you Taf. TNT it's Dynomite! Markiss, you are such an amazing surprise God gave me this year that I'm so thankful for. You came in and made me remember why I love doing what I do. I'm so excited to watch you grow into becoming everything you are destined to be!!! Nalgas! xxx

Nicole, Julie, David, Gayle, and Mel B. at William Morris, thank you for providing the opportunities to reach every star I'm aiming for. I love you guys. David you still owe me a round of golf :) David L, thanks so much for making sure that I am taken care of and being on my team. Julia, thank you so much for pairing up with me to do this book. I never thought that this was a dream that could ever come true until I met you! You are amazing in every way! I had such a great time working with you and learned so much! Thank you, thank you, thank you!!!! Mel . . . how can I even begin to thank my partner in action!?! I love you and thank you for everything you do. You gave me the courage to take my idea, put it on a piece of paper, and make it happen. There's so much for us to conquer and God is going to continue to help us make all of our dreams come true. Thank you so much, I couldn't have done this without you! Pura Vida :)

To the fans! Thank you all so much. You have always been so supportive, which has allowed more doors to open for me. All of your love inspires me to continue to keep making more projects that hopefully show you that you really can do anything you want as long as you work your hardest for it. So, dream big!!! I love you! Muah!

Xoxo,
Sabrina

And the above is why I'm proud to have written a book with Sabrina.

Sabrina, I remember when I first met you how you were getting your first taste of fame. You were so gracious to your fans and everyone around you, and I love how that hasn't changed as you've become such a shining star. It's so fun that I now get to thank you for being my insightful, articulate, hilarious, and talented co-AUTHOR!!!

Melissa Wiechmann, producer and visionary . . . Sabrina eloquently thanked you, but I get my turn, too. This book wouldn't exist without you! Mel, you're brilliant! My family: Dave, Quinn, and Jack DeVillers . . . Mom, Jennifer Roy (my twin sister and the songwriter behind Griffin's lyrics), Adam Roy, and Amy Rozines . . . so much love!

And I have the honor of thanking the team at MTV Books, especially Jennifer Heddle, Anthony Ziccardi, Jacob Hoye, Erica Feldon, Lisa Litwack, and Kerrie Loyd. And one more shout-out to Mel Berger at William Morris . . . You rock.

While the characters and scenarios in this book are fiction, the fan love was inspired by Sabrina's fans. Team Sabrina . . . thanks.

Julia

PRINCESS OF

gossip

1

MySpace BULLETIN

From: Avery [inLA]
Date: October 11—3:45 p.m.
Subject: Vote in my poll!!

I survived the school day! Now where should I go? All you have to do is vote & I pinky-swear to give you the *exclusive inside details* every step of the way!

- Shopping in Beverly Hills—Celebrity views + Jimmy Choos all in one place!
- A concert at the Hollywood Bowl—I'll take pics for you guys from the front row—*and* backstage after the show!
- The set of a TV show at the studios—What's gonna happen on our favorite show next season? I'll watch them film it—& give you all the spoilers!
- A movie premiere and after-party—Let's walk down the red carpet . . . & hit the VIP after-party later!

No matter what you choose, I'll give you all the celebrity sightings & all access—

*R*rrrring!

Dang it. The phone rang, completely interrupting my train of thought. I put the laptop down on the round, furry chair I'd been sitting on and got up to look for the phone. I could hear it ringing from somewhere in my bedroom. Dang it again, I tripped over a cardboard box that was marked *Avery/Magazines*.

We'd moved into this house almost a month ago and a lot of my stuff was still in boxes, waiting for me to put it someplace. I'd convinced my parents before we moved to ditch my old bedroom furniture I'd had since I was eight. They had promised me I could get new furniture, including a bookcase just to hold all my magazines. But we hadn't even started shopping yet. All I had right now was a mattress, my old turquoise comforter set, and boxes. My room theme could be called Modern Cardboard Box. I kicked one of the boxes off to the side.

Rrrrring!

Rrrrring!

I narrowed the ringing noise down to somewhere on my bed. I moved a pile of clothes, my backpack, some pillows . . . and there it was. I saw my mom's cell number on the caller ID.

"Hi, Mom," I said.

"Hi, honey. I just wanted to let you know that Dad and I are working late tonight. Did you finish your homework?"

Um . . .

"Avery? Your homework is done, correct?" my mom said.

Uh . . .

Then I heard a phone ringing in the background on her end. Excellent. It was perfect timing for my mom's business line to be interrupting our call.

"Oh, I have to take this," she said. "Love you!"

I heard a click as she hung up. Yes! Thank you, customer, for interrupting us, as well as—I hoped—buying products from my parents' new company. I went back over to my chair and set my laptop back on my knees. But I was no longer in the mood to write any more of the MySpace bulletin; my mom's call had snapped me back into reality.

I reread my poll. Shopping! Concerts! TV sets! Movie premieres! Oh, the glam possibilities of life in Los Angeles. Unfortunately, those were options in somebody else's life, not mine.

It's pretty pathetic when the most exciting thing that happens in my day is making up a fake fantasy bulletin.

I held down the delete button and erased everything I'd typed. My parents always said I had an active imagination. I started a new bulletin and typed in a real poll.

MySpace BULLETIN

From: Avery [inLA]
Date: October 11—3:45 p.m.
Subject: Vote in my poll!!

I survived the school day! Now what?!

- Do my homework!
- Do some laundry!
- Make ramen noodles for dinner!
- Wait for you guys to text me!

Yes, those were my real choices. I clicked send and watched my lame bulletin pop up on my bulletin list. My life pretty much consisted of school, homework, and being online. Shopping in Beverly Hills? A concert? I had no ride and no money. The TV set or movie premiere? Right . . . like I had any clue how to even find them, much less get into them.

MySpace BULLETIN

From: Avery [inLA]
Date: October 11—4:10 p.m.
Subject: asfgdsl

  boredom sux
  please start a conversation with me
  now!!!!

Hello . . . people? Where were my Ohio friends in my time of need? It was around dinnertime there, so somebody should've been available to chat with me.

I felt a pang knowing that if I was back in Ohio, I'd be there with them, planning for homecoming. I couldn't tell them I was feeling left out, though. I tried that a couple days ago, and Nicole said, "What do *you* have to complain about? You live in L.A.!" And a month ago, I would have thought the same thing. I still couldn't believe I actually lived in one of the most exciting cities on earth. My parents had worked in regular sales jobs back in Ohio, but then someone my mom worked with told her about a business franchise they could start up in California.

They'd called me into our dining room to discuss, as they put it, a major life decision. How did I feel about uprooting our family and taking a risk to start a new life in Los Angeles?

"We might *move* to L.A.?" I asked, not sure if I was hearing them right. "You mean *live* there?"

"Yes, we would live in a suburb of Los Angeles," my dad said. "I know you've never been to L.A. . . ."

Well, no, I'd never been to L.A. in real life, but I'd definitely been there in my dream life. I'd been semiobsessed with celebrities since, well, pretty much forever. Even back in fifth grade, before I was allowed free reign on the Internet, I spent all my allowance on popstar magazines. I was my friends' go-to person for the star gossip and the newest posters to put up on our walls.

So of course, Hollywood was somewhere I'd always hoped to go. But I was thinking more along the lines of a weekend visit, like if my dad had a sales conference there instead of the usual places, like Des Moines. And then I'd convince him to take me with him and I would have the chance to stalk the stars' homes from a tour bus and put my feet in the cement footprints on the Walk of Fame. And then I'd go back home to Ohio for the rest of my life.

I never even remotely thought there was a chance my parents would move us there.

"I know this is the only home you've ever known, sweetie," my mom said. "And you've never been to California, so if you want a few days to think about it before you weigh in with your answer—"

"Mom! Dad!" I interrupted. "The answer is heck, yeah! Let's move to L.A.!!"

"Well, breaking the news to Avery went far better than I'd expected," my dad said dryly, as he whisked my mom out of the dining room before I could change my mind.

However, breaking the news to my friends didn't go quite as I'd envisioned. I was preparing myself for some tears, declarations of how much I'd be missed, and maybe some drama about how they couldn't go on without me. I'd called an emergency meeting at Starbucks.

"I have major news," I announced. "I'm moving to L.A. in a couple weeks."

"No *way*!" Nicole said. "That is *amazing*!"

"I know," I said. "It's—"

Wait. Did she say amazing?

"Ahem," I said. "I said I was *moving* to L.A. Moving, as in leaving here? Permanently?"

"L.A.! Ohmygosh! You have to get me Shiloh's autograph!" Kendall squealed.

"Shiloh's autograph?" I asked. "I'm moving to L.A. and you ask for Shiloh's autograph?"

"Seriously, Kendall," Nicole said. "Give poor Avery a break. I mean, Shiloh's autograph?"

Thank you. After all, I'd just announced I was leaving Ohio forever.

"Shiloh isn't even old enough to sign an autograph," Nicole continued. "Avery, try to get us Zahara's instead."

"Is anyone understanding that I'm leaving?" I said. "We've been friends since second grade. And I'm leaving."

"Well, officially, Lexa's only been friends with us since fourth grade," Nicole said.

"No, it was third," Lexa insisted.

"Not really," Nicole said. "You only thought you were in third. Really, we were only using you for your Bratz dolls."

"What?" Lexa sputtered.

"I'm just kidding," Nicole said. "Kind of."

"You guys!" I said. "Focus! I'm leaving in just a few weeks! This is one of the last times we'll all be sitting here on our couch at Starbucks together."

"Oh, Avery," Kendall said. She reached out and grabbed my hand. I started to get a little lump in my throat as I looked around at the friends I'd known almost forever.

"Okay, this is touching and all," Nicole said. "But a little too *Sisterhood of the Traveling Pants* for me. I feel like we're about to swear our allegiance to our friendship and pledge that nothing can tear us apart."

"Would that be so bad?" I asked.

"Not if we got a pair of magic jeans that would fit all of us like they did in *Traveling Pants*," Lexa said. "That would be sweet."

"Ooh, can they be True Religions?" Kendall said. "Or Rich & Skinny."

"Those *would* be magic jeans if they made *you* look rich and skinny," Nicole said. Lexa snorted.

"You guys!" I said, a little too loudly. Everyone stopped and looked at me. "I need your support here."

"You're right" Nicole said. "You do need our support. Okay, guys, we need to rally around Avery."

Finally, someone was listening to me.

"We have to get Avery ready to go out there and represent us!" Nicole continued. "She doesn't have much time. She's going to have to go all Ashlee and make some facial tweaks. I wonder if we have enough time to get Avery on *I Want a Famous Face*?!"

"Ooh, make yourself into L.C.!" Kendall turned to me. "I love *The Hills*!"

"You think?" Lexa said. "She might be able to pull off Audrina, but I can't see her as a Heidi."

"Boobs!" Nicole yelled so loud that the guy at the table next to us spilled his coffee. "You need boobs!"

I sat there, slightly stunned, as my friends made a to-do list:

- Choose famous face and find plastic surgeon
- Get TanTastic's thirty-day all-you-can-spray tan special
- Dye my hair platinum
- Get clothes other than my usual earth-toned Hollister/AE/Abercrombie basics
- Get veneers for my teeth
- And, of course, the boob job

On the bright side, it made what I'd thought was going to be a traumatically emotional announcement a little less emotional. And the fact that there was so little drama made leaving my friends a little easier to take, too. It was like they were moving on from me already. If I was totally honest with myself, they'd probably been moving on from me for a few years now, but when you've been friends since first grade, you kind of get in a rut.

Despite their compelling suggestions, I decided to disregard the list and go to L.A. as myself: red hair, pale skin, more butt than boobs. I was well aware I didn't look like a star. My friends and I had once asked one another: "Which star do I look most like?" Nicole had been Rihanna, Kendall was Taylor Swift, and after some debate, we chose Demi Lovato for Lexa.

For me, though, they were stumped.

"Well, your hair color is Lindsay-ish," Kendall said. "In its natural state. And the style is a little Miley Cyrus."

"More like Billy Ray," Nicole added. "Just kidding!"

"Avery doesn't really look like any star," Lexa said, and everyone had agreed and moved on.

So I'm not delusional. I knew all along that I wasn't just going to arrive in L.A. and suddenly break into a celebrity world. I wasn't planning to become a star. But I did kind of think I'd at least *see* a couple stars.

I've been here a month. Ask me how many stars I've seen since I moved here.

Zero.

How was it possible that I lived less than an hour away from the Hollywood sign for a month but hadn't seen any celebrities? For one thing, my parents were busy 24/7 starting their new business and while it might not sound too tragic to be virtually parentless, I'm fifteen. So I had no driver's license, no parents to drive me, and no friends who lived in this state. Basically, if I wasn't in school, I was stuck in my house. It was seriously pathetic.

I was hoping that sometime soon, things would pick up a little in my life. So were my friends back home. As a going-away present, the girls had made me a Ning. It's a social network as easy to sign up for as MySpace, but Nicole told me it was the new hot place where you could blog, put up videos, and talk to your friends. And when she made a big show of how it could keep us all so connected, I felt the love—for a second, until she explained I was to put all my Hollywood experiences and celebrity gossip on the site and then network them into it, so we would have our own celebrity gossip world.

The Ning itself was very cool. I'd written: "Stay tuned for the Celebrity Gossip!" I'd gotten excited to develop it. But I had nothing to put on it. I'd had a lot of visitors the first couple weeks, as people from home checked to see what I was up to. After that, though, the site just sat there, taunting me.

I was ready at any time to get something—*anything*—to post on the blog. If I could get out of my house, that is. I'd been keeping a checklist of places I'd read about in the tabloids that I couldn't wait to see in person. I'd started that list back in Ohio, when I thought I actually would be leaving my house in L.A. and going places.

The Ivy restaurant—lunch place where the paparazzi hung out [　]
Beverly Center—a mall where celebrities shopped [　]
Pink's hot dogs—lines down the block [　]
Robertson Blvd.—Rodeo Drive was mostly for tourists but the real stars shop here [　]
The Coffee Bean & Tea Leaf—for caffeine breaks [　]
Chateau Marmont—the hotel to hide out from the paparazzi and trash your room at night [　]
The Grove—an outdoor mall where celebrities shopped and went to the movies [　]

Notice that not one of the places on my checklist had a check mark next to it. It was incredibly frustrating . . . and yes, pathetic. Holly-wood was so close . . . but totally inaccessible to me.

At least in real life.

So I stayed connected to Hollywood the same way I did when I was thousands of miles away from it: online. Yes, pretty much my only connection to the world of Hollywood was through my computer. But it was better than nothing. Gossip blogs! Celebrity websites! Fan sites and fan forums!

I might not be a part of the scene, but at least I could read about it. I leaned back on my big orange pillow and made myself comfortable. I closed out of MySpace and pulled down my Favorites menu, where I had all the best gossip sites bookmarked for quick access. I settled in to read the latest.

STARS SHINE AT PREMIERE!
Natalie Portman and her costars were in L.A. for the premiere of her new movie. A source close to the actor said that it was one of the best times she's had filming. "They were like family on the set," Portman said, according to the source.

I smiled as I saw the pictures of the cast hugging one another. I read how they hoped there would be a sequel, so they could all share those fun times again. Yes, I'd imagine it would be fun hanging out all day with one of the hottest actors on the planet as your pretend boyfriend. And with makeup, hair, and wardrobe on standby to make sure you looked fabulous all the time and personal assistants and a huge paycheck . . . Sign me up for that.

I scrolled down farther and saw a poll.

HOT OR NOT?
Michael Cera at the awards show last night.

I love me some Michael Cera. I clicked on HOT!

What? He was only at 65 percent hot? Those results are flipping ridiculous. Michael Cera is smart, funny, adorable . . . what's not to love? I voted HOT a few more times to get his ranking up.

Who looks hotter at the Young Hollywood Awards: Ashley T or Selena G or Baby V?

Hello, Ashley Tisdale, Selena Gomez, Vanessa Hudgens are all gorgeous. I didn't think people should compare them, jeesh. I split my votes equally among all of them.

BLIND ITEM GOSSIP!

I love blind items. Blind items are the gossip stories that are so scandalous that the gossiper won't reveal names, so you have to guess who they're talking about. Sometimes they're obvious and you can figure them out.

> Blind Item: Which singer hasn't announced it yet . . . but she's pregnant! She and her hubby are thrilled to welcome their first bundle of joy.

Well, that wouldn't be a blind item too long, since it becomes a little obvious. Like when JLo and Christina Aguilera didn't admit they were pregnant but their growing bellies couldn't be ignored.

> Blind Item: Backstabbing BFF
> Which former reality show star is making a move on her BFF's boyfriend—but the friend has no clue? Our star was seen in a heavy-duty makeout session at a club while the BFF went to the ladies' room. And sources tell us it's not the first time . . .

Meow! Who? Okay, as much as I love blind items, they're also very frustrating because most of the time the answer isn't obvious. And then I'm left dying to know the answer.

I clicked onto another website:

NEW COUPLE ALERT?!

Cruz Ramirez, lead singer of the Statement, was caught cud-
dling with TV sitcom star Perth Hampton last night at Nobu.
"They were laughing and it looked like they were holding
hands," said a fellow diner. "I couldn't tell for sure, but I
thought they might have kissed!"

What? No way! Now this was some juicy gossip. Cruz was uber-
hot, and Perth was not only pretty, she was also hilarious in her
new show. Cruz and Perth would be an adorable couple. I clicked
around and didn't see anyone else mentioning it. I found a post on
the Statement's fan forum saying that there was a rumor that Perth
was going to be in his next music video. So maybe they were only
having a business dinner, and the holding-hands-and-kissing was
wishful thinking on somebody's part. But maybe it was a little of
both.

I could just picture how it might have happened. Maybe they
were talking about the music video—at first. Then Cruz might have
sang a little of his new song to her. She couldn't stop looking into his
gorgeous eyes as he sang to her and leaned in and their hands accidentally touched and . . . sparks flew. And they knew they were
meant to be. How romantic was that?

Apparently I needed to put Nobu on my list of places to go
see. I Googled it and discovered it was a restaurant in Malibu
known for its famous chef and sushi. Malibu was only about forty-
five minutes away from where I was. Things were happening out
there, people! Fabulous, glamorous, star-studded things! And I
was stuck in my house, alone. Which completely and totally
sucked.

MySpace BULLETIN

From: Avery [inLA]
Date: October 11—5:12 p.m.
Subject: Obviously I did not make myself clear

    Text me. comment me. message me. it is essential to my survival. i am
lonely and bored, people! be a true friend and reply.

I sent off that bulletin to my friends list. Surely, somebody would
answer that plea. And then I got a new-message alert. Thank you! It
was nice to know that at least one of my friends was there for me in
my time of need. Was it Nicole? Kendall? Lexa? I clicked on the
email to see who was going to cheer me up out of my loneliness.

```
From: DMB Records
Date: October 11-5:15 p.m.
Subject: New artist

Introducing Marisa! Rising star
Marisa is preparing to release her
debut album, Emerald City, so look
out! Marisa is coming!
```

The email was just some promotion from one of the music labels I'd added to my friends list. I sighed and halfheartedly clicked on the web link to see who this Marisa was. I'd check her out while I waited for one of my friends to reply to my bulletin.

The link took me to the DMB site. There was a picture of a girl with long, honey-blond hair, wearing a pretty deep green, flowing dress.

```
Click the link to check out Marisa's
debut song "The Girl Who."
```

I clicked and listened to the song.

They say I'm this
They say I'm that
I'm nothing special
I just fall flat

But I don't care
I just won't share
And give away
What makes me me
And sets me free

Wow, I really, really liked the song so far. I paused it and read the
little sidebar on Marisa.

```
With her voice, guitar skills,
and dance moves, Marisa is a triple
threat. Combining the early attitude
of No Doubt Gwen Stefani, the
esoteric emo-girl vibe of Lisa
Loeb, the vocal feel of Chan Mar-
shall from Cat Power, and the sweet
genuineness and crowd-pleasing
dance moves of early-and we mean
early-Britney, Marisa's unique
voice has positioned her for future
success.
```

Cool. I clicked the song back on and leaned into my pillow. I closed
my eyes and listened.

I'm the girl who
Won't do what they tell me to
The girl who has no place to hide
The girl who won't just go along for the ride

Because I'm the girl who
I'm the girl who
You'll wish you knew

The girl who will make you feel
Nothing you thought was real
Will show you the inside out
I really have no doubt
I'm the girl who you can't do without

I'm the girl who
The girl who
I'm the girl who
You'll wish you knew . . .

The song ended and I opened my eyes. I loved it. If the rest of her album was anything like this song, she wouldn't be unknown for long. I turned back to the website to read more.

`Like what you heard? Be the first to know about Marisa with updates!`

I'd liked what I heard. I clicked the link to sign up for Marisa updates, but I got an error message. I hated when that happened. I almost gave up and moved on, but then I saw an email address at the bottom of the page, so I wrote a quick email:

```
To: DMB Record Label
From: AJohnson@zmail.la.com


Please send me the latest updates on
Marisa!
```

I had just hit the send key when I heard the garage door opening. My parents were home.

"Avery!" came my father's voice from downstairs. "Come on down! We've got a good story for you!"

I put my laptop on my desk and reluctantly headed downstairs. I could only imagine what kind of story my parents would have from their workday. Their new business was called JohnsonPromos and they were really excited about it. I was excited they were excited, but honestly, their business wasn't exactly enthralling. You know how you go to, say, your dentist, and he gives you a toothbrush that has his name on it? Well, when a business wants its name and logo or happy saying on a stress ball or a water bottle or a calendar, they can call my parents' company.

So far, it seems to be going well, but my parents' work stories usually involve mass orders of toothbrushes or pens, so they aren't exactly fascinating.

"Hi!" I said, walking into the kitchen. My parents were standing there, wearing white JohnsonPromos polo shirts, and had huge grins on their faces.

"Do we have a story for you!" my father said. "Patty, go ahead. You can tell her."

"You'll love this, Avery," my mother said. "So we stopped on the way home for a cup of coffee—"

"And we met someone famous!" my dad interrupted. "We met a celebrity!"

"Great!" I said, trying to sound enthusiastic. Knowing my parents, I could only imagine who it was. Probably someone I'd never heard of who was famous decades ago. I plastered on a fake smile so I wouldn't spoil their fun.

"It was this young lady with an unusual outfit and white hair," Dad explained. "The coffee worker told me it was Jen Stephanie. He said she goes there all the time. Ever hear of her?"

"No, I don't know who Jen Stephanie is," I said. "Sorry, Dad."

"Ste-*fah*-nee," my mother corrected him. "It's Jen Ste-*fah*-nee. Here, I took a picture with my cell phone."

"Wait, what? Jen what?" I said. No . . . it couldn't be. I grabbed my mom's cell phone and looked. There was a picture of my dad with his arm around Gwen Stefani.

Wait a minute.

Gwen Stefani??! I looked closer. It was! It was Gwen Stefani! "You and Dad met Gwen Stefani?" I shrieked.

"Oh, it's *Gwen*," my dad said. "I must have misunderstood the clerk."

"Oh dear, Albert, you called her the wrong name," Mom said to him.

"Dad actually talked to Gwen Stefani?!" I could not believe this.

"Yes, and she was very lovely. She even took a badge for JohnsonPromos that Dad gave her," Mom said.

"You gave Gwen Stefani one of your badges?" I asked, stunned.

"And your dad encouraged her to put it right on her jacket and she started to pin it on!" my mother said. "Until her extremely large husband took it away from her to hold."

:"Um, her husband is not extremely large," I said. And then I thought of something. "Oh, jeez, Dad. That was her bodyguard."

"That makes more sense, Albert," my mom said. "That's why he said something about sharp objects and safety precautions and they left so quickly."

I could not believe my parents talked to—and scared away—Gwen Stefani.

"Tell me more! What did she order?" I needed details.

"She ordered a soy latte," my father said. "I know, because then I ordered one, too. I figured if someone who looked as good as she did drinks it, then—"

"He didn't particularly care for it," my mother added. "We should have brought you something, Avery, but things got a little chaotic with your father and his celebrity encounter. You can imagine. I'm just sorry you missed it."

Me, too. Oh, me, too. I looked at the picture again. There was Gwen Stefani and my pasty, redheaded dad beaming with his arm around her. I got my looks from my dad—at least the red hair and pale skin that burned instead of tanned. My mom also had pale skin, but she had medium-length brown hair that she'd recently learned frizzed like crazy in the California heat, so she cut it short.

Gwen, on the other hand, had perfect hair . . . perfect skin . . . Man, I wished I had been there in real life, standing with them. No, make that replacing my father in the picture completely, and then Gavin Rossdale would walk in holding Kingston's hand. But suddenly Kingston would come running over to me, and Gwen would gush how he'd never taken to a stranger like that before and could I babysit for her and Gavin while they went to the MTV Awards. But then they'd have an extra ticket and invite me to go with them and—

"We feel bad you missed the excitement, so we decided to do something special tonight. Something California-ish!" my dad said. "How does that sound, Avery?"

How did that sound? Actually, that sounded like a decent plan. And I had a brilliant idea. We could go to the restaurant Cruz Ramirez and Perth Hampton were at last night. And maybe Gwen "Jen" Stefani would still be hanging around nearby. I opened my mouth to make the suggestion.

"Let's get cooking!" my dad announced before I could say anything. "We finally found the box with the wok in it, so we can make a stir-fry and the pièce de résistance—we brought home California rolls! Get it?"

"Wait, we're staying home?" I asked.

"Oh yes, your father and I had a long day at work," my mom said. "And I for one am a little worn out after our celebrity encounter."

"It'll be a night of fun-filled family dinner and Wii competition!" my dad crowed. "Look out, I'm ready to kick butt in bowling!"

"Nice trash-talking!" my mom said. "But you're going down, mister!"

Oh, you've got to be kidding.

"I'm going to make a Jen Stefani Mii," my dad announced.

"You know, as fun as that sounds I really do have . . . stuff . . . to do in my room," I said. I longingly looked at the picture of my dad with Gwen and clicked to send it to my email address, since I knew he would probably delete it by accident. I put the phone down on the table and started inching my way subtly toward the stairs.

"But we're having our first Family Night, California style," my mom said.

My parents looked at me incredibly sadly, as if I'd just crushed their souls.

"Maybe we're not cool enough for her, Patty," my dad said. "I know! We can play Dance Dance Revolution instead. That's in with you teen girls, right, Avery? We can shake our booties! And your mom looks finer than Jen Stefani when she shakes her—"

He started shaking his, er, booty.

"Dad!" I protested.

"Oh, Albert," my mom said. "I do appreciate the compliment, but I think you're embarrassing your daughter. Avery, how about you go finish your homework while your dad and I whip up some chicken stir-fry. We'll call you down when dinner's ready."

"Yeah, thanks, Mom," I said, and bolted up the stairs before my dad started shaking it again. I sighed as I went into my room and sat down at my computer.

I pulled up one of the gossip sites and saw a cute picture of Will Smith and Jada taking their kids to a Hollywood premiere. Bruce Willis and Demi Moore take their kids to celebrity parties with Ashton Kutcher. And my "Hollywood parents"? Their idea of a California night is to get California rolls and make Jen Stefani Miis.

I scrolled down to the next story. Celebrity sighting! Ashley and Vanessa going to the gym. Ashley in a baseball hat, Vanessa in a ponytail, both in workout gear.

I can't believe my parents met Gwen Stefani without me, while I'm in the house reading about celebrity sightings online, exactly like I did back in Ohio.

Hey, wait. My parents had a real celebrity sighting that was just as cool as spotting Ashley and Baby V, right? I actually had some real celebrity gossip of my own for once in my life. Well, it was really my parents' gossip, but let's disregard that fact because of its sheer lameness. I started typing into a Word document.

Gwen Stefani was spotted at Coffee Bean tonight with her bodyguard. That was possibly the lamest piece of gossip ever. I needed to spice it up a little.

Gwen Stefani Almost Stabbed by Fan?

Rock royalty Gwen Stefani was whisked out of a coffee shop by her bodyguard after a crazed fan shoved what turned out to be a pinned badge at her. "He was harmless," said a bystander. "But who could blame them for taking all safety precautions when a man with a sharp object comes at Gwen?"

That actually sounded pretty juicy, didn't it. For a moment I felt like a real gossip blogger with a real piece of gossip. I pulled up the picture of my dad and Gwen that I'd sent to my email and Photoshopped a big white blur over my dad's face. I put the picture next to the gossip item and smiled. Ha, it looked like a real gossip site entry. I should send it to Nicole and everyone back in Ohio. They'd think it was kind of cool.

A knock on my door startled me. My dad stuck his head in.

"Dinner will be ready in five minutes," he said. "What are you up to?"

"Oh, the usual," I said, leaning forward to make sure my screen was blocked. "Just emailing friends."

"Speaking of which, I got the cell phone bill from last month," he said. "Calls to Ohio are mighty pricey, you know."

"Yeah." I winced. "Well, I'm not really talking to people back home so much anymore, so I don't think it's going to be a problem."

"How's it going making new friends here?" he asked.

"Oh, you know," I said, trying to sound like it was no big deal. "It takes a little time."

"Well, here's a piece of advice from your old man on making new friends," he said cheerfully. "Just smile and say hello and you'll have so many friends in no time, you'll be princess of the prom!"

Er, yeah. Okay, Dad. I'll definitely take that advice under consideration, especially since coming from a guy who scared off Gwen Stefani. I looked at my gossip entry and had an idea. I pulled up the empty Ning site that my friends in Ohio had made for me. I pasted my gossip entry into it. There. Now I just needed a title for my page.

I'd never be princess of the prom, but at least I could be princess of my own gossip blog, right? I typed in a user name:

`Princess of Gossip`

I used an icon of a tiara as my picture, then added one of my favorite Gwen songs, which reminded me of sleepovers and good times with my friends a long time ago. It almost looked like a real blog, other than the fact that there was only one piece of lame celebrity gossip on it—and that gossip was actually told to me by my parents.

Yeah, I take that back—this lame page didn't look like a real gossip site. It just looked stupid. I started to delete it when my dad's voice startled me.

"Avery! Didn't you hear me calling you? It's time for dinner."

"Oh!" I said. "Sorry, I was so into what I was doing that I totally spaced."

"Well, dinner is waiting and then it's—" My dad paused dramatically. "The First Ultimate Johnson Family Wii Bowling Challenge! I've got my Jen Stefani Mii all set up and I'm ready to kick your butt, Princess!"

The thought of my dad as a Gwen Mii was seriously disturbing. I'd delete the blog later. For now, I followed my happy father out of my bedroom and prepared for a very long night.

3

Mrs. Chace Crawford
Chace and Avery Crawford

I was sitting in English class, trying to cover up my yawns. I didn't exactly get premium sleep last night. My father got crazy competitive and refused to let me quit until his Jen Stefani Mii had beaten me and my mom.

My teacher, Miss Schmitt, was talking about the conflicts between characters in *Lord of the Flies,* but I was only half listening. I'd done *Lord of the Flies* last year in my old school, which meant that if all went well, I'd remember the setting, protagonists, plot, theme, and hopefully all of the answers to the test we were having later in the week. So I wasn't really paying attention to her.

Avery Elizabeth Crawford
Chace + Avery =

I wondered what Chace's and my celebrity couple name would be:
Chavery?
Averace?
ChacAvery?

Those didn't quite have the Zanessa/Brangelina catchiness going for them. I entertained myself by imagining fantasy gossip items for my Princess of Gossip blog. Like this one:

Chace Crawford confirms hot romance with new redhead in town, Avery Johnson. In an exclusive interview for Princess of Gossip, Chace says it was love at first sight when he spotted Avery at the Coffee Bean & Tea Leaf. "I fell for her natural beauty," Chace said. "She's the girl who made me feel nothing that I knew was real. I really have no doubt, she's the girl I can't do without."

Okay, those were the lyrics from that Marisa song that kept running through my head. But they worked really well in my fantasy.

"Class! May I please have your attention!" Fantasy over. Miss Schmitt's voice suddenly pierced through my daydream. "You're now going to partner up and quiz each other on the vocabulary words using your flash cards from last night's homework. I'm assigning partners alphabetically to ensure this is not a time to chat with friends."

The class groaned.

Well, that last part didn't really affect me. In my case, it would be impossible to assign me to a friend, anyway. We've already established that the number of celebrities I've talked to since I've moved here is exactly zero. Now, let's be a little less ambitious and discuss how many real people I've talked to since I moved here.

That would be pretty much close to zero as well. Moving during the middle of the school year is not ideal, I've learned. Lunch tables are already chosen, BFFs already long determined, boyfriends and girlfriends already attached at the lips. I thought maybe my appearance would elicit a little bit of buzz: who's the new girl? But apparently, in a school of two thousand people, it's easy to be unnoticeable.

The first few weeks I'd tried. I'd worn my cutest outfits and rocked my best hair. And yes, I kind of tried my father's dorky idea of smiling and saying hi, but the response was lukewarm at best. I quickly figured out I was destined for oblivion, so I didn't even bother anymore. I accepted my destiny as anono-girl.

HOT OR NOT!
NEW GIRL IN SCHOOL AVERY JOHNSON
In her blah-boring gray tee, white tank, denim mini, sneakers, and her hair thrown up in a ponytail, is Avery Johnson Hot or Not?

100% NOT
0% HOT

"When I announce your names, please move your desks together," Miss Schmitt said. "Abbott and Aquino. Bautista and Chavez."

I wish someone would want to know me. At least my partner would talk to me, because you *have* to talk to your partner if you're working together, right? I waited and listened for the teacher to call my last name.

"Horowitz and James, Johnson and King . . ."

Johnson and King. Okay, who's King? I looked around until I saw a guy looking around, too. He raised his eyebrow at me and mouthed, "Johnson?"

HOT OR NOT!
MY NEW PARTNER: SOMEBODY KING
In his chocolate-brown hoodie, beat-up army jacket, and Chuck Taylors, and his light brown surferish hair, is King Hot or Not?

I'd vote Hot. He was cute, although not as gorgeous as some of the other guys around the school, with excellent clothes and hair. Oh, and he was now getting bonus points in hotness since he was smiling at me. So few guys had acknowledged my presence since I moved here, it felt like a bigger deal than it was.

So maybe this was it, that moment in the movies where the dorky girl meets her perfect guy and everything changes—she falls in love, becomes popular, and gets a makeover. He'd be impressed with my knowledge of *Lord of the Flies*. We'd study so quickly, we'd have time to discover our shared love of new music and mocha chip ice cream. He'd put pink roses in my locker and text me that he never knew he could feel this way. And when we became famous, we'd tell our story to the magazine that paid us the most for it and donate the money to charity.

"It all started when we were put together as partners in English class," we'd say. "As we quizzed each other in vocabulary, we fell in love."

Our Zanessa/Brangelina name could be JoKing. Or maybe not.

"Miss Schmitt?" A girl a few rows over put her hand in the air. I knew her name was Cecilia Singer. She was one of those people who stood out immediately, since she was gorgeous and dressed to channel Nicole Richie, down to the huge white sunglasses currently perched on her head. Her makeup and skin were flawless, her tan the right amount of spray without being too orange or too brown. Her strawberry-blond hair was highlighted and streaky. She was always giggling loudly with people around her, so we'd all look and be jealous that we weren't her. We went to a public school, and not one where there were any recognizable celebrities, but Cecilia looked—and acted—like she should be a star.

SABRINA BRYAN AND JULIA DeVILLERS

"Yes, Miss Singer?" the teacher said.

"Griffin and I already started our studying together to get a head start," she said. "May we continue working together?"

"I do like to reward students who take initiative in my class, so that will be fine," the teacher said. "You may work together."

Cecilia smiled and casually pulled up a chair to King's desk.

"Griffin, you're all mine!" Cecilia said. Oh, fantastic. Cecilia was talking about my partner. But excuse me, he'd be *our* partner, I believe.

"Hey, Cici." I saw Griffin flash the hottie smile at her, too.

I sighed and pulled my chair up to Griffin's desk.

"Yes?" Cecilia asked.

"Um, I think we're all partners?" I said. "I'm Johnson? I was with King?"

"Oh, I think Miss Schmitt switched us," she said, smiling sweetly. "It's King and Singer now."

And she moved her chair so her back was to me

"Nice, Cici." Griffin pushed his chair back. "Of course she can be in our group."

I looked around to see if there was another option. Everyone seemed pretty settled with their partners. Nobody was calling out that they needed somebody. I cautiously pulled my chair farther in with them and put my flash cards on the desk.

"Um, hi," I said. "I'm Avery."

"I'm Griffin," Griffin said.

There was a pause as I waited for Cecilia to introduce herself. She examined one of her nails.

"Do not go to Lisa for your nails," Cecilia said, looking disgusted. "I'm chipping already."

"I'll take that under advisement." Griffin turned to me. "That's

Cecilia, my next-door neighbor. She's been giving me valuable advice since we were five. So, I guess we should start studying."

"I'm ready, I brought my flash cards," Cecilia said cheerfully. She reached down and pulled out a black Botkier bag from under her chair. I knew what it was because I'd seen a picture of Jessica Alba carrying it in *OK* or *Us* or somewhere, although I didn't exactly know how to pronounce Botkier. Bot-k-yur? Botkee-er? I certainly wasn't going to ask Cecilia.

Cecilia pulled out a stack of rubber-banded flash cards and put them on her desk.

"You can use my flash cards," Cecilia said. "They rock."

"Those are some serious flash cards," Griffin said. I picked one up and saw they were computer-designed and apparently color-coded.

"I was up all night making them," Cecilia said.

"You can tell," I said, actually impressed. "They're really detailed."

"That was a joke," Cecilia said, turning to look at me. "The only thing I was up all night doing was something that innocent children like you should not know about. Griffy, you never come out with us."

"I tend to do radical things like study and sleep on school nights," Griffin said. "Unlike you, Cici, I won't have a movie-star salary, so I'd like to go to college. And pass this test."

"You can totally pass this test," Cecilia said. "Keep my sister's flash cards. She had Schmitt two years ago and bought them off some genius guy who graduated the year before her."

"I'll stick with mine," Griffin said, holding up some much less impressive-looking cards.

"Fine," Cecilia said, rolling her eyes. "But you'll be jealous when my flash cards help me ace this *Lord of the Rings* test."

SABRINA BRYAN AND JULIA DeVILLERS

"Um," I said. "It's *Lord of the Flies.*"

"Whatever." Cecilia waved her hand. Then she peered at me like I was under a microscope. "And wait. Who are you? Where did you come from anyway?"

HOT GOSSIP!

Who is the mysterious new redhead at school? Everyone's dying to know! The buzz in the halls is that she's moved here to be the newest It Girl in Hollywood. First she'll conquer the school . . . and then Tinseltown!

"I'm new," I said. "I just moved here from Ohio."

"Ohio!" Cecilia said, rolling her eyes again. "You *lived* there? Harsh."

"It's not that bad," I said. "There are a lot of nice people—"

I was interrupted by a girl with long black hair who was attempting to channel Nicole Richie as well, though much less successfully than Cecilia. She kneeled next to the desk and looked up at Cecilia.

"Cecilia, you should have told Schmitt you wanted to work with me," she whined. "I wanted to hear all about your night out at Villa. I'm dying to go there."

"Miss Floyd!" Miss Schmitt boomed. "No socializing! Please return to your partner!"

The girl scurried back to the other side of the room.

"For once Schmitt comes in handy," Cecilia said, sighing. "Like that girl could even get past the door at Villa. Thank Gawd you're in here, Griffin. There's *nobody* in this class. I didn't even want to think about who I was supposed to be partnered with."

"I think you'd survive," Griffin said. "Like Avery said, there are a lot of nice people around."

"Nice? Nice doesn't get you past the red rope at Villa, babe," Cecilia said. "Being with me and having a fake ID will, though."

I felt a ping of envy at Cecilia's ease at getting into Villa, one of the exclusive celebrity hot spots mentioned on the gossip sites. I wished I could ask her what it was like, but I knew I'd only get dismissed like Miss Floyd.

"Class! I need to meet with some of you individually in the hallway to discuss your homework," Mrs. Schmitt said. "You will continue to study as if I were here breathing down your necks. Mr. King, please see me."

"I'm first? This can't be good," Griffin groaned, rising from his chair. "Cecilia, be nice to Avery while I'm gone. Lose the 'tude, she's new here."

And he left me alone with Cecilia Singer. Cecilia didn't acknowledge my presence, but picked up the flash cards.

"Do you want to quiz me or something?" I asked.

"I don't need to study," Cecilia said, slipping the cards into her bag. "I also have my sister's old tests. Schmitt uses the same ones every year."

She pulled out lip gloss from her bag and started applying it. I stared at my vocabulary words sheet and tried to look like I was engrossed in it and too busy to bother with Cecilia. I remained cool until something hit me in the cheek.

"Ow!" I yelped.

A folded-up piece of paper fell on the desk. I hoped that the person who had thrown it merely had bad aim and wasn't intentionally trying to hit me in the face.

I looked around to see a guy making hand motions at me. I moved my head up and down, but apparently that wasn't what he meant. The guy sighed and got up from his desk. He was short, with shaggy black hair and sideburns. He was wearing a black T-shirt, blazer and jeans.

"I need you to move your head farther to the right," the guy said. "It's blocking our light."

"Your light?" I asked him, completely confused.

"I want to get some film of Cecilia putting on lip gloss," he said, pointing across the room. I looked over to see a round guy with curly hair sticking out of a baseball cap aiming a small video camera our way.

"Willie, no," Cecilia said. "This is *not* a photo op. And I also want you to take down that heinous picture of me from homeroom this morning off your Facebook. Immediately."

"There's no such thing as a heinous picture of you, Cecilia," the guy said. "Now smile."

"Emagawd, Willie, will you stop," Cecilia said.

But she tilted her head and gave a big smile as he took the picture.

"Oh, and I'm not Willie anymore. I'm going by Willie.i.am," the guy said.

"Willie," she groaned. "Ripping off a Black Eyed Pea. You can do better."

"Come on," he complained. "I thought I'd be Willie.i.am and you could be Cici-licious. Fine. I'll be William, as in Will*yum*."

I tried to stifle my laugh but didn't do a good job of it, half snorting.

"Sorry," I said, and tried to act engrossed in my vocabulary words.

"Who's she? Is she anybody?" William asked Cecilia.

"No, she's from Idaho," Cecilia said.

"Ohio," I corrected her.

William pointed me out to his video-toting friend and made a slicing motion across his neck. Apparently I was not worthy of screen time.

"Cecilia, how about an interview with Cam," William said. "Did you hook up at Villa last night? Who's the lucky guy? What did you wear?"

"What are you, the school paparazzi?" I couldn't help but ask him.

"I'm *not* paparazzi," William said indignantly. "I'm the chief chronicler of the Beautiful People. My videos are my art. And Cecilia is my muse. She's the Heidi to my Spencer. The Scarlett to my Woody."

"Ha," the guy next to us said. "He said 'woody.'"

Cecilia giggled.

"I meant Woody Allen," William said, annoyed. "ScarJo is his muse for his movies like Cecilia is mine and—oh, Schmitt!" William suddenly ducked behind my seat, but not quickly enough. Miss Schmitt had stuck her head back in the room and seen him.

"Mr. Shaw!" Miss Schmitt's voice rang out across the classroom. "Return to your own partner immediately and stop with your nonsense in my classroom."

"But Miss Schmitt, don't you want me to prepare for my future career as the premier celebrity chronicler?" he protested. "Isn't that what we're here for, preparing for our future?"

"Your future in detention," she said. "If you do not return to your seat."

She glared and went back out to the hallway.

SABRINA BRYAN AND JULIA DeVILLERS

35

"I'll have to find out who's who in detention and see if I should go," William grumbled, heading back to his seat.

"Is that guy for real?" I asked her.

"He's a baby paparazzi wannabe," Cecilia said. "Aka Willie Jr., who's been stalking me since sixth grade. It's a total headache, y'know?"

I didn't, actually. I watched as Cecilia pulled a little mirror out of her bag. I decided to try to keep the conversation going because, well, I'd like to say it was to avoid awkward silences, but how often did I have the school It Girl to myself. I admit I wanted to impress her a little bit.

"I guess you could be flattered," I offered.

"Well," Cecilia said. "It *is* practice for my future fame, I guess."

She smiled at me. It seemed like she was warming up to me. I suddenly envisioned us bonding. She'd invite me to hang with her friends. We'd be BFF and do everything together. Just imagine the parties, the VIP backstage lifestyle I could finally lead. We'd have a joint sweet sixteen party next year and be on *My Super Sweet 16* together. It wasn't that far-fetched, other than that last part. I mean, in Ohio I'd been in one of the popular groups. Okay, maybe it was because I'd hung around with them since we were six—and because of my Bratz collection—but still. Cecilia had her paparazzi and her fans; maybe she needed a new groupie.

"William and his idiot cameraperson need to give me some warning," Cecilia muttered. "My hair is stupid."

I knew exactly what to do. I'd coddled Queen Bee Nicole's need for admiration to perfection since second grade.

"Oh, puh-lease," I said. "You look amazing."

Cecilia looked puh-leased. See, I knew what I was doing.

"I'm sure everyone's told you that you look just like Taylor Momsen," I continued, referring to the *Gossip Girl* star.

"What?" She sat up straight and slammed her palm down on the table. "That's so mean."

"No!" I protested. "Wait! What? I meant that as a compliment! She's gorgeous! Everyone knows she's gorgeous!"

"Oh, just rub it in a little more." Cecilia slumped down into a full-on pout. "I *had* that role. Everyone knows I was meant to be Jenny."

Oops. I wasn't expecting that one.

"I was totally sabotaged in the callbacks," Cecilia kept complaining. "Great. Now you've totally put me in a heinous mood. I need gum. Do you have gum?"

I shook my head no.

She opened her bag and started shuffling things around. She looked really pissed off. Obviously, I hadn't meant to ruin her mood with that comment. I wished someone would tell me I looked like Taylor Momsen.

"Hey, I'm sorry," I said. "I—"

"Oh, yay!" Cecilia suddenly smiled. "I found my gum."

She opened a tin of spearmint gum and popped a piece in her mouth. Then she played with the foil wrapper, ignoring me. I wasn't sure if she was ignoring me because I'd pissed her off with the whole Taylor Momsen compliment/insult, or because she'd forgotten I'd existed and had gone back to her happy place.

NOT-SO-HOT GOSSIP

Who is that mysterious new redhead at school who tried to start a conversation with It Girl Cecilia Singer? Stand in line, girl. Puh-lease, who does she think she is? (We know who she is . . . nobody! That's who!)

And that's when I noticed a hand stamp on the back of Cecilia's hand. It was the logo for a new indie band that I'd read about on one of my gossip sites. Nobody back home had heard of them, but they had a couple really good songs. And I bet I knew something about them she didn't.

"Hey, you like University of Hard?" I asked her. "I love their song 'Dress Up Games.' Did you go to their show?"

"That's usually what a hand stamp means," Cecilia said, not looking particularly interested. I needed to reel her in.

"I heard this story about Shade, the lead singer," I said.

Ha! That got Cecilia's attention. She looked up at me.

"What did you hear?"

"I heard that this weekend Shade was kissing this girl who he picked up after the show, even though he's supposed to be practically engaged," I told her.

"Whatever. You can't believe the tabloids," Cecilia said.

"No, there's proof. The girl's friend sent a picture of it to this gossip site and I saw it," I insisted. "Shade and this girl were totally going at it. But I guess it's no surprise."

"What do you mean by that?" Cecilia said.

"I assumed he got his nickname because he was shady," I said. "Plus, you have to admit that he seems like a major player who totally would cheat on his girlfriend."

"His girlfriend is my *sister*," Cecilia said.

Huh? I processed that information for a minute and decided I'd misheard what she said.

"I'm talking about Shade, the singer from University of Hard?" I clarified.

"Shade, my sister Delilah's boyfriend," Cecilia also clarified.

Crap. Well, that had never happened to me before. In Ohio, when you discuss celebrity gossip chances are extremely slim that you'll be sharing it with someone who is somehow involved with the celebrity you just dissed. Much less their sister who is being cheated on.

"Err," I said.

"Ms. Johnson!" Miss Schmitt walked back into the room, followed by Griffin. "Please see me to discuss your essay."

Thank you! My new savior, Miss Schmitt.

"Gotta go!" I tried to smile at Cecilia, as if I hadn't just accidentally dissed her future brother-in-law. It was time to get away from Ms. Singer as quickly as possible. So when I jumped out of my seat, I didn't think to check if her Botkier tote bag was leaning into the aisle.

I fell over it backward and went down. I couldn't have possibly made any more noise, since I grabbed onto the chair handle and took the chair down with me. Everyone in the vicinity gasped, and then started cracking up as I lay on the floor awkwardly.

I looked up to see Cecilia rolling her eyes at me.

Then William's voice rang out.

"Move out of the way, people!" He shouted and waved to his camera-guy sidekick. I closed my eyes. Now I was newsworthy enough to be filmed.

4

If only I were a celebrity, I could use what happened as one of those most embarrassing moments in the magazines to show that even though I'm a star, I'm *just like you*.

SUPERSTAR AVERY JOHNSON REMEMBERS HER MOST EMBARRASSING MOMENT:

"I had just accidentally insulted the school It Girl's future brother-in-law and then tripped over her designer tote bag. I was flat on the floor, as the whole class laughed at me. Except the It Girl, who didn't even notice."

But seeing as I'm not a celebrity, only an insanely embarrassed nobody, there was absolutely nothing redeeming about my embarrassing moment. For once I was glad I wasn't famous. I mean, celebrities lose roles and they lose their husbands to other famous stars. Their movies bomb and they're featured as fashion don'ts in magazines. At least my humiliations aren't covered in the tabloids.

That is, if Willie.i.am Jr. wasn't affiliated with any tabloids. He couldn't be, could he? I supposed anything was possible in this town. I kept my head down as I headed to my next period, which was lunch. I would just lie low, eat, and hope that my fall would be as ignored as I had been so far.

I stepped out to the lunch area and felt a teeny bit better. The weather was California-gorgeous and the sun's warmth on my sleeveless arms felt good. In Ohio, I'd probably be wearing a hoodie by now. And in Ohio, the cafeteria was a room with long rectangular tables and gray walls, and it smelled like old soup. In California, we ate outside in the sunshine. After the first day of squinting my way through lunch, I realized sunglasses were a must-have.

That was the good thing about lunchtime here. The rest of it, not so much. The first day of school, I hadn't been naive enough to expect to have friends to sit with at lunch. I'd gone into the cafeteria planning to sit alone, observing the scene until I'd made some friends. What I hadn't expected to find were little round tables of eight, meaning there was no sitting by yourself. I sat down on the low stone wall that surrounded the courtyard. I soon learned why people didn't sit there, as the skater dudes attempted to do jumps over me on their skateboards and Rollerblades.

So on the second day, I scoped out the table scene. There was the middle see-and-be-seen section, with Cecilia Singer and her groupies. The second tier surrounding them, and so on. It didn't take much to figure out that the least desirable seats were near the garbage cans, so I headed that way and took a seat at an obvious outcast table. And not the emo one or the indie cool one or the Goth one. I found a table of girls who . . . let's just say they looked like they were in their own world. They were just eating their food silently, not talking or looking at one another. They never even acknowledged my presence, or one another's. They sat there in silence the whole lunch period, reading or studying or who knew what. So I plugged into my iPod and listened to music. It seemed to be fine with them.

Today I sat down at my usual seat and put my earphones in. I'd just clicked to a Camp Rock song to cheer me up when the girl sitting next to me waved her hand in front of my face to get my attention. I pulled out my earphones and smiled.

"Hi," I said, surprised.

"You're in my English class," the girl said, looking concerned. "I saw what happened."

"Oh, you did?" I said. So much for nobody noticing. "That was really embarrassing."

I thought about what my father said about making new friends at school. Obviously these awkward girls had experienced their own embarrassing moments and maybe they were sympathizing with me. Maybe this was an opportunity for a little bonding.

"Yeah, it was," the girl said. "So, you don't mind moving seats?"

"Move seats?" I asked. "Why?"

"What if Cecilia Singer sees our table and then realizes you're sitting with us?" another girl said.

All of the girls swung around to look at Cecilia, who was sitting on a hot guy's lap and feeding him French fries. I doubted this lunch table or any of the girls at it would be on Cecilia's radar, but how could I phrase that delicately?

"Honestly, I really don't think Cecilia Singer is too concerned with this lunch table," I said carefully.

"Well what if she is," the first girl said. "And then she sees you. I mean, that would be embarrassing for our whole lunch table."

The girls all nodded in agreement.

I'd embarrass *this* lunch table? That was it. I'd sunk to a whole new low. I've read that Jennifer Garner said she was a geek in school. And Jennifer Aniston was insecure and uncool. Yeah, yeah, yeah.

The difference between them and me? Well, they're looking way back in time. I'm living it now, present tense. And what about the millions of us who do *not* get to chuckle about their days of loser-dom in magazine interviews?

Apparently we're looking for a new lunch seat.

5

There was no way I was going to approach a new lunch table, so I went back into the building and headed for the only place I could think of to hide—the girl's bathroom. I walked into the room and leaned against some graffiti on the pale green walls.

> *Connor + Jamie 4 eva!*
> *Angela hearts Issam*
> *Angela is a—*

I'll just stop there. Let's just say someone wasn't too happy with Angela. I felt bad for Angela and tried rubbing the words off, but the marker was permanent. I still had a half hour to kill so I pulled out my iPod touch and turned on some music. Marisa's song came up on my playlist.

The girl who . . . has no place left to hide.

That lyric of Marisa's was certainly appropriate. Well, at least I had one place left to hide, even if it was the girls' bathroom. And I had a magazine with me, so I could catch up on some gossip to cheer me up.

BLIND ITEMS!

Which movie star is about to get canned? He's been showing up late or not at all to his sets, claiming "exhaustion." Gee, it must be exhausting staying out all night at the clubs. His late nights have caused his costars to complain that he's holding up filming and costing time and moolah.

MINE-MINE-MINE

Which supermodel stormed off the set when one of the photographer's assistants on the shoot dared to say hello? Apparently she has a "don't look at me or talk to me" policy. She refused to come back until the assistant had been fired—in front of everyone.

Ugh. Those did the opposite of cheer me up. It was a little hard to understand why the stars who have everything act like that. I'm standing in a bathroom, all alone, after my complete embarrassment, having no life, while they have fabulous friends, money, access to all the fun, boy toys, looks . . .

I looked at myself in the mirror. It didn't look like the face of a movie star, but I didn't think it looked like the face of a total loser, either. But I remembered what my friends in Ohio had said about me not fitting in in L.A., and after today's humiliations, I guess they were right. I couldn't help it—I started to tear up. I tried to compose myself so I didn't lose it in the girls' room. I sniffled and went into the stall to get some tissue to blow my nose.

Then I heard the door open and someone come in.

"Ohmygosh!" the girl said. "I'm sorry! I'm sorry! Didn't mean to interrupt!"

"It's okay!" I said. I came out of the stall. "I was just blowing my nose."

"Look, I'll just pretend I didn't see anything, okay?" she said. "Don't worry."

"Um, I'm not worried," I said. "I was seriously just blowing my nose. It's fine."

"No, really! I'm outta here!" she said. "You can go back to doing your thing!"

The girl backed out toward the door. She reminded me of a shorter, curvier Amanda Bynes with her big eyes and wavy golden-brown hair. She was wearing a pumpkin-colored floaty tank, jeans, and boots in a very Anthropologie–meets–Free People style.

"Look," I said. "What *do* you think I'm doing in here?"

"Smoking," she said tentatively. "Or worse."

"I was not!" I protested.

"Then you were puking up your lunch," she said. "Look, it's none of my business, but it's really bad for you. Like it can wreck your teeth and your stomach—"

"I wasn't doing anything." I looked at the girl squarely in the eye. "Honestly, I was just blowing my nose."

She didn't look convinced.

"Okay, fine, I was kind of crying because I'm having a bad day," I admitted. "That's why I needed to blow my nose and that's why I'm here, hiding in the girls' room."

"Oh. That stinks." The girl looked genuinely sympathetic. "What's the matter?"

"It's so embarrassing it's stupid." I waved like it was nothing and tried to dismiss it.

"You want to talk embarrassing?" the girl said. "I'm in here because in computer lab there's this guy Yuri—ohmygosh, he has these Zac Efron eyes and Nick Jonas hair. So anyway, he's at the computer lab next to me and all of a sudden my stomach makes this loud grumbling noise."

"Did he hear it?" I asked.

"Maybe not the first time, but definitely the second time it happened," she said. "I hate not having lunch till sixth period. So I went to my locker and tried to eat a cookie from my lunch bag and this teacher was like blah-blah go back to class no eating in the halls. So I snuck in here to eat. You want a piece of my snicker-doodle?"

I shook my head no.

"So why are you in here?" she asked, before biting into her cookie.

"Oh, I just tripped and fell," I said.

"Oh, that's nothing," she said reassuringly. "So many people trip and fall. Like if they're trying to pull off Jimmy Choo stilettos for the first time. Bam! And come on, people love a funny fall. Remember Lizzie McGuire?"

"Well, it wasn't only a fall," I said. "There was this girl Cecilia—"

"Ooh!" the girl squealed. "I think I heard about you! Were you the girl who tried to take Cecilia Singer's stuff out of her Botkier bag and then Cecilia tripped you?"

"Wait, what?" I sighed. "What did you hear?"

"I heard that this girl begged her way into a study group with Cecilia so she could try to be friends with her," she said breathlessly, "and when Cecilia let her down kindly, the girl started to cry, fell to her knees, and stole lip gloss from her purse, just to have a small piece of Cecilia. And then Cecilia tripped her to try to stop her."

HOT GOSSIP UPDATE!

OH NO SHE DIDN'T!

Did that new redhead—we forgot her name already—stalk and steal from Cecilia's bag just to get some attention? What a wannabe!

"No!" I said. "That's not even close to what happened! I got assigned to work with her and—okay, this sucks. Do you really believe that?"

"Well, it's happened before." The girl shrugged. "Cecilia always has stalkers and groupies. Boys want her, girls want to be her. That's Cecilia's motto."

"Great, so I'm going to be infamous for being Avery Johnson, the girl who stalked and stole from Cecilia Singer." I leaned against the sink. "I've only lived here for three weeks and I've already destroyed my reputation."

"No worries," the girl said calmly. "For one thing, she thought your name was Agatha. For another thing, the gossip mill has already moved on. Megan Morgan was making out with the math sub in the supply room, so everyone's talking about that now."

I should've been relieved I was off the gossip radar. But it was kind of pathetic that I was such a nobody, even gossip about me was irrelevant.

"This kid who thinks he's paparazzi did get his friend to take a video of me falling," I said. "Is that going up on YouTube?"

"Oh, was that William Shaw?" the girl said. "Don't worry. If you're a nobody, he'll delete it."

Again, relief or self-pity? Not so sure.

"I don't mean that as an insult," the girl hurriedly reassured me. "I'm a nobody, too. I'm Jenna. I'm not even remotely part of the Cecilia Brat Pack. Miya is her best friend. Miya's dad is cousins or something with Johnny Depp. And William is totally one of Cecilia's entourage even though she pretends she hates it. He's like her mascot with his camera guy, Cam. Cecilia eats up the attention. So now you know who to avoid or suck up to, depending on your agenda."

"Me? I'm agenda-less," I said. "I confess I did try the suck-up and it didn't work out too well. I tried to compliment her by telling her she looks like Taylor Momsen and—"

"Oh no you didn't!" Jenna gasped. "Dude, Cecilia was up for the Jenny role and she got a callback and totally thought she had it. Then Taylor Momsen got the part and . . . ouch."

"Great," I sighed. "In Ohio, my friends *wanted* to look like celebrities. It didn't occur to me people here would actually be competing with them."

"Oh, Cecilia's probably auditioned for every role out there since she was eight," Jenna said. "She gets a lot of commercials and little parts but nothing major. She's gotten cast in pilots but they never make it on the air."

"That's kind of cool, though," I said. "Back home, nobody was ever on TV except the local news."

"Welcome to the fringes of L.A.," Jenna said. "We're close enough for people to go to auditions, but pretty much all the people who make it are at Crossroads or Lycée Français or tutored on their sets or home-schooled. There are a lot of frustrated wannabe stars here. Like Cecilia Singer. Although in this school, she's treated like a star."

"No kidding," I said. From what I could tell, Cecilia's family had enough money to send her to private school. But she probably got more attention here, surrounded by everyday people. In private school, there were probably a lot of Cecilias fighting their way to the It Girl spot.

"Cecilia does look like a bargain version of Taylor, doesn't she," Jenna giggled. "Momsen Lite. You should see Cecilia's sister, Delilah. Guys think she's the hottest thing. Her boyfriend is a singer in this band. Have you ever heard of University of Hard?"

"Can we not go there?" I groaned.

Suddenly Jenna's cell phone rang.

Don't cha wish your girlfriend was hot like me! Don't cha!

"Okay, that was loud," Jenna said, fumbling in her bag to turn off the phone.

"But I do love that song," I said.

"A classic," Jenna agreed, smiling. Then she looked at her cell and frowned.

"Ugh," she said. "My loser brother is paging me. He's a senior and in charge of my computer lab this period—and the bathroom pass. I have to get back." She picked up her bag and then turned to me.

"What class are you hiding out from right now?" she asked.

"Lunch," I said. "I'm just going to hang here."

"In the bathroom? You should just come with me to computer lab."

"That's okay," I said. "I don't want to get in trouble."

"You'll probably get busted here anyway," she said. "The teachers patrol the girls' room looking for smokers and pukers, so you might as well come with me. Plus, like I said, my brother's in charge of the lab this period."

It did sound way better than the bathroom. It was worth a shot.

"Okay," I said to her. "Thanks."

"No problem," she said. "When we go in, check out Yuri without being too obvious. But if you hear my stomach make noises, drop a book or something to distract him for me, 'kay?"

"Deal," I said, and I followed her out of the girls' room.

6

We entered the computer lab, and Jenna was right. Nobody even looked up when we walked in. People were working at computers in separate study carrels, but other than the tapping of keys, the place was silent. Jenna pointed to an empty computer station for me to take. When she went to sit at hers, I made a point to look at the guy sitting next to her.

Yup, he did have Zac Efron eyes and Nick Jonas hair. And an Abercrombie model body. If I were the one sitting next to him, my stomach would have butterflies, too. Fortunately, or unfortunately, I was sitting next to a guy who didn't have the same effect on me. I needed a good distraction to take my mind off the events of the morning.

Maybe I had some good comments on MySpace to cheer me up a little. I waited for my lime-green background to load and my Paramore song to start cranking. *Unable to load at this time.*

Figures. That went along with my sucky day. I'd have to try again later. I logged off and then signed on to my email.

I was deleting spam when I saw this.

```
From: FFranklin@DMBrecords.com
To: Group email
Cc: Ashley Johnson, Publicity
Subject: Promotions update


Marisa appearance details will be
sent by end of day.
```

Obviously, this email was sent to me by mistake. I remembered sending an email asking for info on Marisa, but I guess they thought I was someone else. Ashley Johnson, Avery Johnson—easy to get mixed up. I'd have to email the record label back and tell them that. I clicked to save it as new so I'd remember it later, and then I went back to my MySpace. *Unable to load at this time.*

Yeesh. There must be a problem with MySpace or the Internet connection. I was like the girl who . . . had nothing right working for her today.

I'd much rather be the girl who you can't do without, like in Marisa's song.

> *The girl who will make you feel*
> *Nothing you thought was real*
> *Will show you the inside out*
> *I really have no doubt*
> *I'm the girl who you can't do without*

I really did love that song. I wondered if Marisa wrote it herself. I'd kill a couple of minutes checking her out. I clicked over to Wikipedia.

```
Marisa (born Marisa Garcia-Myers) is
an American singer. She signed with
DMB Records this year. Her first
single, "The Girl Who," will be re-
leased later this month.
```

That didn't tell me much. I tried IMDb.

```
Marisa (pronounced Ma-ree-sa)
Date of Birth: September 16
Portland, Oregon

Singer, songwriter
```

Now I was curious. I delved deeper. A Google search for Marisa
Garcia-Myers brought up her high school page from a couple
years ago.

```
Marisa Garcia-Myers
Drama Club: Leads in Bye Bye Birdie,
Oklahoma
Service Club: President, Vice Presi-
dent
Quote: "I just want to be the girl
who helps people have better lives."
```

Wow, it was crazy to think that just a couple years ago she was a
normal high school student. I wondered if that was where she got
her "Girl Who" song title from. I pictured Marisa in high school,
doodling lyrics on the back of her notebook.

There was one more link to a Marisa story from a couple years ago in her college newspaper.

One standout in this season's choir concert this past weekend was freshman music major Marisa Garcia-Myers, who sang a solo she had written herself.

Marisa told us this was actually her first school performance since middle school. She's been writing songs, but only recently convinced herself to sing in public.

"I was too self-conscious to try out for solos or plays in high school," Marisa said. "I went to a huge high school where I felt lonely and left out. I guess I didn't audition because I couldn't face any more embarrassment or rejection."

I'm right there with you, sister. I totally could relate to her song, and now I could relate to her. I couldn't face any more embarrassment, like this morning, or rejection, like how MySpace wasn't working for me. Speaking of which, my MySpace page better be back up by now. I checked it and saw:

Your account has been deleted.

My account what? I hit refresh.

Your account has been deleted.

Uh . . . no, my account can't be deleted. Refresh.

Your account has been deleted.

My MySpace has been deleted? That can't be right. I have all of my videos, photos, and polls there. All of my friends. My friends! I can't lose my friends! I have 425 friends!

Your account has been deleted.

I've had that space for two years! I'm a loyal customer! Everyone else switched to Facebook but I've remained loyal!!! Tom! Tom! You can't just erase me!

This user has been deleted.

I quickly went to the help page and read the FAQ. Yes, Tom Anderson *could* just erase my existence. I guess when Tom invented MySpace he made it so that he could erase me. Could my page really be gone for good?

I put my head down in agony and banged my head against the keyboard.

"Excuse me," a voice said over my shoulder. I looked up to see a tall guy with very short dirty-blond hair and silvery metal glasses. He was wearing a Caltech T-shirt and skinny jeans. He peered at my screen. "Are you having computer problems I can help you with?"

"No!" I said, picking my head up off the keyboard. "Well, yes, I'm having computer problems. But nothing you can help me with. Unless you know how to fix a MySpace that was deleted."

"You're not supposed to be on MySpace in here," he said.

Oh, crap.

"Are *you* even supposed to be in here?" he asked. "I don't recognize you."

Double crap. I looked wildly at Jenna for help, but the guy was blocking my view of her.

"Follow me," he said.

I got up and followed him into a small office at the back of the room. He shut the door behind us.

"Are you a regular student in this lab?" the guy asked.

"I'm sorry," I said. "I just . . . I mean . . . I'll just leave. I'm new and I swear I never got in trouble at my old school but I—"

The door opened and Jenna walked in.

"Sebastian!" Jenna said brightly. "This is Avery."

"Ah. Let me guess," Sebastian said. "My sister said you could come into computer lab because her brother wouldn't notice."

Well, yeah.

"Jenna doesn't always think of the consequences," Sebastian continued. "To herself and others."

"Look, I don't want to get anyone in trouble," I said, backing toward the door. "I'll just go to lunch now."

"Nobody will get in trouble," Jenna scoffed. "That is, unless Sebastian turns into Tattle McTattleson."

"And why shouldn't I report an offender?" Sebastian asked, crossing his arms.

"Because Avery needs to be here. She needs a place to recuperate," Jenna said. "She's new and she already got publicly humiliated in English this morning."

"And that happens to some of us on a daily basis," Sebastian said. "Welcome to the club. Now, you may go to your regularly scheduled classes."

"Cecilia Singer totally humiliated her," Jenna said. "Delilah Singer's sister."

Sebastian paused for a second. I caught a glimpse of something—sympathy? No, it was more like disgust. But then he shrugged and turned around.

Giving up, I turned to leave, but Jenna grabbed my arm to stop me.

"Sebastian, you are a cold, cold person," Jenna said. "I should have known better than to try to appeal to your emotions. Because you don't have any."

She picked up an iPhone off the desk and held it up in the air.

"Give me my phone," Sebastian said.

"After I tell Mom about Vida Segunda," Jenna said, moving away from him.

"What about Vida?" Sebastian said.

"About the fact that she doesn't exist! Ha!" Jenna turned to me. "My parents are worried about Sebastian's social life so he told them he had a girlfriend, Vida. He tells them he's going on dates but really goes to the Cyber Café by himself."

"How did you figure that out?" Sebastian groaned. He sank down into his chair.

"Hello? Vida Segunda means 'Second Life' in Spanish," Jenna said. "Just because I don't get straight A's like you doesn't mean I'm an idiot—"

"Um, maybe you two should talk in private," I interrupted.

"Avery, don't you think Vida should come over to our house for dinner? I'm going to suggest that it's time for Mom and Dad to meet her." Jenna held up the phone and speed-dialed.

"This is blackmail," Sebastian grumbled.

"Avery gets to come to the computer lab every day, or else I'm telling!" Jenna's voice changed as she talked into the phone. "Hi, Mommy!"

"Don't even think about—" Sebastian said.

"Mommy, I just wanted to tell you that—"

"Fine, she can stay!" Sebastian said.

"—Sebastian is going to give me a ride home today. I'm not going to stay after. Okay, bye!"

Jenna hung up and grinned.

"Giving you a ride home wasn't part of the bargain," Sebastian grumped.

"Next time be nicer to my friends right away and you won't have to be punished," Jenna said. "Avery, do you need a ride home? Sebastian has a new car. Well, it's an old car. A Prius. Not the new cool kind. It's the old kind that doesn't even have power windows, but still—"

"I'm fine," I interrupted. I inched my way to the door. "Thanks again for letting me stay in the lab."

"Like I had a choice," Sebastian snorted.

"Don't be offended, Avery. My brother is totally antisocial," Jenna said. "You have to be an avatar to get a civil response from him."

"Yo, computer dork! My computer's effed up!" some guy called out from the lab.

"And *that's* why I don't like people," Sebastian said, and walked past me and Jenna out of the office.

"Sorry, I didn't know that was going to be such a problem," I said to Jenna.

"What problem?" Jenna shrugged. "That was no problem. Besides, I'm stoked I don't have to take the bus home today."

We both walked back to our computer stations.

This was huge, to be able to skip lunch and come to the lab every day. I smiled as I logged back into the computer. I should probably do school stuff but . . . I was dying to know if my MySpace was back up. Maybe my luck was changing. I looked around to see if any of the computer lab people were watching. Sebastian was still trying to help that one guy with his computer. I signed into my MySpace.

This user has been deleted.

Ugh. I decided to email Tom and tell him there had been a mistake. Maybe my site was just in MySpace limbo and could be pulled back up as if it had never been missing. I signed on to my email and saw I had a couple new messages in my in-box.

Oh, they were both from Marisa's record label. I still had to let them know that I was mistakenly getting their emails.

```
To: Group@dmbrecords.com
Cc: Publicity
From: AJohnson@DMBrecords.com
Subject: Buzz

Marisa's appearance is in 2 days and
I haven't heard any promotion? We'd
like people to show. Please advise.

Ashley

Los Angeles: October 4
```

Poor Marisa. And I thought I had it bad not having anyone to sit with at lunch. It would be way worse to be a singer and have nobody show up at your appearance. I wondered why nobody was getting any buzz out there for Marisa. Her song rocked.

```
To: Group@dmbrecords.com
Cc: Publicity
From: AJohnson@DMBrecords.com
Subject: Buzz

Mall appearance schedule attached.
Is anyone working on buzz for
Marisa? Please advise. Attachment is
the mp3 of "The Girl Who."

Ashley

Los Angeles: October 4
```

Mall appearance? *Mall* appearance? Who's going to see something in a mall? My mom saw Tiffany in the mall twenty years ago. I like retro, but that's just outdated. Not only did Marisa have to suffer the indignity of doing a mall appearance, but without publicity it would be a mall appearance where nobody showed up.

And I thought *I* had an embarrassing moment today.

I should show up and support her. But then again, I had no friends to bring and just me showing up by myself wouldn't be too helpful. I didn't even know how I would get there.

I felt useless.

I Googled to see if Marisa had gotten some more buzz and found nothing. Where was Marisa's website? Her MySpace or Facebook or *something*?

I thought about the line in Marisa's song: *I'm the girl who you wish you knew.* Marisa deserved more than this. People should wish they knew her. The girl needed some buzz. I couldn't believe her label hadn't set her up with a MySpace. I mean, there's a whole section of MySpace *dedicated* to musicians, people.

An idea occurred to me. I'd make her a page! I'd give her some buzz! I'd be Marisa's street team! Okay, an unofficial street team, just one fan out to promote Marisa and make her the star that she deserves to be.

I'd be . . . Team Marisa!

Team of one, maybe, but that's better than zero, right? Okay, I needed to start a new blog. I still had that account where I made that stupid page the other night about Gwen Stefani. But that blog was called Princess of Gossip, which wouldn't work. And music industry people were all on MySpace, so that was probably the best place to be. Plus, I had my password and I knew how to do the layouts . . . as long as Tom didn't delete my account again.

I looked up at the clock. I didn't have much time left in class to sign up for new accounts elsewhere, so MySpace it was:

www.MySpace.com/teammarisa

I went to my favorite layout page and considered my options. Marisa had been wearing a pink shirt that looked really pretty with her hair color. And since her album was called *Emerald City,* I thought of green. I chose a pink layout with green music notes. I used the picture of Marisa from the record label website as the profile picture.

Now I would need to invite some friends, bump Tom off the Top 16, and start building buzz for Marisa. As the finishing touch, I uploaded the clip of Marisa's new song to use as the music.

I put in the code and Marisa's song started playing loudly. Oops. I didn't realize the audio was on. People who didn't have headphones on looked up to see what was happening. Then the bell rang and fortunately covered up the music until I could hit the mute button. People started getting together their things and heading for their next class.

"What was that?" Jenna's voice startled me.

I quickly closed out of MySpace, snapping back to reality— the reality where my MySpaces got deleted, I had pretty much no life, and I was an L.A. loser. It suddenly seemed kind of stupid to start the page for Marisa. It wasn't like anyone would ever come to it.

"Um, what?" I said, grabbing my tote bag off the floor.

"What was that song you were playing on your computer? It sounded cool."

"Oh, it's by this new singer named Marisa," I said, following her out of the room.

"Never heard of her."

No. Not yet. But maybe soon . . . who knows?

First blog entry:

Presenting . . . Team Marisa's MySpace! Welcome to the place where Marisa's fans can come together and support Marisa as her amazing single, "The Girl Who," debuts. Let's put the "team" in Team Marisa!

How?

1) Add Marisa to your friends list!
2) Tell your friends to check out Team Marisa MySpace! Spread the word!
3) Call radio stations! Indie 103.1 and KISS 102.7 and request "The Girl Who."
4) Go see Marisa's mall appearance! For now, the mall. Next up—anything's possible!

Especially with your help! Join Team Marisa now!

7

```
Text Message
To: Avery's friends list
From: Avery [inLA]
Date: October 12-8:45 p.m.
Subject:

My MySpace is down! But don't panic,
I'm still here. Text me, call me.
```

I tossed my phone on the bed as I walked into my room and turned on my computer. I changed into a tank top, since I'd gotten my shirt all disgusting from sweating on the bus ride home. I lived too far away from school to walk or ride a bike, like I used to do in Ohio, so I was stuck taking the bus.

I pulled up my go-to-first gossip site.

LINDSAY CRASHES CAR!

Again? It was hard to summon up some sympathy for that one. These people did not know how good they had it. They could be me, with no car or ride, forced to take the sweaty and disgusting school bus home. I pictured Lindsay on a school bus. Heh.

PDA FOR PERTH AND CRUZ!

Perth Hampton and Cruz Ramirez were spotted kissing backstage after the Statement's show at Crash Mansion near the Staples Center in downtown L.A. "Perth was on Cruz's lap, and they didn't seem to care that other people were watching them," said a source. "They looked really cute together!"

The duo hasn't made their romance public, but it's going to be hard to stay undercover now that we're onto them!

Those two were so cute together. Someday, somehow, I was going to get myself to the Statement's concert. I had a list of concerts I wanted to see, and the Statement was one of them. I mentally added Marisa to the list and hoped that someday she'd be playing a major place like Crash Mansion—or even the Staples Center. I really thought Marisa was good enough to play someplace huge like the Staples Center, maybe even sell out like Kanye's show did. Marisa could become huge. She had so much potential.

It was probably stupid that I thought she needed me, a fan, to put up a MySpace for her. I should probably take it down. I signed in and went to my home page.

You have 31 Comments.
You have 42 Friend Requests.
You have 28 Messages.

SABRINA BRYAN AND JULIA DeVILLERS

Really? Since this morning? Were they all spam? I clicked over to Marisa's profile.

> Thx for telling us about the mall show! My friends and I will be there!
>
> I can't go to the mall but I called in to request Marisa's song!
>
> Please add me! "The Girl Who" rocks!
>
> Add me to Friends! I want more Marisa!

I sat back against my bedroom wall, rather pleased with myself. Maybe I actually could play a small part in getting people to go see Marisa at the mall. Maybe I could help her in her rise to stardom.

And she deserved to be a star. Unlike some people (cough * Cecilia * cough).

> Add to Friends:
>
> Accept
>
> Accept
>
> Accept

I was still adding friends when my phone rang.

"Hi, honey!" my mom said when I answered it. "What are you up to?"

"Hi," I said distractedly. "Adding friends."

"Wonderful!" my mom said. "I knew you'd make new friends! Are they from your classes?"

"Well," I said cautiously. "They're on my team."

"Wonderful!" she said again. "You joined a team! You'll have to tell your dad all about it when we get home. We'll be a little late.

Your father wants to stop by the coffee shop for the second time today in case Gwen Stefani is there. I told him I would do that one more time but after that he moves into stalker status."

"Please promise me you'll call me if she's there," I said. "And then order really slow and block her so she can't leave until I've had time to call a cab and get there. Okay?"

"We'll be home soon," Mom said. "Enjoy your new friends."

I hung up and went back to adding everyone who looked semi-sane to my friends list. While I was adding, I got another email.

```
To: Groupmarisa@dmbrecords.com
From: AJohnson@DMBrecords.com


Marisa meet-and-greet prior to mall
appearance. Please insert into press
releases. Marisa's official bio at-
tached.
```

Wow! I needed to let Team Marisa know! This was so cool. Marisa would be signing autographs and meeting her fans before the mall appearance! That meant I could actually go meet Marisa in person. She'd sign her autograph, I could tell her about Team Marisa, and she'd probably thank me for the support.

Reality check. There were at least two reasons that wasn't going to happen: (1) Once anyone saw Team Marisa was being run by a fifteen-year-old nobody, it would crash and burn; and (2) I had no ride to a mall two hours away.

There was no way I'd be meeting Marisa. But that didn't mean her other fans couldn't. So right now, I'd live vicariously through the reports from Team Marisa people. I had a lot of work ahead of me. I'd have to put all this new information on the Team Marisa MySpace. Post Marisa's official bio. Add my friends. Reply to messages. There was a lot to do, and I was excited to do it. And I got even more excited after I started reading what people had sent me.

Leslie sent a link to her MySpace background of Marisa, which was totally cool.

Anniebananie sent a photo of Marisa I'd never seen before.

Ivomarie sent a banner with Marisa's name in sparkling letters on it.

And Swaywithme sent a YouTube video with pictures of Marisa in a montage, set to "The Girl Who"! It was so cool that I put it right in the middle of the Team Marisa MySpace page.

I was just sending out a bulletin to tell everyone to check out the new page when I heard the garage door open. Wow. My parents were home already? What time was it? I looked at the clock to see that an hour and a half had passed. I'd totally lost track of time. I hadn't even started my homework yet.

"Avery!" my dad called. "Come tell us about the new team you joined!"

The team I'd joined? I flexed my fingers, which were sore from typing. I grasped for an explanation as I got up and headed downstairs.

"Hey," I said, walking into the kitchen.

"Brought you a little treat from your father's favorite coffee place," Mom said, handing me a little paper bag. Mmm, pumpkin bread.

"No Jen Stefani sightings." My father sounded disappointed. "I'd been hoping that was her regular thing, going to the Coffee Leafy Tea Beany place at eight."

"Wow, Dad," I said, sitting down and taking a bite of the pumpkin bread. "Don't make Mom jealous."

"Doesn't bother me," my mother said. "Especially since I heard that George Clooney has been there, so I'm hoping for my own sighting."

"Pfft." My dad waved his hand in the air. "I'm better looking than that old guy. And I bet I could take him in Wii boxing. Anyone up for a game?"

"Er, I would," I said, thinking quickly. "But I still have homework to finish, so I can't."

"So wait, Avery," my mom said. "Tell us about the team you joined."

"Well, I made up my own team. It's kind of a music team," I said.

Then I thought about Sebastian lying to his parents about his virtual girlfriend and felt a little guilty.

"It's mostly online." I injected some honesty to compensate. "But I'm trying to make it real-world, too. This is only just a start."

That was all the truth.

"And you said you're making this with friends?" my dad asked.

"Yes! I've got forty-three friends!" I said proudly. "And counting!"

"Well, I'm happy to hear you're enjoying yourself," my mother said. "And while you're doing your homework, I'm going to whup your father in boxing."

"I love a woman who gives me a challenge," my dad said.

"Gross, guys," I said, swallowing the last piece of pumpkin bread and heading upstairs to my room. I had a team who needed me.

BULLETIN from Team Marisa

From: Team Marisa
Date: October 13—9:30 p.m.
Subject: Marisa update on my blog!!

New blog entry:

Team Marisa Update

Going to see Marisa at the mall? GO EARLY! She'll be signing autographs at a meet-and-greet BEFORE the show!

Get to Know Marisa:

Marisa was born on September 16 in Portland, Oregon. She picked up a guitar when she was five and begged her parents to let her take lessons. She began taking dance lessons when she was six and took ballet, jazz, and hip-hop throughout school. In high school, she was voted Most Musical and Most Likely to Save the World.

She attended college in Northern California, majoring in social work. Her college roommate invited Marisa to play at her younger brother's bar mitzvah. A music producer, a family friend, was in the audience and saw her potential. Impressed with her vocal range, guitar technique, and dance moves, he invited her to go around to music labels. DMB Records quickly signed her and she began recording her first single.

"I want to create music people relate to," Marisa said. "I want everybody to find a little piece of themselves in my songs. My songs are about real emotions. They're my emotions now, my emotions as I was struggling through my teen years. But they're emotions we all feel inside."

Marisa's album, *Emerald City*, is titled after a necklace with an emerald guitar pendant her father gave her after she recorded her first song.

"My dad told me that in ancient times, emeralds were supposed to ward off negativity and transform it into positive energy," Marisa said.

She says she wears the necklace all the time as a reminder to keep positive people around her.

"My family keeps me grounded," she said. "My friends keep me true. And anyone who takes the time to listen to me sing, well, they're the ones who keep me inspired to create music that really speaks to their hearts."

Her debut single "The Girl Who," was released by DMB Records.

8

Avery Johnson + Chris Brown =
    Avris?

JohnBrown?

No. I still hadn't found my Brad to my Angelina. How would we become the It couple of Hollywood without our cute Brangelina couple nickname? Sorry, Chris, I needed to move on.

Avery Johnson + Penn Badgley

Pavery?

Avadgley?

Oh my gosh, no. Could there be any worse celebrity name than Avadgley? The press would nickname us Vadge and—

"Your test on *The Lord of the Flies* will be tomorrow. Please return to the same groups from yesterday and quiz each other from the review paper," Miss Schmitt said.

Oh, no. Not the same groups.

Johnson + King + Singer = JoKing Singer

As in you've got to be *joking* if you think I'm working with Cecilia Singer again. Everyone started moving their desks around. I was stuck.

"I'll switch with you," a voice said in my ear.

I turned around to see William, the paparazzi wannabe, with Cam standing behind him.

"I need some close-ups," William said. "Cecilia's looking so hot today it gives me chills. I could totally sell some video to the freshmen."

"You *sell* your pictures?" I asked him, horrified.

"Yeah," he said. "This is my career, dollface. There's demand around here for my Cecilia close-ups. Freshmen don't usually get to be close to her."

I didn't know what to say, so I just got up and walked over to where Griffin and Cecilia were already sitting. William and Cam followed me, and Cam shoved his camera in Cecilia's face.

"Dude," Griffin said. "Get out of her face, okay?"

"Mr. Shaw!" Miss Schmitt called out. "Is there a problem?"

"Yes," William muttered. "You." But he headed over to the other side of the classroom, with Cam following.

"Thanks for being my bodyguard," Cecilia said to Griffin.

Great. She's got paparazzi *and* bodyguards.

Cecilia extended her legs over Griffin's desk, effectively blocking me out.

"We missed you this weekend, Griffy," Cecilia said. "After the U of Hard concert we went to the Four Seasons. It was crazy."

Actually, I knew a little bit about that. I had read that Shade had been partying at the bar at the Four Seasons and was seen kissing an anonymous girl with black hair. But I didn't plan to share that last piece of information.

"That reminds me," Cecilia continued. "Mark Ryan's uncle is screening his new movie, *Trail of Entrails III*, Friday night. Want to go, Griffin?"

"Maybe," Griffin said. "So Avery, do you like horror movies?"

Thank you, Griffin, for acknowledging my presence.

"I'm a love-it-at-the-time type," I said. "But then they give me nightmares."

"Living in Idaho would give *me* nightmares," Cecilia said. "But, Griff, let me know—"

"Ms. Singer, please see me for your essay critique," Miss Schmitt called out, interrupting her.

"Time to collect my A minus," Cecilia said. "That was the grade she gave my sister *and* the senior Delilah bought the paper from."

Cecilia slid off Griffin's desk and went to the front of the room.

"Ohio's not so bad," I said, half to myself.

"You don't have to convince me." Griffin smiled and stretched his hands behind his back. His longish dark blond hair was extra messy in that cute way. He was wearing a torn black hoodie with an army/navy-style jacket over it, and washed-out jeans. I couldn't help but notice he was looking really good.

"I wouldn't bother trying to convince Cecilia, though," Griffin continued. "But don't take her personally. Cecilia lives in her own little world."

"Yeah, I wouldn't mind living in Cecilia World." I couldn't help but sigh. "Being worshipped by the masses."

"It's not as perfect as it seems," Griffin said.

I snorted.

"Come on," Griffin said. "Don't you want to hear about how you're supposed to feel sorry for her because of her notoriously workaholic father, her plastic-surgery-obsessed mother, and her stagnant acting career? And how being worshipped by the masses at school is her only source of happiness?"

"No," I said. "It's hard to feel sorry for someone who looks that good. I'd rather think of her as just a cold, callous wench."

Oops, that just slipped out. Should I have said that about Cecilia, much less to her friend?

Griffin laughed.

"I like that," he said. "Can I use that as a song title? 'Cold, Callous Wench' is kind of catchy."

"You're into music?" I asked him.

"Writing it," he said. "The lyrics and the tunes. But not playing it. I am slowly improving on Guitar Hero II, though."

"Well, when 'Cold, Callous Wench' hits the charts, please don't let Cecilia know it's named after her," I said.

"She'd probably be flattered," Griffin said. "See, you had to put up with a few insults, but you got your muse for our hit song. We could make millions and you'll be forever grateful for being assigned to our study group."

HOT GOSSIP!

"Cold, Callous Wench" hits #1 on iTunes! Who *is* the cold, callous wench who inspired this huge hit? Paris wants the title, but it's not hers . . .

"I like it." I smiled. "So what kind of music do you write?"

"Oh, that question makes me so sound like a cliché," he said. "Indie rock. Like if Bob Dylan's DNA crossed with Jack White's."

"Is that what you're writing?" I pointed to a notebook on his desk with writing and doodled music notes on the back.

"Yeah," he said. "It's in progress. I'm just playing around. I'm trying to think of a good title for it."

" 'Cold, Callous Wench' doesn't fit?" I asked.

He smiled and shook his head, then slid the notebook over to me.

> *There's more to you*
> *Than meets the eye*
> *I don't know why*
> *You hide your light*
> *So deep inside*

> *I want to shatter the myth*
> *That is you*
> *And find the girl*
> *That's true*

> *Whatever you're going through*
> *I'll be there, too*
> *Let the stars in my eyes light the way*

I didn't say anything at first. I thought about what it would be like to have someone write a song about me like that. I could just picture a guy thinking about me at home at night and taking out his English notebook. I peeked at Griffin, who was shuffling his flash cards. I thought about how it would feel if Griffin had written that about me. Not that he had, of course, since he just met me. But I had a flash of fantasy as I pictured Griffin staring at me across the classroom, wondering secretly who the new girl was.

HOT GOSSIP

That new song "Redheaded Girl," rising rapidly up the *Billboard* charts, was written about which new girl at school?

Maybe nobody else noticed her, but Griffin King saw her light hiding deep inside . . . and turned it into a megahit!

I sighed.

"It sucks, doesn't it?" Griffin said.

"Huh?" I snapped back to reality. "Oh, no! I was sighing because . . . I was thinking about . . . I mean your song, I mean . . . it's good!"

All right, that didn't come out very convincing. I blushed. Obviously I should change that Hot Gossip to "Which new girl has the obvious signs of a new crush on a guy who writes songs?"

I took a deep breath and continued.

"Really, I like it. And you're right: 'Cold, Callous Wench' doesn't work for the title. Who's your song about? Maybe you could use her name for the title," I said.

"That's been done," Cecilia said, sliding into her seat. I hadn't known she was behind me. "There's already a song called 'Hey there, Delilah.' "

"Who said I wrote the song about Delilah?" Griffin asked her.

"Oh, give it up, Griffin. You have a collection of songs written about my sister. Remember the first song you wrote about her?" Cecilia continued. "It was something like Delilah, I love your smile-ah."

"That was in fifth grade," Griffin said. "I hope my songwriting skills have improved since then."

I did notice he was blushing a little. Apparently Griffin had a thing for Cecilia's sister. My own blush quickly subsided.

"That reminds me. Griffin, you missed this weekend, which means you also missed the unveiling of Delilah!" Cecilia said. "Check her out!"

Cecilia waved her iPhone in Griffin's face. I caught a glimpse of a girl who resembled Paris Hilton, but with a much bigger chest, which she was showing off in her low-cut shirt.

"What do you think, Griffy?" Cecilia asked. "It was a surprise present from Shade. She's a D cup now."

Griffin's face turned redder.

"I think we should study now," Griffin said, looking away.

I sighed. Griffin was smart and cute, and he wrote song lyrics about a girl that's true. Unfortunately, the girl he wrote about seemed to have gotten less true and more silicone over the weekend. I wouldn't have thought his taste ran toward older, plastic-looking Barbie doll types, but then he was a guy. So in hindsight, I guess it was silly to think that he wouldn't.

"Studying's overrated," Cecilia said. "What else did I miss while I was getting my A, besides your latest love song to Delilah?"

"We also came up with a song title and *you* were our muse for that one," Griffin said, winking at me. I hoped he wasn't going to share that it was "Cold, Callous Wench."

"Shut up," Cecilia said.

"Okay, don't believe me." Griffin shrugged. "We're not cutting you in on the royalties, then."

I suppressed a grin.

"You two bore me," Cecilia said casually. "My Twitter fans are waiting for an update on my interesting life. Neither of you two will make the cut."

Cecilia started tapping on her iPhone under the desk.

"Avery, I guess that means we can study in peace," Griffin said to me. "First question. Is the name of the book we read *Lord of the Flies* or *Lord of the Rings*?"

9

Jenna met me at my locker after English class so we could walk to computer lab together. I was at my locker inhaling a chocolate s'mores protein bar to hold me over. My locker was now full of protein bars, fruit, crackers, and individual-size peanut butter things I could eat while still avoiding the cafeteria area. I also had a lot of breath mints.

"Well, I just survived another group session with Cecilia Singer," I said.

"Really? Two days in a row in her presence? Wow. Did she invite you into her inner circle of VIP rooms and nightclubbing?"

"Gee," I said. "That would be no. She does sound like she has a cool life. She was talking about these places she goes to with the guy in our group, Griffin."

"Griffin King? He's nice," Jenna said. "He was in some of my classes last year. The poor guy has a massive crush on Cecilia's sister, though."

"Oh, you know about that?" I asked.

I found myself disappointed that it was such common knowledge. If everyone knew about it, he must be pretty into her. Oh well. Griffin was the first guy who I'd really talked to this year, so naturally I'd developed a little teeny crush on him.

"Yeah," Jenna said. "He wrote a song about it a couple years ago and he played it at the Singers' holiday party. It ended poorly when everyone turned around to look at Delilah and she was making out with the bartender."

"Yikes, that's painful," I said. "I just wouldn't think Delilah is Griffin's type. Not that I know her. I saw pictures of her new, um, surgical enhancements."

"What?" Jenna said, rolling her eyes. "Like she didn't make the boys drool as it was?"

I had a fleeting thought about how it would be nice to have guys drool over me. I'd had one boyfriend in Ohio. Nicole had decided we'd look cute together, so we went along with it. Other than some IMing and a dance where we barely talked to each other, it wasn't much of a relationship. He dumped me. I ate ice cream and moved on.

"It's too bad, Griffin King is too nice to like a Singer," Jenna said. "And, ohmygosh, he has the best clothes. He has the biggest collection of hoodies and his jackets are to die for. And he writes music that the eighth-grade band played at the concert last year."

Definitely out of my league. If I was going to crush, I'd need to find someone who was less talented, less cute, and had lower aspirations for his girlfriend's appearance. I obviously could never compete with Delilah Singer.

We walked down the hall. A couple people said hi to Jenna as we walked by.

"You know a lot of people," I said.

"I've lived here forever, that's all," Jenna said. "Some people you don't want to know, trust me. But others . . ."

She tilted her head to indicate a cute guy walking by.

"Others, you definitely *do* want to know. Like Joe Williams. Do you recognize him from the deodorant commercial? We do have some hot guys in this school," she said. Then she frowned. "However, *that* is not one of them."

Sebastian was standing at the door of the computer lab. I couldn't help but notice he had his shirt buttoned wrong, as he pointed to a large orange watch that had a calculator on it.

"You're almost late," Sebastian said. "If you're going to sneak people in here, Jenna, the least you can do is be on time."

"The least you can do is button your shirt correctly." Jenna stuck out her tongue at him and headed into the room.

"Sorry we're late!" I meekly apologized to him as I walked by. I definitely didn't want to risk getting kicked out of computer lab, especially today. I had a lot to do online. I couldn't wait to check in on Team Marisa, *Billboard* online, and the music-label emails. I followed Jenna over to an empty computer station and got to work.

I signed on to Team Marisa first. I'd set a goal to get at least twenty-five or thirty more friends today.

You have 475 Friend Requests.

What the . . . ? How was that possible? I also had 275 messages? How had these people found me? I searched through a few messages and found the answer.

```
To: Team Marisa MySpace owner
From: Krickett


Guess what? The midnight DJ at Indie
103.1 played "The Girl Who" last
```

```
night!! And he added it to his hot
playlist on his MySpace!
```

Seriously? I clicked on the link Krickett had sent me. It was true! He had added "The Girl Who" to his favorites list! Awesome! I sent him a message to add him as one of my friends. Marisa had gotten some airplay! I wondered if the DMB people knew about it. I wanted to let Ashley Johnson, the other AJohnson, know, except I didn't want to give myself away. In the meantime, I couldn't wait to let all of Team Marisa know that "The Girl Who" was on the air. I had more than a hundred new comments.

> This song is so special! It makes me cry! MinnieM
> Please add more to this MySpace! I heart Marisa! Hotsme1
> I asked a guy to homecoming today and he said no. I thought of the line "I'm the girl you'll wish you knew" and that made me feel better. DCimo

I couldn't help but smile. Marisa's song had meant something to other people, too. It was so weird how you could turn on a song and it seemed to say exactly what you were feeling. I decided to answer everyone at home when I had more time. I checked my email. There was something from DMB in my in-box.

```
To: Groupmarisa@dmbrecords.com
From: AJohnson@zmx.com

Change in mall appearance setup.
Marisa stage moved to upstairs level
near parking garage. Mall owner's
```

```
son needs atrium for fifth birthday
party's petting zoo. Won't budge.
Upstairs has minimal audio but will
do best we can.
```

What? Marisa was bumped so a five-year-old could have a petting zoo? It's not bad enough she is doing a mall appearance with little promotion, but now she has to do one in a place with bad audio so a kindergartener can have a petting zoo?

What was wrong with these people? Marisa deserved better than this! I needed to rally Team Marisa to . . . to . . . I didn't know what we should do.

All of this made me even more convinced the girl needed to get more airplay. Her song wasn't on the radio as far as I could tell, except for that one time. She wasn't getting famous. But what could I do? I had no idea how music people got famous, other than be on *American Idol.* Colbie Caillat got a ton of buzz, but then I'd read her father was some music producer. How did Sara Bareilles get her song to hit the top on iTunes? How did Ingrid Michaelson get her song everywhere, even an Old Navy commercial? Well, we definitely didn't want Marisa to go the Tila Tequila route, that much I did know.

So that left me with . . . what? My father was not a music producer like Colbie's. I knew nobody in the music business. I was just one fan, could I really make a difference? I pulled up my Team Marisa site. I closed my eyes and thought of Marisa's song. *The girl who, the girl who, the girl who you'll wish you knew.*

I wanted people to know Marisa, and to love her music like I did. I needed a flash of inspiration of how I could make that happen.

Suddenly, there was a flash. But it wasn't a flash of inspiration, it was a white flash on the computer screen, accompanied by a little zapping noise.

And then the screen went black. The computer had completely crashed.

10

Crud. This was no time for my computer to crash. I hit the power button, but the screen stayed black. Apparently this *was* a time for my computer to crash. I sighed. Maybe that was a message from the computer gods to just give up on the whole Marisa inspiration thing.

I got up and looked around for the nearest computer lab monitor. I spotted Sebastian sitting in the office.

"Sebastian?" I tapped on the office door as I opened it.

"Mmm-hmm?" He was typing on his computer and didn't take his eyes off the screen.

"My computer crashed," I said. "I think it needs you."

"Were you working on two screens with extensive graphics at one time?" he asked without looking up.

"Kind of," I said. "Is that a problem?"

"These are school computers," Sebastian groaned. "What do you people think they're capable of? Everything overloads them."

He rolled his chair away from the computer and stood up. He stomped out of the office, and I turned to follow him. But something caught my eye.

Sebastian's computer screen was filled with bright lights. There was an elaborate background scene that looked like the ground was the moon, with bright stars blinking in the sky. It was pretty cool.

I leaned in closer and watched as a manga-looking girl avatar with blue hair and three arms popped onto the screen. She floated around in space.

Then another avatar, this time a guy with a normal number of limbs but wearing an outfit reminiscent of *Star Wars* popped onto the screen. He floated over to the girl and a speech bubble appeared over her head that said "Hi."

Heh. It looked like Sebastian was playing some kind of Second Life or a Sims game. The guy avatar looked familiar for some reason. And then it hit me. It was Sebastian, but with black hair and in costume. Which made me guess who the other character might be.

Suddenly the girl avatar disappeared. Then she reappeared, disappeared, and reappeared again.

"Your computer just needed a restart," Sebastian said, startling me as he came back into the office. "You're back in business. Don't do it again."

"Is that Vida?" I asked Sebastian.

"What?" Sebastian said, and looked over at his monitor. "Man, didn't the screen saver go on?"

He looked frustrated and tapped a few keys. "No, that's not Vida. Vida has three *eyes,* not arms."

Oh. Sounds attractive. I watched, fascinated, as the background turned to silver tiles and the avatar disappeared.

"Is that Second Life?" I asked him.

"No," Sebastian said abruptly.

"It's kind of cool," I told him. "The background looks so real."

"Yeah, I'm sure you really think so," Sebastian muttered skeptically.

"No, I do." I leaned in closer. "Why does she keep disappearing?"

"I'm trying to make it so the characters actually can move between layers," Sebastian said. "But my coding isn't working right . . . and why am I telling you this?"

"You're coding that?" I said. I sat down on a chair and rolled over next to him. "As in, making up that program?"

"Yeah," he said. "It's part of my application to Caltech. I'm making a new online world and putting it up on a website. I applied for a patent for part of it but—"

"Like Club Penguin?" I asked. "I love Club Penguin."

"No, not like Club Penguin, jeez," he said. "Okay, maybe in theory, but more like Second Life or World of Warcraft."

"Or like Webkinz," I said.

Sebastian gave me a look.

"I'm just kidding!" I said. "Really, this is cool. I mean, I was impressed with myself that I can make MySpace layouts, and here you are creating an entire world. What can you do with it?"

Sebastian actually smiled a little. "If you really want to know, the characters are the avatars, the people who populate the world. They can talk in speech bubbles. I haven't figured out how to do audio, so at this stage it's all text. I can play music in the background, though."

"Who draws the artwork?" I said. The avatars were very manga-inspired and simple, but also kind of cool.

"Me," he said. "Yes, I'm not only a computer geek but I draw manga. Continue your inner laughter."

"I'm not laughing at you," I said. And I wasn't. Because this was starting to get interesting. Geeky, but interesting. An idea percolated in my brain.

"What are you going to do with the world?" I asked him.

"Well," he said. "I have a website that will be devoted to my virtual world. Next, I have to find real people to go online to be the avatars and interact on the site. However, I have to do all this by next week for early admission, so thanks for stressing me out."

Hm. Real people. A virtual world. What if, along with a MySpace, instead of just leaving comments and messages . . . we could make a virtual online world. What if I could make . . .

A Marisa World. I could call it M World City, which sounded like Emerald City, the title of Marisa's album! It was brilliant. I'd call it M World for short.

I had more than five hundred Team Marisa people who were asking to help promote Marisa. And Sebastian had a virtual world to populate.

"Sebastian," I said. "We might be able to help each other out."

"Not to sound cynical, but you think you can help me how?" he said.

"Well, I want to throw a virtual party," I said. "So maybe I could use your site for it."

"A party? This is a serious, intense project. And how is that helping me?"

"I could bring real people online, to be your avatars," I said, and then paused dramatically. "Would five hundred be enough?"

"You can get five hundred people to come to my virtual world?" he asked suspiciously.

"Yes," I said. "I can. And just think, you'd have your virtual world for a real cause. So that would make it even more impressive for the Caltech people, right?"

"I guess you're right," Sebastian said. "That would be more impressive . . ."

My mind reeled with the possibilities. I'd throw a party online in a virtual M World. This was way bigger than just a MySpace. Way bigger and way cooler.

"All right, let's do it," Sebastian said.

The door opened behind me, and I turned to see Jenna in the doorway.

"Avery, is my brother giving you a hard time about being in lab again?" she asked.

"No, it's all good," I said. "I needed help with a computer project. And Sebastian is going to help me."

"You're working on a project with my brother?" she said. "Gross. Wait, you didn't blackmail her to do this with you, did you, Sebastian?"

"No. Perhaps you don't recall, but you are the blackmailer in our family," Sebastian said. "I am the computer genius."

"And I really need his computer genius to make my project happen," I said.

"Is it a search engine to help me find all the vintage bargains and sample sales in Los Angeles?" Jenna asked.

"No," I said.

"Is it a Stardoll version of me I can dress up in fabulous costumes online?" Jenna asked.

"Um, no," I said.

"Darn," Jenna said.

"It's not something you'd be interested in or would likely understand," Sebastian said. "It's a virtual-world thing."

"Oh, come on, let me play, too," Jenna said.

"Why, so you can blackmail me about it?" Sebastian said. "So you can sabotage my Caltech chances?"

"No," Jenna said. "Because I want to hang out with you guys."

She put on a sad puppy-dog face.

"Sebastian, how can you say no to that?" I asked.

"Wait, a few minutes ago I was working alone and happy about it," Sebastian said. "Maybe I should reconsider."

"I guess I won't bring my five hundred people, then. It's going to be pretty lonely with just your avatar in there," I reminded him.

"Fine, fine, whatever!" Sebastian threw up his hands in defeat. "You can fill her in."

He got up and left the office.

"So what are we doing?" Jenna asked.

I suddenly had a moment of doubt. What if our idea was idiotic and completely crazy? Making a virtual world because of a song by a singer who had never heard of me?

"Listen to this," I said. I went over to the computer and brought up Team Marisa. I clicked on the song and turned up the volume. It wasn't exactly like she had to pass a test or anything, but I wanted to hear what Jenna's reaction would be to the whole Marisa thing. If she wanted to help, it would probably be better if she at least liked the song.

"Hey, isn't that the song you blasted on your computer by accident?" Jenna asked.

I nodded and waited.

"This song rocks," Jenna said, and started singing along. "*The girl who . . . the girl who . . . you wish you knew*. Who sings it again?"

She passed the test.

"Jenna, meet Team Marisa."

11

BULLETIN from Team Marisa

From: Team Marisa
Date: October 15—4:30 p.m.
Subject: Something big is happening

Something big is happening on Team Marisa.
It's called M World.
If you thought Team Marisa was rocking now, wait till you come to
M World. As Team Marisa's humble messenger, I'm sworn to secrecy,
but I can tell you to be ready on Thursday night for something big.

I thought that made M World sound pretty cool and mysterious. Now I just had to figure out what M World was really going to be and we'd be in business. After I'd told Jenna about Team Marisa and M World, she'd gotten me even more psyched. I'd spent the remaining class periods obsessing over it.

As I clicked to send the bulletin to Team Marisa, my cell phone rang. I moved my laptop off my lap, slid off my bed, and kicked a box of old magazines marked *Teen Vogues* and *Teen Peoples* out of the way. I grabbed my cell off my desk, where it was charging.

"Hi!" Jenna said. "What are you doing?"

"I'm working on Team Marisa," I said. It was nice to have a real person to talk to about all this.

"I just posted a bulletin," I continued. "And I'm about to post a new interview with Marisa I found online."

I read the article to Jenna.

IN THE SPOTLIGHT: MARISA

Rising star Marisa has the whole package. She writes her own songs, sings, plays the guitar, works hard, and wants to do good things for the world. Her debut single "The Girl Who" has just been released.

Q: MARISA, WHEN DID YOU START PLAYING MUSIC?

A: *My parents say I was always singing when I was little. I was four when I picked up a guitar from my uncle's house and my parents said I begged to take it home. My parents never pushed me into it, but I was pretty obsessed all on my own.*

Q: DO YOU THINK "THE GIRL WHO" COULD BE A HIT SONG?

A: *Well, I always try to think positive, but the music business is tough. What I love is just playing my guitar and singing, and anyone hearing it is just a bonus. Of course a hit song would be awesome. But honestly, I'm truly happy when anyone enjoys my music.*

"I love her," I sighed. "She's so inspiring."

"What? Sorry, hang on, my mom is yelling something," Jenna said.

I could hear muffled shouting.

"Ugh, I have to go. Marisa is so lucky her parents never pushed her," Jenna said. "My mother is pushing me into something right now. She's got some advisor coming over to help me with, quote, planning my future, unquote."

"You mean college stuff?" I asked her.

"I wish. You haven't met my mother," Jenna said. "No, it's my new psychic advisor."

"A psychic advisor?" I thought it was weird enough when some of my friends in Ohio started meeting with college advisors and PSAT tutors. Jenna had a psychic advisor?

"Trust me, I'm not happy about it," Jenna said. "This lady's supposed to read my future and tell me what I'm supposed to be doing to prepare for it. My mom's all happy because she thinks she can convince me to go back into dancing or something."

"You were a dancer?" I said.

"Oh, you don't even know," Jenna groaned. "My mother had me in insane lessons and things. I'm still trying to block them out of my memory. So anyway, Sebastian said he'd be able to do M World later tonight."

"Cool," I said. "Hey, if you have a chance, ask your psychic if Marisa is going to have a number one hit. If she says yes, I can put that on the Team Marisa space."

Jenna laughed, and we hung up. I sat back down on my bed and pulled over my laptop. A psychic? Dancing? There was obviously a lot I didn't know about Jenna's life. I guess it was unusual that I never heard Jenna talk about doing anything after school. I mean, most people were sucked into sports, orchestra, tutoring, jobs. Back in Ohio, I was too uncoordinated for sports, but I used to be in choir and the service club. I wondered what Jenna had meant by "insane lessons and things."

I checked the messages I'd gotten from Team Marisa.

Marisa is an amazing singer! I'm trying out for school jazz choir but I'm so nervous! I wish I could sing as great as Marisa, then I wouldn't have to be nervous at all. Gymfan66

I knew how to answer this question, because Marisa talked about it in the article I'd been reading to Jenna.

Marisa would tell you that no matter how good a singer you are, that doesn't mean you don't get butterflies. She said, "It's never easy because I'm always nervous before I perform, because I want to do a good job. But I take a deep breath and then give it my all." Good luck with the tryouts!

I sent that answer and read the next message.

Hi, Team Marisa person!! One of my friends doesn't like the music I listen to. She won't even listen to "The Girl Who" even though I told her it's special to me. It's kind of hurting my feelings. DanceSassy

Everyone has their own tastes and opinions and that's okay. But why not tell her Team Marisa is important to you and maybe she'll get it? Tell her I sent you :) If she doesn't like "The Girl Who," well, that's her bad right? lol!

Hi Team Marisa
Marisa is so talented. I have no talent and am afraid I'm going to be a nobody. Did Marisa ever feel this way? DCIMO

I could relate to that one.

I don't know if Marisa ever did, but I know what you're saying. I'm not coordinated. I can't dance. I can't sing. I can't play the guitar. I guess it's one of the reasons I worship the talent of people who do, like Marisa. And we can cheer her on together! Team Marisa rocks!

I read the next message.

Guess what! I MET MARISA! I was at Urth Caffé and she was in line and she was soooo nice! We both ordered flourless chocolate cake! And Marisa signed an autograph for me! Brenda

That was very cool. I loved when stars were nice to their fans. Marisa seemed so down to earth, even if she became a huge star, she'd probably still be nice to her fans.

"Avery!" My mom's voice made me jump.

I opened my eyes and saw my mom in the doorway.

"Ohmygosh!" I said. "I didn't even hear you guys come home. I was focused on . . . my homework."

"Good for you," she said. "And now it's time for a break. Dad and I are taking you out to dinner."

"Any other night that would be great," I said, "but I have a *ton* of homework to do."

I did have a ton of homework. However, I also had a ton of Team Marisa and M World to do, which was what I was really thinking about.

"That's exactly why we decided you needed a break," my mom said. "We came home early to take you out to dinner and that's what we're going to do."

"I'm good, I ate ramen when I got home," I said.

"Then we'll have some dessert," my mom said firmly. "Put on some shoes and come on down."

She wasn't budging. Well, I do like dessert. I plugged my laptop in to charge it. It was going to be getting a lot of use tonight. I had to plan the launch party scene, figure out what to do with this list, keep the buzz going on Team Marisa MySpace. And do my homework. I headed downstairs and went into the kitchen.

"Hi, Dad," I said. "So. Where are we going?"

"Your mother and I thought you might like to pick the place," he said.

"Really?" That cheered me up. I thought about the latest Marisa sighting. Maybe going to one of Marisa's favorite places would inspire me. "How about Urth?"

"Yes, dear, on the planet earth," my mom said. "Honey, are you sure you haven't been studying too hard?"

"Mom, Urth is the name of a café!" I said. "It's about twenty minutes from here. And Dad, I hear Gwen Stefani sometimes goes there."

"Ooh-la-la!" my dad said. "Then let's boogie!"

I put my earphones in and cranked up "The Girl Who" on my iPod. I leaned back on the seat of the car and started to relax when I noticed my mother turning around and mouthing something to me.

"What?" I asked, clicking off the song.

"Does George Clooney ever to go Planet Urth?" my mom asked.

"It's Urth Caffé," I corrected her. "And maybe, a lot of celebrities do."

"I hope so! He's on my Freebie Three!" my mom said cheerfully.

"What?!" my dad said. "We made those up in Ohio. That doesn't count anymore."

"What's the Freebie Three?" I asked them.

"It's a list your mother and I made as a *joke* back in Ohio," my father said.

"We each got to pick three celebrities that if we ever met in person we were allowed to . . . kiss!" my mother said. "Even though we're married! My list is George Clooney, McDreamy, and Wayne Newton."

"Ew!" I was horrified. "*Mom! Dad!* That's disgusting!"

"We said it as a *joke,*" my father protested. "When we didn't know we were moving to a place where we might actually run into celebrities. People like Wayne Newton."

"Ooh, do you think Wayne Newton goes to Urth?" my mom said.

"Stop!" I yelped. "My ears! My ears!"

This was so not what I wanted to hear from my parents. Fortunately, my dad announced we were arriving at Urth. I got kind of excited when we pulled up to park. Finally, I was going to get to go someplace on my celebrity hit list. I'd been waiting a long time for this.

"If I see George Clooney, we're leaving," my dad muttered.

We walked into the café and went to stand in a long line to order. I tried to see if I could spot any celebrities, but nobody looked familiar. Everyone looked beautiful, though. I looked down at my sweats and wished I'd thought to change into something a little cuter. Oh well, it wasn't like anyone was going to notice me.

SEEN ON THE SCENE

What up-and-coming star was spotted in Urth, disguised in casual clothes and hiding under red tresses and big shades? With her star quality, will she be able to stay invisible for much longer?

"Why don't you grab a table outside, Avery," my dad suggested. "I'll place the order. What would you like?"

"I'll have a flourless chocolate cake," I said, and left my parents in line and walked out to the patio. I snagged a table from some people who were leaving and sat down. Everything was very green, with vines climbing along the walls. There was a fountain with running water. A heat lamp was on and I felt cozy and . . . maybe it had been a good idea to get out of the house. I felt more chill than I had in weeks.

"Avery! Avery!" My father's voice broke through the peace and quiet. "Celebrity! Celebrity alert!"

OMG. I scrunched down and pretended I didn't know him.

"Avery!" My father came over to me, followed by my mom.

"Shh, Albert, you're disturbing people," my mom said, putting a number on our table so the server could find us. "Avery, go with your father so he can show you."

"Come on, Avery," my dad whispered loudly. "This is your chance."

He gestured for me to follow him. Despite the fact that people were probably rolling their eyes at us, I started to feel a little excited.

I mean, this was it. The moment I'd been dreaming of forever. After a lifetime of online celebrity stalking in Ohio, and a month living near them in L.A., I was finally going to see an actual celebrity.

I hoped it was someone good.

"Who is it?" I whispered to him.

"The Hilton girl," my dad whispered back.

Paris Hilton? Now, that was a good celebrity spotting! My dad pointed toward the counter. I saw a group of girls standing together. I totally squealed when I saw the tall blonde standing in the middle.

I walked over to the counter and pretended to be checking out the salads. I couldn't see Paris's face because she was turned the other way. Her hair was darker than I'd expected. I made a mental note of her outfit so I could tell everyone. She was wearing a tight black tank, jeans, and high, high heels.

I'd need to stay cool. I didn't want to be one of those fans who made the star feel awkward. I wanted to be chill, like someone she'd want to hang out with. Then she'd invite me to sit with her outside (instead of my parents, thank you) . . . I'd get her autograph for my Ohio friends . . .

I moved casually closer. And then a voice boomed out.

"Excuse me!"

That would be my dad. Who apparently was right behind me.

"My daughter is too shy to speak up, but she would love an autograph!"

"Dad!" I hissed. I looked for an escape route, but he pushed me forward.

And then, in what was like a horror movie of epic embarrassment, the girl with blond hair turned around. As did the girl standing next to her. The girl with blond hair was not Paris Hilton. But I recognized her from her picture—Delilah Singer.

And the other girl was Cecilia. Cecilia gave me a catlike grin and stepped forward.

"That's so precious," Cecilia said. "Your daughter wants my autograph?"

"Oh, are you someone famous, too?" my dad asked her. "Like I told my daughter, you never know who you are going to see here in L.A.!"

"That's so true!" Cecilia said, flashing a fake smile.

Just shoot me now. I felt my face turn a burning red.

"I also met Gwen Stephanie in the coffee place," my dad continued. "I am a celebrity magnet!"

"I'm sure you're a chick magnet, too," Cecilia said, acting cute.

"Dad," I whispered. "They're really not stars."

"I know, I know, they're people just like us." My father smiled patronizingly at me. "My daughter wants to play it cool, but I know she'd love a picture with you two," he said to Cecilia.

"No, Dad, really," I said. "They're not who you think they are."

"I know, stars are like everyday people," my dad said, totally missing the point. "But humor me for a photo opportunity."

"Did someone say photo opportunity?" William Shaw popped out of nowhere with his ubiquitous cameraperson.

Oh, come on, could this be any more cliché?

"Look! The paparazzi is here!" my dad said. "That's what happens in these hip celeb hot spots, right, Avery?"

Right.

"Say cheesy," William said. "Cam, get the shot. I'll do the interview." Cecilia and Delilah both put their arms around me as my father took pictures and Cam shot video.

"This is flippin' hilarious," Cecilia said to me under her breath, keeping her fake smile.

"Are we finished? My ice blended should be ready at the counter," Delilah said.

"I'll get it, Paris!" My dad practically skipped with glee over to the counter.

"Paris?" William looked around hopefully.

"Paris isn't here," I said, exasperated.

"Who are you?" Delilah asked me. "And why do you still have your arm around me?"

I did? I quickly dropped my arm.

"Delilah, did you meet Agatha? She goes to my school and says she's a big fan of Shade. Right, Agatha?" Cecilia said slyly.

Oh, crap. I looked at her sister to see if she knew I was the one who had been talking about her allegedly cheating boyfriend. Delilah Singer looked either very bored or just very clueless as she ignored all that was going on around her. I had to admit, my dad wasn't completely wrong mistaking her for Paris. Even her vacant expression was Parislike.

"Girls, where are you going tonight?" William said, and cued his cameraman to move in closer.

"We're going to a University of Hard rehearsal," Cecilia explained to the camera.

"You didn't invite me?" William groaned. "Think of the photo opportunity!"

Speaking of photo opportunity, my father was walking toward us carrying the tea. I tried to think of a good escape line.

"Here's your drink, Paris," my dad said graciously. "It's been a pleasure meeting you ladies. And your paparazzi."

"Actually, I prefer celebrity chronicler," William said.

"The pleasure was all ours!" Cecilia flashed her best fake smile at my dad, and then at me.

I wanted. To. *Die*. We started walking away. But not before I heard Cecilia talking to her sister.

"How funny was that? That girl goes to our school," Cecilia said. "She's from Iowa, so that's why she's all like that."

Oy.

NOT-SO-BLIND ITEM

What new redhead in town was excited when her father pointed out a Paris Hilton sighting at Urth? Her hopes were dashed when it wasn't the celebutante It Girl, but her own school's It Girl. And the wannabe paparazzi now has the pictures to prove it!

"Good-bye! Good-bye!" My father continued the humiliation until the last possible second. I kept my head down as I followed him to the outdoor patio, where my mom was waiting for us.

"Well, did that make your night or what?" my father asked.

Made it a nightmare was more like it. I opened my mouth to break it to him that they weren't celebrities, except maybe in their own minds. But my dad looked so excited, I decided to let him have his moment of glory. There was no need to share the humiliation, I supposed.

"Avery has just witnessed the magic of my celebrity radar!" my dad said to my mom, and held out his cell phone so she could see.

"That's Paris Hilton?" my mom said, squinting at it. "Goodness, she got . . . larger in the bust area. I don't know why these girls aren't satisfied with their looks and have to have all of that surgery. She made herself look like a different person!"

"The other girl was a celebrity, too!" my dad announced. "Did you know who she was, Avery?"

Yeah, Dad. I knew who she was. Unfortunately, I knew.

12

The Ivy restaurant—lunch place where the paparazzi hung out [   ]

Beverly Center—a mall where celebrities shopped [   ]

Pink's hot dogs—lines down the block [   ]

Robertson Blvd.—Rodeo Drive was mostly for tourists but the real stars shop here [   ]

The Coffee Bean & Tea Leaf—for caffeine breaks [   ]

Chateau Marmont—the hotel to hide out from the paparazzi and trash your room at night

The Grove—an outdoor mall where celebrities shopped and went to the movies [   ]

Well, at least I'd been to one celeb hot spot. Of course, it had been a total *fiasco*. I felt my face get red just thinking about Cecilia and her glee at my humiliation. I texted Jenna to call me, so I could tell her what happened. Just as I sent the text, I received one. I was surprised to see it was from Nicole.

We r thinking of u. we r at the library talking about u.

Aw, that cheered me up a little bit. That was really good timing for them to text me. I thought back about how we all used to sit around the library table. Good times. I texted back

I miss u guys too.

Two seconds later I got another text from Nicole.

We were talking about how u didn't send the autographs! We're waiting to see u on a gossip site, hanging with the stars.

Well, so much for cheering me up. They didn't miss me, they were talking about me because they wanted autographs and celebrity gossip. They wanted to see me in pictures with stars and on gossip sites.

The only gossip site I was on was my own Princess of Gossip Ning site. I smiled for a second, thinking of sending them the site with the picture of my dad and Gwen Stefani on it. I clicked over to it.

Yes, the Princess of Gossip site was really rocking. My blurred-out dad and Gwen. I was definitely the Princess of Gossip, wasn't I? It was so ridiculous it was almost funny.

I turned back to my slightly more successful site: Team Marisa.

I'm the girl who . . . is happy whenever I hear that song. Keep strong!
PurplePenguin12

This song is so meaningful. I don't have too many real friends right now. It's a long story but there was this girl who turned everyone against me and "The Girl Who" reminds me that "I'm the girl you wish you knew."
DivaGirl

"That's the power of Marisa's song," I wrote back to DivaGirl. "I feel it, too. I'm kind of alone, too, but now we have Team Marisa!"

Team Marisa was up to 1,175 friends. We had friends from all over the country. I decided to add famous people to the MySpace, hoping they'd see Marisa and love her, too. I added all the info I was getting from the music label emails.

Then Jenna's name came up on my iChat. I clicked on the chat icon and her face popped up on the video screen.

"You are so not going to believe what happened to me tonight," Jenna said. "It was painful and humiliating."

"You are so not going to believe what happened to *me* tonight," I said. "It was painful and humiliating. But you go first."

"Okay, I met with my mom's so-called psychic advisor, Madame Courtney," Jenna said. "She read my palm and my tea leaves and my aura. Don't ask. She then told me I needed to take dancing and acting classes, and that she saw a lot of weight loss coming for me."

"That was your future?" I said. "That seems a little shallow."

"Well, then Madame Courtney turned on the lights and my mom was there, conveniently holding a diet book and flyers for dance and acting classes."

"Wow, is your mom psychic, too?" I asked her.

"It was a total setup," Jenna groaned. "My mother told her to say those things, because that's what she wants me to do. It couldn't have been more obvious. I mean, what psychic is named Courtney anyway. My mother is out of control."

"If it makes you feel any better, my father was completely embarrassing tonight." I told Jenna about the Urth Caffé fiasco, with Cecilia, Delilah, and William capturing it all on video.

"You should have heard my father thanking them for their time speaking to nobodies like me," I said. "He was groveling and Cecilia was eating it up."

"Okay, ouch," Jenna said. "That must have been ugly. They are so lucky they're going to that show."

"I know," I sighed. "And backstage."

"Those Singers get everything," Jenna grumbled. "Backstage passes, celebrity boyfriends, boob jobs from boyfriends."

"Well, I'll take the first ones but I'll pass on the boob job from my boyfriend." I shuddered. Not that I wasn't lacking in that department, but I'd rather get like, jewelry or something. "Seriously, they're so huge I'm surprised she can stand upright. But I guess now she's every guy's dream."

Just then a random screen name came up on my iChat: Green-DayGriff. I was about to deny it when I realized who it might be.

"Speaking of guys dreaming of Delilah, I'm getting a message from a GreenDayGriff," I said. "Do you think that's Griffin King?"

"Griffin King wears Green Day shirts," Jenna said. "He wore a black one with this deconstructed blazer once that—"

While Jenna was giving me the fashion report, I clicked to accept the iChat.

Hey, it's Griffin King. Do you know which pages we have to do for English?

I went back to Jenna's screen.

"It's Griffin and he needs help with English," I told her.

"No problem," she said. "I've got math to finish. Madame Courtney did predict if I didn't try harder in math, my grades would be in trouble. That I did believe."

She signed off and I went back to Griffin. I cut and pasted the vocabulary list into the text box for him.

It's pages 28–32 in the green workbook.

Which green one? The dark or light?

I looked at the cover. It was kind of medium green.

It has a design on it that looks like a squiggle.

I think both do.

Can you turn on your video chat? Then I'll show you.

I turned on my video chat and waited for it to connect. Then I saw myself in the screen and realized that my face was about to appear on a guy's monitor.

"Hang on!" I said, disabling the video. "Be right back!"

I was wearing a pajama top so I needed to change. Not that I really cared what Griffin thought of me or anything. No, I didn't, really. I threw on an Ohio State sweatshirt and brushed my hair. And put on a little lipstick so I didn't look too washed out.

"Hi," I said, as Griffin's face popped up on the screen. He looked good. His blondish brown hair was set off by the lighting. He smiled when he saw me. His smile lit up his whole face and his eyes got a little crinkly and—okay, moving on.

"How was Urth?" Griffin said.

"Urth was interesting. Wait," I said. "How'd you know I was at Urth?"

"Willie Shaw told me," Griffin said. "I ran into him on my way home from work. Actually, I almost ran him over with my dad's car because Willie is sitting out on the curb near my house right now."

"Why is he sitting on your curb?" I asked.

"Good view of the neighbor's," Griffin said.

"Oh, that's right," I realized. "You live next door to the Singers."

"Yeah, it's not an uncommon occurrence for Willie and sometimes his camera guy to stalk them," Griffin said. "Sometimes my mom feels bad for him and brings him something to drink. Anyway, William said he wants to scoop the competition and get an interview with Cecilia and Delilah about what happened at the University of Hard rehearsal."

"What competition?" I asked.

"He said you were at Urth with another paparazzi who was following the Singers, too," Griffin said.

"He said what? He must have meant my father! He's not a paparazzi. He just keeps thinking he sees celebrities so he takes pictures. He hasn't been out of Ohio for long, it's embarrassing."

"That's funny." Griffin grinned. "Willie is out there now in the darkness, all proud of himself for beating out your father for the scoop. Anyway, I'm glad you were online. Willie didn't know what the homework was when I asked him."

"Is he still out there?" I asked.

Griffin stood up and walked over to a window. I could see the background for the first time. He was obviously in his room. There were a couple posters on the wall: Killers, Flyleaf, and a UCLA poster.

"Yep, he's still there," he said. As he sat down, I noticed his shirt said CREW on it.

"Where do you work?" I asked him. "I see your CREW shirt."

"At a roller-skating place," Griffin said. "I know, it sounds stupid, but it's pretty retro and fun. You know how everyone's into bowling now? I think roller skating is next. Have you ever skated?"

"Um, I could say yes and just drop it," I said. "But I also could show you the scar I have on my ankle from when my first boyfriend ran over me during couples skate. It was ugly."

"We still have couples skate," Griffin said. "And the big disco ball that we turn on for moonlight skate. But we also have some bands play there on a stage, and some cool music. Well, I say that because I'm the DJ a couple nights a week."

"Really?" I asked him. "That does sound kind of cool."

I had a fleeting thought of Marisa playing on the roller rink stage while Griffin announced her act from the DJ booth. The place would be skating-room only with Team Marisa fans and—

"I know why you're smiling," Griffin said. "You're picturing the debut of our hit song, 'Cold, Callous Wench,' aren't you?"

What? I came back to reality.

"I guess we need more than just a title," he continued, "Hm, 'Cold, Callous Wench.' What should be the next line? 'Cold, callous wench, are you French?' No. How about 'We go together like a hammer and a wrench'? No. 'We're stuck in a trench'? "On a bench'?"

"No offense but those lyrics stink," I said. "No, wait, I got it. 'Cold, callous wench, you have an awful stench.' "

Griffin laughed.

"Too bad we aren't writing song lyrics for English class," Griffin said. "We'd get an A. Oh man, I better get working on that homework. Which workbook is it?"

I held up the workbook so he could see the cover.

"Cool, thanks," Griffin said. "I'm glad you're in our class so I have someone to ask. I have to leave early a couple days a week for this service project I'm doing and Schmitt's not exactly supportive. Cecilia never knows what the homework is; she just takes her sister's old papers and then hands in the one that's due."

"I guess that's one way to do it," I said. "I, however, have no older sisters and sadly, I do have ethics."

"Same," Griffin said.

"What's the project you're doing?" I asked him.

"It's this poetry slam we're setting up for the elementary school for community service," Griffin said. "I'm helping them write their poems, which probably sounds kind of stupid."

"Actually, it sounds great," I said.

"Yeah, well, some of the kids thought it was stupid, so I told them that song lyrics were poetry. Now I'm helping them write song lyrics and they like it. Miss Schmitt said I have to find out the home-work on my own, since I have the nerve to leave her class five minutes early. You'd think she'd appreciate how I'm passing an interest in English on to her future students."

"That is ridiculous," I said. He was so sweet for helping with the poetry slam.

"Hang on, someone's AIMing me," Griffin said. "Oh, it's Delilah from next door. I have to take it, sorry."

"That's okay," I said. But I was disappointed, I admit. His video chat closed out and his face disappeared. On the plus side, I'd just had a conversation with a cute guy, something I hadn't been particularly adept at when I was back in Ohio, much less here. Video chat was easier than face-to-face, but still. On the minus side, I was bumped for his real crush. On the plus side, it made it easier for me not to crush on him. On the minus side, who wouldn't rather look at Delilah on video chat than my face? On the plus side—okay, obviously I needed to stop overthinking this and do my homework.

I opened my English workbook and turned to the homework page. I turned my iPod on and "The Girl Who" came right up. I tried to concentrate, but my mind suddenly wandered and I pictured Griffin and I holding hands for a couples skate at the rink, while Marisa sang onstage in the background. I smiled at the thought and that's when it hit me.

Griffin said roller rinks were the next big thing? That's what I would do with the virtual world that Sebastian was making. We would have a virtual concert in a virtual roller rink with virtual fans skating around.

```
Genius.
From: TeamMarisaMySpace
Subject: MarisaWorld CONCERT
```

Spread the word! Virtual Marisa*
will be performing LIVE and in virtual person! Meet other Team Marisa
fans online and listen to "The Girl
Who" together in a secret (virtual)
location.

When: Thursday night
7:00 p.m. PST
10:00 p.m. EST
Where: Virtual MarisaWorld

Trust me, you have never, EVER seen
anything like this. More deets to
come!!

* It's not the real Marisa. But it
will be her real song.

13

Sebastian was pretty stoked about the roller rink idea when I told him.

"You really like it?" I asked him. I was a little surprised. His earlier suggestion had been a *Star Wars* scene, with the avatars carrying light sabers to wave at the concert like glow sticks. Clever, perhaps, but not exactly our audience.

"Sebastian's secret favorite movie is *Roller Girls*," Jenna laughed.

"No," Sebastian grumbled. "It's number seven in my top ten."

"Someone told me roller skating was getting hot again. Plus, it would give the avatars something different to do while the music played," I explained.

"I have to make avatars skate?" Sebastian shook his head.

"I love it!" Jenna said. "Can you make it sparkly with disco lights?"

"Frak," Sebastian said. "Did anyone warn me I'd be doing sparkly disco for my Caltech project? No."

"Did he just say frak?" I asked Jenna.

"Geek speak," she said. "I won't translate it but it means what it sounds like."

We'd been working on M World pretty much nonstop, and I was

pretty impressed at what Sebastian had accomplished. I looked over his shoulder at the computer monitor, where he'd set up the virtual world background for me to see.

Picture a Sims scene, or a Second Life scene of a roller rink with a giant stage in the middle of it. The floor of the rink wasn't ordinary wood, but jewel-toned emerald. And when Sebastian turned the virtual lights down and made the giant disco ball start turning, the emerald floor sparkled like green diamonds. The effect was pretty amazing.

There was also a bar and an area for virtual food and drinks off to one side. And a massive DJ booth off to the other side. Sebastian had told me to make up a playlist so that people could have a free skate after the show.

"Dang, it looks *real*," I told Sebastian. "It's awesome."

We grinned at each other.

"Ok, *gag*," Jenna said behind us.

"Hey, Jenna," I greeted her.

"I hope I'm not interrupting a *moment* between you two," she said.

"You know we're working on our project," I said.

"It's just unnerving. My brother is actually smiling and talking to a female who's not a teacher," Jenna said.

Jenna was looking more colorful than usual. She wore a pretty green top that had a silk-screened peace sign on it. She paired it with skinny jeans and cream-colored wedges with a yellow and green pattern. A green pendant dangled from a chain around her neck.

"Shut it," Sebastian started to say, but his voice was drowned out by the last-period bell.

"I have to go," I said. "Sadly, the bus driver doesn't recognize he's my personal chauffeur and that he should wait for me if I'm late."

"You can't take the bus and go home," Jenna said. "We have a party to coordinate and not much time to do it! Come on, Sebastian will give you a ride."

"I live on the east side of town," I said. "It's not that close."

"It's fine, I have some questions about M World, anyway. I have to close down the computers first, though," Sebastian said. "You guys can meet me at my car."

"That sounds great," I said. "I hate the bus."

"Ah, good ole bus memories. Like people tripping you while you're going down the aisle, and leaning over the seat to hit you on the head," Sebastian said. "Too bad Jenna doesn't appreciate that I drive her home from school and she doesn't have to take the bus."

"It's punishment enough being in a car with you," Jenna said.

"Shush, don't ruin my chances at a ride home," I said. "Sebastian, we'll meet you outside."

Jenna and I headed out to the senior parking lot.

"I can't wait to turn sixteen in January and get my own car," Jenna said cheerfully. "My stepfather said we're all doomed once I'm on the road. He owns a BMW dealership, so I think I convinced him to get me a little white convertible."

That was one of the things I liked about California—more year-round convertible use.

"Lucky you," I said. My birthday was in March. I definitely wouldn't be getting a car from my parents, I was going to have to save up to buy one on my own. And since I had no job, not even babysitting like I did back in Ohio, I had a feeling it was going to be a while before I could get anything at all.

We walked over to Sebastian's car, which looked like it had seen better days, especially compared to the new cars in the lot, which I could see included a Ferrari, a Hummer, a Smart car, hybrids, and many convertibles. Jenna sat on the hood of Sebastian's car and I leaned against it.

"Did your stepfather get Sebastian this car?" I asked.

"No, Sebastian saved up for it himself. Sebastian says he won't take anything from my stepfather because the guy's a jerk." Jenna frowned. "But I think that's all the more reason to take it."

"Oh," I said. I knew Jenna and Sebastian's mother had remarried a couple years ago. I knew they lived in the same elementary school area as Cecilia. I didn't know much more than that.

"Sorry it's not a cooler car," Jenna said.

"Are you kidding? I'm just happy I don't have to take the bus," I said. It was the perfect day not to take the bus, actually. The sky was a bright blue with one or two puffy white clouds floating by. The smog level was low, and it was the kind of day that made me happy to be living in California. In a few months, it would be beach weather. If Jenna and I stayed friends, maybe we'd drive to the ocean sometime. There were no oceans in Ohio. I leaned back on the car and closed my eyes in the sun. It was really relaxing.

Until the car alarm on the silver Range Rover next to us went off loudly. Jenna and I both jumped.

"Oh, yuck," Jenna said. She tilted her head and I turned to see Cecilia and Miya walking toward us. Jenna closed her eyes and leaned back on the car.

"Oopsie!" Miya was walking toward us and holding out her Chanel key ring. "I guess I hit the wrong button."

"Did that old car finally break down?" Cecilia asked. "Are you waiting for Triple A?"

They both giggled, and Jenna and I pretended to ignore them. I did notice Miya's attempt at channeling Blair Waldorf in her argyle and headband wear, while Cecilia was wearing a University of Hard

T-shirt with a very, very short mini. We continued to ignore them as they got in Miya's car. I thought they were going to leave us in peace, but no such luck.

"Jenna, I forgot to tell you the rumor I heard!" Cecilia called out through the open window. "My agent told me rumor has it the Remington sisters are being killed off in a horrible flesh-eating plague. It's airing during sweeps week!"

Jenna flinched but didn't open her eyes.

"I wonder if they'll show them rotting away," Cecilia said. "That would be pretty grisly. And flippin' awesome."

Miya gunned her engine and then the car sped off.

"Hate," Jenna said. "Hate her."

"Okay, I think I'm missing something," I said. "Was she talking about the Remington sisters of *One Life I Breathe*? You and Cecilia discuss soap opera plots? I'm lost."

"It's complicated," Jenna said. "I wouldn't even know where to start."

"Let me guess," I said. "You and Cecilia used to be BFF and you'd watch soap operas after school together. And then Cecilia got hot and dropped you for the popular crowd."

"Buzz," Jenna said. "Wrong. Cecilia and I were never friends. She hates me. I hate her."

"But why? You wrote mean things about her in a slam book?" I tried. "You choreographed the holiday dance every year but then she spread a rumor that you were in love with her?"

"That was *Mean Girls*." Jenna smiled.

"Just spill it," I said.

"Okay," Jenna said with a sigh. "My best friends were these sisters, Alice and Ann. They were really sweet. Ann, Cecilia, and I were in this acting class together after school. There was a casting call for sisters for a TV movie and I talked Alice and Ann into trying out for it." She sat up on the hood of the car and looked into the sun. "I went to the audition with them. Except Cecilia and Delilah Singer were in the waiting room, auditioning, too."

"So Alice and Ann got the job and Cecilia hated you for it?" I asked her.

"No, they didn't get that job," Jenna said. "Danielle and Kay Panabaker got it and they were awesome. But the casting director loved Alice and Ann so much she cast them in *One Life I Breathe*."

"So Alice and Ann are Aliceandra and Anntoinette Sanders?" I said. "That's so cool!"

"I know! I was really happy for them," Jenna said. "But of course Cecilia and Delilah were pissed. And then Cecilia froze me out. She threw a spontaneous party the night of my bat mitzvah and invited the whole grade. And everyone bailed on my party at the last minute."

"They skipped your bat mitzvah?" I asked.

"Her father got Jesse McCartney to sing at her party," Jenna said. "I had a guy making balloons. You do the math."

"Wait," I said. "All you did was help your friends go to an audition? That was it?"

"Avery," Jenna said. "This is L.A. It's *all* about the business. My friends became stars. Cecilia is still here, auditioning for pilots that don't get picked up. That was enough."

"Harsh," I said.

"And since Alice and Ann moved to New York for the soap, there went my friends in school," Jenna said. "Blah-blah, the end."

"That's a bummer," I said. "And now you're sworn mortal enemies with Cecilia."

"Actually, usually I'm just ignored," Jenna said. "But obviously

Cecilia wanted to rub that piece of gossip in my face. I hope she was lying about the twins getting killed off by a flesh-eating plague and leaving the show. And speaking of flesh-eating plagues, here's my brother."

I looked up to see Sebastian crossing the parking lot, carrying a huge backpack on his shoulders.

"Get off my car, Jenna," Sebastian said. "You're defiling it."

"My chauffeur is being disrespectful," Jenna said to me.

"Your chauffeur is about to quit and leave you stranded," Sebastian said. But he opened the car doors for us. Jenna let me have shotgun and she got in the back.

"I've been thinking about M World," Sebastian said. "I've got the background and the platform. But what kind of avatars do you want? You've got the audience, what do you want them to look like?"

"They have to look hawt," Jenna said, sticking her head up front. "You could dress them in Marc Jacobs's new line and—"

"It's not a fashion show," Sebastian said. "I was thinking more along the lines of aliens and a *Battlestar Galactica* futuristic feel."

"What?" Jenna said. "It's a concert for Marisa! There's no *Battlestar Galactica* feel. I was thinking Avery's character should be wearing a LaROK dress with Christian Louboutins and carrying a Botkier bag."

Oh, so that's how you pronounce it, *bot-key-air.*

"Guys—" I tried to interrupt but they were in full-on sibling mode.

"This is not a fashion show," Sebastian said. "This is my project for Caltech. I take it seriously."

"*Battlestar Galactica* people are serious?" Jenna protested.

"I think you missed the turn to my house!" I said loudly. "I have no clue where we are."

"Frak!" Sebastian said. "I forgot we were taking you home. Can you just come to our house and we can work on M World?"

"I guess," I said. "If it's okay with Jenna and your mom or who-ever."

"Come over!" Jenna said. "Call your parents and see."

I called to check with my parents, as Jenna and Sebastian continued to argue about the look of the avatars.

"My mom says yes," I said. "If you don't mind bringing me home later. My parents are working late tonight."

"Speaking of mothers," Jenna said. "I apologize for my mother in advance. And just hope my stepfather doesn't come home early."

"That's okay," I said. "I'm sure she can't be any more embarrassing than my parents."

I told Jenna about my dad and his "Jen Stephanie" meeting, and she and Sebastian dissolved into laughter. I looked out the window and realized we were in a neighborhood I hadn't been to before. The yards got bigger and bigger, and soon the houses became gated. Sebastian clicked a remote on his car and one of the gates opened.

"Wow," I said, as he parked the car in a circular driveway surrounded by fruit trees. I looked up at a large white Mediterranean-style house.

"Welcome to our home," Jenna said. We walked past a gazebo with a trickling fountain and up the steps to the front door. Inside, the foyer was huge. The house was huge. It had three-story windows that went from the ground to the rooftop, and the sun shone through the glass, casting a golden light on the tiles below. There was a spiral staircase with a large chandelier overhead. I followed Jenna and Sebastian into a room that wasn't really a room but more an outdoor garden with furniture.

One thing I loved about California houses was that they had actual rooms outside. For example, you'd be in the kitchen, but to get to the living room you'd go through an outside garden like this one and then the house would start up again.

"Mom! We're home!" Jenna yelled.

"Your house is gorgeous," I said in awe.

A woman walked in the room. I saw where Sebastian got his height and bony look. She was wearing a gauzy white tunic shirt, white drawstring floaty pants, and very high gold stilettos. She looked sculpted, tan, and wrinkle-free.

"And that's what you're supposed to feel like, darling," she said. "This is supposed to be the Garden of Eden. You must be Vida. It's so nice to meet you."

"Um, no," I said. "I'm Avery."

"Sea Bass!" she said. "You didn't tell me you broke up with Vida and found a new girlfriend! You're turning into quite a stud-muffin."

She turned to me.

"Stewie and I were getting a little concerned about his social skills," she said. "It's nice to see him bring girls home."

"Mom!" Sebastian said. "She's not—"

"What's your last name, dear?" his mom asked me.

"Johnson," I told her.

"Oh!" she squealed. "Are you Dr. Lou Johnson's daughter? He did my forehead the second time. And the fifth."

"Er, no," I said.

"Is the producer Greg Johnson your father?" she tried. "Dr. Johnson the cosmetic dentist? I heard he was good. I'm not too happy with my veneers."

"No, but my parents do put the smiley face on Dr. Johnson's toothbrush," I said. "They own a promotions company that does advertising things."

"Avery just moved here from Ohio, Mom," Jenna said. "So you won't know her parents from the circuit."

"Ohio," her mom said; she couldn't quite place it. "Well, do tell them we're happy to advise which clubs are best. Stewie and I could play a foursome with them at our club."

"I'll be sure to tell them," I said.

"Louise will get you some appetizers," she said. "She made some delightful tofu canapés. I had a nibble, but I have to watch my girlish figure! It's so nice to meet you, Vida!"

I watched their mother sweep away off down a hall.

"Wow," I said. "Your mother seems—"

"Yes, we know," Jenna interrupted, rolling her eyes. "She's a total stereotype. I worry that the Botox or the plastic surgery is impairing her brain cells."

"The only good part is I got the extra brain cells she's missing" Sebastian said.

"So, should I call you Sea Bass?" I asked him.

"I swear Mom named him after the trendiest food at the time, Chilean sea bass." Jenna laughed. "Good thing she wasn't into tofu back then like she is now. You could be Tofu Alexander Martin instead of Sea Bass."

"Call me Sea Bass one more time and your avatar will appear as a toad on M World," he said. "Let's get to work."

"We're not going to your bedroom," Jenna said to her brother.

"As much as Mom would love you to finally have a girl in there. It smells like sock. Let's go to mine."

"Agreed," said Sebastian. "I'll bring my stuff over."

We walked through a huge room filled with white furniture and a white baby grand piano, then up some short steps and over a bridge with a little stream below.

NEXT EPISODE OF *CRIBS*!
Kristen Bell's swimming pool, Bow Wow's party room, and Jenna's home spa.

"Wow, you have an outdoor spa?" I asked her. I touched a message table with a soft fluffy cover and a mirror next to it. "Can I just lie down and take a nap and never leave? Will a masseuse come and pamper me into oblivion?"

"Not on that table," Jenna said. "That's my mom's injection table for Botox."

"Oh," I said. I pointed to another one questioningly.

"Wax table," Jenna said. "Brazilians a specialty."

"Okay, I'm out." I backed away. "So this is just right here in the middle of everything?"

"That's one reason I called before we showed up," Jenna said. "I didn't want to scare you. I hate when I come home and my mom has friends over and they're all getting what she calls 'treatments.' "

"Right. Let's change the subject," I said, stopping to look over the bridge. "This is pretty. Are those real fish in there?"

"Koi," she said. "Mean little suckers, too. Don't get too close."

"I don't mean to be nosy," I said. "But with Sebastian's brains and your family's, you know, money, why are you at our public school?"

"Because our stepfather went to public school and look how

great he grew up!" she said. "That's his party line. It's actually just because he's a cheapo and won't spend any money on us. He won't pay for Sebastian's college because, frankly, they hate each other. That's why it's so important Sebastian gets an academic scholarship to college, because he obviously won't get financial aid."

"Well, I hope the M World project helps him out," I said.

"My real dad has no money," Jenna continued. "On purpose. He unloaded all of his material possessions and went off to Tibet to find himself a few years ago. I guess he still hasn't found himself, since he hasn't come back."

Ouch.

We walked down a hallway and I came face-to-face with a giant framed picture that was almost as tall as the wall. The picture was of a little girl with white-blond hair, holding up a box of bandages. It looked oddly familiar.

"And here's my room," Jenna was saying. Then she turned around and noticed I'd stopped. "Oh, I should have had you close your eyes when you walked down the hallway of lost souls. I've tried to forget all this is here."

"Wait, this one's from a commercial," I remembered.

"Ding, ding, ding!" Sebastian said, coming up from behind us. "You're right. And for the million dollars, what was the theme song of the commercial?"

I thought hard.

" '*When I get an owie, my mom knows what to do!*' " I sang, off-key but with enthusiasm as I remembered the words. " '*She puts on my Band-Aid and no more boo-boo boo-hoo!*' "

"Don't forget the little dance she did," Sebastian said. He did an over-the-top twirl and jazz hands, ending in a cute pose.

"Come on," Jenna said. "I was five."

"Oh my gosh, that's you?" I gaped at Jenna. I looked at the picture and then back at her.

"Oh, you hadn't figured that out?" she said. "I know, I'm not as cute anymore."

"It's just that in Ohio, nobody is on TV, so it didn't occur to me," I said. "I can't believe you're the boo-boo boo-hoo girl. I loved that commercial."

"And I hated it," Jenna shuddered.

"She also was in a commercial for those CDs full of kids singing cheesy songs," Sebastian said. "That picture's over here on Jenna's Wall of Fame. My mom won't let her take it down."

I looked and saw a few more ads with little Jennas in them.

"Wow," I said. I was still in shock that my new friend was the boo-boo boo-hoo girl. "I didn't know you were famous."

"Shut *up*," Jenna said. "That was a long time ago. I think I was twelve in the most recent picture."

"So you don't act at all anymore?" It seemed from the jobs she'd landed that she must have been pretty good. "Why not?"

"Well," Jenna said. "It stops being fun when your mother starts to get pissed off when you don't book jobs, because you go through puberty and you get zits and suddenly your round cute look isn't considered so cute anymore. And then Mother gets all Barry's Bootcamp on your butt since she can't pimp you out anymore."

Sebastian and I were completely silent.

"That's why I don't audition anymore," Jenna said. "So disregard the pictures in the hallway and let's move on."

Sebastian and I looked at each other awkwardly and followed her.

"There's something better to see." Jenna pointed down the hall and a white and brown fluffy shih tzu dog came racing toward us.

"This is Rocky," she cooed, and picked up the dog. You could see all her tension fall away as Jenna cuddled with her puppy. Rocky gave her a kiss and panted excitedly. Then he ran to Sebastian, who scratched him on the belly. Then he came up to me.

"Oh, he's so cute!" I said, as Jenna showed me how Rocky shook hands and rolled over.

"Come on, Rocky," she said. "You can help us with M World."

The little dog followed us into her bedroom, which was gorgeous. The walls were pale purple, and she had an enormous, elegant bed with a gold canopy draped over it. Her comforter was gold, too, and purple pillows decorated the bed. She had an old-fashioned phone next to her bed and an antique-looking ottoman.

A glittery chandelier hung over the bed, and on the other side of the room a pink disco ball hung over a vanity. An Andy Warhol–style print of Marilyn Monroe was mounted over her computer desk.

"Your room's amazing," I said. "And spotless."

"Thanks to Louise," Sebastian said. "Jenna's a pig."

Jenna stuck her tongue out at him. There was a knock on the door. Sebastian opened it and an older woman walked in the room carrying a tray.

"Thanks, Louise," Sebastian said, taking the tray from her. "These look awesome."

"Speaking of Louise," Jenna said. "Louise, this is Avery."

Louise smiled and said hello.

"You have a cook?" I asked them, after Louise excused herself.

"She's our housekeeper," Jenna said. "But she also feeds me and Sebastian. Our stepfather, thankfully, never eats dinner at home. My mom only eats her Zone delivery or Master Cleanse."

"Master what?" I asked.

"It's some drink made of lemonade, pepper, and maple syrup or something," Jenna said. "My mother's doing it to lose probably half a centimeter to fit into a dress for this weekend."

Eww.

"This side is mother-approved." Jenna pointed to the tray. "Tofu and celery roll-ups. I'd recommend the minipizzas over on that side, though. Louise sneaks us the good stuff."

I took two pizzas. Sebastian stuffed some food in his mouth as he set up his laptop.

"Ready for work?" Sebastian asked. I nodded, my mouth full of pizza.

"I'll help!" Jenna said. "Just make me my avatar with a fabulous outfit first."

"Jenna is overly obsessed with the trivial and superficial," Sebastian said. "Caltech is not interested in fashion."

"No, but Team Marisa is, right, Avery?" They both looked at me for the decision.

"Can you just teach Jenna how to make her own avatar?" I asked him. "That would probably save us a lot of begging."

"Pleeease," Jenna said dramatically. "Pretty please! I want to make my own avatar."

"I never thought I'd hear that out of your mouth," said Sebastian. "I'm going to have to get used to the fact that you can even pronounce avatar."

"I promise to never make fun of your virtual world again," Jenna said. "Well, except for the one where you're a knight fighting flying dragons. That one is seriously stupid."

Sebastian gave her an evil eye.

"I'll make some good ones. I'm kind of famous on Polyvore and Stardoll for my outfit choices," Jenna said reassuringly.

"This is not paper dolls," Sebastian said.

"Just let her try it," I said. "She'll get started on the avatars, you work on the background, and I'll make a script for what's going to happen. Sound cool?"

"I can make a hot outfit for Vida Segunda," Jenna said coyly.

"Well," Sebastian said. "All right, then."

14

WHICH REDHEAD HAS FIFTEEN MINUTES TO FINISH HER MATH HOMEWORK BEFORE THE BUS COMES?

That would be me. But first, I had to do a quick check of my email. And Team Marisa.

```
To: Group@dmbrecords.com
From: AJohnson@DMBrecords.com
Subject: Marisa in weekender this
weekend

Marisa's interview will be in the
newspaper this weekend. Attached is
a sneak preview.
```

I hit the download and felt a little chill that I could get a sneak preview before anyone else. It was a thrill to know that I was in the inner circle, even secretly. I pulled up the interview to read.

NEW SINGER MARISA HAS BEEN WRITING SONG LYRICS SINCE SHE WAS IN HIGH SCHOOL.

Q: HOW DID YOU COME UP WITH THE IDEA FOR "THE GIRL WHO"?

A: *"The Girl Who" is just me being me. When you're being you, you'll be the person everyone wants to know. By being yourself and not being anyone else, people will want to get to know you. Maybe it won't always seems that way, like if you're in high school where people think they need to conform. Keep looking and you'll find your people. Eventually if stay true to yourself, like my song says, you'll be someone people will wish they knew.*

Love her.

I closed out of email and checked my Team Marisa messages. I had a couple minutes to answer a few people. I'd do my homework on the bus.

> *Marisa is so confident! I want to try out for jazz band but we have so many good musicians in my school. I'm scared to audition!*

> Marisa says that she gets nervous whenever she performs, because she wants to do a good job. Being nervous shows you care. Go out there and try your best—the only way you can fail is if you don't try!

I sat back and reread what I wrote. It sounded pretty good. I wondered if the last sentence was too hokey, because it was something my father always said. In fact, my parents had printed calendars for some doctor's office with that saying on it. But I knew Marisa would agree, so I left it on there.

Marisa fans are the best. I feel like we all would support each other as much as we support Marisa. I hope someday I can meet other Team Marisa fans! Monica

Come to M World . . . it's all going to be blowing up there!

I smiled after I answered that one. I completely agreed with her, that Team Marisa was turning out to be a place where people were really supportive. We had a couple trolls being obnoxious about Marisa's song, but people rallied against them so fast they didn't stick around. Team Marisa was a place where I felt safe.

I feel like I'm a fake. My friends and I are popular, and we wear certain clothes and like certain guys, but I'm starting to feel like I want to have an identity that's more me. But what if nobody likes it? JennieG

I knew what Marisa's advice would be, because she gave it in the interview I just read. I changed the words a little and wrote back.

By being yourself and not being anyone else, people will want to get to know you. Eventually if you stay true to yourself, like my song says, you'll be someone people will wish they knew. Think of the line in "The Girl Who" and be the girl who won't just go along for the ride.

My ride! Crud! The bus! I'd completely lost track of time. I ran downstairs and grabbed my tote bag and bolted out the door to see the bus at the stop down the street.

"Hey!" I yelled to the other people who were getting on the bus and apparently not hearing me as I ran across my lawn. Then I heard that terrible sound of the bus door closing and—

Dang it. I watched as the bus pulled away, completely ignoring the fact that I was supposed to be on it. Sigh. I'd have to call my parents and make them come get me. They were going to kill me. I took my phone out of my pocket and my Paramore ringtone went off, startling me. My parents must've had their parent radar on.

"Yes, Mom, I missed the bus," I said into the phone.

"Uh, Avery?"

The voice was not a parent.

"It's Griffin King," the voice continued.

"Oh, hi!" I said. "Sorry, I didn't check to see who was calling. I thought you were one of the parentals."

"I had a question about the English homework," he said. "Did you just say you missed the bus?"

Sigh again. Not only did I have to confess I take the bus (uncool), but also that I missed it (uncooler).

"Yeah," I admitted. "So anyway, what's your question? I've got time now that I have to wait for my parents."

"We can pick you up," he said. "Where do you live?"

"You don't have to do that," I said. "But then again that would save me from calling my parents and hearing the responsibility lecture."

"You help figure out the homework, I'll get you a ride," he said.

I told him where I lived and he said they were on their way. I went back and sat down on my front step to wait. Griffin had said "they" would pick me up. I realized that probably didn't mean his mother. It might mean his next-door neighbor, Cecilia, or one of her friends. Maybe I'd made a mistake to say yes.

I suddenly felt nervous. I looked at my house, which wasn't anywhere near the league of Griffin's or Cecilia's, I was certain. They were probably going way out of their way. I sat down and worked on my health homework while I waited.

I looked up when a silver BMW convertible pulled up in front of my house, with Cecilia's friend Miya driving it. I saw Cecilia in the shotgun seat, Griffin and another guy I didn't recognize in the back. This should be interesting. I put on my sunglasses and walked down the sidewalk to the car.

"Hi," I said, giving a little wave and trying to sound confident.

"Hurry up," Cecilia said. "We're going to be late. I didn't know we'd be driving way out to the boonies. Even Miya's GPS didn't know where we are."

I blushed, feeling not confident at all.

"Her GPS knew where we were," Griffin said. "Maybe you're just not smart enough to read it."

"Ooh, burn!" Miya said.

It made me feel a little bit better that Griffin stuck up for me, but I was still standing there awkwardly, noticing there were basically two seats in the back, with just a bump in the middle.

"I'm Javier," the other guy said to me. I knew that, from Jenna's "Hot Guys in School" reports. Jenna also called him "Sexy Beast." And he was that, with his jet-black hair and gray T-shirt molded to his tan muscles.

"I can sit in the middle," I said, starting to get into the backseat.

"No, I'll sit on the bump," Griffin said.

"Nah, she can have the comfortable seat," Javier said. Before I knew what was going on, he reached out and pulled me onto his lap. Oh. My. "Now you're riding in style, baby."

"When Miya drives, it's always in style," Miya said casually. The car raced off down the street, and the momentum threw me forward a bit.

"Don't worry, I'll hold you safely," Javier said, and actually wrapped his arms around me.

I felt my face flush red and I stared straight ahead.

"Watch out for Javier, he's a dog," Griffin said. He smiled, but I noticed he sounded a little testy.

"Yes, I'm like a sweet puppy," Javier said. "Will you take me home with you?"

The girls laughed. Griffin rolled his eyes.

"You should have seen Javier last night," Miya said. "He was hitting on every girl in the In-N-Out line. I was like, dude, just get your burger."

I turned around to see if Javier was offended but he was smiling.

"Griffin, listen to this," Cecilia said, handing him her iPod. He put in the earphones and started listening.

"It was a good burger," Javier said.

"I've never been," I said.

"They don't have In-N-Out burgers in Idaho?" Miya asked. "You have to try one."

"You're from Idaho?" Javier asked me. "Then you like potatoes. In-N-Out has excellent fries, too."

"Here's a good story for you guys," Cecilia said, before I could clarify the Idaho thing. "Avery's father was in Urth, and he thought Delilah was Paris Hilton. Right, Avery?"

I looked over at Griffin, but he was in his own little world, listening to the iPod.

"Um, yeah," I said. "He was kind of embarrassing."

"I know, right?" She laughed. "And he thought I was Paris's sister, and of course I am so not Nicky, puh-lease. Willie took pictures and we were all like, that guy is so from Idaho."

My face turned red as everyone laughed. Griffin took his head-phones off.

"What's so funny?" he asked.

"Nothing," I sighed. I was sure William would leak the pictures and Griffin would get the full horror story. I shifted uncomfortably on Javier's lap.

"I liked the third track best," Griffin said. "The first one I thought was weakest. Avery, you'll have to hear this. It's University of Hard's new songs they're trying out."

"Shade likes to get Griffin's opinions," Cecilia said.

"That's so cool," I said, impressed.

"That's just spin," Griffin said to me. "Shade doesn't know who I am. He asks Delilah's opinion and she tells him what I said."

"Oh, you knew that?" Cecilia said. "I thought you bought the whole Shade-values-your-opinion thing."

"Well, he should," I said. "Griffin knows his music."

"Thanks," Griffin said. "So do you. And we're almost at school, so can you fill me in on the project? I had to leave class early so I missed it. Schmitt needs to get into the twenty-first century and update her webpage with the homework."

"Well, we have to do a project to show one of the objects that represent the thematic concepts," I said. "There are all these objects that mean something, like the conch shell or the glasses one of the characters wears. We have to pick one today."

"Is this our English class?" Cecilia asked. "We have to do a project on *Lord of the Rings*?"

"You get to read *Lord of the Rings*?" Miya said. "You're so lucky. In my English class we're reading *Lord of the Flies*."

"That's what Cecilia means, she just doesn't know it," Griffin told her, scanning the list of topics.

"Crap, I better find out what my sister did hers on," Cecilia said. "Griffy, do you know what Delilah did?"

Griffin gave me a sly grin.

"The sow," he said. "I think she did the sow."

I started to laugh and then covered it up by turning it into a cough.

"Okay, I'll do the sow, whatever that is," Cecilia said. She turned to Miya and started talking about how cute Miya's earrings were.

"A sow? Isn't that a pig?" Javier whispered into my ear.

"Yeah," I said, shifting around on Javier's lap. It was a little difficult to concentrate when Javier was leaning into me like that. "Um, a pig's head embodies the human impulse toward violence and savagery that exists within every person."

Obviously, I needed to stop babbling now.

"You're a smart girl as well?" Javier asked me. "I find that very sexy."

"Yeah, talking about pig's heads and savages always does that to me, too," Griffin said, rolling his eyes. "But it's true, Avery is smart. She's like a *Lord of the Flies* expert."

"Well, I did that book in my old school so I already studied it," I said. "Are you going to tell Cecilia that her sister probably didn't do that for a project? Particularly since the symbol is a pig's head impaled on a stake?"

"Should I enlighten her?" Griffin asked me. "I was thinking it would be really interesting to see her do that topic."

Yeah, that could be pretty entertaining. I thought about Cecilia laughing at my father and decided we could keep it to ourselves.

"Finally, we're at school," Cecilia announced. "That took forever. Avery might as well still live in Idaho, it seemed that far."

"Cece, stop rolling your eyes. You're about to be snapped," Miya said.

Cecilia started smiling and rolled down the window. I watched as William and Cam came over and started filming.

"Cecilia! Where'd you go last night?" William asked. "What were you wearing? Did you see Shade? Did you—"

"No comment. I have to get to class," Cecilia said, keeping the smile on.

"That means she only did something lame last night and doesn't want to admit it," Miya translated.

"In-N-Out burger doesn't sound lame to me," I muttered.

"I will take you there on our next date!" Javier told me. "You will sit on my lap again!"

"Enough with the sitting on your lap," Griffin said.

"Perhaps you want her to sit in your lap?" Javier said.

I blushed. If I felt light-headed about sitting on Javier's lap, the thought of Griffin's was putting me over the edge.

"Don't think so," Cecilia cut in. "Griffin wants Delilah on his lap. You know it's true, Griffin."

"Cecilia, your sister has a boyfriend who I'm sure would not be happy to hear you saying things like that," Griffin said.

"Dude, did you see Delilah's new boobies yet?" Javier asked.

That was definitely my cue to leave.

"Thanks for the ride," I said, although nobody paid much attention. I slid off Javier's lap and not very gracefully climbed out of the car.

"Hey! What's she doing getting a ride from you?" I heard William ask. "She's a nobody! If you had room in the car for someone, why didn't you pick me up?"

I looked straight ahead, to avoid anyone thinking I was remotely bothered by being called a nobody, and probably on film at that.

I hurried into school and found Jenna waiting for me at my locker.

"Good morning!" Jenna said, and shoved some magazine pages into my face.

"You're awfully chipper today," I said, taking the magazines.

"I am so excited about M World. I circled potential outfits for the avatars. Tell me if you hate them, I mean, I tried to go *Gossip Girl* meets *Project Runway* meets Prada meets *Teen Vogue*, with a little Hello Kitty thrown in."

I had no clue what she was trying to say, but I nodded enthusiastically.

"Do you like what I'm wearing? I thought we could do this as an avatar, too. It's Alice + Olivia, Ella Moss, and Free People inspired."

"Awesome." I nodded, overwhelmed, and then saw Jenna's face fold into a confused look that probably matched mine.

"Idaho! Idaho! I have a few questions to ask you." William came up to me, with Cam filming close behind. "How did you get Miya and Cecilia to give you a ride to school?"

"You got a ride to school with who?" Jenna said.

"What were you really doing in the backseat with two of our school's own hotties? Aren't there only two seats in there?" William asked.

"I was helping Griffin with his homework," I said. "That's all."

"Oh, helping with homework?" William said, making little quote fingers in the air. He turned to the camera. "She claims she was helping Griffin King with his homework. Is *that* what they call it in Idaho these days?"

"I'm from *Ohio*," I said. "O-H-I-O. Not Idaho or Iowa."

"Get a close-up, Cam," William said. "Get her looking mad."

"Oh my gosh, get out of here," Jenna said. "She has no comment for you."

"Her publicist is claiming no comment," William said. "What are they covering up?"

I stuck my head in my locker until they left.

"That boy is truly annoying," Jenna said. "But don't think you're off the hook answering those questions. I don't give up as easily as William. Did you really drive here with Cecilia, and who exactly were these hotties?"

"I missed the bus," I said. "Griffin King just happened to call at the exact moment I missed the bus, and he said they'd come pick me up. And 'they' turned out to be Miya and well, we were squashed in the back and I had to sit on Javier Rodriguez's lap."

"You sat on Sexy Beast's lap?" Jenna's jaw dropped open. "He is hotter than hot. What was it like?"

"He was cheesy," I said. "But still, hot cheese."

"I want to know everything. What it felt like. What everyone talked about. Was there any good gossip? Ooh, if you infiltrate the inner-circle car pool, I bet you can become the princess of gossip."

I half smiled as I thought of the random blog I'd started and left untouched.

"I don't think I have any gossip that worthy," I said. "But I will describe the feel of Javier's arms around me and what it was like when he whispered cheesy pickup lines into my ear."

"You are so flippin' lucky," she squealed. "Was Cecilia nice to you?"

"Not exactly," I said. "The whole thing was a little stressful. I feel a little worn-out already and the day hasn't even started."

"You better not be tired," Sebastian said as he walked up to my locker. "We have a lot to do for tomorrow night."

"I know," I said. "I'm starting to get nervous."

"We can meet in the computer lab today," Sebastian said. "Avery, I need you to double-check the storyboard to see if I've got everything in sequence."

"And I'm going to unveil my avatars for your viewing enjoyment," Jenna said proudly. "At least I hope you'll like them."

"I can't wait until computer lab to see them," I said honestly.

We'd all worked together to design an avatar for Marisa. She was going to look amazing. We'd modeled it on a picture of her rocking out that we'd taken from her album cover. She was wearing a casual floaty emerald-green dress with a circle pattern on it, bangles on her wrist, and of course her emerald guitar pendant. Her long hair was down and wavy. I pictured Marisa on the stage, with avatars cheering her on, and smiled.

And then the early bell rang and startled me back to reality. The reality of school starting and the fact that I hadn't finished my math homework.

"What's the matter?" Jenna asked. "You suddenly look like you're going to puke."

"I just realized I never finished my math homework. I don't even understand it, I'm so screwed."

"What period do you have it?" Sebastian asked, coming up behind me. "I can help you with it in lab."

"No, it's already late from yesterday," I groaned. "So, thanks, but I have to turn it in before first period or I get a zero. I'll try to whip it off in homeroom."

"Let me take a look at it. I'm not giving you the answers so don't get too stoked, but maybe I can see what you're doing wrong," Sebastian said.

I pulled out my homework sheet and handed it to Sebastian. He moved a few lockers down and started looking at my paper.

"Okay, I can't take it anymore," Jenna said suddenly. "I'm just going to come out and ask you. Do you like him?"

I looked around to see who she was talking about. She was looking at her brother.

"Wait, your brother? You think I like him? Like, *like* him like him?" I said.

I shuddered at the thought. I mean, I like Michael Cera, who is an ubersmart geek type, but at least he can button his shirt correctly.

"Well, you're pretty much the first real live girl he'll talk to. So I figured you'll date him and then I'll be on my own."

I lowered my voice so as not to hurt Sebastian's feelings.

"Jenna? I don't like him like him. We're just doing M World."

"Are you sure?" she said. "You don't have one of those secret crushes that friends are supposed to have on other girls' older brothers? I wouldn't know how to recognize it, since it's never happened. But I suppose someone lonely and desperate could fall for him."

I looked at her. I'm sure if my life was a movie, I might have suddenly realized that even though he was a computer geek, he was the one for me, and we'd end up getting married and he'd be a gazillionaire like Bill Gates. But in reality, while the last part was likely to happen, there had to be something there for me to like him. And there wasn't, at least more than a friend.

"Not that you're lonely and desperate," she stammered. "I mean, maybe lonely, since you moved from Ohio and don't know anyone, but you're not desperate."

"You should probably just be quiet now," Sebastian said from where he was standing.

"Oh, no," Jenna said. "You could hear us?"

"Yes, and while Avery may find me irresistible, our relationship is purely professional. Avery is not my type," Sebastian said.

"I'm not?" I asked. I felt mildly insulted. I mean, *he* was the geeky loner.

"No offense, Avery, but when I found out you didn't even know how to defrag the computer, I knew you weren't the one for me."

"That's your criteria for a girl?" I said. Suddenly I stopped feeling insulted. "See? We're not a love match."

"Defrag is so basic," Sebastian said, shaking his head. "Reducing the amount of fragmentation in a file—"

"Well!" Jenna interrupted the lecture. "I feel so much better now that I can see there's no chemistry between you two. Avery probably got enough chemistry from sitting on hot Javier's lap this morning. Next time you're calling me and I get to sit on Javier's lap, okay?"

I had to admit my fleeting thought was that if Jenna had been there to sit on Javier's lap, I could have sat on Griffin's.

"Ooh, she's blushing," Jenna said in a singsong voice. "Avery's felt the heat of hot-hot Javier."

I'd let her believe that was it. Much easier that way.

15

"My new collection is inspired by the sparkling of emeralds, the truthful vibe of Marisa, and the cutting edge of technology. It is the return to empowered femininity with a rocker vibe and—"

"This is not hackin' *Project Runway*," Sebastian grumbled. "It's my Caltech project."

I let the siblings have their rivalry as I pulled over a chair to a spot where I could see the computer screen. I'd survived a boring and uneventful morning at school. Well, except for the part when Cecilia had selected "the sow" as her project for *Lord of the Flies*. Griffin had caught my eye, but I'd had to look away to stop myself from laughing out loud and I hadn't seen him since.

Now we were in the computer lab, about to see the M World avatars for the first time. I was a little nervous. Avatars were obviously a critical part of M World. I mean, they were the characters who would represent the people of Team Marisa. When you went on Sims, or on Wii, you spent a long time picking out who your characters would be. I thought of my dad and his Gwen Stefani Mii fetish. Of course I'd seen Sebastian's manga people and trusted Jenna's taste, but I was anxious.

"Don't worry, it is going to be fierce," Jenna said. "Now shush. Everyone will be wearing a Team Marisa VIP badge around their neck. I divided the avatars up into different categories. First up are what I call Cool People."

I watched the screen as the first avatars popped up. They were in the style of Sebastian's anime cartoons, and featured guys and girls in all colors of the rainbow—including violet and orange. Their outfits ranged from rocker to boho to T-shirt casual to a girl in a ski outfit. They all wore lanyards with a small badge that said Team Marisa.

"Wow," I said. And I meant it. The avatars looked fabulous.

"Thank you." Jenna smiled. "And here is what I call the Jenna Collection. Starting with my avatar in her fabulous Jenna Couture gown."

The avatar shockingly resembled her, and was wearing a fuchsia off-the-shoulder gown with long gloves.

"Sweet," I said. "But you do know we're having a roller rink tonight?"

"Avatar Jenna is so talented she can skate in a ball gown," Jenna said. "And here is the rest of the Jenna Collection."

And suddenly a Zac Efron avatar popped up. The face was cut from a real picture and the body was done in Sebastian's manga style. He was wearing a Team Marisa T-shirt and roller skates.

"Okay, that is beyond cool," I said.

"Doesn't he make a cute Team Marisa fan?" Jenna asked. "And look who else is coming tomorrow night!"

More avatars popped up. They were all wearing Team Marisa T-shirts and roller skates: Joe Jonas, Jason Dolley, Corbin Bleu.

"All my sweeties will be there," she said. "I've promised them each a couples skate."

"All right," Sebastian suddenly said, standing up. "This is abuse of my avatars. I didn't want all of your pop-star pretty boys taking over my world."

"Come on, Sebastian, these are unbelievable!" I said. "I can't believe you taught her to do that. Team Marisa is going to love it. And then Caltech will be impressed that you're connecting with your audience."

Sebastian made a noise of frustration, but sank back down in his seat. "Well, I draw the line at that stupid top hat. At least crop out that stupid top hat."

"Agreed," Jenna said. "Joe can lose the hat. Maybe I should debut the next collection. I call it the Sea Bass Collection."

She clicked her mouse and more avatars popped up: Angelina in her Lara Croft outfit, Princess Leia in her slave outfit, and Captain Picard from *Star Trek*.

"I'm appeased," Sebastian said.

"I thought so," Jenna said triumphantly. "Avery, I made some for you but they'll be surprise guest appearances. So I'm not telling. But we do need to figure out what your own avatar will look like."

"I'll think about it," I said.

"And there's one more category," Jenna said. "Randoms."

A page full of avatars came up on the screen and I laughed. They weren't even people—there was an alien, a robot, several superheroes, and even a cheetah.

"Using nonpeople was Sebastian's idea," Jenna said. "Well, I picked the cheetah. I like cheetahs."

"I thought it would be more interesting to explore outside the human realm," Sebastian agreed. "Makes it more surreal."

"So there might be an alien roller skating with Joe Jonas while Marisa is singing?" I shook my head in disbelief. That was definitely surreal. "I think Marisa would be thrilled. And slightly weirded out. But mostly thrilled."

16

```
From: TeamMarisaMySpace
Subject: M World Launch Party


14 minutes until MWorld
Let the countdown begin
```

Team Marisa MySpace was blowing up with excitement. I read the comments people were posting and they were dying of suspense. So was I.

From StarTrekSeb:

> Be on standby. I will open the room for u to see in a minute.

"Jenna!" I said. "We've got thirteen minutes left."

I looked at Jenna, who was across the room. We were in her bedroom and I was sitting at her computer desk, on her computer with the huge monitor. She was sitting in her round chair, with her laptop on standby.

"Avery, this is hugely major," Jenna said. "Are you sure you don't want some guacamole? Louise makes the best guacamole."

She held out a tray of blue tortilla chips.

"Another time," I said. "I'm so nervous I think I'm going to throw up."

"Don't be nervous!" Jenna said. "Look, worst-case scenario nobody shows up. Or no, worst case is people come and it doesn't work at all. No, worst would be if people came and everything crashed and—"

"You are so not helping," I groaned, suddenly having second thoughts about the whole thing.

"Look, this whole thing is anonymous," Jenna said. "If it doesn't work, then nobody knows it's you, right?"

"Yeah, that doesn't even feel important to me," I said. "I want Marisa, I want *Team* Marisa, to have something special. I want this to be a virtual party that gets people psyched up for Marisa."

"And, ahem, you want Sebastian's project to get him a full scholarship to Caltech, thank you," Sebastian said, coming into the room.

"That, too," I said, nodding. "You guys, you really did an awesome job on this. I mean it."

"Aw, that's so sweet," Jenna said. She came over and gave me a big hug.

"That's touching," Sebastian said. "But there's no time for sentimental bonding now. You guys need to sign in for a test run now. Avery, you go in first."

Sebastian left the room, and Jenna and I focused on our computers.

"It's ready!" Sebastian yelled from his room down the hall.

I crossed my fingers and clicked on the link that Sebastian had emailed me. *Please work. Please work.*

`Would you like to enter M WORLD?`

Yes. Yes, I would! I clicked on the yes button and a new screen popped up.

A big, burly avatar with SECURITY on his T-shirt appeared on the screen.

His speech bubble said:

Choose your avatar.

A screen full of Jenna's avatar choices popped up. Everyone would get to choose one, and the cool thing was that once you picked one, nobody else could select the same one—everyone would have their own individual identity.

I scrolled down and found the avatar Jenna had designed for me.

And, I have to say, I looked hot. Just because I was short, pasty, and had frizzy red hair in real life didn't mean I had to look like that in virtual life. In Marisa World, I had long, shimmery silver-metallic hair with a pink streak (Marisa's favorite color!). I also had big manga-style eyes that were bright green.

I wore a black T-shirt that said Team Marisa on it in emerald and silver, a cropped vest over it, a miniskirt, and tall silver boots that doubled as roller skates.

Yes, I was seriously cute. I clicked on the avatar.

The security avatar's speech bubble popped up and said:

Let me see if you are cool enough
for this party.

There was a pause and a virtual red rope opened on-screen.

Okay, you're in.

The screen went black, and then I was in . . .

M WORLD!

My avatar stood inside the roller rink. I moved my mouse and my avatar skated gracefully around. I turned my character view so I could see the performance stage up close.

This was flipping unreal.

I clicked a button and my avatar was standing on the stage. In a few minutes I'd be up here introducing Virtual Marisa online to a room full of people. Well, hopefully a room full of people. Or at least a decent-size crowd of people. Because what if nobody showed up? I shuddered.

Well, no matter what, we would pack the rink because Sebastian had made it so that with a press of a button it looked like the place was full. But I hoped Team Marisa people would really come. I wanted to share it with them.

Suddenly, Sebastian's avatar popped up into the room. I stifled a laugh. Okay, it wasn't nice to make fun of anyone's alter ego, but . . . Sebastian's avatar had spiky black hair and huge, huge muscles. Basically, he was the anti-Sebastian.

Then I looked at myself standing on the stage and realized that he probably resembled his avatar more than I did mine. Never mind.

"hi," Sebastian-avatar said in a speech bubble.

"i m freaking out!" I typed back.

"don't say that," Sebastian-avatar said. "the Caltech people will be here soon. compliments only."

"Then Sebastian: You're a genius."

17

Jenna's avatar appeared in the roller rink, wearing the long fuschia dress. Glittery emerald skates peeked out from under the hem.

"Wow," Jenna said out loud, from over on her bed. "This is fun."

"Can u test out different avatars, Jenna?" Sebastian's avatar speech bubble said.

"Coming right up!" Jenna said. I heard her type something into her computer and suddenly a Chris Brown avatar appeared.

"Chris Brown is in da house!" Chris said, and roller-skated across the roller rink until he went up to my avatar.

"u r so hot, avery," Chris's speech bubble said. "let's make out."

"Stop that," I scolded Jenna. "That is not allowed in Marisa World. Your avatars have to behave themselves. Even Chris Brown."

"I know," Jenna said. "But it's just us in there for five more minutes. I thought we could play. Doesn't it seem like Chris really is talking to you? The virtual you, I mean, with the silver hair and the Team Marisa Captain T-shirt. It gives me chills."

This whole thing was giving me chills.

"Okay, what are you doing?" Sebastian stomped into Jenna's

room. "I saw that. There will be *no* comments about making out. I will have enough problems making sure this place stays clean without you causing problems."

"Sebastian is policing this," I said. "Unlike some celebrities in real life, ours will behave."

"Okay, okay," Jenna said. "But one favor before anyone else gets in here. Can you pleaaase let Joe Jonas kiss my avatar?"

"No," Sebastian said. "I have two words for you. Cal and Tech." He stormed out of Jenna's room.

"Fine," she sighed. "No kissing avatars. Let's bring in a little Bono."

"hello avery," said Bono's avatar. "will u help me with the crisis in Africa?"

"Yeah, except can you not use my real name, please?" I said out loud to Jenna.

"hello no name," said an Angelina Jolie avatar as she roller-skated into the room. "u r so cute. can I adopt u? I will name u a super kewl name like Vivienne." I couldn't help but laugh. Then Sebastian's avatar came over to us and said, "It's time to get serious. M World is going to open in three minutes."

Jenna and I looked at each other and sobered immediately. I took a deep breath and watched as Sebastian flashed words on the screen:

```
WELCOME TO M WORLD
THE ROLLER RINK!
```

I smiled as the roller rink lit up. Sebastian had designed some serious special effects. Disco ball and strobe lights. Confetti. Balloons.

For one long, horrible moment, nothing happened. And then

suddenly, another avatar popped in the room. It was one of Sebastian's designs—a girl with curly hair and a rocker outfit. Then another avatar—a hipster guy. Then another.

People were here!

"Welcome to M World!" my avatar walked around saying to people.

More avatars arrived, including an alien, a robot, and the cheetah.

"Growl," said the cheetah. "This place is too cool."

It felt like a mix of Sims Nightlife, Second Life, and Club Penguin. And suddenly the place was packed. And everyone was talking in their speech bubbles:

```
where is marisa
Watch me skate!
i want a smoothie
Team Marisa rox!
```

M World was rocking. It was a scene. Avatars were skating around or talking to each other. Two of them were holding hands. People were on a virtual date in M World? Wow.

"Did you notice the DJ?" Jenna said. I skated over to the DJ booth and saw a virtual Mark Ronson spinning away.

"And now, I'm going to walk in with Bono!" Jenna said, obviously having fun with this.

"look, it's bono!" Avatars flocked around the virtual star.

"r u the opening act?"

"do u heart Marisa, too, bono?"

"Jenna, be good," I warned. "It's Bono. He's sacred. No asking for kisses."

"I know," Jenna said. "Watch and learn."

"I am a fan of Marisa," Bono answered. "I am here to ask all team Marisa fans to donate to Darfer."

"See," Jenna said, leaning over past her computer screen. "That's cool, isn't it?"

"Yeah, but it's Dar*fur*, with a *u*," I said.

"Darfur!" Bono said. "Donate to Darfur."

Bono skated off the screen and disappeared.

All of a sudden Kristi Yamaguchi skated by on ice skates, wearing a sparkly ice-blue skating outfit.

"You made a Kristi Yamaguchi?" I asked Jenna, laughing. "On ice skates?"

"Roller skating, ice skating, practically the same thing. She's my favorite skater," Jenna said. "Want to see my triple-triple and double salchow?"

Just then signs started flashing along the top of the screen.

```
Welcome to M World! Marisa will be
onstage in 3 minutes!
```

People seemed to be really digging the roller-rink idea. Some avatars were even skating on the rink walls and on the ceiling.

"Um, Sebastian?" I called out. "Are people supposed to be skating upside down on the ceiling?"

I heard footsteps and Sebastian stuck his head in the door.

"I'm having an issue with the platform. I can't keep everyone on the floor," he said.

"Wheee!" Jenna said. "Look at me! I'm skating on the ceiling with Kristi Yamaguchi!"

"As long as Marisa can get to the stage, we're golden," I said, making my own avatar skate on the ceiling, next to Batman.

I smiled, then laughed out loud when I saw a new avatar skate by me.

"I am oprah! and I am here!" said an Oprah avatar wearing a Team Marisa shirt and a tiara on her head.

Avatars started surrounding Oprah, chanting: "Oprah! Oprah! Oprah!"

"You are good," I told her. "Oprah is a hit."

"Thank you, thank you," Jenna said modestly.

An AIM came on my screen from Sebastian:

`Virtual Marisa is ready!`

Signs started flashing:

`TAKE A SEAT * TAKE A SEAT *`

"Why don't you have Oprah go up onstage and introduce Marisa?"

"Okay," Jenna said. "I'll have Bono join her."

Avatar Oprah and Avatar Bono went up onstage. Jenna maneuvered them so they looked like they were holding hands.

"hello! I am Oprah! And this is my pal Bono! We are together to support our new favorite artist: MARISA!"

The crowd cheered.

"Who wants to hear Marisa?" the Oprah avatar said.

Some of the avatars started jumping up and down. Speech bubbles started flashing:

```
I heart Marisa!
We want Marisa!
Marisa rox!
```

Jenna typed: "Then let's give it up for (Virtual) MARISA!"

Sebastian's avatar's speech bubble popped up first: "Clap clap clap!"

The other avatars joined in: "Woot!" "Clap clap!" "Marisa!" "MARISA! MARISA!"

And suddenly Marisa's avatar appeared, with her guitar. On the ceiling.

"She's upside down!" I yelled to Sebastian. "Marisa's on the ceiling!"

We heard Sebastian curse from down the hall.

Even upside down, Marisa looked amazing. She had her emerald guitar necklace and was holding her guitar, and on her feet were emerald-green roller skates, of course. Oh well, how many musicians could perform upside down on a ceiling of a roller rink, right?

"The Girl Who" music started playing in the background as Virtual Marisa played the guitar.

> *They say I'm this*
> *They say I'm that*
> *I'm nothing special*
> *I just fall flat*

The crowd was "dancing" and "clapping" and "cheering." Avatars in the audience swayed back and forth in unison. I actually choked up for a minute. I felt the love. I was pretty proud of myself that I put this together. I caught a glimpse of my real face reflected in the screen and I realized I had a goofy grin going. Well, come on. M World was a success.

> *I really have no doubt*
> *I'm the girl who you can't do without*
> *The girl who*
> *The girl who*
> *I'm the girl who*
> *You'll wish you knew . . .*

Marisa's song ended and the crowd went wild. I sat back and enjoyed the moment.

I'd written a speech for Virtual Marisa and it popped up in a speech bubble over her head.

```
Hi I'm virtual Marisa
Not the real one
But that WAS Marisa's real song
"The Girl Who"
Hope u liked it!
Thanks for being awesome fans!
Team Marisa rocks!
```

The Marisa avatar bowed and then . . . poof! Virtual Marisa disappeared.

And then *fireworks* went off! This was a surprise to me. Sebastian had kept that part a secret. Colors filled the screen—emerald green, pink, silver, gold. There were popping noises and everything. And then the fireworks spelled:

SABRINA BRYAN AND JULIA DeVILLERS

Afterward I watched as avatars stayed behind and chatted with each other, some even introducing themselves as Team Marisa members. A few avatars were dancing. I saw Sebastian's avatar getting a smoothie. There was even a line for the virtual girls' room.

"They love us," Jenna sighed. "This is truly cool."

"I know," I said. "Hey, where's your avatar?"

"Don't tell Sebastian but I'm in the corner holding hands with Jason Dolley," Jenna said, giggling. "Uh—*Hey!* My Jason Dolley just disappeared."

She leaned over and yelled out the door.

"Sebastian! Did you make my Jason disappear? We weren't kissing! That's not fair!"

"No kissing allowed," Sebastian's avatar popped on to the screen to announce.

"Fine!" Jenna typed back. "Then you will miss out on THIS!"

Suddenly Scarlett Johanson popped onto the screen next to Sebastian. She was wearing a long red evening gown with exaggerated cleavage.

"Do you like the plumpness of my lips and my sexy pose?" Scarlett asked Sebastian. "Too bad you will not be my virtual boyfriend because you are so mean."

Jenna and I giggled as Sebastian's avatar stomped off to another room.

"Here's one for you, Avery," Jenna said, and James McAvoy popped into the room.

"Och!" James's speech bubble said. "I am a truly hot Scot. Do you like my lilting Scottish brogue?"

"You are crazy." I shook my head, smiling. "But in a very good way. Now, let me focus on Team Marisa here and stop distracting me with your crazy."

"Aye!" James's speech bubble said, and he disappeared.

Suddenly a giant spotlight aimed itself over my virtual head and words popped up.

GIVE PROPS TO YOUR HOST FOR THE EVE-NING

Aw, that was really nice. People surrounded me and clapped and cheered. I typed in thank-yous and everyone told me how much fun they had.

"Don't forget to support Marisa!" I said. "Request 'The Girl Who' on the radio! Spread the buzz!"

A guy avatar skated over my head and his speech bubble went up. "i am a music journalist. I would like to do a story on M World."

"Sure, why not," I typed back. I turned to Jenna. "Someone's pretending he's a music journalist. People are seriously into this."

"This is even better than Sims2," Jenna said. "Especially because you don't have to deal with the fuzzed-out people parts when they go to the bathroom. And now, I will make it even better!"

Brad Pitt suddenly appeared in front of me.

"Oh my gosh, Jenna," I said. "You made a Brad Pitt, too?"

"I m a big fan of Marisa," the Brad avatar said. "Will u ask her to help me rebuild New Orleans? If she's as handy with a hammer as she is with her voice, we'll have it done in a week."

I looked over at Jenna, who was cracking herself up.

Okay, this *was* truly cool.

MySpace BULLETIN

From: Team Marisa
Date: October 22
Subject: Marisa World Listening Party

The M World Party ROCKED!
Team Marisa fans really know how to bring it!
And we're just getting started!

18

I looked at myself in my locker mirror and had a mixed reaction. On the one hand, I was still smiling because of the M World success last night. On the other, I looked seriously exhausted. After I'd gotten home from Jenna's house, I'd stayed up late hyperactively reading the comments Team Marisa and other new fans had left on MySpace about M World.

I quickly put on some lip gloss and smoothed down my hair, but it was pretty much hopeless. I was wearing an Ohio State T-shirt, shorts, and sneakers because I unfortunately had gym later. So basically, I pretty much looked like a wreck.

"You did look much better in M World last night," Jenna's voice said from behind me.

"Harsh," I said, turning around. "I know, I'm a mess, but—"

"No!" Jenna cut me off, laughing. "I didn't mean it to come out like that. I was just fishing for compliments about my personal styling last night."

"You don't have to fish," I said. "Everyone looked amazing. I am in awe of your skills. In fact, a couple people made requests for next time, so you may be making a Ryan Sheckler, a Hermione, and a Blake Lively."

We walked into the computer lab, and found Sebastian in the office.

"Hi, Fellow M Worldian," I said to him. "I feel like we need a secret handshake or something. Or a hand signal like this."

I folded my pinky down with my thumb to make a sign of an M.

Sebastian looked at me with a bemused expression.

"Okay, I'm a little punchy today," I said. "You would be, too, if you stayed up reading all the compliments we got last night. People loved it."

"May we please use your computer so we can read all the compliments?" Jenna asked her brother.

"Yeah," Sebastian sighed. "I didn't hear anything from the Caltech guy so I don't even know if he bothered to show up."

"Oh," I said. "Well, I could cut and paste all the compliments and at least they'd see what a great reaction we had."

"Sure, whatever," Sebastian said, heading out the office door. "If you need me, I'll be helping people whose computers are blowing up and calling me a geek in the meantime."

"I need to find a message to cheer him up," I told Jenna. I knew Sebastian was only doing this for his college application, but still I felt like he should be in a good mood about it. It had been a huge success.

"Let me know when you find a good message," Jenna said, taking some paper out of the computer printer and sitting on the low bookshelf near the window. "I'm going to sketch some ideas for my next M World outfit."

I signed onto the computer and went straight to my MySpace to see what else people were saying about M World. I had a lot of new comments and messages and friends.

Add me to your friends please! serrabear

Marisa rocks! annawowo

I called the radio stations to request "The Girl Who"! mayapapaya

And then I read a message that made my jaw drop. Someone from Team Marissa had sent me the link to a music journalist's website, where there was a new story posted this morning.

A NEW WAY TO BUZZ AN ARTIST

Promoters for a new artist have taken an unusual approach to promoting her debut. They gave her a listening party—at a roller-skating rink. Not a real rink, however, but a virtual one online.

Marisa, a singer/songwriter who has just released her debut single, is with DMB Records. The music label is using a grassroots effort online to drum up a fan base, with a Team Marisa MySpace and last night's virtual listening party.

Hundreds of people, in the form of avatars, attended the show. Said one attendee, in the form of a giant penguin, "Marisa's song is amazing and everyone had a rocking time."

"Come see this," I said to Jenna. "There must have been a music journalist there."

"That's amazing he or she wrote a story about you!" Jenna said, reading over my shoulder for a minute before going back to her seat.

"Well, not me," I said. "He thinks the music label made up Team Marisa."

And that was kind of annoying. Not that I needed the credit. But I made up everything because the record label was being so lame in the first place. So giving them the props for it bugged me. But still, it was cool that a journalist had been there. I wondered which avatar he or she was. One of the hip, slightly emo avatars? Or a space alien?

I forwarded the article to Sebastian. He'd be pretty psyched to read it, and it was definitely something that he could send to Caltech to impress them, right?

I opened a few more messages and thanked the fans for coming to M World. And then I opened a message titled "From an M World guest." I clicked on a graphic of an envelope and suddenly Rihanna's latest blasted across the room.

"What the hell!" I said, hitting the mute button as fast as I could.

An invitation unfolded on my computer screen.

"Jenna?" I said cautiously. "Come look at this."

To: Marisa and Marisa's Team
Please join us
For a launch party to celebrate the newest phone
At *Intermix*
Robertson Blvd., Beverly Hills
Wednesday evening
RSVP

"Oh my gosh!" Jenna said. "It's a launch party for the new T-Mobile! And we're invited!"

"*We're* not invited," I said. "They think we're Marisa's people."

"It says Team Marisa," Jenna pointed out.

"Marisa's team," I said. "Not Team Marisa. They're referring to assistants or managers or her people."

"That's not how I see it," Jenna said. "We're all on the same team. Team Marisa! Go team! And we should represent her at the T-Mobile launch party at Intermix."

"We're fifteen-year-old high schoolers," I said to her. "Why would they want us there?"

"You're right," Jenna said. "We should just send the invitation to her music label people who were written up in a music magazine for creating M World, right?"

"When you put it that way . . ." I said. "We created M World."

"Which is pretty much the biggest buzz Marisa has gotten so far," Jenna said. "Oh, come on! Let's go! I went to a couple launch parties when I was doing that acting thing and the food was yummy, but other than that I was miserable and I hated them."

"So I guess I'm missing the point a little about why you want to go?" I asked her.

"Because I was nine and my mom would push me to go 'schmooze' and 'network' with grown-ups in the hopes they would hire me for a job," Jenna said. "She wouldn't let me eat the food because I was getting chubby. She would keep the goody bags for herself. So I want to finally go to a launch party and have fun."

I saw her point.

"Come on, we'll give the party some buzz on M World so it's not like we won't be going for no reason!" Jenna pleaded.

"No," I said. "We won't be going because we won't be going. Because seriously, how are we going to get to the Intermix store in Beverly Hills on a Wednesday night?"

Jenna looked disappointed, but my argument was compelling. Of course I'd love to go. But we couldn't go to a launch party. It was ridiculous. I focused on my emails again.

"Hey, listen to this email I got," I said, and read it to Jenna.

```
Dear Team Marisa,
M World Party was fun! I talked to
fake Bono and guess what? My friends
and I are going to have a candy sale
in school on Friday and raise $ for
the Global Fund. Check out the fan
video we made.
```

I clicked on her video. It was a montage of pictures of Marisa, some of which I hadn't even seen yet. Marisa singing. Marisa signing an autograph. Marisa and her mom, smiling. She looked really pretty in all of them.

"The Girl Who" was playing in the background. And then, the last frame came up:

```
TEAM MARISA CARES
About Africa
```

"See, that is amazing," Jenna said. "Look at the good you are doing with M World."

"Wow," I said. "That's seriously cool."

It was. I mean, this girl was raising money because of Team Marisa. I bet Marisa would be really happy to know that because of her song, all this was happening.

"You get a lot of credit for this one," I said to Jenna. "Your Bono was genius."

"Thank you, thank you," she said. "And you can show your appreciation by taking me to the T-Mobile party."

"Nice try," I said. "We should probably just forward the invitation over to DMB Records. They'll probably want to go, it sounds like an awesome party."

"I can't believe they invited us," Jenna said.

"I can't either," a voice said behind us. I swiveled the desk chair around to see Cecilia, Miya, and William walking into the office. I quickly minimized my screen so they wouldn't see what we were working on. But I accidentally clicked on the email and the Rihanna song blasted again.

"Are you guys having a party in here?" Miya asked.

"They're probably dancing," Cecilia said. "Oh, wait, Jenna doesn't dance anymore. Her mom told my mom she stopped dancing because she didn't look good in the leotards. Jenna did have that big-booty dance situation."

I was about to stick up for her, but was dumbstruck when Cecilia started doing a slightly bizarre dance. She waved her hands in the air and did an awkward booty shake. William started laughing and did it, too.

I glanced at Jenna. She wasn't laughing.

"I don't get it," Miya said, wrinkling her brow.

"Before you moved here," Cecilia stopped laughing to explain, "Jenna did a toilet paper commercial where she had to do this crazy dance."

"And her dance partner was toilet paper," William said. "And she had pulled it out of the roll and said 'This toilet paper is so soft!' And she shook her booty at the camera."

Now all three of them laughed.

"I wonder if it's on YouTube," William said. "We should check."

"Hey, we're busy in here," I said, trying to sound more confident than I felt. "We'll let you know when we're finished."

"You're finished now," Cecilia said.

"Actually," I said, "we're in the middle of something. There are lots of computers out there in the lab."

"Let me spell something out for you," Cecilia said. She smoothed her long hair as she talked. "It's like if you were at a club. You got there early and sat down at a table. But I'm a VIP, so if I want your table, I get your table."

"There's no such thing as VIP in the computer lab," I said just as Sebastian walked into the office.

"Uh, you guys have to leave," he said to Jenna and me. "Cecilia has a pass to be in here."

Maybe there is such a thing as VIP in the computer lab. I reluctantly closed out of everything on the computer and stood up.

"You're a doll," Cecilia said, blowing a kiss to Sebastian. "Sorry, girls, VIPs coming through. TP people out, VIP people in."

"Ha!" William laughed a stupidly loud laugh. "TP versus VIP."

Just then, an Atreyu ringtone started playing and Cecilia pulled her cell phone out of her bag.

"That's a sweet phone," Sebastian blurted out.

"It's the newest T-Mobile," Cecilia said, popping it back in her bag. "So cute, right? And hm, are you two still here?"

Jenna and I didn't look at each other as we slunk out of the office into the computer lab. I found an empty carrel, and Jenna kneeled down next to me.

"I hate that," Jenna said. "It's like I'm a total nobody. She just waltzes in and we have to leave. It's like Heidi Klum. You're either in or you're out. And we, Avery, are out."

"I know," I said. "It's depressing."

I understood there were VIPs at clubs and restaurants and concerts. Even the lunch tables had their VIP sections. But a computer lab? That should be VIP-free. What's next, a red carpet and swag bags for the popular people? At least in the virtual world last night, I was a somebody. Then I had to come back to reality for this.

"I hate that Cecilia thinks I'm such a nobody she can rag on me," Jenna said. "And I definitely hate that toilet paper dance."

I looked at Jenna and tried to think of something I could say to cheer her up.

"Hey, sorry about that," Sebastian said as he came over to us. "They had a pass from the principal, so what could I do?"

"Well, for one thing you could not give her any more compliments. It's bad enough Cecilia bumped us for her 'VIP status,'" Jenna said. "Did you have to go and give her a compliment? 'Cecilia! That's a sweeeeet phone.'"

Sebastian turned red. "Sorry, I choked. Technology blinds me. That phone *is* sweet. It's T-Mobile's newest model."

No, it's not the newest model. The newest is the one being launched at the party we got invited to.

"Augh!" we heard someone yell. "My computer blew up! Computer Geekaleak, I need you!"

"Could we be any more abused today?" Jenna sighed. "That's us, Geekaleak and TP."

"Oh, was she doing her thing about the toilet paper commercial?" Sebastian said. Just because she didn't get the part and you did, doesn't mean she should abuse you for it."

"It doesn't matter," Jenna said, but I could tell she didn't mean it.

I looked at Jenna and Sebastian. And the words just blurted out.

"So. You guys free Thursday night?"

```
To: TMobile Launch party people

RSVP: We will be delighted to attend
the launch party.
Team Marisa, 3 guests.
```

Okay, so maybe I got a little caught up in the heat of the moment when I told Jenna I'd changed my mind about the launch party. But she was so excited, there was no way I was going to back out now. She asked Sebastian if he'd be willing to take us there and he said first he'd check to see that it wasn't an over-twenty-one thing, but he said yes so quickly I realized he was just as psyched to go so he could see the new phone.

AVERY'S FASHION TRANSFORMATION
On Tuesday, she was the girl next door. But on Thursday, after up-and-coming personal stylist Jenna took over, she was a glam style icon! Her own style icon? Audrey Hepburn, of course.

I finished putting on makeup and looked in the mirror. I was as ready as I was going to get for the launch party. I'd taken Jenna's fashion advice on what to wear tonight. "I miss the days where I could waltz into Limited Too and know I'd have the right outfit," I stressed.

"Jenna to the rescue!" she said cheerfully.

"You want to be cool enough to fit in. And casual enough to blend in."

Jenna had helped me pick out a cheap version of a Holly Go-lightly–inspired H&M black dress and pearl choker. I'd put my hair up in a bun but little frizzies kept escaping. Sigh. Someday I'd have a stylist who would use the perfect product and technique to make my frizzy hair the sleek envy of all. For now, I smoothed my hair one more time and headed downstairs. I wanted to be there to intercept Jenna and Sebastian before my parents got to them.

My parents were so happy I was finally being social that I was afraid they were going to attack Jenna and Sebastian and smother them with gratefulness for being their lonely daughter's friends.

"Where are you all going?" my mom asked.

I didn't want to lie, so I said I was going to try to spot celebrities in Beverly Hills. Which was true, right? I just didn't mention that I was going to an invitation-only launch party. Besides, once they saw the three of us, I didn't think we'd be allowed in the party in the first place, and we really *would* be on the street trying to spot celebrities.

The doorbell rang just as I made it to the front hallway. I ran and opened the door.

"Wow, Jenna, you look awesome."

She really did. Jenna definitely wasn't planning to stay under the radar. She was wearing a yellow ruched bodice shroom bubble dress and cute deep lavender heels. She looked really bright and sunny.

"Hello!" My mom came up behind me. "I'm Mrs. Johnson!"

"Hi!" Jenna said in her bubbly way. "It's nice to meet you. Avery, you look chic!"

"Mom, Dad, this is Jenna and Sebastian," I said. Sebastian's hair was spiked up more than usual. Otherwise, in his button-down shirt and jeans, he looked like he could be going to school.

"Hello," Sebastian said.

"And I'm Mr. Johnson," my dad said. "We're happy Avery finally has friends!"

Everyone stood there awkwardly for a moment. I thought about Jenna's glamorous mother standing in her enormous lobby. If Jenna's house was *Cribs*, mine wasn't quite ready for *Extreme Makeover*, but it could have used some *Trading Spaces*.

"So, son, you're the driver," my father said to Sebastian. "Have you ever had a ticket or caused an accident? Have you ever broken the driving laws of the state? Do you talk on your cell phone while driving, which quadruples your chances of being in an accident and is now illegal in this state?"

"No," Sebastian said. "I'm a careful driver."

"And he's very responsible. He's going to be valedictorian of his class," Jenna assured my dad.

"And he's probably going to Caltech," I said.

"Well, please drive carefully," my mom said. "Do you have your cell phone, Avery?"

"Don't worry, Mrs. Johnson," Jenna said. "We'll be *surrounded* by cell phones." She gave me a wink.

"Wow, you have the Beaver Cleaver family," Jenna said as we walked to Sebastian's car. "They're so normal. Your mom doesn't even Botox or anything. And I mean that as a good thing."

"Well, thanks for being so clean-cut and wholesome and parent-approved that I can finally leave my house for a social event," I said.

"Parents love Sebastian," Jenna said. "He's the perfect foil to any plan."

"Ahem. Feel free to thank me for being such an upstanding citizen that parents trust me," Sebastian said. "However, if you two do anything to damage my reputation—"

"We're not going to be any trouble," I said. "We're going to hide in the background and just watch the launch party. That is, if we even get in."

"It's not like we're trying to go clubbing," Jenna said. "We don't need fake IDs. We have the invitation right here. It's real and it's ours!"

She kissed the invitation.

I didn't feel so confident, though, as I climbed into the backseat of Sebastian's Prius. I couldn't help but feel I didn't belong.

Jenna climbed in next to me. Sebastian turned up the music. I stared out the window and watched as streets I'd only read about passed by. Hollywood Boulevard, Sunset Boulevard, Santa Monica Boulevard. I watched the palm trees lining the streets swaying, and for the first time I truly felt like I was part of L.A.

"I can't believe I'm going to a launch party," I sighed.

"I can't either, I'm having flashbacks," Sebastian said from the front seat. "I got dragged along to some of those with the little actress."

"Hey, I didn't know what I was doing, I was ten years old. I do remember one of them that had the best cupcakes—"

"But mainly they're pretentious and boring, and if this one doesn't have good phones for me to check out, then we are so out of there," Sebastian announced.

"Oh, chill," Jenna said. "It's not like you have anything better to do. This is going to be fun. I'm stoked."

"I can't believe I might see stars in real life," I said. "This is huge for me."

"Yeah," Jenna said. "I mean, I've lived here all my life so I want to say I'm kind of used to it. But really, it's so cool and yet so freakish when they're right there in front of you. And you're staring at them and they have to pretend not to notice you."

"Or maybe they really don't notice you, Jenna," Sebastian said.

"Shut up," Jenna said.

"Okay, you guys, no sibling bickering right now. I am seriously freaking out," I said. "I think I'm going to hyperventilate and pass out at the door and get carted off to Cedars-Sinai. But if I do, you guys go into the party without me."

"You'll be fine," Jenna said. "And if you're nervous, just take a couple deep breaths. Pretend you're chill, they're not going to mess with you. Avery turns into Avril. You're confident and nobody can mess with you."

Jenna sat up straighter and looked me up and down coolly. She even sneered a little bit.

"That's a good impression," I said. She barely looked like herself. I suddenly saw the actress side of her.

"You try," she said.

I sat up straight, looked at her, and started laughing.

"No, no, you're a Hollywood VIP," Jenna said in a snobby voice. "No laughing. Don't look the door guy in the eye. Look slightly over his head. Shoulders straight, and walk on in."

"I have an idea," I said. "You go first."

"I'm sure Mom will be glad all those childhood acting classes paid off," Sebastian said. "Get ready to use them. We're almost here."

"I can't believe it," I said.

"Believe it, sister. Because you're officially now in Beverly Hills," Jenna said. "Look!"

I looked out the window and stared. Palm trees, roses, and philodendron, and gates along the road blocking the sprawling houses from view. I wondered who actually lived behind those trees and gates among celebrities like it was an everyday thing.

"We're a couple minutes early," Jenna said. "So you know what we have to see, Sebastian?"

"The Apple Store?" Sebastian offered.

"Nice try. Go to Rodeo Drive." Jenna ignored Sebastian's sigh. I watched as we passed by hotels I'd only read about in the tabloids. Restaurants where stars at that very moment might be eating.

I beamed when I saw the street sign: Rodeo Drive. *The* Rodeo Drive, entrance to one of the most famous, expensive streets in the world. Chanel, Dolce&Gabbana, the Juicy flagship store, Tiffany's, Gucci! Palm trees lined the sides of the cobblestone road full of shops I could never afford.

"You guys don't know how long I've been dreaming of this," I told them. "Ever since I got my first *Teen Vogue* magazine, I've been imagining the day when I could drive to Rodeo. Of course, in my fantasy I was in a stretch limo and could afford anything I wanted. And back then, my dream boyfriend was that Ricky guy from *Phil of the Future*. I've been imagining this day forever."

I watched out the window and realized what was missing.

"Where are the people?" I asked her. "The streets are practically empty."

"In their cars," Jenna said. "They drive. Shop. Put their stuff in the car. Drive away. But we'll come back and walk around," Jenna said. "When Sebastian isn't here to whine about it."

"Thank you," Sebastian said. "I appreciate not being a part of any girly shopping expeditions."

We passed Melrose Avenue, home of the hipster secondhand stores I was dying to get to because I might actually be able to buy something there! And then we passed Robertson, where I paid a silent homage to Kitson, the store I'd read about on the gossip blogs.

"Turn left in one-fifth of a mile!" Sebastian's GPS system announced loudly. "You have arrived at your destination."

I tried to put on my Avril face and stay cool as we pulled up behind a silver Lexus. There was a row of cars—a Maserati, a Jag, a Porsche. People were stepping out of them and being ushered to the front door of the store. Our car inched closer and closer to the valet. And that's when it hit me what we were about to do.

"Jenna," I said. "I feel kind of sick."

I could see the headline now:

SIDEKICK CRASHERS SIDEKICKED TO THE CURB

Who were the newcomers who tried to crash the T-Mobile launch party? Did they think they were up-and-comers? Because when they got rejected, they were up-and goers . . . buh-bye, nice try!

"Oh, no!" Jenna said, looking at me. "You can't chicken out. Take a deep breath and listen."

Jenna pulled her iPod out of her bag and turned it on. And suddenly, Marisa's voice filled the car.

The girl who will make you feel
Nothing you thought was real

Will show you the inside out
I really have no doubt
I'm the girl who you can't do without

Jenna and I both sang along, letting the words fill us with confidence.

I'm the girl who
The girl who
I'm the girl who
You'll wish you knew . . .

"We're going to represent Team Marisa!" Jenna said in her best cheerleader voice. "We need to go in and make Team Marisa proud, right?"

"Right," I said weakly. "I guess."

The valet opened my door and held out a hand to help me out. And I hesitated.

"Avery," Jenna whispered. "All those times back in Ohio, you probably imagined people going to these VIP parties. And now it's your turn! You deserve this, and I'm not just saying that because I want to go to the party. You're working hard for Team Marisa."

"This is all very touching and inspiring," Sebastian interrupted. "But if you guys don't get yourselves out of this car, the Hummer behind us is going to run us over."

I turned around to see some annoyed people scowling at us from a ginormous yellow Hummer.

"Right!" I said. I felt kind of stupid to be nervous, but then I also realized something else. I really, really wanted to get past the door people and go to this party. I got out of the car and took a deep breath. We walked up the sidewalk and stood in a small line of people at the door of the store. Gold velvet ropes blocked the way in.

"Okay, here's the plan," Jenna whispered. "I've got the invitation. I'll hold it out to the bouncer and look slightly past him nonchalantly. You walk on in like it's no big deal."

I tried to smile confidently.

"How's this?" I asked.

"Cheesy," Sebastian said. "Just give me the invitation and I'll handle it."

He grabbed the invitation out of Jenna's hand before she could protest. He walked up to the door guy and handed him the invitation.

"Three of us," Sebastian said casually.

Jenna and I walked up and stood behind him. Jenna did her Avril. I bit my lip and did my nervous Avery. The door guy looked at us. I tried not to think about how crazy it was that I was even trying to get into a VIP party. I wasn't anyone famous. I wasn't anyone at all and—

The guy tilted his head to the door and held out his hand to the guy behind me.

"We're in!" Jenna whispered, and gave me a little shove forward. Sebastian was already walking past the rope. And we were in! I looked down at my feet and gasped. We were on a real, live red carpet! About to be with Real. Live. Celebrities.

I seriously needed to calm down a bit. I took a deep breath and controlled myself as we turned a corner toward the entrance of the store. There was a tent covering a walkway with another real red carpet.

And that's when I heard it. The paparazzi calling people's names.

The sound that I'd read about on the blogs, in the magazines. Then under a tented walkway, I saw flashes go off from their cameras. There was *People* magazine, *Us, In Touch*, the TV shows, the websites, the newspapers. And where the paparazzi were . . . there were celebrities. This was it. I was about to see my first celebrity. I felt the chills on my bare arms. I got closer and could hear the noise. Who was going to be my first celebrity sighting?

"Hayden! Hayden! Over here!"

"Is that a real Hayden?" I grabbed Jenna's arm. "Which one?"

I looked and saw Hayden Panettiere, smiling and posing for the photographers. She was wearing a white flowy dress and her hair was wavy and long. Her tan skin glowed.

"Hayden! Turn left! Over here! Over here, Hayden!"

Hayden looked over her shoulder. Jenna and I gaped at her.

"Hayden Panettiere is here," I said. "Now *that* is the perfect first celebrity sighting."

"Please pause for a moment to commemorate Avery's first celebrity sighting," Jenna said.

We paused and bowed our heads solemnly.

20

"Excuse me, but you're blocking the line," said a girl said behind us, who obviously had seen celebrities before and was not interested in celebrating with us.

"Oh, sorry, sorry," I said, and tore myself away from my Hayden worshipping.

We walked into the front lobby area, past the walls with the names of the sponsors on them, and into the party.

"We did it," Jenna squealed, and hugged me. I felt a huge, goofy grin spread across my face.

"Look, over there," Sebastian said, pointing.

"Who is it?" I didn't recognize anyone.

"The new phone!" Sebastian said. "Let's go check it out."

"Gee, Sebastian?" Jenna said. "You go check out the phones. Avery and I have more important things to check out. Like the crowd."

I looked around. I was surrounded by rich, beautiful, famous and not-so-famous but still cool people in their designer clothes. They were talking to one another, laughing, having a good time. I tried to act casual. I knew when you saw a celebrity at a VIP launch party, you should act cool, like they were just regular people. Even though they weren't.

"Now remember," I said to Jenna. "We're supposed to be staying below the radar. We're barely supposed to be here. Team Marisa undercover, right?"

"Right," said Jenna.

We'd just go get some sodas and stand quietly off to the side and watch the show. Then we'd sneak out before anyone knew we were there. It wasn't like anyone was noticing us. They were busy noticing people like—

Pete Wentz.

I was an early fan of Fall Out Boy. I was one of the first people to download their songs and put them on MySpace, back in Ohio. I was standing near greatness. And, I have to add, hotness.

"Jenna," I whispered, trying not to hyperventilate. "It's . . . it's . . ."

"What?" Jenna said, and then figured out what I was trying to say.

"No way," Jenna said, looking. "Come on, let's get closer."

We wove through the crowd toward Pete Wentz until we'd maneuvered right behind him. If I moved six inches to the left, I'd actually be touching him. Not that I was really going to touch him. That would be stalkerish and would probably get me tossed out by security. I tried to play it cool, like I was so used to being around famous people that I was just standing there because I felt like standing there. And not because Pete just happened to coincidentally be standing there.

And not because I was secretly daydreaming that he would suddenly see me and our eyes would meet. He'd look at me and say, "There's something compelling about you. I must write a song about you. Meet me in the studio. Fall Out Boy's next song will be named after my new muse, Avery."

"Stand closer," Jenna whispered in my ear. "I'll get a picture of him with you in the background."

I was about to tell her not to push it, but she pulled her cell phone out of her bag and aimed it without anyone seeing it. Fine, we were totally stalkers. But stalkers who got a picture of Pete Wentz.

When it was over Jenna and I fled to the side of the room, where I basically collapsed against the wall.

"I can't believe I didn't faint," I said.

Jenna held up her cell phone. There, in living color, was a picture of Pete Wentz, up close and personal. And next to him was my arm, also up close and personal.

"Sorry, I couldn't get you in the shot," Jenna said.

"Who cares," I told her. "You got Pete, and my arm is proof that I was standing there. That's what's most important. But I think we should lie low on the pictures. I don't want us to get kicked out or anything for being William Shaw wannabes."

"But tell me that risk wasn't worth it. I told you we had to come here tonight," Jenna teased. "Repeat after me, Jenna was right and I was wrong."

"Agreed," I said. "I'm beyond grateful to you. Seriously, this is the best night of my life."

"Mine, too," Sebastian said dryly, joining us.

"Really?" Jenna asked him.

"No," Sebastian said. "Not really. I've eaten unidentifiable finger food. I've been ignored by famous people. So now that Avery is fulfilled, can we take off?"

"What? No, we just started," Jenna said. "Don't spoil our good time."

"While you're here, why don't you get some ideas for Marisa

World?" I asked Sebastian. "Maybe we can do a launch party that looks like this. You have to admit, it's a cool party."

"Well, I do have to admit that the phones are sweet," Sebastian said. "When my plan runs out I might actually get one. You know what, I'll go ask the T-Mobile person if this has compatibility with—"

His techno-speak trailed off as he wandered over to the phone display table and started talking to the person standing behind it. Who looked slightly familiar. She had long, platinum-blond hair and was wearing a red and black long shirt over skinny jeans and black heels. Wait a minute.

"Hey, Jenna," I said. "Who's Sebastian talking to?"

"The phone seller person," Jenna said. Then she did a double take.

"He thinks she's the phone seller person," I said. "But isn't that Candee-Amber Lee?"

"Candee-Amber Lee?" Jenna said. "From *Valley Passions*, the cheesetastic soap opera? It is! It's Candee-Amber Lee! Ha! My brother is such a dork."

"She's such a ditz on that show," I said. "But look how serious Sebastian is, trying to talk about the phone with her."

"That's so funny," Jenna said. "Candee-Amber is probably thinking, 'What is this geek talking about? Just give me my shiny phone!'"

Jenna and I were still laughing when Sebastian rejoined us.

"She didn't know the compatibility so she had to check it out," Sebastian said. "Why are you laughing?"

"No reason," Jenna said innocently. "Oh, look. Here comes the girl who . . . works with the phones."

Candee-Amber walked up to Sebastian, holding one of the phones.

"I figured it out," she said to Sebastian. "You have to hit this button and then click here."

"Okay, cool," Sebastian said.

Jenna and I looked at each other.

"Um, aren't you Candee-Amber Lee?" I blurted out.

"Yup," she said, with a small smile.

"I'm really sorry, but my brother thinks you work here and knows about these phones," Jenna said.

"Well," she said. "I don't work here, but I do know a little about phones."

"You don't work here?" Sebastian said.

"She's an actress, you idiot," Jenna said. "She stars in *Valley Passions* every Monday night at ten?"

Sebastian's face dropped in horror.

"Candy-Amber plays identical twins CarrieAnn and MaryAnn Peterson," Jenna said. "So airheaded that sometimes they don't even know who's who. She's been on it since she was like six."

"That's just my character," Candee-Amber said. "Don't hold it against me, it's just my day job. And please just call me Lee. My real name is LeeAnn, not Candee-Amber Lee. I so wish I hadn't gotten to choose my own stage name when I was six. Candee-Amber is painful."

"Yeah, at that age I probably would have been Ariel Tinkerbell," I said. Candy-Amber smiled.

"Please continue thinking I'm a technology person," she said to Sebastian. "I'm stuck here and I really am tired of talking about who made my dress or whether my character really is dating quadruplets. My publicist is here and she made me promise to stay for an hour."

Sebastian looked uncomfortable.

"They gave me a free phone," Lee said, holding it out. "You can help me program it. I have a kick-ass new *Star Wars* pic that George Lucas's assistant sent me. I want to use it as the screen saver."

That got Sebastian's attention. They both leaned over the phone intently.

"Quick, let's go walk around while Sebastian's occupied," Jenna said.

"That was so wild," I said to Jenna as we made our escape.

"I know," she said. "Sebastian's talked to you and Candee-Amber. I mean Lee. That's more girls than he's talked to before in his whole life."

"No, I mean that she's so not ditzy in real life," I said. "Technology? *Star Wars*?"

"That's acting," Jenna said. "Most people aren't like their characters. Look, there's that very serious Oscar winner shaking his booty on the dance floor. Or attempting to."

Yeah, that looked a little painful. Good acting doesn't translate to good dancing, I guess.

"The DJ is so hot," Jenna said. "Look at those arm muscles as he spins his mix."

"Too bad he couldn't play 'The Girl Who,' " I said.

"Ooh, maybe he could," Jenna said. "I'm going to go request it. That's what we're here for, right, to support Marisa. And bonus, I'll get to be up close and personal with Mark Ronson 2.0. Be right back."

Before I could say anything, Jenna took off. I watched her go up to the DJ booth and wait in line behind a couple people waiting to make requests.

That left me by myself. Now what? Some people left one of the tall bar-style tables and nobody seemed to be taking it. I went over and sat on one of the stools. I sipped my water and tried to look comfortable sitting there by myself. I tried to memorize every detail of the celebrities to tell my friends back in Ohio. I so wished I could take pictures.

And that's when I saw her. One of my favorite singers: Haley Lane. Her black hair was longer than it had been when I saw her on TV at the video music awards and she had fringy bangs. But I could tell it was her. She was wearing a red sleeveless dress and a bunch of giant silver chains around her neck. She was texting someone, and smiling.

"Do you mind if I put my things on your table?" a lady who looked like she was in her twenties came over and asked me. She was perfectly golden, with black straight hair chopped in blunt bangs that almost covered her eyes. She was wearing a black suit and stacked deep red heels. "So are you a fan?"

"Um, excuse me?" I asked her.

"Are you a fan of Haley Lane?" she asked. "I saw you watching her. We were in the recording studio all day and I've got to tell you, her new song for her next TV movie is going to blow you away."

"You work with Haley?" I asked her.

She nodded. "Oh, I assist her with parties and things."

She was one of Haley Lane's personal assistants?

"That's so cool," I said. "You must see celebrities all the time. But I don't. I still can't believe I'm in the same room as these people."

"Let me guess, is this your first launch party?" She smiled at me.

"I guess it's pretty obvious," I said. "Sorry. It's actually my first party of any kind in L.A. I moved here from Ohio and I've never met a celebrity or even seen one before today and now, oh my gosh, I'm standing in a room full of them. It's just weird. Sorry. I'm babbling."

"You can stop saying you're sorry," she said. "It's actually refreshing to talk to someone fresh off the boat."

"Thanks," I said. "I think."

"So how did you score an invite here?" she asked. "This is a pretty big get."

I set my water glass down on the table so hard it sloshed over. She wasn't going to report me or anything, was she?

"I kinda write for this Internet thing," I stammered.

"Oh, you're a celebrity blogger!" she said. "Do you know Perez?"

Do I know who Perez is? Sure, he's got one of the most read celebrity blogs in the world. I nodded.

"You know him?" she said. "You'll have to tell him I say hi! I haven't seen him in weeks!"

"I didn't mean—" I started to tell her I didn't mean I *knew* him knew him, but she looked at her BlackBerry and interrupted me.

"Hang on, do you mind if I leave my stuff here for a second?" she asked, pointing to the drink and a couple gift bag–style bags she'd put on the table. "I need to call someone and I can't get a signal here."

"Um, sure," I said. "No problem."

I wondered what was in the gift bags. Probably swag, the free stuff given out to celebrities and VIPs at these things. I was tempted to peek but I controlled myself. I looked at the line in front of the DJ booth for Jenna. She was finally talking to the DJ.

The woman came back and smiled at me. "Thanks. Hey, I'll do you a favor. If you have a camera phone I'll sneak a picture of you. I was new to this scene a couple years ago and I wish I'd taken pictures of my big moments."

"Hey, thanks," I said. I handed her my camera.

"There are too many flashing lights here," the woman said, pointing to the strobe lights. "How about standing over there, by the hallway?"

I went over and stood in a darker part of the room. I smiled kind of awkwardly as she snapped a few pictures.

"Oh!" She gasped as she noticed something behind me.

I turned around and looked. Two people were in a corner, holding hands. And kissing.

It was Haley Lane! And then the kiss ended and the guy looked up at me and I saw who she was kissing: Kevin Webber. Kevin Webber, the R & B singer. He leaned in toward her and they kissed again. Haley Lane was kissing Kevin Webber! I'd had no idea there was anything going on with them. I realized I was staring, so I quickly turned around and started walking away to give them some privacy.

"Wait! Wait!" Haley's assistant was running after me, holding out my cell.

"Oh, yeah, my phone," I said. "Thanks."

"I guess you probably saw that," she sighed. "Haley and Kevin. Well, it was bound to get out sooner or later. I guess sooner, with that kind of PDA."

"So, they're like dating or something?" I asked her.

"Yes," she said. "It's been a whirlwind romance and they're so in love. They were planning to go public any moment now. Guess you're the first to know."

Wow!

"I'm being paged," she said, looking at her BlackBerry and turning back to me. "I need to go."

"I need to go, too," I stammered.

I needed to go, all right. I needed to go tell Jenna what I just saw! Haley Lane and Kevin Webber! Jenna was going to die! I started walking through the crowds until I found Jenna, who was holding a plate full of snacks.

"I was bringing us treats!" she said brightly.

"Come here." I pulled her arm until we were off to the side by the dessert table. It was the emptiest spot in the place.

"Ooh, cupcakes from Sprinkles," Jenna said, reaching for one. "You have to try the red velvet ones."

"You're killing me here, I have a major scoop!" I insisted. "I have to tell you something. Haley Lane is hooking up with Kevin Webber!"

"What? Who told you that?" she said.

"Nobody told me," I said. "I saw them making out in the corner."

"Are you sure it was them?" Jenna said.

"Yes, very sure because I was with Haley's assistant," I said. "She confirmed it. She said they were going to go public soon. The assistant was taking my picture with my cell phone when we saw them."

I held out my cell to Jenna.

"Wow," Jenna said, clicking it on. "That's insane. And you're the first to know?"

Okay, that just sunk in. I was apparently one of the first people in the universe to know that Haley Lane and Kevin Webber were together. Before the tabloids. Before the paparazzi. Before the blogs. I was the first to know celebrity gossip!

"Are you going to post this on the Internet or what?" Jenna said.

"Who's going to believe me?" I said. "It'll just be a random rumor from a nobody."

"Holy moley. It won't be if it's accompanied by a picture," Jenna said. "Like *this*."

She held out my cell phone. I looked and saw a really dumb picture of myself posing like a goofball.

"Ouch I have to delete that picture," I said. "I'm hideous."

"No!" Jenna practically screamed. "Look at the background!"

I magnified the picture and I saw what she was talking about. Haley and Kevin were leaning toward each other. They were holding hands and definitely looked like they were about to kiss.

And I had it on camera.

"There's your exclusive," Jenna whispered. "What are you going to do with it?"

I thought about all the times I'd gone online to read exclusives on the blogs. I had a gossip exclusive. And it was even approved to go by the celebrity's assistant. Could this night have gone any better?

"We should find Sebastian and leave now," Jenna said. "You've got a scoop in that camera that needs to get out."

I nodded and started to follow her through the crowd, then suddenly stopped. The DJ was playing a new song.

> *They say I'm this*
> *They say I'm that . . .*

"He's playing Marisa!" Jenna and I looked at each other and grinned. And we stood there, smiling and watching famous and nonfamous people out on the dance floor of a launch party, dancing to Marisa's song.

21

I think we've done Team Marisa proud," Jenna said after the song ended. "Let's go get Sebastian so you can get your exclusive scoop out there."

We finally found Sebastian by one of the phone tables. He was looking at a red phone and clicking on the buttons.

"Are you ready to go?" Jenna asked him.

"Sure," he said. "In a minute. I'm checking the ergonomic feel of this phone."

"Sebastian," I said. "I have something we need to do right away. You can play with the phone another time, right?"

"I don't think he wants to play with the phone." Jenna nudged me to show that Lee was walking back up to him. "I think he wants to play with Lee."

"Hey, Lee," Sebastian said, conveniently ignoring his sister's comments. "We're taking off."

"It was nice to meet you guys," Lee said. "Don't forget your bags."

"I've got mine." I held up my purse.

"I meant the swag bag." Lee smiled. "Don't forget to grab yours."

She pointed to a table covered in gold and red gift bags. Jenna and I looked at each other.

"Really?" I asked. "We're not stars or VIPs or anything."

"The celebrities got ones with the phones during the photo ops in the red carpet area. So you guys are *supposed* to take those—that's what they're there for."

"Ready, set, go!" Jenna said. We went over to the swag table and each grabbed a bag. Then Jenna took an extra for Sebastian.

"Are you guys ready?" Sebastian said. "See ya, Lee."

Lee waved, turned, and walked away.

"Well, that was a quick and lame good-bye," I said to Sebastian as we headed toward the doorway. "Considering you hung out with her all evening."

"Puh-lease," Jenna scoffed. "This is my brother. Before you came along, Vida Segunda was the only girl he ever talked to. What, did you think he'd get her phone number?"

"I didn't get her phone number," Sebastian said.

"See?" Jenna said.

"I got her phone."

Sebastian held up a black Sidekick and then shoved it in his pocket.

"Did you steal that?" Jenna asked him.

"No, of course not," he said. "She gave it to me from her, what do you call those things, swag bag. She got the celebrity one, I guess. I tried to refuse, but she said she feels guilty about the number of phones she's been given and that I'd appreciate it more."

"Shut up! No flipping way! Give me that," Jenna said. She took the phone and looked at it. "Wait, it gets crazier. She put her phone number in there with a picture of herself making a call-me sign! Oh my gosh! You got Candy-Amber Lee's digits!"

"Really?" Sebastian said. "Huh."

"All right, this night is getting too unbelievable for me," Jenna said. "Let's go."

I scanned the crowd to get one last look. Hayden Panettiere was surrounded by people. It looked like Jordin Sparks was on the dance floor. I saw Haley Lane talking to some other girls. Across the room, seemingly not paying attention, was her *new boyfriend*, Kevin Webber!

I closed my eyes to capture this moment in my memory.

THE NEW GIRL IN TOWN

Who's the hottest new celebrity gossip blogger in town? It's Avery, with all the inside scoop from one of the hottest parties around. It was Avery who broke it to the world about Haley and Kevin's überhot new romance. And that's only the beginning!

"Wake up." Jenna grabbed my hand and dragged me to the door.

"I'm just capturing this moment in my memory," I told her.

"You've got a more important memory captured on your camera, remember?" Jenna said. "And it has to go out to the public. So come on! Sebastian went ahead to get the valet."

We found Sebastian out front, oblivious to the fact that he was standing next to someone who was once on *American Idol*. After the singer's Mercedes pulled up, Sebastian's Prius was next. Jenna slid into the backseat next to me.

"Wow," I said. "That was awesome."

"Chauffeur! Chauffeur, I have a request," Jenna said.

"I can't hear you," Sebastian said, holding up his cell. "I'm too busy talking on my *new phone*."

"That excuse would be more believable if you had friends to call," Jenna said. "I still can't believe you got that phone. Now aren't you glad you came with us? Can I say I told you so? Be a good chauffeur and play some Marisa music off my iPod so our goody-bag celebration can begin."

"The Girl Who" blasted in the car as we drove through the streets of Beverly Hills.

"That was so awesome you got the DJ to play her song," I said. "I can't wait to post that on Team Marisa. They're going to be really excited to hear that. I've got a lot of posting to do tonight."

"Good thing you've got sugar to keep you going." Jenna pulled something out of the swag bag and held it like a QVC model. "We have fabulous chocolates in the shape of the new Sidekick."

"Yum," I said. I reached into my bag and pulled out . . .

"A lovely red soy candle," I announced. I sniffed it and read the label. "The pomegranate scent will add to the atmosphere in my room as I post my news to Team Marisa."

"Next up is a travel collection with body lotions and lip gloss!" Jenna slicked some of the gloss on her lips as I reached in my bag and opened an envelope.

"A gift certificate for an online music store," I said. "I think I'll be using that for Marisa's new songs, which with our street team in action will all hit number one."

"*Magazines.*" Jenna held them up.

"A cute bottle of perfume," I said, spritzing it on myself. Mmm.

"And, last but not least," Jenna announced. "A little red velvet bag with a card that says, 'A unique gift item to celebrate the launch of the blah-blah-blah from T-Mobile.' And it's . . . a key chain! Excellent, I'll use it when I get my first car and am liberated from this Prius, which is only months away."

She held up a silver key chain with a little Sidekick in rhinestones dangling from it.

"Cute," I said. I opened my velvet bag. But it didn't have a key chain in it. It had a pair of sunglasses.

"Whoa," I said, holding up a pair of metallic aviator sunglasses. "I have sunglasses."

"Score!" Jenna said. "Those are supersweet."

"You should have these," I said, tossing them to her. "If it weren't for you, we wouldn't have gone tonight."

"Thanks, but they're definitely you," Jenna said, looking at them and handing them back. "For two reasons. First, check out what they say on the side."

"Ray-Ban?" I asked.

"No, the other side!" Jenna said. "They're like made for you, it's spooky! TM! For Team Marisa!"

"The TM is for T-Mobile, you airhead," Sebastian said from the front seat.

"Oh, yeah." Jenna laughed. "Well, it's still a coincidence."

"I like it as Team Marisa," I said. "What's the other reason they're mine?"

"You know those sunglasses you've been wearing to school?" she said. "These Wayfarers make you look way hotter."

"Thanks," I said. I put the sunglasses on my head. "Hey, Sebastian, can you make these sunglasses on my avatar for the next M World?"

"Man, a launch party, an M World party," Sebastian fake-complained. "No wonder I don't hang out with girls. They're always nagging me to do things."

"We're bringing out your secret party animal, Sebastian," Jenna said to him. "I mean, look at tonight. You talked to a real girl—a celebrity—and went to a real live party. That's more excitement than you've ever had in your life."

"We're almost to your house, Avery," Sebastian said. "Feel free to take my sister with you and keep her."

"Happy to," I said. I smiled at Jenna. Our first social event together had definitely been a success. I started packing up my coat and swag bag as the car pulled onto my street.

"I feel like Cinderella coming back from the ball," I said. "Now I have to turn from a princess into a regular nobody."

"Well, you didn't bag a prince, but you've got major celebrity gossip," Jenna said. "AIM me when you get back and tell me what you're going to do with it so I can see!"

"Okay," I said. The car slowed down in front of my house. "I'm going to go in, light my pomegranate candle, eat the chocolate, and post some gossip. Thanks, you guys. Tonight was awesome."

"Later," Sebastian said.

"When can we do another M World?" Jenna said. "That launch party gave me some cool ideas. I'm going to make a new avatar for Hayden Panettiere wearing that cute dress she had on—"

"Enough about the dresses," Sebastian interrupted. "Avery, we'll talk."

I watched their car pull away and practically skipped up the driveway like I was five years old. It was late enough that I wouldn't get in trouble, but that my parents *might* have already gone to bed. I opened the door quietly, just in case. I wanted to get to the Internet as fast as possible.

"Avery!"

Dang it.

"Hi, Dad," I said. He was in the living room, watching TV.

"Did you have fun tonight, princess?" he asked.

"Yeah," I said, holding my swag bag behind my back. "It was

great. I don't want to interrupt your show, so I'm going to head right to my room."

"I paused it," he said, holding up the remote. "Talk to your dear old dad, who was charged with waiting up for you since your mother fell asleep."

"Well," I said, and then grinned. "I had my first celebrity sighting. *And* my first celebrity conversation. I don't think they were anyone you would know. But it was cool."

"I'm glad you enjoyed yourself," he said. "Well, it's late, so you need to get your beauty sleep, princess."

"Good night, Dad," I said. I ran upstairs to my room and immediately turned on my laptop. I pulled up my picture of me with Haley and Kevin in the background. I cropped myself out and zoomed in on the couple. You could definitely tell it was them.

Haley Lane and Kevin Webber were a couple. And only a few people in the world knew, and I was one of them. But not for long.

22

So, once you have exclusive celebrity gossip, what exactly are you supposed to do with it? As I stared at the computer screen, I tried to figure out the best way to get the scoop out on the Internet. I felt like I should give Team Marisa the scoop first. I mean, it was thanks to the site that I even went to the party. Maybe I'd email the picture to one of my favorite websites anonymously. They'd post the news and everyone would know. Then I remembered my Ning site, where I was supposed to be posting all the celebrity gossip. It was time to take it out of hibernation.

As the site was loading, I heard a quiet knock on my bedroom door.

My dad stuck his head in the door. "I'm heading to bed. I'm glad you had a good time tonight."

"Thanks, Dad," I said. I spun my chair around and smiled at him. "I can't believe I saw my first celebrities tonight. I'm emailing some of the gossip to my . . . um . . . friends online."

"Now remember, don't get too starstruck," Dad warned.

"This coming from you, Mr. Jen Stefani?" I laughed.

"Well." He grinned. "You know what I mean. Don't get too caught up in the celebrity L.A. scene. It's not always pretty."

"I know, Dad," I said. "I'll stay away from the wild rehab celebrity scene, I promise. All my gossip stays clean. It's not even really gossip, it's just scoop."

"Well, as the pencils that we made for a client to give out today said, *Stay Positive!*"

"Thanks for the pencil advice," I said.

"Don't stay up too late, princess. Sweet dreams."

"Good night, Dad," I said.

I turned back to my computer.

```
Princess of Gossip
Exclusive

A match made in heaven...or shall
we say, HEVIN?

Haley Lane
+
Kevin Webber

Check out the hot picture of two of
our fave stars at a launch party to-
night—as a couple!! Just a few hours
ago, a source close to the duo con-
firmed there's something going on
there. What is it? See for yourself
in my Princess of Gossip PHOTO EX-
CLUSIVE below!!!
```

It was looking good, I thought. I had one last thing to post, however. I needed to let Team Marisa know about the scoop first, but I wanted to keep myself anonymous. I went over to Team Marisa MySpace and posted a blog, a bulletin, and the link:

> Which two music stars are making music together—a real-life love song? Check out the new website Princess of Gossip for the exclusive scoop.

CHAPTER

23

I was front row at a Chris Brown concert, sitting next to Haley and Kevin, who were holding hands. Chris reached down into the audience, looking to pull a girl up onstage to dance with him. I waved my hand in the air, hoping to catch his attention.

"I love you, Chris!" I yelled.

And then the audience started laughing. Why was the audience laughing?

I opened my eyes. Because I was in English class, not at a Chris Brown concert. I must have fallen asleep in class. And now people were looking at me and laughing.

"May I ask why you're interrupting my lesson, Miss . . ." Miss Schmitt referred to her seating cheat sheet. "Miss Johnson?"

Oh jeez. Did I say something out loud?

"Um," I stammered. "Uh."

"Miss Schmitt." Griffin raised his hand. "Perhaps you didn't hear what Avery said. She called out 'I love . . . this!' Obviously your teaching, um, inspired her."

Miss Schmitt looked at me.

"Um, yeah," I said weakly, playing along with it. "I just couldn't control myself from saying I love this . . . lesson."

"Ah." Miss Schmitt looked pleased. "I, too, remember when I felt the inspiration of grammar. Then I'm pleased that my class on participial phrases caused you such joy."

I tried to will my face not to blush as I heard people quietly laughing around me.

"As I was saying, a participial phrase is a . . ." Miss Schmitt continued the lesson that had inspired me to fall asleep and humiliate myself. I tried to pretend to pay attention, while at the same time ignoring my classmates, who were probably still laughing at me. I tried to focus, since unlike with *Lord of the Flies,* we hadn't done dangling participial phrases like this in my old school. And I was getting a little overwhelmed with my homework lately. Fortunately the bell rang, so I didn't have to keep up the guise anymore.

"Do pages eighty-five and eighty-six in your grammar workbook!" Miss Schmitt shouted over the noise of everyone shuffling about. I started to make my escape out of the class but I saw Griffin look up at me and smile. I decided to go over and thank him for getting me out of trouble with Schmitt.

I caught up with him as he was putting his books into his backpack.

"Thanks for the rescue," I said. "I'm glad you didn't have to leave class early today for the poetry, or I really would have been screwed."

"Sorry I couldn't think of anything less lame," Griffin answered. "I wasn't prepared to come up with an excuse for someone yelling 'I love you, Chris!' in the middle of the dangling participial lecture."

"I was totally asleep," I said. "And obviously that was totally embarrassing."

"Yet entertaining." Cecilia came up behind us. "Although, *I* thought you said 'I love you, Miss Schmitt!'"

"I said I love you, *Chris*!" I defended myself. "I was up late last night so I fell asleep and was dreaming I was at a Chris Brown concert. I said Chris! Not Miss Schmitt!"

Oh, this was fantastic. People now thought I yelled either that I loved a grammar lesson or that I loved Miss Schmitt.

"You can tell you were up late," Cecilia said. "You have these huge black circles under your eyes. Maybe you need to go to bed earlier instead of staying up dreaming about Miss Schmitt."

If only she knew I was up late at a launch party, thank you very much. But did I really have huge black circles under my eyes? Ugh. I pulled my new TM sunglasses out of my bag so I could put them on in the hallway—until I could check a mirror. I stuck them on my head. My outfit today wasn't exactly cool enough for them—a navy hooded sweatshirt, a white T-shirt, and jeans.

They would have much better matched Cecilia, in her chocolate brown slip dress, bomber jacket thrown over it, and bronze lace-up sandals.

But they were mine, and I was glad about that.

"Griffin falls asleep all the time in class," Cecilia said. "And he yells, 'I love you, Delilah! I love you, Delilah!' "

"I do not. Stop picking on us," Griffin said, grinning. "Right, Avery? Should I share how Cecilia doesn't dream, she just snores?"

"Riiiight," Cecilia said. "You wish you knew what I was like when I'm sleeping."

Let the flirtatious banter begin. At least the focus was off me. I started following them out the door.

"Hey." Cecilia had turned around and stopped. She was looking at me. "Where'd you get those Wayfarers?"

At the VIP invitation-only Sidekick launch party. Just thinking that was enough to give me a confident smile.

"I just got them last night," I said. "They were a gift."

Cecilia looked at me questioningly for a second, but didn't say anything. We all walked out the door, and I practically ran into Jenna waiting for me.

"Later, Avery," Griffin said.

"Bye," Cecilia said, waggling her fingers at me as she walked off down the hall with Griffin. "Don't stay up so late tonight!"

Well, well, well. I rated an actual good-bye?

"Hi," I said to Jenna. "Ready to go to computer lab?"

"Sure," Jenna said, and started walking.

"You wouldn't believe what happened to me in English," I said, catching up with her.

"Let me guess. You became BFF with Cecilia." Jenna stopped walking. She looked down and picked some imaginary lint off her long turquoise T-shirt.

"What?" I said. "No, I fell asleep and—"

"So you told Cecilia?" Jenna interrupted. "I thought we weren't going to tell anyone."

"I told her what?" I asked her. "What are you talking about?"

"You were walking out with Cecilia and Griffin? Cecilia told you not to stay up so late tonight?" Jenna said, speaking all in a rush. "And she was all friendly? That's what I'm talking about. So you told her about the launch party? Did you tell her about Haley and Kevin? Team Marisa?"

"Jenna," I said. "Why the heck would I do that?"

"Gee, I don't know," she said. "Because it could be your chance to become friends with popular people, instead of just me and my brother? You were new, didn't know anyone, and I was fine for a starter friend. But now you've seen that I'm a nobody and if you're friends with Cecilia, you can ditch me and have the glamorous and fabulous life."

She looked seriously miserable.

"First of all, I didn't say anything at all to Cecilia," I said. "Except I had to tell her I was up late because I fell asleep in class and totally humiliated myself by calling out that I love Chris Brown in the middle of class. And she thought I was calling out that I loved my teacher, so I needed to clarify that."

"Are you kidding me?" Jenna said, and I could see her trying not to smile.

"And second, hello? You and I—and even your brother—did the most glamorous and fabulous thing that I've ever done in my life together last night? Without Cecilia and her faux Cecilias," I said. "And I wouldn't have been there if you hadn't talked me into it."

She did start to smile this time.

"So, what were you saying about me ditching you?" I said.

"Nothing!" Jenna grinned, looking a lot happier now. "Nothing at all."

"That's what I thought. We have no time for insecurity, we have more important things to do." I lowered my voice so nobody around could hear. "I want to show you the Princess of Gossip site."

I hadn't had the chance to even check the site yet today, because I'd slept until the last minute. I wanted to see if anyone checked it out, because although I had a breaking exclusive, it didn't mean anyone would notice. Jenna and I walked into the computer lab and back to the office where Sebastian was working.

"Hey, Sebastian," Jenna said as we walked into the office. "We need the computer office for Team Marisa stuff, so can we use it?"

We hadn't told Sebastian about the website. Somehow, I didn't think a Princess of Gossip blog was going to be his thing, like M World was.

"Yes, because I'm in a particularly good mood," he said.

"Is it because you had bonding time with a cute nighttime soap actress whose name rhymes with Wii?" Jenna said. "And you got the new phone?"

"No," Sebastian said. "It's because the Caltech guy emailed me that he wanted to invite one of his professors to see M World. That could be very influential to my scholarship chances. So, Avery, I wanted to see if we can do another M World."

"Definitely," I told him. "I was thinking that we could make an M World launch party like we went to. So Team Marisa fans could see what it was like."

"That's cool," Jenna said. "What are you going to launch? Virtual-world cell phones?"

No, not cell phones. It would have to be something Marisa-ish. I'd have to think about it. I shrugged.

"Text me," Sebastian said. Then he held up his hand and separated his fingers in the Spock Vulcan hand salute. "Live long and prosper."

"Okay, just when I start thinking you have a chance at coolness," Jenna sighed. "You remind me that you're hopeless."

Sebastian grinned and left.

Jenna slid into one of the chairs at the computer. I sat down on the other one and started signing in.

"Okay, just so you know, it isn't much yet," I said to her. "I mean, who knows if anybody has seen it or if anybody cares."

"Okay," Jenna said.

"It's not that great yet," I said. "I've got to add a lot to it."

"Now who's insecure?" Jenna said. "Just pull it up and let me see."

Princess of Gossip, the website, came up. A giant picture of Haley and Kevin loaded onto the screen. They really were an adorable couple.

"Sweet background," Jenna said. "I like the pink. You've got a lot of people in your group."

"Holy moley!" I said. "I've got four hundred and forty-two friend requests already!"

"Just since last night?" Jenna asked.

"I can't believe it," I said. "For someone who has so few friends in real life, I get popular pretty fast online."

I scanned the friend requests.

"They're mostly Team Marisa people," I said. "But there are some new people I don't recognize. This is great!"

"You do have some excellent scoop," Jenna said. "If you think about it, this is kind of insane. Can you believe you are breaking the story of Haley and Kevin? Did you make up the name Hevin?"

"Yup," I said, somewhat proudly. "A match made in Hevin."

"Catchy."

I had a ton of comments.

Is this 4 real? I hope it's true! It would be HEVIN! SandeeSunshine

omg you don't understand how much i luv these 2! SweetCaro

This is the cutest couple EVER!!!!!!! Danceyfan

Awesome! Give us some more gossip! KimberleyBB

"So what else are you going to put up there?" Jenna asked. "Are you posting anything else from last night?"

"What, isn't it enough I just broke a major exclusive? That's my gossip. I'm done. People can comment and speculate and I know that it's because of me!"

"Are you crazy?" Jenna said. "You've got a captive audience here. You can make this thing huge. I thought you were the gossip website guru."

"I *read* them," I said. "If you haven't noticed, other than last night I'm not exactly in the middle of things out here. The only gossip I know is from other websites and I'm not going to steal theirs."

"You have Marisa exclusives," Jenna reminded me.

"True," I said. "But that's all."

"No, it's not!" Jenna smiled. "Because remember when you told me not to take pictures last night in case it was against the rules?"

"Yeah," I said. "And because I didn't want us to call attention to ourselves."

"Well, it wasn't against the rules! And I, um, ignored you," Jenna said. She pulled her cell phone out of her pocket and handed it to me. "Check it out."

I pulled up the first picture. It was of Hayden Panettiere as she was posing for a picture with the phone. There were a couple of Pete Wentz looking really, really cute. There was one of Haley Lane on the dance floor (without Kevin). A crowd shot with—

"Hey," I said. I enlarged the picture. "There are two *America's Next Top Model* people in the crowd."

Jenna peered closely.

"You're right!" she said. "I didn't even know they were there!"

The next picture was of Jenna smiling with the DJ.

"I had someone take that for me," Jenna said. "He was so hot, I couldn't resist. You can crop me out and use his picture, though. He did play 'The Girl Who,' so he needs some love. Now, aren't you glad I ignored you and took the pictures? You can use them, and then you'll have a real gossip blog."

I flipped through the pictures again. They definitely gave an insider look. For the last eight years I'd been an outsider reading all of the celebrity gossip and wishing I could be on the inside of it all. This was my big chance. I knew how to do this.

"You're smiling!" Jenna clapped her hands. "So that means you're going to do it?"

"Thanks to you," I said. "You are witnessing the official launch of the Princess of Gossip blog."

Just then the office door swung open. William Shaw stuck his head in and raised his camera to his eye.

"Oh," he said, obviously disappointed. "It's just you two. I thought something scoopworthy was happening here."

His head disappeared. Jenna and I looked at each other and laughed.

Princess of Gossip

I've got the scoop

All you have to do is ADD ME AS A FRIEND & I pinky-swear to give you the *exclusive inside details* every step of the way!

24

"Avery!" my mom called. "Time to wake up!"

She stuck her head in my bedroom.

"Honey, it's— Oh!" my mom said. "You're already up. And dressed."

"Yeah," I said, yawning, as I finished putting on an earring. "I had extra homework to do so I got up early."

"Well, I'm glad you're taking it seriously," she said. "But you were up so late doing your homework last night. Is your new school getting too difficult? Are they assigning too much homework? Should I call to have a teacher conference?"

I hadn't actually gotten up early to do my homework. I just wanted to have a little time to check my Princess of Gossip blog and Team Marisa before school.

"No," I said. "I'm good. I'll get everything done before the bus comes."

I did have a lot of homework to do for math and chemistry. But the only chemistry I'd been focusing on last night was the sparks between Haley and Kevin.

"Dad and I are heading out to work," my mom said, blowing me a kiss. "Keep an eye on the time."

I turned on my computer and checked myself in the mirror as I waited for it to load. I was dressed for school in an outfit that would particularly match my TM sunglasses: a steel-gray jacket, a white tank, skinny dark jeans, and silvery gray flats with bows on them. I felt like it was the school version of the outfit I wore for the launch party and was definitely more chic than what I usually wore. I also put on an emerald-colored ring in honor of Marisa. Maybe my blog was anonymous, but I was feeling like I could add a little something to myself today. After all, I was the Princess of Gossip.

First, I checked my email.

```
To: Group email
From: AJohnson@DMBrecords.com
Subject: Access

Exciting news! In talks for Marisa
to be interviewed on Access Holly-
wood!
Ashley
```

That was great news for Marisa! I crossed my fingers that the interview would happen. I signed on to Princess of Gossip and—

I had 2,345 friend requests.

What?! Was I on some kind of spam list? I checked my comments to see what the heck was going on.

Cool blog! I just saw you on the *People* site and I had to check it out!

Huh?

Someone saw me on *People*'s website? What was she talking

about? I clicked over to People.com and my jaw dropped practically onto my keyboard.

There, on People.com, the world-famous website of one of my favorite magazines, was my picture of Haley and Kevin, with a short article.

KEVIN AND HALEY: HOT NEW COUPLE?

New gossip blog from music insider Princess of Gossip is reporting that costars Kevin Webber and Haley Lane were spotted together at the T-Mobile Sidekick launch party and that Haley's rep confirmed the match.

Check out pics of the match made in "Hevin" and more hot photos from the launch.

Princess of Gossip is on People.com. And they called me a music insider! I clicked on the link that took me directly to my website. I clicked again: People.com. And back to my website. I kept clicking back and forth, amazed.

Holy moley. I had gossip that was good enough to be linked to *People*.

I looked at their pictures of Haley and Kevin from the launch party. Haley posing with the new phone. Kevin holding up the new phone. Haley wearing the sunglasses from the swag bag. Hey, I had those sunglasses, too. They had pictures of Haley and Kevin individually, but I was the only person who had them together.

Heck yeah. I *am* the Princess of Gossip. I grinned as I slid my own launch party sunglasses back on my head and leaned back in my chair. I wanted to savor this moment. I'd never felt cooler in my entire life.

Well, not counting the fact that I was about to get on a school bus. I walked down my front steps and was slightly taken aback by the car sitting at the curb.

"Hurry up, we don't have all day," Miya called out her window.

"Are you guys waiting for me?" I asked, confused.

"Come on," Cecilia said.

All righty, I guess I was getting in Miya's car.

"Didn't you get my text?" Griffin asked me. "We had to come out this way so I said we'd pick you up."

"I didn't get it," I said. "But thanks."

I slid into the car, this time awkwardly climbing over Javier and aiming for the middle bump. I was sorry to disappoint Jenna, but I wasn't mentally prepared to sit on Javier's lap again.

"I can sit there," Griffin said. "You take this seat."

"I'm okay," I said. "I'm just happy I don't have to take the bus."

"We had to drive out this way to pick up one of my kids' poetry slam pieces, so I thought we'd pick you up if you needed a ride," Griffin said.

"That's cool," I said. "I'd like to read it."

"So, did you have any dreams about Miss Schmitt last night?" Cecilia said. Then she explained to everyone her version of the story as I sat there, blushing. I had to remind myself that I was the Princess of Gossip, and mere high school hierarchy wasn't going to make me feel insecure. I reached into my tote bag, slid out my new sunglasses, and put them on. There, I felt more confident now. I had to admit I still carried some of the swag around in my tote bag, in case I needed reassurance that all of this had happened. I pulled out the minivial of perfume and spritzed some on my wrist.

"I dreamed about Chris Brown," I said. "Not Miss Schmitt."

"So Chris Brown is your type?" Javier asked. "I'm tall, dark, and handsome, too."

"Everybody is Javier's type," Griffin said.

"What's your type, Griffin?" Javier asked him.

"Blond and smoking-hot like Delilah," Cecilia called out from the front seat. I glanced at Griffin and he shrugged, like yeah, what can you do.

"I like redheads, too. Mmm, you smell good," Javier said, leaning over to me.

"It's my new perfume." I shifted away from him. "I think it's called Wishes."

"You have Wishes?" Miya said. "It's not even out yet. Let me smell."

I leaned forward and held up my wrist so Miya could sniff.

"I love that!" Miya said.

"I have more if you want some." I opened my tote bag and pulled out the little bottle.

"I love it, too," Javier said in a seductive voice.

Both Griffin and Cecilia rolled their eyes. I sort of did inwardly, but it wasn't often—or ever—that I got compliments, however cheesy, from a hot guy, so it wasn't a complete eye roll.

"Hot sunglasses," Miya said. "Did I see those at Kitson? No, wait, Lisa Kline? I feel like I just saw those. I know! Haley Lane was wearing them! I saw it online in that picture of her and Kevin Webber."

"Kevin is hot," Cecilia said. "He might be my type."

"Too late, he's taken. Did you see their nickname? Hevin? How cute is that?" Miya said. "I read it on People.com."

This was getting a little too close for comfort. I started to feel like I was going to break out in a sweat, sitting in a car with Griffin, Javier, and two girls who were talking about my gossip.

I was saved by my phone going off. It was my ringtone of "The Girl Who," which meant it was Jenna. I clicked it off, but would have to text her as soon as I got to school and ask her to meet me so

I could tell her about this interesting ride. We pulled into the school parking lot.

"What's that song on your phone?" Miya asked. "It sounds good."

"It's by this singer called Marisa," I told her. "You should look her up. She's really good."

"Avery has excellent taste in music," Griffin said.

"Thanks," I said. "Marisa's going to be big. It's still in talks, but she's probably going to be on *Access Hollywood* this week. I'll send you the YouTube clips when she does."

"Does she perform live?" Griffin asked.

"Yes," I said. "She does shows." Well, so far just at the mall, but . . .

"I have to get my daddy to get us tickets!" Miya squealed. "Or wait, Avery. Do you get front row or VIP? I'll go with you!"

"I'm sure I can get tickets from Shade," Cecilia said. "You can go with me. Are your parents in the business, Avery?"

"No. I just, um, have my sources," I said.

"Well, aren't you the little early adopter for someone fresh off the boat from Ohio," Cecilia said. "You've got the perfume, the sunglasses, the new music. What other treats do you have for us?"

I could feel everyone looking at me expectantly. Part of me wanted to say screw you. I don't have to prove myself to you with my swag and my cool new knowledge.

But of course that was only a small part of me. The other part of me was thinking, *In your face! I'll show you who's in the inner circles.* I weighed my gossip stories, remembering what happened the first time I'd shared gossip with Cecilia.

I reached into my bag and pulled out the red lipstick, then held it up so they could see it in the front seat.

"Ooh, the new Chanel color!" Miya said. "There's a waiting list for that!"

"Here's a little thank-you for driving me to school," I said. I dropped the lipstick onto Miya's lap. I opened the car door and stepped out smoothly as Miya let out a happy squeal.

"Let me see that," I heard Cecilia say.

"It's mine," Miya said. "She gave it to me."

Well! That was a surprise success! Sure, it was thanks to a swag bag, but at this point I'd take whatever school cool I could get.

"Avery," Javier said. "I missed the lap dance this time. Maybe next time—"

"Ew, Javier," Miya said. "Avery is so not into you. Stick with me and Cecilia, Avery, we'll protect you from him."

She grabbed my arm, and I found myself walking into school between Miya and Cecilia. Moments later, William was there with Cam, trailing, ready to take some video.

25

WHICH FORMERLY UNKNOWN GIRL FROM
THE MIDWEST HAS ANONYMOUSLY TAKEN
TINSELTOWN BY STORM WITH HER NEW TELL-ALL
GOSSIP BLOG? HOW DID SHE GO FROM A HIGH
SCHOOL GIRL NOBODY TO A GO-TO PERSON FOR
BEHIND-THE-SCENES GOSSIP ABOUT YOUR
FAVORITE CELEBRITIES? SHH! THAT'S ONE GOSSIP
SECRET WE'RE NOT SHARING!

So I've learned that once your blog gets a major mention on a site like, say, People.com, you get a little attention online. I'd put a few more stories on my Princess of Gossip site. And I'd posted the People.com mention right up top:

New gossip blog from music insider Princess of Gossip reports . . .

"Whoa," Jenna said, looking over my shoulder. "This thing is blowing up."

We were staring at the monitor in the computer lab office after school, looking at our results of Googling "Princess of Gossip."

Not only was Princess of Gossip mentioned on People.com, it was all over the place. For example, *another* major celebrity news site said:

"It's true," a rep for Haley Lane said. "Haley and Kevin had been having feelings for each other. But it wasn't until the T-Mobile launch party that they admitted their feelings. And you got a glimpse of their true feelings in the picture."

"The picture" refers to the candid behind-the-scenes photo of the couple kissing. (See Princess of Gossip link.)

"Even Haley's rep says it's all you!" Jenna said. "How cool is that?"

"Well, Haley's assistant knew it was me that took the picture," I said. Then I gasped. "Do you think she knows I'm Princess of Gossip?"

"Nah, she probably thinks you sold the picture," Jenna said. "And you're now living the life of luxury from the profits."

"Yeah, that's it, life of luxury," I said.

"Does anyone realize this is *my* office?" Sebastian stood in the doorway with his arms crossed.

"Oh, Sebastian." Jenna shook her head in mock pity. "Don't you know this is headquarters for Princess of Gossip now?"

"And M World," Sebastian said. "Avery, we have to get a plan. I've got more Caltech people coming to our next one. My friend Vida Verdad is going, too."

"You made up a new virtual girlfriend?" Jenna laughed. "Vida Verdad? Did Mom fall for that one, too?"

"Just let me know," I said. But I was already distracted by another Princess of Gossip sighting:

Who's the new behind-the-scenes "Gossip Girl" in town? Princess of Gossip? She brings us the buzz that only a music industry insider can bring.

"They think I'm a music industry insider," I said.

"Well, you put that People.com review on your blog," Jenna said. "It called you a music industry insider."

"Yeah, maybe I shouldn't have posted that," I said. "Obviously I'm not really an insider of anything except my bedroom."

"You're nobody until rumors fly around you, dahling," Jenna said. "Let's plant another one about you. Let's say you're a sexy music insider who dates the hottest celebrities and you're now single so guys should send you their phone numbers. And you have a friend . . . Oh my gosh, look!" Jenna pointed at another one of my messages. "It's from Indie 103.1! Open it!"

"Just one second, Sebastian?" I pleaded. I opened the email and scanned it. "They want my address so they can courier over tickets to something."

"Ohmygosh?" Jenna said. "That's awesome!"

"No, it's not," I said. "I can't give away my address. They'll know who I am. Plus, I'm not allowed to give out my address online, blah-blah Internet Safety 101. My parents would kill me."

"But you *can* give them a P.O. box number," Jenna said. "A post office mailbox is anonymous."

"I don't have a P.O. box number," I said. "And I think if I asked my parents to get one they'd be slightly suspicious."

"No problem," Jenna said. "Sebastian has one."

We turned to look at Sebastian standing by the door.

"How do you know that?" Sebastian groaned and threw up his hands. "Can I have any privacy in my life?"

"I'm concerned he's using it to order X-rated materials," Jenna said. "Maybe I should let my parents know my concerns."

"Jeez, it's not for that," Sebastian said. "It's part of my *Star Trek* swap. We swap copies of our manga books and—"

"It's not just comics." Jenna laughed. "It must be where he gets his Spock costumes I've seen in his closet. I think he secretly dresses up and plays *Star Trek* at night."

"First off, they're not Spock, they're Captain Picards," Sebastian defended himself. "And second, I don't wear them. I'm saving them for the reenactment convention. If I get enough points, I can be Picard."

"Okay, okay, leave the poor guy alone," I said.

"Thank you," Sebastian growled. "I wonder if my sister realizes that if she shares my personal stories, I can do the same?"

"Oopsie! I'll be quiet now. But can you let Avery use the box number?" Jenna asked. "Just for this one little thing? Please? Pretty please with sugar on top?"

"On one condition," Sebastian said. "Don't mess with my stuff."

"I'll try to keep myself from trying on the Captain Picard costumes," Jenna said.

"Give me one second to reply to this email." I turned back to the computer and typed in the P.O. box number Sebastian gave me.

"Post it on the website just in case more DJs want to give us tickets," Jenna said. "I heard Jonas Brothers are touring again. Maybe I'll get backstage and meet Kevin, Joe, and Nick."

She pretended to faint.

"People," Sebastian muttered. "It's *my* lab. *I'm* the senior lab monitor."

"Yes, you are," Jenna said, soothingly patting him on the shoulder.

Just then, a student stuck her head in the office.

"Are you the computer lab monitor?" she asked. "Can you come help me?"

"Jeez!" Sebastian said. He threw up his hands and left the office to us.

"Okay, read me more Princess of Gossip stuff, I'm dying here," Jenna said. She looked over my shoulder. "What's that message?"

I clicked on the icon.

> *Dear Princess of Gossip,*
>
> *Thank you for the kind coverage of my client, Kevin Webber. He is a sweet young man who is new to the Hollywood dating scene. Your support of his new relationship is appreciated. We'd like to send a promotional kit with photos and a thank-you to your post office box, if you have one.*

"What the—?" I said. "I've been thanked by Kevin Webber people! They give thank-yous to gossip blogs?"

"Good thing you got Sebastian's P.O. box," Jenna said. "If the pictures are autographed, can I have one for my locker?"

"Of course," I said, scanning emails. "Listen to this one."

> *Who's the one to watch? Princess of Gossip broke the story of Haley Lane and Kevin Webber. And her picture of Pete Wentz posing is hot, hot, hot! What's next from this new gossip insider?*

"That is so cool!" Jenna said.

"And so stressful!" I told her. "What's next? What am I supposed to do now, crash another launch party? I have no insider gossip, since I'm not really a gossip insider."

"Come on, if you can do M World, you can totally make a gossip site," Jenna said. "You've got your whole gossip thing. Just do that."

"I can't make up gossip."

"All right, so let's think," Jenna said. She sat down on the low bookshelf and swung her legs. "What's on gossip sites?"

"Well, I'm definitely not doing 'whose cellulite is this' or people with their butt cracks hanging out," I said. "And I'm not voting which celebrity baby is cuter. I don't want to be responsible for scarring some poor child for life."

"Agreed," Jenna said.

"Hot stars," I said. "Polls. Couple names. Cute celebrity outfits. Kevin Webber publicity photos. Marisa . . ."

"See? Easy-peasy," Jenna said. She leaned back on the counter and pulled a lipstick out of her tote bag. "You may have gotten the sunglasses but I definitely got the better color of Chanel lipstick."

"Oh, actually, I gave my lipstick away," I said. "But it was for a good cause. I gave it to Miya as a thanks for the ride this morning. I mean, I would have given it to you but it's a terrible color for both of us."

"Well. Miya is okay considering she hangs out with Cecilia," Jenna said. "She's clueless, not evil. And she did give you a ride this morning. I think I will make a Javier avatar for our next Marisa World. Then my avatar can sit on his lap. So there!"

I noticed there was a new email from DMB Records.

```
To: Group email
From: AJohnson@DMBrecords.com
Subject: Play


Got word that "The Girl Who" was
played at a T-Mobile launch party!
We've sent a thank-you to the DJ.
```

"Hey, that's us!" I said. "That was thanks to us! Well, actually you, since you had the nerve to request it from the DJ."

"They're thanking the DJ, but they should be thanking us," Jenna said.

"We're anonymous, remember?" I said. "If they find out they sent two fifteen-year-old nobodies to the launch party, we're toast."

"You're right, you're right," Jenna sighed.

"There's another email from DMB," I said.

```
To: Group email
From: Exec@DMBrecords.com
Subject: Truthful


Clip of Marisa's next single release
attached. It's called "Truthful."


Drop date to be discussed.


Feel free to distribute clip with
press kit tomorrow.
```

"Jenna, I think we've got something big for Team Marisa," I said. I clicked on the link and Marisa sang in a slow, soulful voice.

I'm tired of the lies
I can't sympathize
Anymore

I have one thing to say
Or get out of my way
Always be truthful
With me

"That's pretty. What's that?" Jenna said.

"That's Marisa's next song," I said. "And we get to play it tomorrow at M World. We get to make M World a music launch of Marisa's second song!"

We sat there, grinning, as Marisa's voice sang over the computer. And then I opened the next email.

```
To: Group email
From: Exec@DMBrecords.com
Subject: Goal


Rumor is Kevin Webber and Timbaland
will be guest DJs tonight at Con-
stellation★, the new club. We are
working on having "The Girl Who" on
the playlist. My source tells me
Haley Lane, Perth and Cruz, and Ash-
lee Simpson will be there as well.
```

"And we have another scoop for the Princess of Gossip site," I said. I quickly posted the scoop onto the blog. As I was doing so, a message showed up marked Urgent: Princess of Gossip.

"Ew, look. Someone wants to know what size I am," I said. "Creep."

"Wait, don't delete that," Jenna said. "They probably want to make you a Princess of Gossip T-shirt. Just tell them a size."

"Oh, I guess that would be cool," I said, typing it in, and then getting up from the chair.

"We'd better go meet Sebastian in the parking lot," Jenna said, looking at the clock.

Sebastian was going to drive me home, which overall made it a good bus-free day for me. Jenna and I walked out to the parking lot silently. I was deep in thought, planning how to post my new gossip.

"Let's listen to a little Marisa, shall we?" Jenna pulled her iPod and her mini speakers out of her backpack and set them up on the car. We leaned back, enjoying "The Girl Who" and the sunshine.

"Hey!" I turned around and squinted in the sunlight. I recognized Griffin's gray hoodie and leather jacket walking toward us. Javier was a few steps behind him.

"You guys need a ride home?" Griffin called to us.

"We're good!" I called back. "We're waiting for our ride."

"Maybe we should go with them. Would I get to sit on Javier's lap this time?" Jenna asked. "Look how cute he is. I swear his muscles gleam."

The guys came closer.

"You don't want to come? You can sit on my lap again," Javier said, his white teeth also gleaming as he smiled. Then he looked at Jenna. "And who is this babe?"

Ay-yai-yai. I looked at Jenna to see if she was falling for it. She smiled, but also muttered under her breath to me, "I know. Cheesy. But hot."

"I'm Jenna," she said to him.

"We're waiting for our ride, too," Griffin said. "I get my license next month and then no more waiting for rides."

"Are you getting a car?" Jenna asked. "I think I've got my mom and stepfather talked into a MINI Cooper."

"I've been saving up for one for years," Griffin said. "I should be able to get a decent used one. Hey, Avery, will you read something for me if I give it to you? It's some of the poetry jams the kids wrote. I'm trying to figure out which ones would be good to use as song lyrics."

"Sure," I said, flattered he'd want my opinion. I took the folder he was holding out and slipped it into my tote bag.

"So, what song are you guys listening to?" Griffin asked. Jenna held up her headphones so he and Javier could hear it. "Hey, isn't this the song by Marisa? I downloaded her song after you told me about it, Avery," Griffin said. "Do you know she has a Team Marisa MySpace? You should check it out."

"Great!" I said in a strangled voice, willing Jenna to be quiet. Thankfully, she didn't even look at me. "Anyway, I think your ride is here."

Cecilia, Miya, and William were walking toward us.

"Hey, all," Miya said.

"Change of plans," Cecilia said to Griffin and Javier. "You guys want to go see Shade rehearse? My sister's going to be here in a minute, so we can follow her to his place."

"Sweet," Javier said.

"Hey, Avery and Avery's friend? Do you want to come?" Miya said. "Have you ever heard of the University of Hard?"

Erm, yeah.

"Yeah, you guys should come," Griffin said.

"I would invite them but . . ." Cecilia said, stalling for a decent excuse. "We don't have enough room in the car."

"The girls can sit in my lap," Javier offered. "Or we can dump William."

"I don't think so!" William said indignantly. "Cecilia said that her sister might let me take some pictures of Shade. Maybe he'll do something scandalous I can sell to the paparazzi."

"It's okay, we've got plans," I said. So maybe our plans involved going to the post office and then I was going home to watch a show I DVR'd, but hey.

"I don't think Avery's a fan anyway," Cecilia said, looking at me. "Do you have any new gossip to share about Shade?"

I bit my tongue. Because the rumors were flying that he was hooking up with groupies all over the place. But I wasn't going to say that. Maybe William would get his scandalous pictures, but I wasn't going to make that mistake again.

"Nothing?" Cecilia said. "All out of gossip?"

"Avery is never out of gossip," Jenna blurted out. "Tell Cecilia about Constellation★."

"Well, there's this new restaurant/club called Constellation★ opening tonight," I said.

"I heard the commercial for that place!" Miya said. "Constellation★—a galaxy of stars."

"That's gossip?" Cecilia said. "Boring."

"Well, Kevin Webber and Timbaland are going to be the surprise DJs tonight," I said. "There's supposed to be a lot of stars there. Like Ashlee Simpson and I bet Kevin will bring Haley Lane with him."

"She's hot," Javier said.

"*He's* hot," Miya said. "I love Kevin Webber! We should go."

"It's the opening night," I warned them. "It's probably impossible to get in."

"Anyway, hello? We're going to University of Hard's rehearsal," Cecilia said.

"Are you guys going?" Griffin asked me.

"Pssht," Cecilia said. "She just said it's impossible for *us* to get in."

Before Griffin could say anything, a Porsche Boxster convertible sped into the parking lot. A University of Hard song was blasting out the windows. Two girls with straight blond hair and huge black sunglasses sat in the front seat. I recognized the girl in the passenger seat as Cecilia's sister.

"Let's bounce," said the driver.

"Griffin, why don't you go with Delilah," Cecilia said, giving him an exaggerated wink.

"I'm okay," Griffin said.

"Griffy, come on!" Delilah yelled.

Griffin shrugged and went to sit in the teeny backseat of the Porsche.

"Griffin so loves Delilah," Cecilia sighed. "It's so sweet, yet so hopeless. Just like Avery's little crush on Griffin."

"What?" I said.

"Oh, Avery, it's so obvious," Cecilia said, shaking her head. "Too bad you're the opposite of his type."

We all looked at Griffin, who was laughing with Delilah and her friend.

"This has potential for a story," William said. "Girl loves boy who loves other girl who loves other boy. Especially if someone turns violent. Let me get some pictures. Avery, look at Griffin with lust and jealousy."

"What?" I said. "No!"

"You can look at *me* lustfully," Javier said.

"Wait, no!" I said.

"Okay, then your friend can." Javier looked at Jenna. "I see she is undressing me with her eyes."

"Will you stop that," Cecilia said to Javier. "You're ridonkulous. We're leaving."

The Porsche's horn beeped.

Just then, Sebastian started walking through the parking lot.

"Hey! Is that Sea Bass?" Cecilia's sister called out, waving. "Wooo! Sea Bass! Slimy Sea Bass!"

"Oh, crap," Jenna said. "Sebastian is going to flip when he sees her."

Sebastian stopped for a second and looked in Delilah's direction. His face visibly reddened and he walked quickly toward us.

"Delilah knows Sebastian?" I asked her.

"This isn't good," Jenna said, picking up her iPod and her tote bag. "Get ready to make a break for it."

Sebastian stomped over to us. "What is going on?" he asked Jenna.

"Time to go!" Jenna said. "Bye, all!"

Sebastian went into the car and leaned over to open the back door. Jenna and I slid into the seat. As Sebastian started his car, I watched out the window as everyone else got into Miya's car. I saw Miya wave to us, and then Miya's car followed Delilah's out of the parking lot.

"Whew! Sorry," Jenna said. "Obviously, we didn't plan to be stuck in the parking lot with the Singers."

"Thanks for the added humiliation in my day," Sebastian said.

"You weren't the only one embarrassed, Sebastian," I said. "Cecilia announced I had a crush on somebody for no reason."

Jenna snorted.

"What?" I said.

"There's reason," Jenna said. "I hate to give Cecilia any credit, but you do have a crush on Griffin King."

"I do not!" I said. I thought about Griffin sitting in the back of the convertible, in his leather jacket and hoodie. "Well, okay. Maybe a teeny bit. But probably because he's the only guy in school who talks to me."

"I talk to you," Sebastian said, sounding insulted.

"Javier talks to you," Jenna teased me.

"Yeah, well, I'm sure Javier *talks* to many girls, if you get my drift," I said. "I definitely do not have a crush on Javier or Sebastian. No offense, Sebastian."

"None taken," he said.

"But thanks for taking us to the post office," I said. "Sorry you had to run into Delilah on the way."

I paused.

"Oh, fine," Sebastian said. "You can tell her."

"Okay, this is what happened," Jenna said. "You know how I used to do those commercials and Cecilia and I would audition for the same ones? Sebastian would have to come wait in the waiting room, like all the brothers and sisters."

"And since I had to wait at all the auditions, even though I was old enough to be home by myself"—Sebastian glared at Jenna—"the rumor was I went because I was obsessed with Delilah. All the stage mothers were like oh, it's so cute but so pathetic. Sebastian the geek loves Delilah."

"It's not my fault!" Jenna protested. "My mom was delusional and only got the it's-so-sweet part. She didn't get the joke and was always pushing them together. Delilah heard my mom call him Sea Bass. And when they toilet-papered my house, they also left sea bass on our front step. It smelled disgusting for a week."

"So. The moral of this story is the Singers are not our friends," Sebastian said.

"No kidding," I said. Harsh.

"So that's the sad tale," Sebastian said. "Finished just in time to pull into the post office."

I looked out the window and saw we were in a shopping plaza with a post office in it. Just then an old-fashioned-phone ringtone went off.

"I need to take this call," Sebastian said. "Take the key and get the stuff out of the box."

Jenna took the key and we got out of the car.

"Hey," I said to Jenna as we headed to the post office. "I'm sorry about all that happening to you."

"Oh!" she said. "I'm over it. Well, not really. But I'm ignoring it as much as possible. It's been a lot easier lately, since I feel like a little less of a nobody. I mean, we have our secret lives of M World and Princess of Gossip, right?"

"Right," I said. That was exactly how I felt.

"I wonder what they sent me," I said, using Sebastian's key to the little post office box. I pulled out an envelope and a little yellow card.

"It's for Princess of Gossip," I said.

"Poor Sebastian, nothing for him," Jenna said cheerfully. "While he's waiting in his car, hoping in vain we'll come out with a *Star Trek* costume."

"There's a package that's too large to fit in the box," I read from the yellow slip. "Maybe that's for him. We have to go to the counter."

I handed the man behind the counter the yellow ticket, and he gave me some rubber-banded envelopes in return.

"Whoa, " I said. "That's a lot."

"There's more," he said, and handed me a stack of packages.

"This is fun," I said, handing off some of the packages to Jenna. The clerk then handed me a long box.

"That's gotta be Sebastian's costume," I said.

"Let's go find out," Jenna said.

We brought the packages out to the car, where Sebastian was texting on his Sidekick.

"Here, this small one and the costume one is for you," I said, handing them to Sebastian. "The rest is for me."

"Yes! My new manga and my Captain Picard costume. But who's Princess of Gossip?" Sebastian asked, picking up a package I laid on the seat next to me and reading off the label.

"Nobody!" Jenna and I said at the same time. I'd forgotten to hide it from him.

"Whatever. Anything with the words 'princess' or 'gossip' in it doesn't interest me," Sebastian said. "Is there any food in those packages? I'm starving."

"If there is, we're not eating it," I said. "I don't know who sent these things."

"I'm dying to see what you got," Jenna said. "I don't want to wait to drive all the way home. Sebastian, I'll buy you lunch if we can go right there."

She pointed at a Mexican restaurant across the street.

"Deal," Sebastian said.

We drove across the street and parked. Sebastian helped us carry the boxes and mail into the restaurant and put them in one of the booths. We went up to the counter. Jenna ordered a chicken burrito, and I ordered a quesadilla with a side of guacamole.

We carried our trays back to the booth and Jenna slid in across from me. Sebastian sat at another table away from us and pulled out his manga to read as he ate his tacos.

I took a bite of quesadilla.

"Let's take turns opening them," I suggested. I picked up a large envelope from the top. "This one is from a publicity agency," I said. I pulled out some headshots of a girl and a page that said: "Bio for Jocie Belle."

"Do you know who Jocie Belle is?"

"Nope," Jenna said.

"Well, I'll have to listen to this tape and find out," I said, holding up a CD.

"That's cool. Maybe you'll discover the next Marisa," Jenna said. She picked up another letter and started reading.

" 'Dear Princess of Gossip, I love Kevin Webber and am a bigger fan than you. I'm his number one fan. Can you get me backstage tickets to his next concert?' " Jenna looked at me.

"Um, sorry to disappoint. But that girl just wasted a stamp," I said. "Maybe I should add to the site that I don't get tickets or any freebies or—"

"Ooh!" Jenna squealed. "You got free makeup!"

She held up a cute pink and black makeup kit. I recognized the makeup company's name. I guess I do get freebies.

"I should probably return that," I said. "They probably want me to give them a plug on Princess of Gossip. I can't go there."

"Oh, but the colors are so cute," Jenna said. She scanned the letter that came with it. "It says to take it with their compliments. And that maybe sometime you'll wear it to another event. It doesn't say you have to promote it on your site. I guess you're just supposed to wear it and look glamorous."

"Really?" I said. "Well, if we ever have another event to go to, maybe we'll use it. Maybe. I'm not sure if I should."

"Oh, come on," Jenna said. "It's like the swag bags. These companies want famous people using their products. It's good for business."

"Except I'm not famous," I said.

"Well, being the Princess of Gossip obviously is enough for them," Jenna said. "Or they wouldn't be sending you things like . . . this!"

She waved a card in front of my face. I took it from her and read out loud.

" 'Princess of Gossip. Please accept a gift certificate courtesy of Haley Lane for spa treatments. We have enclosed a gift certificate with a number on it, so your name does not need to be identified. We hope you enjoy your spa experience.' "

"Seven hundred and fifty dollars?" I said. "It's for seven hundred and fifty dollars' worth of treatments. That would be amazing. But I can't accept it."

"Why not?" Jenna asked. "It's just a thank-you. You can still be anonymous. Anonymous, with better skin and nails."

"It stresses me out," I said. "These companies think that I'm somebody I'm not. I'm not Marisa's assistant or from her record label. I'm not a real gossip columnist."

"Perception is everything in this town," Jenna said. "As I well know, you might as well grab it while it's hot. In Hollywood, nothing is guaranteed to last."

I looked up to see Sebastian standing over us. He was holding the long box and his phone.

"Mom's on the phone," he said to Jenna, handing the phone to her. "She wants to talk to you. She said your phone is off."

"Purposely," Jenna sighed. She stood up. "I'll be right back."

"Can I ask you a question?" I asked Sebastian. "About Jenna."

"What's up," he said, putting down the box and sliding into the booth.

"Jenna is really friendly and funny and nice," I said. "People are always saying hi to her and stuff. So why doesn't she, well . . ."

"Have any friends?" Sebastian finished. "Hang out with people besides her brother? And now you?"

I nodded.

"Jenna used to have lots of friends," Sebastian said. "Unlike me. She was my mother's great hope as a stage mom-ager, and living vicariously through her child. Then her agent told her she was cute when she was little but not so much anymore and dumped her. And my mom was crushed and kept asking her, 'Why don't you go on a diet?' 'How about a nose job?' "

Ouch.

"And then the Cecilia toilet-paper cruelty of seventh grade happened, Alice and Ann moved away, and she now has a hard time trusting people."

"Jeez, I see why," I said.

"Well, she seems like she trusts you, so that's cool," Sebastian said. "Maybe because you're so Midwest and not L.A."

"I think that's a compliment," I said.

"And you're not trying to be famous," he added.

We both stopped talking, because Jenna came back and handed Sebastian the phone.

"Mom wants me to come home now." Jenna came back over and slid into the booth. "Her favorite waxer is coming and Mom said if I get rid of my unibrow and mustache I might be able to audition again someday."

Jenna pulled a mirror out of her bag.

"Now I'm paranoid," she said.

"You're blond. You don't have a unibrow or mustache," I said.

"No, I see it," Jenna said. "Ugh."

"You don't have anything wrong with your face," I said. But I took the spa card off the table and gave it to her. "But here. Now you really won't have to worry about it."

"What?" Jenna said. "This is the spa gift certificate."

"Well, it says to make Princess of Gossip happy," I said. "And it would make me happy if you used it."

"Only if by 'you' you mean 'we'!" Jenna squealed, picking up her phone and dialing. "I mean, we both have to go! I'll call and make an appointment before you change your mind. What spa treatments do you want?"

I wouldn't know. I'd never had one. I mean, I'd gotten my nails done and of course my hair cut in Ohio. But I'd read how stars had spa treatments like caviar facials and hot stone massages . . .

"I'm not sure if we should use this—"

"This is how Hollywood works," Jenna said. "Everyone gives out swag, everyone takes it. Avery, you've been working hard. You look tired. You deserve some pampering."

I thought about Cecilia's comment about the black circles under my eyes from being tired. Any misgivings I had about using the gift certificate disappeared.

"Fine, whatever you think," I said.

I dug the last tortilla chip into the guacamole.

"We have a gift certificate," Jenna was saying into the phone. "Um, it's gold? Oh, you do? We can come today? Great! Hang on."

She turned to Sebastian.

"Um," Jenna said. "Can you drive us to the spa? Like, now? And then pick us up when we're done?"

"What?" Sebastian sputtered. "Do we take into consideration that I might have plans? That I am not your driver?"

"Mom gave me some money for weight-loss pills," Jenna said. "If you drive us, you can have it and kill some time in the Apple Store," she said.

"Deal," Sebastian said. "I'm going to text my friend to meet me there."

Jenna turned her back to talk into the phone.

"Your mother gives her money for weight-loss pills?" I asked him.

"Oh yeah, and fake tanning, and I dunno. All that usual girl stuff," Sebastian said.

Um, that wasn't usual girl stuff to me. My parents gave me an allowance for movies or going out to eat. It wasn't much, and I seriously needed to find a babysitting job or something soon, but at least they didn't give me an inferiority complex.

"So do you have a sugar daddy or rich boyfriend back in Ohio or what?" Sebastian said. "Who's sending you the gift cards, the clothes?"

"Not exactly. It's hard to explain," I said. "Wait, what clothes?"

"Oh, this was for you," Sebastian said, pointing to the long box we'd gotten at the post office. "It's not my Captain Picard costume."

What? I read the label. It was addressed to Ms. Princess of Gossip.

I opened the box and pulled out something silver and shimmery. It was a cocktail dress, and it was incredibly gorgeous.

"Whoa," Jenna said, looking at the dress. "That's not Captain

Picard's costume. Unless I missed the episode where he cross-dresses. Where did that come from? Read the card."

I opened a silver envelope, which had "Princess of Gossip" written on it in calligraphy.

> Dear Princess of Gossip,
> Please accept this dress with our compliments for a future event. Call the store to arrange a fitting.
>
> > Best wishes for your continued success,
> > Christian Palandro

"*The* Christian Palandro?" Jenna clapped her hands. "Do you know who wears his dresses? Reese! Cate! Natalie! Anne!"

"Christian Palandro sent me a dress?" I said. "Well, he sent Princess of Gossip a dress."

"Honey, you *are* Princess of Gossip," Jenna said. "It's yours."

"It's probably not my size," I said. "I mean, he dresses size negative-three celebrities."

I looked at the tag. It was my size. How did he know?

"Remember that email asking for your size?" Jenna said. "And we thought it was someone who wanted to make you a T-shirt? It must have been Christian Palandro!"

"Okay, this is getting out of hand. I'm going to use the spa gift certificate," I said. "But we've got to return the dress. I feel too guilty about that one. I don't deserve it."

I looked down at the stack of packages and envelopes lying next to me in the booth. No, I definitely didn't deserve this.

26

Y ou're glowing," Jenna told me later, as we met in the hallway of
the spa.

"*You're* glowing," I said back to her.

"It must have been the seaweed mask," Jenna said. "With its extreme pore-tightening qualities."

She posed in her fluffy white towel.

"Mine is from the white chocolate soothing facial," I said, touching my skin. Which had never felt so soft, I might add.

"Okay, your hair is to die for," Jenna said. "There's no way you're
just going home. We need to celebrate the new us."

"Sure, whatever," I said dreamily. I was still floaty from my shoulder massage.

"So go change into your new dress and let's do something fun,"
Jenna said.

"The dress is in Sebastian's car, with the rest of the stuff," I said
to her.

"Well, actually I kept the dress with us," Jenna confessed.

"What?" I said. "I'm returning it. In fact, I should probably return it now before I damage it. And we're right down the street from
Christian Palandro's flagship store."

"'Oh, okay," Jenna said. "Spoil my fun. But after that we're going window-shopping."

We started walking down the boulevard. I held up the dress in its bag so it wouldn't wrinkle. I kept a lookout for stars, but it was slightly difficult with the dress bag, which was almost as tall as me. Anyway, there weren't many people walking around the streets. In L.A., everyone pretty much stays in their cars.

We walked into the tiny shop. It was small but colorful, with the walls lined with formal and party-style dresses. There was a lavender couch in the center of the room, and a deep wood checkout table that matched the hardwood floors.

"This is gorgeous," I said, touching the silk of a deep red dress.

"May I help you?" a salesperson came up and said skeptically.

She looked us up and down. I caught a glimpse of myself in the mirror and realized that despite my great (for me) hair and our glowing faces, Jenna and I were wearing sweatshirts and shorts. We definitely didn't look like good customers.

I placed the bag on the counter.

"Good-bye, dress," Jenna said wistfully.

"I need to return one of your dresses," I said to the saleslady.

"Where's the receipt?" she asked.

"I don't have a receipt," I said.

"We clearly state the policy," she said. "No receipt, no returns. No exchanges, no store credit. We consider our dresses couture and made especially for each customer. You touch, it's yours."

"Oh, I'm not asking for money back or anything," I quickly explained. "I got this as a gift and feel I should return it."

"Sorry," she said. "We can't take it back. No returns."

Great.

"They're not even letting me return it," I said to Jenna, who was gazing adoringly at a white dress with a black sash. "They said each dress was especially made for one person. Maybe I should just leave it here and we can run."

"What? It means the dress is meant to be," Jenna said. "It's yours. You have to keep it!"

The saleslady came over.

"Have you tried it on yet?" the woman said. "Come to the private dressing room. We'll see if you need a fitting."

Before I could protest, she led me to the dressing room. Well, what the heck. Can't hurt to try it on. I slipped off my sweatshirt and shorts. I slid the dress over my head and—

Hello. You know when you're trying on clothes and you put something on and realize you never want to take it off because you love it so much?

"Let me see!" said Jenna. "Let me see!"

And add to that the fact that you've just had a relaxing facial and massage. And a professional salon blowout and makeup application? Yes, this was definitely the best I'd ever looked in my entire life.

I stepped out of the room to show Jenna. She gasped.

"Ohmygosh, it's gorgeous!" she said.

"It is," I said, twirling the skirt a little. "It totally is."

"It fits you very nicely," the saleslady said. "We will take it up just a drop and in just a pinch."

"Oh, that's okay," I said.

"Christian himself would insist it fit you perfectly," she said. She lowered her voice. "One reason celebrities look so good in their clothes is because they have them fitted exactly to flatter their bodies. Our tailor, Ilana, will be back from break in a few minutes to fit you."

"Okay," I said.

"I'm going to try some on, too," Jenna said. "Just for fun."

She took the white dress with the black sash off the rack and went into the dressing room.

I couldn't stop looking at myself in the mirror. I slid on one of the pairs of heels that they had out to try on looks. I twirled the skirt a little.

"That's the one," a voice behind me said. "That looks great on you."

I turned around to see a cute guy standing there, carrying some bags.

"Um, thanks," I said. And then I blurted out, *"Oh!"*

Because the guy wasn't just any guy. It was Beckett Howard! Beckett Howard, the "celebutoy." Nicknamed that by the gossip blogs, because he was the new arm candy for the younger sisters of celebutantes.

Oh, and he was really, really good-looking. He had sandy blond hair and a deep tan. He was wearing a Pink Floyd vintage-looking gray T-shirt and jeans that were a little baggy.

"You're going to buy that dress, right? It looks great on you," he said.

"Well, actually I didn't buy it. The designer sent it to me," I blurted out. "It's like a gift, like swag. I'm just waiting to get it fitted."

Okay, I was babbling. He was just that cute.

"The designer sent it to you?" he said. "That's cool. By the way, I'm Beckett Howard."

"I'm Avery. And I know who you are," I said. "You're a little famous."

"Oh," he said. "Darn. I hoped I could start fresh without the tabloid reputation. You look like someone who maybe didn't read that stuff."

Um, yeah. I definitely wasn't going to mention that I wrote that stuff, too. Including about him.

"Beckett! Give me one minute and I'll go get the dresses," the saleswoman said to him.

I wondered who he was picking up the dresses for. Maybe the young ingenue Oscar nominee he'd taken to an awards ceremony? The hip-hop singer he'd dated who put him in her latest video? The girl from Nickelodeon who showed up with him at a movie premiere?

"I'm just here picking up some things for my mom," he said. "See? My life isn't really too glamorous."

"Mine isn't either," I said. "I just moved here from Ohio, so this is all new to me."

"New in town and designers sending you dresses," he said. "You must be doing something right. Are you an aspiring actress, singer, or supermodel?"

"Yeah, that's me." I laughed. "A five-foot-two supermodel. No, I'm just aspiring to getting used to living in L.A. No acting or singing talents like the girls you go out with."

"Actually, that hasn't worked out so well for me yet," he said. "They're all nice girls, but I haven't really connected with them, you know? Maybe I need to go out with someone who isn't in the business."

I blushed.

"So where are you wearing that dress?" Beckett asked. "That deserves to go somewhere special. What are you doing tonight? I know a party that could be kind of fun."

Uh . . .

"Okay, you don't know me," he said. He turned to the saleswoman, who was walking over to us. "Cheryl, can you vouch for me? Tell Avery that despite what she reads about me in the tabloids, I'm a nice guy. I'm safe to go to a party with."

"He's safe." The saleswoman nodded. "Beckett's been coming here since he was a little boy."

"My mom drags me shopping a lot," Beckett said. "So what do you say? Want to go to a party with me? It's at a restaurant, you don't have to be twenty-one or anything."

Just then Jenna came out of the dressing room, dressed in her normal clothes.

"I just love these dresses. I wish I— He*llo*!" She stopped as she saw who I was standing with. Then she quickly composed herself. "I mean, hello." She shot me a surprised look.

"I was just asking Avery if you guys didn't have any plans tonight, if you want to go to a party with me?" Beckett asked her.

"Well, duh," Jenna stammered. "Yes."

27

So that's how two hours later, Jenna and I were in Sebastian's car, heading to the opening of the new club Constellation★. Yup, the one that I'd been telling Cecilia about earlier. The one Kevin Webber was going to guest DJ with Timbaland. The one that Beckett Howard had invited us to. Jenna had bribed Sebastian to chaperone us, and my mom had said yes, I could go out to a restaurant. Okay, I didn't mention it was a restaurant/club with a guy celebrity where there was a big party, but . . .

"I seriously don't see how Beckett Howard can get us all in," I said.

"I can only hope," Sebastian groaned. "Did I mention I hate parties?"

"I feel a little bad about that," I said to him. "And I'm sorry you had to wait so long for us today."

"That's okay," he said. "I had Apple people to hang with. We figured out how to work something new for the next M World, too."

"Well, cross your fingers!" Jenna said. "We deserve to be out on the town since we look this hawt. Your hair still looks really good, Avery. And that dress is to die for."

I did feel pretty good, for me. I was starting to feel excited as the valet opened the door to let us out in front of Constellation★.

"Beckett said he'd put us on the list," I said. It was crazy that I was going to another event with real paparazzi and stars. Two months ago, I was hundreds of miles away, reading about these celebrities in Ohio. And here I was, getting ready to go to an event with Beckett Howard. I suddenly felt light-headed and grabbed Jenna's arm.

"Avery," Jenna said. "Are you freaking out? Oh, you're freaking out! Okay, just remember your theme song." She started singing quietly:

> I'm the girl who
> You'll wish you knew

I joined in with her.

> The girl who will make you feel
> Nothing you thought was real
> Will show you the inside out
> I really have no doubt
> I'm the girl who you can't do without

"Marisa power!" Jenna said. "Just like the lyrics say, Beckett can't do without you."

"Actually, we can't do it without him," Sebastian said, annoyed. "Let's go give our names and get out of this place."

"Just shut up. Oh! There he is!" Jenna said, nudging me.

"Sweet car," Sebastian said.

Beckett was getting out of a black Aston Martin at the valet stand. He looked around and waved to us to come over.

"Hey," he said. "Sorry I'm late. I got stuck in line, getting this."

And he held out a small bouquet of white daisies to me.

"Oh," I said. "That's so sweet!"

He looked really hot in a navy blazer, white shirt, and jeans. His hair was perfectly gelled and he smiled that famous white-teeth smile.

"You guys ready?" Beckett asked. He took my arm. Jenna and Sebastian started walking toward the line of people waiting to get in.

"Guys, this way," Beckett said, motioning us to follow him the other way, around the corner of the building. "We don't have to wait in line."

"Dude." The big guy at the door at the side of the place gave him some elaborate handshake.

"'Sup, man?" Beckett said back to him. "These are my friends."

The big guy nodded and we went into the side door.

"This is so exciting!" Jenna grabbed my hand and squeezed it. We were walking into a new club opening with Beckett Howard! I silently squeed with excitement, but on the outside played it cool.

We were in a darkish room, with lights blinking. There were deep red chairs at tables, red booths, and a black floor. I saw a dance floor with some people on it, dancing to a Lil Mama song. Other people were standing around, laughing and talking.

Was that Ashton Kutcher? I squinted to see. That could be Demi and Rumer with him! I nudged Jenna so she'd look.

"You guys want a drink?" Beckett asked.

"I can get it," Sebastian said. "They're having soda with nothing in them."

"Dude, no worries," Beckett said. "So am I."

"Beckett!" Some girls came over to him and gave him hugs. Then some guys came over and started talking to him.

Jenna and I moved off to the side, to stay out of his way.

"Ladies!" Beckett said. Oh! He was waving us over to join him. When I walked over, he slung his arm around our shoulders.

"Avery and Jenna," he said. "Meet—"

He ran through a bunch of names I didn't catch. We all said hello. Sebastian came back with two Sprites for me and Jenna.

"We've got your table ready, Mr. Howard," a man with a manager tag came over and told him.

"Thanks, Jimmy," Beckett said. We all walked back to a booth by the dance floor. Sebastian slid in first, uncomfortably. Jenna went next and I followed her. Beckett sat on the end, next to me.

"Nice place, huh?" Beckett said. "Invite only, so everyone's pretty cool."

"Oh my gosh, is that Avril and Deryck?" Jenna asked. I tried to casually look and see them.

"Probably," Beckett said. "So you guys—"

We were interrupted by a group of girls who stopped by to give air kisses to Beckett. I tried to disregard the fact that they were 100 percent more gorgeous than I was, and to stay chill. But I couldn't stay chill when I kicked into celebrity-spotting mode.

"Jenna!" I hissed. "Kate Hudson to your left!"

At the same time Jenna kicked me and whispered, "Duffs to the right!"

The DJ was wrapping up a song, and then made an announcement.

"Let's give it up to our surprise guest DJ . . . Kevin Webber!"

Well, ha! That was no surprise to me, thanks to my Princess of Gossip skills. Everyone in the crowd was cheering, though, and looking surprised. I saw Haley Lane standing with him in the DJ booth. Kevin started playing Kanye and the crowd went pretty crazy.

Okay, this was the coolest night ever. And then it got cooler.

Beckett leaned over and draped his arm around me. Well, it was really around the back of the seat, but it was almost around my shoulders, too.

Jenna kicked me again.

"Oh my gosh, look at the dance floor," Jenna said. "It's the guy from *Dancing with the Stars,* my favorite adorable pro dancer. We have to dance."

"I'm fine," Sebastian said.

"Sebastian, how many years of dance lessons did Mom force me to take?" Jenna asked him. "I can finally put them to use. I have only one dance dream, and that is to dance on the *DWTS* stage with that boy. This is as close as I may ever get, so move your butt, bro."

Sebastian realized he had no say in the matter and stood up. Jenna turned, giving me a meaningful smile, like she was doing me a favor leaving me alone with Beckett Howard.

Alone with Beckett Howard! Well, not really alone. I tried to relax. People kept stopping by to say hello to him. I felt really out of place and awkward. I sipped my Sprite and tried to follow the conversations.

Finally, Beckett turned to me. "Having fun?"

"Yes," I said weakly.

"So tell me a little more about yourself," he said.

"Well, I moved here two months ago from Ohio for my parents' business," I started.

"Ah," he said. "There's no business like show business. Are they agents? Screenwriters?"

I was about to explain when two more girls came up to give Beckett kisses hello. They started talking to him and hanging all over him like I wasn't even sitting there. But then I think he recognized how uncomfortable I was.

"Do you want to dance?" he asked me, to the girls' disappointment.

"Sure," I said. I followed him up to the dance floor, walking through a crowd that included people I recognized from *The Real World* and *Project Runway*. I saw Jenna dancing near the *Dancing with the Stars* guy. I don't think he had any clue she was behind him, but she was smiling like a maniac. She gave me the thumbs-up and did a little cha-cha move behind the oblivious dance pro.

Beckett took my hand and the next thing I knew I was dancing with Beckett Howard. He was a slightly awkward dancer, but we did our best to Lil Mama. And he looked smoking hot no matter what he was doing.

"Excuse me!" I said, bumping into someone.

"That's okay," she said. "Oh, I like your dress."

"Thanks," I said. Ohmygosh! That was America Ferrara! Complimenting my dress! I looked around for Jenna to see if she saw me dancing with Beckett and being bumped by Ugly Betty! Beckett danced along with me and I raised my hands in the air.

"That mix rocked," I said when it was over. "The way they made the songs blend, even I could dance to them."

"You could dance to anything, I'm sure," Beckett asked. "So now I know how you got your Christian Palandro dress."

"How?" I asked.

"You're going to be one of the pros on *Dancing with the Stars* next season, aren't you?" he teased me. "Like the guy Jenna is stalking."

I giggled.

"You wore me out, shawty. I need to sit down," Beckett said. He took my hand and we headed back to our table. Only, some people were sitting at it. I started to look for another seat, but Beckett gestured for me to slide in the booth, so I slid in next to a guy who was talking to someone on his other side.

"Hi!" I said to the guy, since I was practically shoved onto his lap.

"Hey." He smiled. "Didn't mean to take your seat."

"I'm good," I said. And I got a look at his face before he turned back to the conversation. Holy crapoley. I was sitting next to Chace Crawford.

My mouth dropped open. What should I say? Should I tell him that I'd married us off on many of my school notebooks? That although I hadn't any luck with our celebrity Brangelina name, Mrs. Avery Crawford sounded good to me?

"Hi-lo," I said to him. Hi-lo? I meant to say hi. Or hello. Hi-lo? What the heck was that? I'm an idiot. He looked at me like I was slightly strange, but smiled kindly. Then he turned the other way to continue his conversation.

Hi-lo? I giggled. I mean, there was no way I was going to wow Chace Crawford anyway. But maybe I made an impression, even if it was a dorky one.

Beckett was greeting more people. I was sitting between Chace Crawford and Beckett Howard. My life was officially a success. I wished my Ohio friends could see me now. Why couldn't someone take a picture? Where was the paparazzi when I needed them? Couldn't they take a break from stalking Britney or whomever and come out tonight? Nobody would believe this. *I* could hardly believe this. I was smiling into my Sprite when Jenna and Sebastian came back.

"This place is sick," Jenna said. "I totally want to— *Gwah!!*"

Apparently she recognized Chace Crawford. She clutched her brother's arm to steady herself, and then looked at me, her jaw hanging open.

"Hey, Avery, it's getting late," Sebastian said, oblivious to the fact

I was sitting in a spot millions of girls would dream about. "We gotta get going."

Noooo! I never wanted to leave! But I also didn't want to get grounded.

"Oh, hey," Beckett said, looking at his watch. "I don't want you to get in trouble on our first date. But are you sure you can't stay? I could give you a ride home."

Yeeeeees! He called it a date! But nooo! I didn't want to leave. And then my cell phone buzzed. It was my parents calling.

"Hi, I'm fine," I said, plugging my ear. "Yes, I know. I'll be home soon. Yes, Sebastian's driving."

Ugh. Curfew.

"Sorry, Sebastian has to drive me home," I said to Beckett.

"I'll at least walk you out. Just hang on and let me text the door guy that we're heading out." He got up and typed something into his Sidekick.

I slid out of the booth and stood next to Jenna.

"My shoulder touched Chace Crawford," I said to her. "Pinch me. I'm totally dreaming."

"I will pinch you, you brat," Jenna said, but she was grinning. "The only celebrity I got that close to was one of the Bachelors when he tripped on the dance floor."

"Can we please get out of here," Sebastian said. "My online Sudoku opponent from Dubai should be waking up soon. I want to get in a game before he goes to school."

"Please, Sebastian, just for one moment pretend to be a normal person," Jenna said.

"Beckett said to wait and he'd walk us out," I said. And just then a familiar song was coming on as Madonna's voice faded out. "The Girl Who" was being mixed in with a techno beat.

"They're playing Marisa!" Jenna said. "A club remix of Marisa! I requested that! I totally talked to the DJ's assistant person and re-quested they play her!"

"We've got to get this recorded." I reached into my tote bag and clicked my cell to record the music. This was the perfect way to end the night.

"You'll have to put it on Princess of Goss—" Jenna said, and stopped. "Oh, hi, Beckett!"

"Your car's been pulled around," he said. "I'll walk you guys out."

"Thanks so much for taking us to Constellation★," Jenna said as we walked out the door.

"Anytime," Beckett said.

The doorman held the door open, but Beckett held my arm so that Jenna and Sebastian would walk out first.

"I had a great time," he said. And then Beckett leaned in, put his arm around my waist, and kissed me on the lips.

I was kissing Beckett Howard! Beckett Howard was kissing me! At first I froze, but then I melted a little and kissed him gently back. He pulled away and smiled at me.

"I'll text you," he said. And he took my hand to walk me to the car. I slid into the backseat next to Jenna.

"Bye!" I called out. I looked out the window as our car waited in the parking lot behind a line of cars. I watched as Beckett waved in our direction and then turned to head back inside the club.

I leaned back in my seat, grinning.

"Did you just kiss Beckett Howard?" Jenna asked.

"Did you see that?" I asked. "Did you see it?! Please tell me I have witnesses so I'm not losing my mind."

"Well, I didn't stand there and watch the whole thing," Jenna said. "But I did see the lean-in and lip-connect before I turned away."

"It was kind of a blur," I said. "All I could think of was that I was kissing Beckett Howard."

"You kissed a celebrity!" Jenna gave me a high five. "I am officially insanely jealous. I've lived here how long and the closest I've gotten was when I used to kiss my Jesse McCartney poster. I should have just climbed across you in the booth and thrown myself at Chace Crawford. I bet I could have made out with him for a few seconds before he threw me off."

"Can we change this conversation?" Sebastian interrupted. "I'm not interested in hearing my sister's makeout fantasies."

As our car pulled away, I couldn't help but notice some guy totally macking with a girl a few feet from our car where the paparazzi couldn't see him.

"Hey!" I said. "Isn't that Shade from University of Hard?"

"And isn't that *not* Delilah Singer," Jenna said, shaking her head. "Better not tell Princess of Gossip *that* scoop."

We both laughed.

28

"Good morning, sleepyhead!" My mother's voice interrupted my wonderful dream. I'd been sitting between Beckett Howard and Chace Crawford. And then Beckett Howard had kissed me and—

"*Ouch!*" my mother said. "What did I just trip over?"

She opened the shades in my room and sunlight streamed in. I pulled my covers over my head.

"Avery, there's just no excuse for your room to look like this," she said. "I know you're busy with your new social life, but I mean honestly. Avery?"

I groaned and turned the cover down.

"It's ten o'clock. Your father and I wanted to know if you wanted to come help us in the office today. I know you've been saying you could use some spending money and— What is this?"

"It's a box," I said sleepily. "Everything's still in boxes because we still haven't gotten furniture for my room, remember?"

"I mean this dress," my mother said.

Uh-oh. I opened my eyes and peeked. Yup. She was pointing to my silver dress. Apparently I'd forgotten to hide it. She and my dad had worked late last night, so they hadn't seen me in it.

"It's just something I . . . borrowed from Jenna," I said. "Isn't it pretty?"

"It looks very expensive to be tossed on the chair like this," she said disapprovingly. Then she held it up. "Oh! Is it for homecoming? Oh no, I feel terrible!"

"You do?"

"I should be the one taking you shopping for dresses for your first dance in California. You shouldn't have to borrow."

I didn't even know if we had a homecoming dance at school. School social events were almost off my radar right now.

"Ma," I said. "Don't worry. We were just playing around with outfits, that's all."

"Okay," she said. Then she kicked one of the boxes to the side. "We really do have to start your furniture shopping, don't we? Do you want to go today? I can have your dad go to the store without me."

Oh, that figures. Today I had some serious work to do to update my Princess of Gossip blog and my Team Marisa MySpace. I also had a research paper to write for social studies, a math test on Monday, and my English project hanging over my head. I was getting behind in school and I knew I had to get focused. And apparently pick up my room to hide any more traces of my secret life. And spend some time talking to Jenna reminiscing about my unbelievable time last night, of course.

"Can we do it tomorrow?" I asked her.

"Oh, honey, your dad and I are doing inventory tomorrow. But you can come help us."

"Maybe," I said. "It's just that I've got a lot of homework I want to get done today. And stuff for my team thing."

"Don't work too hard," she said. "Although we are certainly proud of you. I look forward to seeing your report card with all this studying."

Uh-oh.

"Good morning, sunshine!" My dad stuck his head in the room. "Are you coming out with us today, Avery?"

"She can't," my mom said. "She's got a lot of schoolwork today."

"Oh." My dad sounded disappointed. "I was looking forward to tracking down celebrities with you. Your mother isn't very good at it. It's been nine days since I saw Gwen Stephanie."

"He's having celebrity withdrawal." My mom shook her head. "Think of poor Avery. She hasn't seen any celebrities other than that one time she met Paris in the Urth Caffé."

I turned my head so they couldn't see me smiling.

"Well, get your homework done early so we can have a Family Night," my dad said. "I bought a new Wii game today and you're gonna love it."

"What is it, Albert?" my mom asked.

"We Cheer!" my dad said. "The Wii cheerleading game. I saw this video of Jen Stefani where she was a cheerleader, so I'm going to make a Jen Stephanie Mii and go b-a-n-a-n-a-s."

I groaned and threw the covers over my head.

"Well, Avery, you have to admit your father is never dull," my mom said, and leaned down and kissed my head. "Call if you need anything."

"Bye," I called. Speaking of calls, I wondered if I had any, well, interesting text messages. You know, from a guy who said he would text me. I leaned down from the bed to get my cell phone off the floor where I'd dropped it last night. There were no messages. Darn.

Well, who was I kidding. Beckett Howard probably went back into the club, was swarmed by all those girls who did not have curfews, and promptly forgot that I existed. Sigh. I checked my phone and realized the ringer was off. I had ten messages from Jenna waiting for me.

"Finally!" Jenna said when she answered.

"Sorry, my ringer was off," I said. "What's up?"

"Did you check your email yet?" she said. "I'm dying to know what you think."

"No, I just woke up," I said. "I'll go on now."

"I'll hold while you look," she said, sounding very cheerful. "I know you said we shouldn't take pictures because we might get busted, and I wasn't sure these would turn out since I was hiding my camera in my bag, but . . ."

I signed on to my email and downloaded a huge file from Jenna. When I opened it I saw pictures of the celebrities at the party last night! There was Hillary. Chace. Ashton. Avril. Two American Idols. Two hot *Dancing with the Stars* pro dancers. An Amazing Racer.

"When did you take pictures?" I asked her.

"When you were snuggling with Beckett," Jenna said. "Don't worry, I only took pictures when they were posing for the paparazzi, so you won't get in trouble for invading their privacy. And a couple of them I even asked, so they're all cool. These are good for Princess of Gossip, right?"

"Jenna, these are amazing!" I said. "Thank you, thank you! I'm glad you didn't listen to me and took pics."

"Yay," Jenna said. "Now go put them up on the site."

I heard someone else pick up.

"Hi, Sebastian," Jenna said. "Stop spying."

"I'm not spying," he said. "I'm first telling Avery that I'm going to the post office. Do you want me to get anything for you from the box?"

"Yeah, that would be great," I said.

"And second," Sebastian said. "I'm reminding you, Jenna, that you've got a lot to do today."

"I'm coming, I'm coming," Jenna groaned.

"What do you have to do?" I asked her.

"Oh, Sebastian's job," Jenna said. "In exchange for driving us last night."

"Oh no," I said. "I thought you just blackmailed him. What job does Sebastian have?"

"He earns gas money by grading papers for one of the math teachers," she said. "I get to grade two hundred and fourteen multiple choice tests today."

"And double-check them for accuracy," Sebastian added.

"Hang up, now," Jenna commanded. We waited till we heard the click.

"I have to come help you with those tests," I said.

"No, you have to put up the pictures on Princess of Gossip," Jenna protested. "We don't want anyone to scoop you!"

"Well, I totally owe you," I said. "I'll make your pictures look good."

"Don't forget to tell Team Marisa we got 'The Girl Who' played at the party."

"I will, it's awesome," I said.

I felt a little guilty when I hung up. And tired. But excited. I had a lot of pictures to choose for Princess of Gossip. I smiled at the one of America dancing. And whoops, there was Shade making out with NotDelilahSinger. I shouldn't post that on the site, although he probably deserved it.

And Chace Crawford smiling for the paparazzi. And Beckett Howard, throwing a peace sign and making a kiss face at the camera.

I stopped on that one for a minute. Because of course it reminded me of when he was making a kiss face at me. I closed my eyes and remembered that moment when he'd pulled me toward him. I'd actually kissed a guy who was known for being gorgeous and a good kisser. It had been a really, really good kiss.

My phone rang, startling me out of my daydream. For a split second I thought it might be Beckett.

"Did you see the picture of Chace?" Jenna said when I answered. "I almost got my camera taken away for that one, but how worth it is it? I might blow it up poster-sized for my room."

"It's crazy hot," I agreed. "I'll put it up on the site right away."

I had fans who would love to see these pictures. My first loyalty was to my Team Marisa fans. Without them none of this would have started, right? So I went onto the Team Marisa page and posted a new blog entry.

"The Girl Who" is getting some play! At the hot Constellation★ party in L.A. last night, DJ Kevin Webber was mixing it up with Mark Ronson and what did stars like America Ferrara, Chace Crawford, and Kate Hudson get to dance to?

"The Girl Who!" Marisa rocked the crowd. Now let's make some noise about Marisa playing LIVE at one of these parties!!

Click the link to hear the mix.

I uploaded the song mix from my cell phone capture to the site. I wondered if DMB Records had found out that "The Girl Who" was played last night. I mean, when Timbaland is DJ, they should take notice, right? I checked my email.

```
To: Group email
From: AJohnson@DMBrecords.com
Subject: Heatseeker

Great news! Due to radio play and
club exposure this weekend—
```

Club exposure? That was because of me and Jenna! I read on.

```
"The Girl Who" is going to be on
Billboard's Heatseeker list this
week! I'll send out a press release
to announce.
Ashley
```

A *Billboard* Heatseeker? That sounded amazing, but . . . I had no clue what it was. I picked up my cell and texted Griffin.

```
Aves: hi—it's Avery. U there?
GreendayGriff: yea— Hey.
Aves: do you know what a Billboard
Heatseeker is?
GreendayGriff: sure. It's Billboard
magazine's weekly list to showcase
hot new music artists.
Aves: kthx
```

Okay, the *Billboard* list was big news. It was scoopworthy for Princess of Gossip! I wanted to post that right away. I jumped back to the Princess of Gossip site to post the new information there.

Could rising star Marisa possibly be Billboard *'s newest Heatseeker? Once she cracks that chart, I'm predicting it's Top 10 all the way!!*

Oh wow, I had so many new messages, comments, and friends to add on Princess of Gossip. And with these new pictures and stories about the party last night, it was going to be a big day.

I brought my laptop over to my desk and moved some papers out of the way to make room for my laptop. And then I saw the folder that Griffin had given me with the poetry slam. I opened the folder and saw little kids' handwritten poems. Then I saw Griffin's own handwriting on the back of the folder.

Light Your Way
By Griffin King

There's more to you
Than meets the eye
I don't know why
You hide your light
So deep inside

I want to shatter the myth
That is you
And find the girl
That's true

Whatever you're going through
I'll be there, too
Let the stars in my eyes light the way

SABRINA BRYAN AND JULIA DeVILLERS

Wow. That was really good. I wondered if that was the song for Delilah that Cecilia had mentioned. It was pretty romantic. I thought about Griffin writing the lyrics, and even if it was about Delilah, I still felt a little crush flush.

```
Aves: u still on? I 4got 2 tell u. I
liked the poetry jams u gave me.
GreendayGriff: cool! Maybe u can
watch the kids show.
Aves: and I liiiiike ur song Light
Your Way.
GreendayGriff: ??
Aves: ur lyrics were on the folder.
I really liked it. We will have to
put that on the album with Cold Cal-
lous Wench.
GreendayGriff: u liked it? Cool.
```

And that's when my phone went off with another text.

```
Any plans for Friday? Want to spend
it with me? Beckett
```

29

"Good morning, sleepyhead!" My mother's voice interrupted my wonderful dream. I was out with Beckett Howard. What was my mother doing on my date?!

I opened my eyes and blinked. Oh shoot, it was Monday morning.

"Avery, you have to get up for school," my mother said. "We have to have a serious discussion about your late nights. They can't be interfering with your schooling—"

Well, actually they can. That is, if your late nights were due not only to chatting with 19,425 of your closest friends on your My-Spaces and blogs, but also texting with Beckett Howard.

I smiled into my pillow.

"Avery, the bus will be here in twelve minutes," my mother said. "Your dad and I have to leave, so you're on your own."

"Oh, crud!" I said. I jumped out of bed and brushed my teeth really quickly. Crud and crud. I also remembered I also had English vocabulary due today I didn't finish. My weekend had gone by in a blur. Every spare minute had been spent updating my sites with all of the scoop coming in.

The pictures of the launch party had gone over really well. Princess of Gossip had been linked to a lot of major gossip sites, and I was going crazy adding new people to my blog list.

And some of my new friends were really unexpected. I was suddenly "friends" with several publicists and people with insider information. I knew that publicists tried to plant gossip to get publicity for their clients, but it still was very weird that it was happening to me.

"*I'm the publicist for Perth Hampton and we wanted to share with you these great shots of her walking her dog, Fritzy, on the beach yesterday. Her bathing suit is by Shoshanna and her sandals are by Michael Kors.*"

"*Why is Kristen Bell having lunch with a director and an up-and-coming star? Could there be a project in the works?*"

"*Here's a picture of David Beckham coming out of the stadium. That boy is on fire!*"

"*What TV star on a new sitcom took her friends out to a $1,000 dinner—and left an enormous tip? What a sweetie!*" And there was a picture of the star, who wasn't exactly known as a sweetie, attached. I had a feeling that one was from a publicist, too.

My cell rang with an unfamiliar number.

"Avery! Are you ready?" someone said to me.

"Um, who is this?" I asked.

"It's Miya, silly! Are you still home? We'll be there in like ten minutes to pick you up for school!"

And the phone clicked off.

I was getting a ride from Miya again today? Well, I could get used to not having to ride the bus. And I could use the extra couple minutes to pick out a cute outfit. Every time I was in that car, I felt pressured to feel confident and cool. Also, the fact that William and the camera guy were always around filming made me doubly self-conscious. A cute outfit would help. Too bad I couldn't wear my silver dress. I put on my Marisa emerald-green and cream top, long silvery gray shorts, and silver flats. I put on a charm bracelet and checked myself in the mirror. With my new haircut, it was as good as it could get. My cell phone went off again, this time to "The Girl Who."

"Hey, it's me," Jenna said. "Do you want a ride to school? We've got time to come get you. We left early because Sebastian thought he had calculus club and now we're just sitting here."

"Uh." I paused. "I would but Miya's going to pick me up."

"Oh," Jenna said. "Okay."

"She just called me out of the blue," I said. "I didn't plan it. I can call her back and change it."

"No, go ahead," Jenna said. "But if there's the chance to sit on Javier's lap, I want to come, too."

I laughed and hung up. I went downstairs to wait on my front step. The infamous L.A. smog made the sky slightly gray and it looked like it might rain. I hoped any rain would wait until after my ride got here.

Then my cell rang again—*I'm the Girl Who*—

"Hi again," I said.

"Hey, Avery!" Jenna was screaming. "You won't believe what I just saw on Sebastian's Sidekick! You—"

"Hey, Avery!" Miya's car was pulling up in front of my house. "Come on! Hurry!"

"I have to go," I said to Jenna apologetically.

"But—"

"I'll meet you at your locker," I told her.

I hung up and put the phone on silent as I went over to the car and saw Miya and Cecilia in the front. The back door opened and Griffin was sitting in the backseat.

"Hey," Griffin said. "Sorry, Javier's not here, so we'll all get to sit in an actual seat. Unless you preferred his lap."

"That's okay." I blushed.

"Get in, girlfriend!" Miya said. "We couldn't wait for you to tell us what happened! We want *all* the details."

"Happened where?" I asked cautiously.

"At Constellation★!" Miya said. "I can't believe it! You told us it was impossible to get tickets and then you were there!"

"You've been holding out on us," Cecilia said drily. "Or are we being punk'd? Or was it Photoshopped? And then you sent it to us and tricked us?"

"It's on Perez," Miya said to her. "How could she make that happen?"

"Can someone fill me in on what we're talking about?" I asked.

Griffin showed me something from the Internet on his iPod touch. And I gasped.

There was a picture from the opening. It showed a crowd, and the focus of the picture was Kevin Webber in the DJ booth. But just off to the side, there I was, dancing with Beckett Howard. I was doing an awkward dance move and he was waving his hands over his head.

I had no idea anyone was even taking that picture. I checked the time and realized it was just posted this morning.

"I did my morning Perez gossip check and I totally love Kevin Webber. So I enlarged the picture and then I was like, hey, isn't that Avery the new girl from Idaho dancing out there near Beckett Howard?" Miya said. "We didn't know you had this secret cool life."

"Didn't take you long to get into the Hollywood scene, did it?" Griffin said.

"I, uh," I stammered. How did this happen? I was supposed to be anonymous. Nobody was supposed to care about me. I couldn't believe my picture was in there!

"So how did you get into that party?" Cecilia asked. "I thought you said it was impossible to get in."

"Well, I guess Beckett Howard can pretty much go anywhere," I said. "I mean, he just took me in the side door and they waved him through like it was nothing."

"You went *with* Beckett Howard?" Cecilia asked.

"Well, yeah," I said. "I mean, it was just a last-minute date and—"

"You were on a date?!" Cecilia and Miya both screamed.

"We thought you were out on the dance floor and then just tried to dance with him," Cecilia said. "And he took pity on you so he danced back."

Gee, thanks.

"So how did you meet Beckett?" Cecilia continued.

"I was in the Christian Palandro shop," I said absentmindedly as I tried to enlarge the picture to see exactly what face I was making in the picture. I looked like I was having fun, but it wasn't exactly pretty since it was in midlaugh. Note to self: Keep mouth shut anywhere the paparazzi could be lurking.

"Was that a Christian Palandro dress you were wearing?" Miya shrieked. "I knew it looked gorgeous. And your hair looked really cute, too."

"So how did you get a Christian Palandro dress?" Cecilia asked. "I haven't seen that one in the store. Is it from his new line? Is it the same place you got those sunglasses? And the lip gloss?"

"Um," I said, my head spinning. "Um, yeah. It's, you know, family connections."

"Griffin!" Cecilia said. "You said she was cool but you didn't tell us Avery had family connections."

I looked at Griffin, who had been sitting there listening to the conversation.

"I said she was cool for other reasons," Griffin said. "I said she was cool for her taste in music. And also for not putting up with Cecilia in English."

"What?" Cecilia said. "I've always been nice to Avery in English. Gawd, I let her in our group even though we thought she was a nobody."

"Hellooo? I'm right here," I said.

"I said Avery was cool, too," Miya said. "Remember? So anyway, I can't believe we were at the University of Hard waiting around forever for Shade, who never showed, and you were at the big party."

I didn't mention that the reason Shade didn't show was because he was also at the launch party with someone else.

"Griffin was glad Shade didn't show, weren't you, Griffy?" Cecilia said. "Then you could comfort my sister in her time of need."

"Cecilia, don't even go there," Griffin said. "Change the subject."

"I will! Avery, did you hook up with Beckett?" Miya asked. "We want full details! Is he as hot as he looks?"

I felt my face turn red just thinking about it. This conversation was going way too fast for me.

"That wasn't the change of subject I was looking for," Griffin said. "Save the kissing conversations for when I leave the car. Which, since we're at school, is now."

That was a relief to me. I still needed to process the fact that my face was on a major gossip website and that everyone in the car knew I'd gone to the party with Beckett Howard.

We got out of the car and Cecilia came over to me.

"Bye, Griffin!" Cecilia said, and took my arm. "Now that Griffin's pure and innocent ears are out of range, tell us what it was like to hook up with Beckett Howard."

"It was just a kiss," I said.

"Eeee! You made out with Beckett Howard!" Miya said. "That's better than *your* celebrity makeout, Cecilia!"

"It is not," Cecilia said. "Mine was a real singer with talent. They told him at the *Idol* tryout he has a good shot of making it next season. What's Beckett's talent?"

"Maybe it's kissing," Miya said. "Is it his kissing? Or just his hotness? Or is it serial dating?"

"Do you know all of the stars he's dated?" Cecilia interrupted. "Why would he go out with you?"

"He said he wanted to hang out with regular people," I said.

"Well, that makes sense." Cecilia seemed satisfied. "You're regular."

"She's not regular," Miya said. "Did you see her dress? And Avery, your hair looks great, too."

"Cecilia!" It was William, coming down the hall toward us. "Smile. I've got time to work on my Facebook so I need today's look."

Cecilia posed and smiled.

"You know who you need to get on your MySpace is Avery," Miya said. "She got snapped by real paparazzi. Check out Perez today."

"I'm not paparazzi, I'm a celebrity chronicler," William said, then looked at me. "Wait. This Avery? Why was she on Perez?"

"She went on a date with Beckett Howard!" Miya squealed. "They went to the Constellation★ party and there's a picture of Avery and Beckett dancing to Kevin Webber!"

"No friggin' way!" William said. "Really?"

I nodded.

"I'm a little hurt," William said. "You know I'm here, waiting for my break to fame, and you didn't let me take a picture of you?"

"You never wanted to," I said defensively.

"Well, let's start now," Cecilia said. She and Miya draped their arms around me and smiled. "Say cheese, Avery."

I smiled awkwardly and I heard someone say, "Who's that girl Cecilia and Miya are hanging all over?"

And so went my first moment of fame at my new school. Yes, Cecilia was using me because of my Beckett Howard moments. But it was a little fun to have some attention.

"Now take just me and Avery for my Facebook," Cecilia commanded.

And the warning bell rang and the photo shoot was over.

"I gotta get to my locker before homeroom," I said. "I have to run."

"See you in English!" Cecilia said to me. "We can be partners!"

Okay, that girl is so fake. But she had that way of totally sucking you in, where you ended up smiling and nodding in agreement even though you knew she was a total phony. I moved as fast as I could to get to my locker and homeroom in time. I went to my locker and dialed my combination. When I opened my locker and pulled out my notebook, the first thing I saw was something I'd written on my notebook.

Avery + Chace Crawford

I grinned. How weird was that. Not long after I'd written that, I'd ended up sitting right next to him and actually talking to him. It was all starting to sink in how much had changed so quickly. And today I was in a gossip blog to prove it.

"Hey," the girl who had the locker next to me said. "Aren't you . . ."

Aren't I . . . ? For a split second I had the feeling that celebrities must have when they're first recognized. What should I say? *Yes, I'm the girl on the gossip site.* Do I look down modestly and smile? Do I share my excitement?

"Aren't you the girl who was walking in with Cecilia Singer this morning?" the girl continued. "Did you come to school with her? Do you know her sister goes out with Shade, from the band the University of Hard?"

Or, I could be famous for that.

30

Oops.

"I'm sorry, I'm sorry," I said to Jenna as she walked up to her locker, where I was waiting for her before computer lab.

"I'm going to forgive you, but first you have to hear me whine about how I had to spend the whole morning ready to burst. How do you think I felt when I saw the picture of you and Beckett and then you hung up on me?" Jenna said.

"I'm sorry!" I said.

"And then I see William showing off pictures of you and Cecilia all BFF from this morning?"

"It's not as bad as it looks!" I protested.

I told her how I found out from Cecilia and Miya that you could see me in the picture. And how Cecilia had glommed onto me not only on the way to school but also in English class, where she sat down at the desk behind me and proceeded to text me and pass a note about how I met Beckett and got to go to the party. All while William was taking our picture and getting us in trouble with Miss Schmitt.

"So seriously, it was a stressful morning," I said. "Not fun at all."

"Okay," Jenna said cheerfully. "You've paid your dues. But now tell me the good stuff. What did you think when you saw that picture? Did you freak?"

"Beyond. In fact, I'm still freaking," I said. "I mean, I don't think most people would really see me in it, do you? People will be looking at Kevin Webber. Then they might notice Beckett Howard. But I'm just some nobody girl who happens to be out there on the dance floor, right?"

"I think so," Jenna said. "Unless the Princess of Gossip runs a story. Like, who is the hot new mystery girl dancing at Constellation★? And the gossip princess becomes the gossip item."

"I wonder if Beckett has seen it yet," I said. "I hope he's okay with it. It doesn't really look like I'm actually with him or anything, right?"

I suddenly had a terrible thought. What if he didn't want our night out in the gossip blogs? I mean, I was a nobody. He might be really embarrassed or pissed about it. I wondered if I should text him to find out.

The warning bell rang.

"We better get to the computer lab," Jenna said. Sebastian was standing at the door when we got there, holding some papers.

"Hi, Sebastian," I said.

"Hey, Avery, I went to the post office box," Sebastian said. "Some of the packages were too big so they're in my car. But I did bring in one envelope that looked like it might be important."

I looked at a large cream envelope that said: URGENT TO PRINCESS OF GOSSIP.

"Who's it from?" Jenna said. Just as I started to check, Miya came walking down the hallway. I hid the envelope in my notebook.

"Hi, aren't you the lab monitor?" Miya came up to Sebastian. "I have a pass to excuse Avery Johnson from this class."

"You do?" Sebastian, Jenna, and I all said at the same time.

"Yes. May I speak with you privately, Avery?" Miya said, and took me aside.

"Just go with it. We're breaking you out of class. I remembered you had computer lab last time we had to use the lab," Miya said quietly. "So Cecilia got a pass to get you out of this period and come to lunch with us."

"I have things to do in computer lab," I said. "I need to stay."

"I'll get you out of it," Miya said before I could protest, and went back to Sebastian and Jenna.

"You got Avery a pass to go to lunch?" Jenna asked her.

"Yes," Miya explained. "Hi, I'm Miya."

"I'm Jenna," Jenna said. "And we've already met before."

"Oh. Sorry. Well, it's very important Avery comes with me," Miya said. "I have a pass."

"She's got a legitimate pass," Sebastian said to me. "You'll have to go with her."

"How can you have a legitimate pass to make me go to lunch?" I asked. "Actually, I already have lunch this period."

"You have lunch?" Miya asked. "Then why are you even in the computer lab in the first place? Are you supposed to be in here?"

Oh, shoot, I just busted myself as hiding out from the cafeteria. I'd almost forgotten that I wasn't officially supposed to be in here. The computer lab had started to feel like my second home, but if I got busted I'd be out.

"No reason," I said. "I'll go to lunch."

"Bye." Jenna waved halfheartedly.

"Wait," I said, realizing that I'd be dissing Jenna once again. "Can Jenna come with us?"

"Yes, please take her. Then I can have my office to myself," Sebastian said, and went back into the room.

"I don't want to go to lunch," Jenna said.

"Please," I said. "I need you."

"Well, I am kind of hungry," Jenna said. "It would give me a chance to hit the snack machine."

"Okay, come on, guys," Miya said, pulling me down the hall. "Cecilia's waiting for us. Oh, she's texting me."

Miya walked and texted, and I dropped behind with Jenna.

"Thanks for coming with me," I whispered to Jenna. "I need help so I don't spew out something stupid. I barely have a cover story for being at Constellation★."

"Thanks for asking me," Jenna said. "Although I'm not sure I can protect you from Cecilia Singer. I don't have a history for standing up to her."

"Don't worry about that," I said. She just wants to be in the know. So this time you have the upper hand."

"Oh yeah," Jenna brightened. "I do!"

We headed into the cafeteria. I thought about the last time I'd walked into the outdoor lunch area and seen Cecilia and her crew at the center table. Now Jenna and I followed Miya over to the long picnic area.

"Avery!" Cecilia said, patting the seat next to her. "Come tell us about the party with Beckett Howard!"

I sat down next to her.

"Can you move over a little bit so Jenna can sit, too?" I said.

"And what is Jenna doing here?"

Cecilia looked quizzically at Miya.

"Jenna was at Constellation★ too," I said cheerfully, shifting over so Jenna could sit beside me as everyone gasped at this apparently shocking news. On Jenna's other side was Javier and two other guys wearing basketball uniforms. And across from me were a few football players and assorted hot people I knew by reputation.

"The party was so fun," I said. "Here's the scoop . . ."

I told everyone my stories and they gasped in all the right places. Chace, Ashton, Kate, Haley, Kevin, reality-show stars, Timbaland . . . everyone at the lunch table was hanging on my every word.

"Avery, I knew you were nice, but didn't know you were so cool!" Miya squealed.

"Well." I shrugged. "There's a lot you don't know about me."

Heck yeah, I'd let them fawn over me. It was certainly preferable to having them making fun of me or ignoring me like a nobody. I casually leaned back in my seat, and in the process knocked my notebook off the table.

"What's that?" Cecilia said, leaning over to look. "Another invitation to a hot party?"

Oh shoot! I gave Jenna a panicked look. She quickly put her foot down on it and slid it out of Cecilia's reach. I grabbed it and ripped it open and shoved the envelope in my pocket.

"I'm not sure what it is," I said casually. "Let's check it out."

I skimmed the invitation and my jaw dropped. It said I was invited to host a party at a hotel in Laguna Beach. Free. It said that I was to be VIP guest of the hotel. I could invite up to fifty friends for a special beach party compliments of the hotel. What the—?

"So," I said, trying to look cool but failing. "I'm, um, having a party."

Cecilia snatched the invitation out of my hand.

"Wow, you're hosting a party at the new Royal Beach hotel?" Cecilia said. "Impressive."

"Yeah." I shrugged.

"Okay, who *are* you?" Cecilia asked. "You obviously have some secret life you're not sharing with us. Dating Beckett Howard, VIP beach parties . . ."

I didn't dare look at Jenna.

"Um, I have, those um, family connections," I stammered.

"That's so cool!" Miya said.

"I admit, I'm kind of impressed," Cecilia said. She leaned over to the guys, who were talking among themselves. "You guys, this hotel is throwing Avery a beach party."

"Awesome!" Javier said. "Do we get to see you lovely ladies in bikinis?"

"Who said you guys are invited?" I blurted out. Everyone turned to look at me because obviously that didn't come out too well. But I choked. I mean, Princess of Gossip was throwing this party, how was I supposed to invite them? Heck, who was I fooling? Sure, I could throw a vitual-world party, but that didn't mean I could have a party as a fifteen-year-old nobody in real life.

"I mean, um, it's not necessarily for people from school," I said lamely. "It might be a family thing and all."

Whew, everyone seemed to buy into that.

"You can adopt me if I can come to your bikini party," Javier said.

"Javier," I said. "Do these lines actually work for you? I mean, have they gotten you a girlfriend?"

"Girlfriend?" He looked taken aback. "I'm too busy for a girlfriend; I have to keep my grades up for Harvard."

"*You're* going to Harvard?" Jenna asked him.

"Yes, premed for neurology," Javier answered. "I don't have time for a girlfriend. I just like to give girls the compliments you all so deserve."

"Cheesy but harmless," Jenna whispered to me. "Yet brilliant. I'm so getting to ride on his lap next time."

And then Jenna's phone vibrated.

"It's my brother," Jenna said. "I left my books back in computer lab. I need to go get them."

She got up and looked at me.

"Okay, I'll see you later," I said, waving as Jenna left. I didn't think she needed me to go with her, and I was kind of shell-shocked from the invitation. I mean, I couldn't really have a beach party, could I? That was ridiculous to even consider.

"Isn't Jenna's brother that computer lab guy?" Miya asked.

"Ugh, yes," Cecilia said. "Major geekazoid. If you want a good story, I have this hilarious one about him from a couple years ago."

"Why don't we—" I interrupted, trying to change the subject, but nobody was listening to me.

"Jenna and I took dance class together," Cecilia continued. "Sebastian had this wicked crush on my sister Delilah. He followed her around, it was squicky. So she pretended she liked him and Sebastian's mom believed it and—"

"Hey! Guys!" I said, a little too loudly. Everyone turned to look at me, kind of annoyed. "I just uh, counted guests at my party and I have room."

Everyone stopped looking annoyed.

"No way!" Miya said. "Really?"

"Yes way," I said. "You're all invited. You can all come to my beach party."

The Sebastian and Delilah gossip story was forgotten as everyone at the table turned toward me.

"I mean, if the beach party goes through. I have to confirm it, of course," I said, backpedaling for a second. "I mean, they might be booked up for a long time and—"

"Oh, let's see!" Cecilia said. She whipped out her cell phone and called the number on the invitation.

"I can just call them later—" I started.

But Cecilia waved me off and got up to talk in a quieter area. Shoot. What did I just get myself into?

"Is Beckett coming to the party?" Miya asked.

"Maybe," I said. Maybe not.

"You guys are a cute couple," Miya said. "I'd love to meet him."

"We're in!" Cecilia said. "I told them about your invitation and they've got a private suite with beachfront access open this Friday. You are having a party, girlfriend!"

She held up her hand to high-five me.

"Friday?" I said weakly. "That's pretty short notice. I have . . . plans."

"Well, break 'em," Cecilia said confidently. "It's party time. Who else should we invite? They said you could have fifty people. Let's start the guest list. Me, Miya, Javier, Griffin—"

"Jenna," I said firmly.

"Oh yeah, I didn't finish that story about Jenna's brother," Cecilia said. "So Delilah heard Sebastian's mother call him Sea Bass as a stupid nickname. So she got one of those fish things that you hang on your wall that sings Elvis songs or whatever. She told Sebastian to meet her in one of the empty dance rooms and she'd give him her first kiss."

I winced, but I knew there was no stopping her now.

"Then what?" Miya asked.

"Delilah picked the dance room with the one-way windows and

got our whole dance class to watch. Then she told him to close his eyes and he kissed the fish!!"

Ouch.

"That's kind of mean," Miya said.

I opened my mouth to agree with her but Cecilia talked first.

"Whatever," she said. "It was hilarious, especially afterward when the fish was set off and started singing Elvis. Delilah's always playing games with the guys who are in love with her. Like they really think they have a chance with her."

"Delilah and Shade are so hot together," Miya said.

"She has him wrapped around her little finger," Cecilia said. "Delilah told me this gossip reporter said she was going to do a story about Shade and Delilah. How cool would that be?"

I looked the other way. I bet the gossip reporter did a story, just not about Delilah. Shade had been spotted with an *America's Next Top Model* contestant, according to another site. So . . .

"Shade is totally whipped," Cecilia said. "But anyway, speaking of sea bass. Let's talk about this beach party. Avery, what's going to be on the menu? What's the music? What are we wearing? Let's do this thing right."

CHAPTER

31

I sat in my room that night, trying not to stress about how to pull off the beach party. I cheered myself up by reading a new interview with Marisa I'd found online. I had a lot to catch up on for Team Marisa. I also had a lot of schoolwork piling up. I'd bombed my chemistry test, I had to do my *Lord of the Flies* project, and a history paper coming up on great inventions of the twentieth century.

One of the great inventions of this past century was definitely the cell phone, I thought as mine rang.

"Hey," Jenna said. "Can I ask you a question?"

"Sure," I said, cutting and pasting the article to save to put on Team Marisa when I had time.

"Were you guys talking about my brother at lunch after I left?" Jenna asked.

"Oh, that," I groaned. "I tried to stop her, but Cecilia kept jumping in with the story of dance class. If it makes you feel any better, Miya called her out on being mean."

"Did you say anything?" Jenna asked.

"I . . . um . . . no, but . . . I did change the subject to the beach party," I said.

"Oh," Jenna said.

"Seriously, I didn't have a chance to stick up for him," I said. "And everyone forgot about it right after."

"No, they didn't," Jenna said quietly. "William was talking about it in math class, and everyone was cracking up, making kissy faces and fish faces at me. I think Sebastian, too, but he wouldn't talk about it when I asked him."

Oh.

"I'm sorry," I said. "Next time I'll say something."

"That would be great," Jenna said. "I just hate that it was all brought up again. People like Delilah and Cecilia just go along and trash everything in their path. I hate that they get away with it. I'm having flashbacks to Delilah in her little ballerina leotard, holding out a fish and laughing. Honestly, I think it's one reason Sebastian doesn't talk to girls."

"That sucks," I said. "It seriously sucks."

And then I made my decision.

"Hey, maybe karma will bite them on their Rich & Skinny butts, okay?"

We hung up. I closed out of my Team Marisa pages and went over to Princess of Gossip. And I posted.

NOT-SO-BLIND ITEM

What singer from a rock band was making out with a girl in the parking lot at the Constellation★ party? Notice that this girl has curly hair—and his girlfriend? She doesn't. Next time, this dude better take his cheating out of the light.

32

I didn't exactly get a good night's sleep. After I hit the post button on the Shade gossip, I almost changed my mind and deleted it. But I left it. I mean, both Shade and Delilah deserved what was coming to them, and besides, who would really know that it was Shade. While I thought my light/shade pun was kind of clever last night, I wasn't so sure about it in the morning.

I thought about the way I hadn't stuck up for Sebastian yesterday and . . . well. Now I felt like at least I did something. But still, I was a little nervous to face Cecilia, given that I'd just posted that about her sister's "loyal" boyfriend. So, I decided it would be better if I took the bus to school. Actually, it would have been best if I didn't go to school at all, since I hadn't gotten too far on my *Lord of the Flies* project and I was starting to fear the moment Schmitt called me for a private conference. Anyway, I left a message on Miya's cell not to come get me.

"Aren't you friends with Cecilia Singer?" a girl waiting at the bus stop asked me.

"Kinda," I nodded, and busied myself on my phone.

"You're so lucky," the girl said. "Did you know her sister goes out with the singer of a band?"

Yeah, thanks for sharing. I tried to smile politely at her, giving the "Please leave me alone" hint.

And then the white Jag convertible pulled up to the curb.

"Avery! What are you doing out here?" It was Miya. The front passenger seat was empty, and Cecilia, Griffin, and Javier were in the back.

"Didn't you get my voice mail?" I said. "It's okay. Go on without me."

"Are you crazy?" the girl said. "Cecilia Singer is in there! Get in the car!"

"You can sit in the front with me," Miya said.

I sighed and got into the front passenger seat. I turned around and saw Griffin, Javier, and Cecilia in the back. Cecilia was sitting on Javier's lap. Griffin rolled his eyes at me. I tried to give a little smile back.

"Watch out, Cecilia's on a rampage," Miya warned me.

Uh-oh.

"I'm trying to comfort her, but it's not working," Javier said.

"Listen to this one," Cecilia said, reading from her iPhone. "What singer is the subject of a not-so-blind item? Rumors of Shade from University of Hard's cheating has been on the DL. Could he be the subject of the rumor on Princess of Gossip?"

"That's ridonk," Miya said. "You said that Delilah and Shade were practically engaged."

"They are," Cecilia said. "Whoever this Princess of Gossip is, she's spreading her lies about the wrong person. I'm so pissed."

"Here, I'll give you a little shoulder massage to make you feel better," Javier cooed.

"The only thing that will make me feel better is when this rumor is exposed as a lie," Cecilia said.

Uh-oh. What had seemed like a good idea last night . . . not so much now.

"Are you sure it's a lie?" I asked cautiously.

"Of course!" Cecilia said. "Shade doesn't cheat on Delilah. If anything, she cheats on him."

"What?" Miya said.

"Nothing," Cecilia said. "Disregard that. The point is, this Princess of Gossip site started a rumor that's so untrue it's like libel or slander or whatever. Miya, your mom's a lawyer. Tell her to sue this Princess of Gossip."

Gulp.

"Well, even if it's the truth, I hate those gossip sites," Griffin said. "I mean, what's cool about tearing celebrities down? Don't these gossip people have their own lives?"

Oookay. Can we please change this subject fast? I shifted uncomfortably in my seat.

"It's not very well written either," Griffin said. "I mean, 'out of the light'? That's kind of stupid."

Hey, I was slightly insulted here. It was late at night and I was tired. It's gossip, I wasn't writing for a Newbery Medal. Jeez. I stayed silent while we pulled into the parking lot. I would just lie low today. As I got out of the car, I noticed Sebastian's car pulling in. Great. I could tell Jenna what I did last night for them, and hoped I'd get a little support.

"Jenna!" I called out, waving.

Jenna turned around and looked at me. Then she looked mad. What? Oh, shoot. She saw me getting out of Miya's car and I must have looked like I was walking in with them even after they spread the Sea Bass story.

"Jenna, wait!" I called out.

"Avery, you can cheer me up," Cecilia said, taking my arm. "Let's talk about your party this weekend."

"Um, I have to talk to Jenna about . . . my homework. It's really important," I said, and in one swift move I detached from her. "I'll catch up with you guys later."

I hurried ahead and caught up with Jenna and Sebastian at their car.

"That is so not what it looked like," I said.

"It looked like you were riding to school with Cecilia and company even after the horrible things she did to me and my brother just yesterday," Jenna said. "Look, I'm really not into this drama."

"Jenna," I said. "Just wait until Cecilia is out of sight and then look at something. Sebastian, can you get the Internet up for me?"

He handed me his iPod.

"Hey, Avery, I went to the post office box," Sebastian said. "A couple of the letters were priority, so I brought them. Hang on, I left them in my backseat."

He went back to his car. And I went online to the Princess of Gossip site. I handed the iPod to Jenna.

I watched as she read the story. And then her face suddenly lit up.

"You did *not*."

"Yup, I did."

She handed the iPod back to her brother and grabbed my arm. She half dragged me to the other side of the car.

"I can't believe you posted that," Jenna said. "What if you get in trouble?"

"Look, we have a picture to prove it's true," I said. "So even if they sued me it doesn't matter because it's true. And Shade knows it, so he won't sue."

"Not about that," Jenna said. "Does Cecilia know? Does Delilah know about this?"

"Um, yeah," I said. "I tried to take the bus but Miya picked me up anyway. It was an extremely uncomfortable car ride. Cecilia is pissed."

"Oh my gosh," Jenna said. "Wow."

"I know." I looked around. "But we have to act normal, okay?"

Jenna nodded.

Sebastian came over, oblivious to what was going on around him. "I have a couple letters for you," he said. "There are some packages, but I'll get those to you later unless you want to put them in your locker."

"No, I'll have to get them later," I said.

"Later," Sebastian said, walking toward the school. Jenna and I followed him slowly as we thumbed through the envelopes.

"Ooh! Here's one from Christian Palandro," Jenna said. "Open it!"

I opened the crisp white envelope.

"Dear Princess of Gossip," I read aloud. "We've been enjoying your site and would like to send you another of my designs from next season. It will arrive tomorrow. I hope you like it. Sincerely, Christian."

"Dude!" Jenna said. "You are so lucky. You know what this means?"

"What?" I asked her.

"You are going to be looking sweet for your beach party," Jenna said.

"Oh yeah, I can wear it Friday!" I said. "Yay!"

"I have no clue what I'm wearing," Jenna said. "Can you go shopping today? I can get Sebastian to drive us. I got my stepfather's credit card, and I saw this adorable Tracy Reese dress I could wear Friday. I could use your opinion."

"I totally would," I said. "But really, I'm dying. I have so much homework and I'm getting behind in everything. Can you take a picture and send it to me from the store?"

"Okay," Jenna said.

"Wait, when you're there can you see if they have any earrings on sale?" I asked. "I guess silver would match any dress, right? I'm thinking about wearing my hair up on Friday."

The warning bell rang and we ran into the school building.

33

WHICH FORMERLY UNKNOWN REDHEAD IS ABOUT TO THROW THE PARTY OF HER LIFE? TOO BAD SHE'S SO NERVOUS, SHE'S ABOUT TO THROW UP INSTEAD.

Chill," Jenna said as she watched me anxiously pacing around the hotel suite. "You have a great hotel suite, the pool, the beach nearby. You picked the music, the food. You have celebrities. You even have swag bags."

Thanks to Jenna and her brilliant idea. She'd sent off an evite to a couple companies that sent things to Princess of Gossip before and we'd gotten overnight shipments for swag bags for everyone, containing a new CD, a magazine subscription, a candle, and some chocolates.

"Relax, Avery," Jenna said. "Look at this place. It's just like Marisa World come to life. It's going to be awesome."

"I *wish* it was a virtual party," I said.

If I was only planning a Marisa World party, it would be so easy. I wouldn't have to worry about my outfit. If the background didn't work, I could have Sebastian just zap it into something new. Jenna could make any celebrity guest I wanted.

Tonight I had invited a celebrity guest: Beckett Howard. I wasn't sure if I was ready for mixing my worlds, but everyone else assumed I would, so I went ahead and did it. And he'd RSVP'd yes.

I started to feel sweaty and faint. Add to that every popular person in school and I was definitely feeling the pressure. The room phone rang, startling both of us.

"Hello?" I answered.

"We have a delivery arriving at your room, Miss Gossip," the hotel staff person said. Just then, the doorbell buzzed.

"That's probably the toothbrush and toothpaste I asked them to bring me," Jenna said. "I asked for an extra for you, since you're the one who will be needing the fresh breath for your kissable Beckett Howard. Take note, there's a little dish of Altoids in the bathroom, too."

The thought of kissing Beckett again, surrounded by people from school, while hosting the party was officially freaking me out. I needed to get some air. I went outside to the private patio area, which was set up with buffet tables with black tablecloths and pink and silver plates and cups piled high. Servers in white jackets were setting up the food.

You could walk past the patio to a private beach area. There was a hot tub bubbling, and although there was no way in heck I was going to put on a bathing suit, I knew others might. A pathway led to the small private pool.

It did look amazing.

"It wasn't the toothbrushes!" Jenna said. "Come see what they brought."

I walked in to see a giant vase of violet and white flowers.

"They're gorgeous," I said. I opened the envelope.

"Can't wait for the party! Love, Beckett."

"Oh my gosh!" I said. "They're from Beckett! He said 'Love, Beckett'!"

"That's so romantic," Jenna said, sitting down in the chair at the desk. "You are so lucky."

"Do I look okay?" I asked her. I checked myself in the mirror. My hair was down, with a slight curl. Whatever the salon had sprayed on me was holding back the frizz even from the ocean humidity.

I was wearing a Christian Palandro, of course. This one was a white silk halter dress that fell just above my knees. It had shimmery pailletes around the neck, which Jenna helpfully pointed out meant large sequins. I wore silver gladiator-style sandals (borrowed from Jenna's closet) that had inset emerald-color fake jewels, and silver earrings with tiny emeralds (Target . . . shh). And I also had a silver necklace that had been given to Princess of Gossip by some place called the Jewels Boutique.

"You look fab," Jenna said. "That dress is so cute and beachy. Do you know how huge it is you have your own Christian Palandro dress? Two of them?"

"I know, it's crazy," I said, and smiled at myself in the mirror. "You look really pretty, too."

She did. She was wearing a swirly print abstract slip dress in raspberry and orange. She had gold bangles on her arm and her hair was down and wavy.

The room phone rang.

"I got it," Jenna said, and leaned over to grab it off the desk. "Hello? No, this is— Oh. Uh-huh. Hang on."

Jenna covered the mouthpiece on the phone and hissed.

"There's someone who wants to drop off something to the Princess of Gossip," she said. "One of the sponsors."

"Uh, can they just leave it at the front desk?" I said. "Or can they have a hotel person send it up?"

Jenna asked and then shook her head no.

"They said they need someone from the Princess of Gossip team to sign for it," she said.

"I don't know," I said worriedly. "If we let them come up here, they could blow my cover. The hotel doesn't know it's me, they only know Princess of Gossip. Our friends only think it's me and can't know about Princess of Gossip. Crap, crappity crap. I can't leave here, I'm the host."

"Look, how about I'll go to the lobby," Jenna said. "I can sign for the package and keep whoever it is away from the party."

"Great," I said. "Wish me luck."

Jenna saluted me and walked out the door. I took a deep breath and looked around at the empty suite, which hopefully wouldn't be empty for long. The music was loud in the background, but I needed a minute to pull myself together. It was time for my theme song. I clicked my iPhone to "The Girl Who."

> *They say I'm this*
> *They say I'm that*
> *I'm nothing special*
> *I just fall flat—*

Tonight I was not "nothing special." When I was living in Ohio, if you'd told me I would be throwing a free beach party, in a free designer dress, for guests Beckett Howard and the popular clique at my L.A. school, I would have laughed.

But it was true, and it was about to happen. And then the first guest walked in the door.

34

"Avery?"

"Oh, hey!" I said, turning around to see Griffin. "Welcome to the party. You're the first person here."

"I know, I'm sorry I'm early," he said. "But I ran into Sebastian at the gas station and he was trying to call you to say he was running late, but he'd be bringing the things you needed. I told him I'd let you know your phone wasn't working."

"I didn't get any calls." I frowned, checking my iPhone, then realized I'd accidentally turned the ringer off. Figures.

"Hey, this place is sweet," he said, looking around. "If I'm in the way, I can leave and come back."

"No, I could use some company," I said. "I'm kind of nervous."

"I brought you these," Griffin said. He handed me a small bunch of flowers.

"Pink roses!" I said, smiling. "They're my favorite."

"Really? I'd pretend I knew that," Griffin said. "But I guess they look pretty weak compared to those."

He pointed to Beckett's huge bouquet.

"No, yours are pretty, too. So where's Cecilia and everybody?" I changed the subject.

"They're on their way in the limo," Griffin said. "I felt like driving myself since, well, I got a new car."

"No way!" I said. "Congratulations! You got your own car?"

"Yeah," Griffin said. "It's not that great. But it's mine."

"Where is it?" I asked him. "I want to see it!"

"Well, you can probably see it out over the balcony," Griffin said.

We went over to the balcony that looked out onto the parking lot. Griffin pointed to a small dark red car.

"Awesome!" I said. "It's cool."

"Nice lie," Griffin said. "It's an old car."

"Hey, it's your own," I said. "You've got freedom now. Trust me, I would be thrilled to have a car like that."

"That's nice to hear," Griffin said. "Cecilia called it the used-and-abused mobile, so I prefer your reaction. I did get my music system hooked up and it rocks," he said. "Feel free to give me some of your new music finds."

"Totally!" I said. "Wait till you hear some of the music tonight. I've got an iPod hooked up to a sweet system out there, and a CD player, too."

"Cool, can't wait," Griffin said.

I smiled at him. He smiled at me. I suddenly felt slightly awkward.

"Well, your guests are arriving," Griffin said, pointing over the railing.

A long white Hummer limo was pulling into a spot below us.

"Avery! Griffy!" Cecilia stepped out of the limo and spotted us. "Griffy, look who's here!"

Delilah slid out of the limo, too. I had a momentary ping. Cecilia looked hot in her cobalt beaded halter dress with a keyhole cutout neckline. But Delilah was smoking in her low-cut clingy top, mini-skirt, and spiky heels.

I didn't even look to see Griffin's reaction to that. I suddenly felt very underwhelming. I mean, Beckett Howard would take one look at them and—

"They look really nice," I blurted out.

"So do you," Griffin said.

"Oh, thanks." I blushed.

"You better go back inside and prepare to get your party started," Griffin said. "Don't be nervous, this place is amazing. It'll be great."

"Thanks," I said. I took a deep breath and walked back into the suite with him, then greeted everyone from the limo as they came through the door.

"This place rocks!" Miya said.

"It's pretty nice." Cecilia nodded. "But it's too quiet. Where's the music?"

"Oh yeah, we need to fix that," I said. "Griffin, can you please go put some music in?"

"Sure," he said.

"Delilah, why don't you help him," Cecilia said.

"Okay," Delilah said, following Griffin out to the patio. I heard her ask him, "Does she have any University of Hard?"

"Hey, look who's here!" Cecilia said. A bunch of people I recognized as seniors came in the door. Cecilia had helped me plan the guest list of see-and-be-seen people, so I was prepared not to know a lot of my guests tonight. Cecilia went up and gave them all air kisses.

"Hi, I'm Avery," I said nervously. "Let me know if you need anything."

"Yeah, can I have a Diet Coke?" one of the girls said. "I'm parched."

"She's not a waitress." Cecilia giggled. "It's her party."

Great.

"Food and drinks are on the patio," I said, pointing to the back.

Suddenly, the room got louder as some Arctic Monkeys started playing. More people I didn't know came in the door, but Cecilia was thrilled to see them.

"Hi!" I put on my best hostess smile. "I'm Avery."

Sebastian came in next, carrying an enormous box. He'd been in charge of picking up the gift bags, which had to be sent to a special place to get ribbons on them, according to the swag sponsor.

"I'm having a hilarious flashback," Sebastian said, grinning. "Your avatar at Marisa World greeting everyone. I almost expected a speech bubble to come out of your head saying 'Hi! Hi!' "

"Shh!" I said, looking around. "Don't say M World! Someone might hear you."

"Jenna says to tell you she's still waiting to get your package in the lobby," Sebastian said. "Where do you want this swag?"

"I want to save it for later," I said. "How about in the closet? Thanks."

"I have to get another box," he said. "I'll be back."

I watched as the place filled up with people from school. Most I recognized. Some I didn't. I went out to the patio and saw Cecilia, Javier, Miya, and Delilah standing around with drinks. Javier was eating a plate of food, and everyone was laughing at something he was saying. Griffin was nearby, mixing some music.

"Hey, you're good," I said to him. "You can be the official DJ. As long as you take my requests."

"I may not be Mark Ronson," he said. "But I have to be as good as that Kevin Webber, right? Maybe?"

"Definitely," I told him. "Do you have any 'Cold, Callous Wench'?"

He grinned at me, and then I felt a bump at my elbow.

"Good food, Avery!" Javier said. "Have a bite."

He held out a mini Kobe beef burger with gorgonzola cheese.

"I'll have some later," I said, waving him off. I was starving but I'd eaten two Altoids and I wasn't risking the breath.

After I said hi to a few more people, I stood off to the side and breathed a sigh of relief. People seemed to be having a good time. I felt one of my phones buzz in my pocket. I pulled it out and saw a text from Jenna.

BECKETT IS HERE!

Beckett was here! I tried to stay calm. Should I go inside and meet him? I didn't want to look too obvious, like I was waiting for him and knew he was coming. Plus, to be honest, I didn't really know anyone inside the suite. I'd rather have Beckett find me out here, laughing away with Cecilia and everyone, looking cool and in. I went over and joined the group and tried to look cool and in.

"Avery!" Cecilia suddenly lit up. "Beckett Howard is here."

"Oh, really?" I said, casually turning toward him. Yes, I was smooth, and oh so casual about all this. At least I hoped I appeared that way. Inside, I was shaky.

"Bring him over and introduce us!" Miya said. "He is so hawt!"

And he was. Beckett was wearing a blue button-down shirt that highlighted his blue eyes, his tan, and his blond hair. Everyone turned and stared at him.

"Hi!" I squeaked.

He leaned in and gave me a kiss on the cheek. I knew everyone was looking at me and watching the kiss. And the music magically mixed into Chris Brown's "Kiss Kiss" song. I turned around and looked at Griffin, who shrugged at me innocently. Griffin was a wiseass.

"I love the flowers," I said to him. "They're so pretty."

"So are you, babe," he said.

Awww. That was so—

"Hi! I'm Miya! Avery's friend!" Miya was gaping.

"I'm Beckett," he said, smiling.

"Do you want to meet more of Avery's friends?" Miya asked. "They're dying to say hi."

She gestured toward everyone. I nearly snorted when I saw Cecilia, looking casual and trying to pretend she didn't put Miya up to this.

Beckett looked at me.

"I'll introduce you," I said. I brought him over to everyone. "This is Cecilia, her sister Delilah, Javier, and that's Griffin on the music."

I watched to see Beckett's reaction, especially to Delilah, who was absentmindedly playing with her hair, but he just smiled a friendly smile at everyone.

"Smile!" I heard the click of a camera and turned around to see William behind us, with of course Cam behind him.

"Babe, I think paparazzi followed you here," Beckett said.

"No, that's just William and Cam," I said. "Paparazzi wannabes."

"Ah, wa-bes," Beckett said. "That's what I call them. Should I throw them out and wait for the real paps?"

"No, he's invited, he goes to my school. If they annoy you, just

let me know. I know from experience they can be annoying, but they're harmless."

"Yo!" William shouted. "Stand close together, you two, and give me a photo op. Make out or something."

"I'll stop him from doing that," I assured Beckett.

"So, who else is here?" Beckett asked. "Anyone I know?"

Um. I didn't exactly have any famous friends. Nobody who ran in his circle.

"Hey, Candee-Amber Lee's here," he said. "I didn't know you were friends with her."

She was? I turned around to look and oh my gosh! Lee was here! She had her hair up in a loose bun and was wearing a teal and green crocheted dress. She looked gorgeous. Where'd she come from?

"Avery, you'll have Beckett all to yourself later." Cecilia came over and linked his arm with hers. "Beckett, come over and tell us about the time you and Paris danced on the table at Les Deux and the paper called you a celebutoy? I want all the deets."

Ugh.

Cecilia led Beckett over to her group while I went over to say hi to Lee, who was standing by herself near the door.

"Hi! Remember me?" I said. "Avery?"

"Hi!" Lee said. "Thanks so much for having me!"

"You're welcome?" I said, still wondering how she'd gotten here. "I can introduce you to some people," I said. "I mean, not that people won't want to talk to you anyway. Of course, because you're you. I mean, they just haven't recognized you yet."

"Trust me, that's a good thing." She laughed. "They can all stay focused on Beckett Howard. Did you see where Sebastian went?"

"Sebastian?" I asked blankly.

"Oh, there you are," Sebastian said, coming out to the patio. "I thought you said you were going outside, so I went out front."

"Good thing he has a GPS on his Sidekick or he'd never find his way around," Lee said, rolling her eyes.

"Wait, are you two here together?" I asked.

"Yeah, you don't mind that I brought her, do you?" Sebastian asked. "You said I could invite anyone."

"Of course not. I just didn't realize you guys were still in touch," I said. "You haven't mentioned her."

Lee laughed.

"Hello?" Sebastian said. "Who do you think I've been texting and meeting at the Apple Store."

"You said her name was Vida Verdad," I said. "Your post—Vida Segunda girlfriend?"

"Vida Verdad *is* Lee. In Spanish, *vida verdad* means 'real life,'" Sebastian said. "I wasn't going to use her real name around my parents; they'd be all up in my business."

"Oh my gosh!" I said. "I thought you made her up like Vida Segunda to fool your parents! She's really Candy-Amber Lee?"

"Yeah," he said. "I do have a life that's not online, you know."

Sebastian reached over and held Lee's hand. Well! I guess so!

"Does Jenna know about this?" I asked.

"No," Sebastian said. "But now she will. I'm sure she'll find a way to blackmail me about it."

"I think she's going to be too shocked for that," I said. "Well. So. I'll leave you two alone to. You know. Whatever."

"Hey, I got more info on the next generation of iPods," Lee was saying to Sebastian as I walked away.

Wowza! Lee was here with Sebastian, I couldn't even begin to process that. I left them alone and walked over toward the patio, where a few people were making a makeshift dance floor and starting to dance.

I looked at Beckett, who was trapped between Cecilia and Miya, with William taking pictures. He made a little face at me and mouthed, "Help!"

That put a smile on my face. I went over to rescue him. Just then, the music changed to a fast song. I recognized it from one of the CDs that a hopeful had sent to Princess of Gossip. I smiled, thinking how I could email that singer's publicist back and say that her song was played at a Princess of Gossip party.

"Let's dance!" Miya whooped and grabbed my hand. She grabbed Cecilia's hand and we formed a chain. Beckett grabbed my other hand and a couple other people joined us.

"This one's for our hostess, Avery Johnson," Griffin announced loudly in a DJ voice. "All friends of Avery hit the dance floor!"

People applauded for me. I blushed. We started dancing in a circle to Fergie. Then Beckett jumped into the circle and started dancing, with us dancing around him. He turned to me and did a little grind, totally embarrassing me. Everyone was cheering us on with "Go Beckett"s and "Go Avery"s. I loved it.

This was what L.A. was supposed to be.

Then the music slowed down and switched to Marisa's "Truthful."

"Oh, I love this song!" I said.

"Cecilia, will you dance with me?" William asked her.

"Go on, Cecilia," Beckett said. "Dance with the poor guy."

"Ick," Cecilia said poutily, but she wasn't going to disregard Beckett's command. William didn't seem to care about the attitude, just that he was holding his muse in a slow dance.

"May I have this dance?" Beckett asked me, and did a cheesy

bow. He put his arms around my waist and I put mine around his neck. We swayed back and forth.

"Isn't Marisa awesome?" I sighed, as I listened to the words. "Be true, be true to what makes you happy."

This night was making me happy. I sighed with contentment.

"I don't know," Beckett said. "Who's Marisa?"

"A singer who means a lot to me," I said. I closed my eyes and thought about how Marisa had been the one who started this all.

We danced past Miya, who was eating a shrimp kebab. She gave me a thumbs-up sign with her other hand.

"I hope my friends aren't embarrassing," I said.

"Where's your friend Jenna?" he asked. "Did you two have an LC/Heidi situation?"

"Oh, crap! I totally forgot about Jenna!" I blurted out. She was probably still in the lobby, waiting to intercept the sponsor. I needed to check what was going on in case there was trouble.

"I need to go get Jenna," I said. "Sorry to interrupt the dance. I'll be right back."

"No, no, I'm good," he said. "Go ahead."

I made my way through the crowd of people and into the suite. I went out and down the hall as fast as I possibly could. Then I slowed down to look casual.

"Heyyyy!" I said when I spotted Jenna standing in the front lobby.

"Oh, good, I almost thought you forgot about me or something." Jenna laughed. "I didn't miss anything, did I?"

"Of course not!" I said guiltily. "The party's just picking up. You know what, I'll just tell the lobby person to text me when the sponsor arrives."

"So how's it going with you and Beckett?" Jenna asked as we walked down the hallway to my room.

"I think good," I said, smiling. "We've been dancing. He's been charming. He looks hot."

"Dude, I wish I'd seen the looks on everyone's faces when Beckett came in the door! Did anyone flip out?"

"Yup," I said proudly. "And did you know there's another celebrity here?" I wondered what she'd think when she saw her brother and Lee.

"No," Jenna said. "Who?"

"It's—"

Jenna opened the door to the suite and Paramore came on full blast.

"Avery!" some girl squealed. "Awesome party!"

"Wow, it's rocking!" Jenna yelled over the noise. "I'm starving. Is the food ready?"

"Yeah," I said. "Let's go get you some."

We went out to the back patio and made our way toward the food table.

"Oh, don't look. Beckett's talking to Delilah." Jenna winced.

I looked over to see how much flirtation was going on, but Beckett saw me and waved me over. Phew. I motioned I'd be over in a second.

"Yummy," Jenna said, filling a plate with appetizers. I was tempted to have something myself, but now that I knew there was kissing involved tonight, I was uberparanoid about my breath. And spilling something on my white Christian Palandro. Jenna put some salmon sashimi on her plate.

"I think the Singers have had enough time with Beckett," Jenna said. "Let's break that up."

We walked over to Beckett, who was standing with Cecilia and Delilah.

"Jenna!" Beckett leaned over and gave Jenna a kiss on the cheek. "I'm glad Avery remembered you!"

"What, did Avery forget about her?" Cecilia snorted.

"You forgot about me?" Jenna turned to me and asked.

"No! Of course not!" I said. "I just—"

Jenna looked skeptical. Before I could explain myself, Miya came running over to us.

"Avery! We just asked Griffin to play more dance music."

"You've been dancing already?" Jenna asked me. "How much of this party did I miss?"

"The 'Friends of Avery' circle dance was fun," Beckett said. I saw Jenna react to that. "I thought you two had an LC/Heidi fight going on. Glad to see it was just that Avery forgot about you." Er. Thanks a lot, Beckett.

"Oh, Avery and Beckett shared a romantic slow song," Cecilia added. "That song should be your new song, Avery. What was it called?"

" 'Truthful,' by Marisa," Beckett said proudly. "Avery told me it was one of her favorites."

"You already danced to Marisa?" Jenna said quietly. "You really did forget about me."

"It got a little crazy," I said. "I was hostessing and—"

"Dancing away, apparently," Jenna said. "With your Friends of Avery."

I couldn't really look at her.

"Jenna, I—"

"Look, I'm going to go find my brother," Jenna said. "You go hostess and I'll be right back."

"He's with Lee," I said. "I saw them out in the hallway."

"Lee?" Jenna asked.

"Yeah, he brought her as a date," I said. "That's what I was going to tell you—"

"Sure you were," Jenna muttered. "After you remembered I existed."

Jenna stomped off toward the door.

She didn't say anything, but walked out the door. I sighed and followed her out. Sebastian and Avery were over near the elevators that went up to the tower levels, talking to a woman I didn't recognize.

"Jenna!" Lee said, coming over and giving her a hug.

"You're here with my brother?" Jenna asked her. "Have you two been hanging out or something?"

"Well, yeah," Lee said, looking confused. "You know that. You've texted me a couple times? I'm Vida."

"I thought Vida was some virtual girl or in Egypt or something!" Jenna said. "I didn't know it was you!"

"Oh, gosh," Lee said. "I hope you don't mind I'm seeing your brother."

"It is a little shocking," Jenna said.

"I think you and Sebastian are great together," I said, trying to warm things up a little. Didn't work. Jenna shot me a dirty look.

"I'm going to the girls' room," she said. "I need a break." She walked to the ladies' room at the end of the hall.

"Is she okay?" Lee asked. "I hope I didn't upset her."

"No, I think I did," I said. "When she cools off, I'll talk to her."

"While we're waiting, come here," Lee said, walking us over to where Sebastian was talking to the mystery woman. "I want to introduce you to someone. This is Avery. And this is my publicist, Monica."

The woman had black straight hair chopped in blunt bangs that almost covered her eyes. I felt like I'd seen her before. It took me a minute and then I placed her. She was the woman from the T-Mobile launch party that had taken the picture of me, with Haley Lane and Kevin Webber. The picture that started all of this.

"Aren't you Haley Lane's assistant?" I blurted out.

"Me?" she laughed. "Close, I'm her publicist. And do you look familiar to me?"

"Yeah, we met at the T-Mobile launch party," I said.

"Yup, Monica had to babysit me that night and make sure I stuck around," Lee said, laughing. "I hate those parties. She's lucky most of her clients love them and had a good time that night."

"Like Haley Lane!" I said. "Remember, she was there? And we accidentally discovered Haley and Kevin kissing, and you said that they'd have to go public as boyfriend and girlfriend! And then I took a picture of them and you said I could go public with it?"

"Oh yes!" Monica said. "You're the gossip blogger who's friends with Perez Hilton! And now you're here, so you must be friends with the Princess of Gossip. That was perfect timing when we met at T-Mobile."

"Monica!" Lee stopped laughing. "You didn't."

"Didn't what?" I asked, confused.

"Oh, Lee, it was an ideal opportunity," Monica said. "She said she was a gossip blogger. And it worked. She got that picture out to Perez, *Us Weekly*, Princess of Gossip, all the big ones."

Sebastian and I made eye contact and looked away.

"I hate that game," Lee said. "I stay as far away from it as possible. Worst part of the business."

"Gossip bloggers?" I cringed.

"That, too," Lee said. "But having fauxmances. Like Haley and Kevin. That was so obvious, Monica."

"Their fauxmance?" I asked. "What are you talking about?"

"Fake romance," Lee said. "Haley and Kevin are both Monica's clients. She has them fake-date for publicity. And it worked, their pictures are everywhere."

"They're not really dating?" I asked.

"I can't tell you, you're a gossip blogger," Monica said.

"She's not a gossip blogger." Sebastian laughed. "She has a fansite for an artist named Marisa. I help her with it."

"Ah, then see? We all stretch the truth, don't we?" Monica said. "Avery pretended she was a gossip blogger and I fell for it."

I tried not to blush.

"Since you're not a gossip blogger, then the truth is that Haley and Kevin had never met before that night," Monica said. "Haley was getting to be a bit of a free spirit with different boys, and I was concerned about her reputation. And Kevin has a new album coming out so they're perfect together. It would help if they liked each other but c'est la vie."

My head was whirling. I'd been set up to take that picture. Haley and Kevin were only fake-dating and I'd broken their fauxmance on Princess of Gossip. And it hit me. Princess of Gossip was based on a lie.

"Is everything in Hollywood a fauxmance?" I asked.

"Of course not," Monica said. "Stars really do meet, sparks fly and the romance is real. Other times, sure, it's an act."

"I'm Monica's worst client, because I won't play that game," Lee teased. "I only have real—and unpublicized—romances."

She and Sebastian looked at each other and smiled.

"I do have some great clients right now. I also represent the Cruz and Perth romance," Monica said proudly. "They're fake—breaking up this weekend. They should be screaming at each other at Urth right about now. That should get some front-page attention for sure."

Cruz and Perth, too?

"I . . . I . . . need to go to the girls' room," I said. My head was spinning. I was trying to process the fact that Princess of Gossip was based entirely on fake romances. Not that I didn't know they existed. Just that I felt really . . . really naive.

I pushed in the girls' room door. Jenna was standing at the mirror, her eyes red.

"I need to tell you something," I said to her.

"Okay," Jenna said, crossing her arms in front of her. "I'm listening."

"I just found out some serious celebrity gossip," I said.

"*That's* what you wanted to tell me?" Jenna said. "I thought you were going to apologize for forgetting about me."

"No! I mean, I'm going to do that, too," I said. "I'm just freaking out about what I just found out about Haley and Kevin—"

"Bad timing," Jenna said, pushing past me to the door. "I'm just not interested, Princess of Gossip." Just then, Miya stuck her head in the door.

"Jenna, Cecilia says to take this to the limo." She held out a shawl. "She's warm enough."

"Why me?" Jenna asked.

"Cecilia said Avery said you are working the front door," Miya said. "Here's a dollar for a tip."

"I'm *supposed* to be a guest here," Jenna said, looking hurt and angry.

"Of course you are—" I protested, but Miya had tossed the shawl at Jenna by then.

"You told people I work for you? I'm over this."

Jenna took off out the door and back over to where Sebastian and Lee were talking. Monica wasn't in sight. I started to follow Jenna over, but William came over and blocked me.

"Hey, one of the servers tipped me off that there was a celebrity in the lobby!" William said, looking around. "Where? All I see is Sebastian and some girl."

"That's just his girlfriend," I said. "Nobody at all."

"I'm going to look around," William said. "I smell a scoop somewhere. Cam, follow me."

Shoot, I didn't want him to recognize Lee or get her on camera. I'd just have to explain it to Jenna and make it up later.

"I saw someone who I think is famous," I improvised, gesturing to the guys to follow me back to the suite. "But she went back toward the party. Let's go find her."

"Who do you think it is?" William asked. "I'm hoping it's one of Beckett Howard's ex-girlfriends coming to cause a scene because he's here."

"Thanks a lot," I said. "That would suck for my party and also for me."

"It's all the nature of the biz." William shrugged. "Scandals create stars for us paparazzi. Imagine the buzz you'd get if you got into a catfight with like an Olsen twin or something."

Yeah, that's what I needed about now.

"If you want your party to really get buzz, someone should go all Paris Hilton," he said. "Ask Beckett. He's a master of going out with girls who know how to work it. You better do something wild or you're going to lose his attention."

"Beckett likes me because I'm a real person," I said. "I wouldn't want that kind of attention. I mean anyone can act skanky and get attention for that, right? Doesn't it mean more if you get attention for being yourself? Beckett has learned that lesson, that's why he's here with me."

I looked for Beckett and found him over by the DJ setup, where her, Cecilia, Delilah, and Miya were talking to Griffin.

"Hey, Avery, how's my spinning?" Griffin asked me cheerfully.

"It's very Ronsonesque," I said. "I'm impressed."

"Your music selection is great," he said. "That helps."

"Griffin, can I make a request?" Delilah asked us. "University of Hard's new song, 'Dress-Up Games.'"

"You like University of Hard?" Beckett asked her. "That guy Shade was at the Constellation★ party last week."

"That wasn't Shade," Delilah said. "He was at rehearsal that night with me, but went home early with a headache."

I elbowed Beckett and gave him a look that said stop talking.

"No, it was Shade from University of Hard," Beckett insisted. "Remember, Avery, how you said you saw him macking on some chick in the parking lot?"

"Um, no," I said, giving him the look.

"Yes, you did. You said Shade is at it again with some curly-haired girl," he said. "And his girlfriend doesn't have curly hair."

Beckett laughed. And Delilah looked at me.

"Avery, tell her it's not true," Cecilia demanded.

I winced. "I'm sorry, it's true. I did see that."

Delilah burst into tears. "I'm so stupid," Delilah cried. "I even brought him Advil the next morning for his headache." She stormed over to an area by the gate to the beach to cry in private.

"Nice job." Cecilia shot me a look, then went after her sister.

"Shade is Delilah's boyfriend," I told a confused Beckett.

"Oops," Beckett said, "My bad."

"It's not your fault," I sighed. "It's happened to me before." I looked over at Cecilia and Delilah. I would try to make things better, but I didn't know how. Then I saw Jenna walk the outskirts of the party and past the Singers. She opened the gate and headed toward the beach.

Oh, good. I could go explain things to Jenna and make it right with her, at least. I opened the gate to the beach and walked out to the sand.

"Hey," I said when I caught up to her. "Look, I'm sorry. I'm really sorry I left you in the lobby during the party."

Jenna was quiet.

"Come on, I'm a terrible party hostess," I said. "I admit it. I'm sorry I forgot about you."

"And . . . ?" Jenna prompted.

"And, um," I said. "I don't know. And what?"

"Any more apologies?" she said.

"Um, for what?"

"Well," Jenna said, crossing her arms. "I was in the lobby, being your slave as usual. You've been treating me like I'm your personal assistant or something. Jenna, go get this. Jenna, go do that. Like I'm nobody and just there to do things for you."

"I didn't mean to—"

"Like when you got your Christian Palandro dress, and you were all like help me get dressed, how do I look? Buy me earrings when you go find something to wear. You, you, you."

Ouch.

"You've changed," Jenna said. "Maybe that sounds stupid because I haven't known you that long. Maybe this *is* the real you."

"Look, I worked hard to pull this all off," I said. "I made Princess of Gossip and Team Marisa and all of this so that we can have this party."

"See, there you go," Jenna said. "I, I, I. I know that Princess of Gossip and Marisa World are yours, but if you haven't noticed, I've worked my butt off on them, too."

"I know that. And I appreciate—" I tried to explain but she cut me off.

"At first you did, but now you just take everything that comes with it. I worked really hard, I took the pictures, I made the avatars. Gawd, I practically started Princess of Gossip with you with my party pictures and talking you into it. It's not like I want credit, but everything good that comes with it, you take right away. Now it's all about you."

"But now we both get to celebrate," I said. "We both get to enjoy what we did with this party and have fun."

"Yeah, it's been a blast for me!" Jenna snorted. "You forget me and leave me in the lobby. And every time you blow me off, your so-called date hits on me."

"What?" I laughed. "Why are you joking like that?"

"I'm not joking," she said. "I'm sorry to break it to you this way, but Beckett's been totally hitting on me."

"Why would he hit on *you*?" I asked. "You must have misunderstood him. He was being nice because you're my friend."

"Of course, the only reason anyone would be nice to me is because I'm *your friend*," Jenna said. "Maybe that's the case with Cecilia, who just uses you anyway. But Beckett Howard is hitting on me."

"Okay, now you're going too far. Maybe you're jealous of me and Beckett," I said. "I would be, too, if I were you. But—"

"You think I'm saying that because I'm jealous of you two?" Jenna screamed. "Oh my Gawd! You are so into yourself!"

She threw her hands up in the air.

"Look, I shouldn't have said it like that," I said. "I just meant I think you misunderstood. Come on."

"Ooh, catfight! Meow!"

I whirled around to see Cecilia and Miya right behind me.

"Sorry to interrupt this juicy fight," Cecilia continued. "But you're needed on the patio, Avery."

"We're not fighting," I said.

"We *are* fighting," Jenna said. "Avery was just saying how much fun we have together. Except I haven't had any fun with you in a while. For one thing, you're always ordering me around. And for another, you're always blowing me off for other people."

She looked pointedly at Cecilia and Miya.

"Ouch," Cecilia said sarcastically. "I wish I could watch this reality show in progress, but you're really needed on the patio, Avery."

"I can't come now," I said.

"I think you'd better," Cecilia said. "The hotel people are here looking for the person whose party it is."

Oh, crap.

"But they're asking for a 'princess'?" Miya added.

Crap crap crap.

"Are you really a princess?" Miya asked eagerly. "That explains why Beckett Howard is going out with you! And how you get all of this stuff! Oh my gosh, what country? Is it someplace in Europe, like Genovia?"

"Did you hear her? The hotel people want to talk to the *princess*," I said to Jenna, lowering my voice. "What do I do?"

"I don't know." Jenna shrugged. "It's all yours. You're the princess."

Oh, boy. I was on my own.

"Okay, I'll be back," I said.

"Oh, no worries. I'll stay and comfort Jenna," Cecilia said. "I already had to help my sister through Avery's crushing deception. Jenna, I think we're all learning that Avery isn't what she appears to be."

"I know! She's a princess!" Miya said.

"Shut up, she is so not a princess," Cecilia was saying.

I walked up to the patio, my heart totally pounding. And standing near the food, there was a man in a hotel uniform, and two women in business suits standing with him.

"Hi," I said, trying to smile. "Can I help you?"

"I'm the hotel manager. We're looking for the host of this party," he said.

"Well, I think she arranged to be anonymous, right?" I said. "So, she sent me to ask if there was a problem. I'm her, um, intern."

"Oh, you're the intern to the Princess of Gossip?" one of the ladies said, too loudly. "I'm Deborah from the hotel chain. We're sponsoring this event for her. I'd love to meet her and ask if everything was to her liking."

Uh-oh.

"I know she loves it. I just don't think she knew anyone was coming to check up on it," I said. "When she turned in the certificate, she was told she could remain anonymous."

"Obviously she didn't expect anyone to check up on it," the younger woman said in a snotty way. "I'm Suzi from the West Boutique. We donated that necklace you're wearing. And while I can't deny it looks lovely with your dress, we expected it to be on the Princess of Gossip. Not her teenage intern."

I fingered the necklace nervously.

"Well, she can be anonymous to the public," Deborah said. "But as sponsors, we obviously would like the opportunity to check on the event. This seems to be a rather young crowd."

"Oh, there's no alcohol," I quickly assured her.

"I don't care about that." Deborah waved like it was a nonissue. "I mean for our publicity purposes. Where are the celebrities? Where's Young Hollywood? Old Hollywood? Any Hollywood."

I was panicking. But at least I could provide a star for her.

"They're here!" I said. "In fact, there's a celebrity now. See? It's Beckett Howard?"

I pointed to the corner where Beckett had been standing. And where Beckett was now standing with his arms wrapped around Delilah Singer. And his lips wrapped around Delilah Singer.

"Oh my gosh, Beckett is making out with her!" I blurted out in horror.

I leaned against the pole as I watched Beckett totally going at it with Delilah. I felt something in the pit of my stomach, watching as Beckett totally betrayed me. I thought he liked me. I thought he wanted a regular girl, which obviously Delilah so was not.

"Beckett Howard is always making out with girls at parties," Suzi said. "I'm surprised as the Princess of Gossip's intern you don't know this. He is nothing but a Z-list celebutoy looking for press with his antics."

"We gave Princess of Gossip our hotel for publicity. This looks like a high school afterparty," Deborah said. "I must insist I meet Princess of Gossip and request answers on how this is going to generate publicity."

I looked at her in horror. I looked at Beckett and Delilah in horror. I looked at Griffin and Miya, who were also looking at Beckett and Delilah in horror. Everything hit me at once. And I cracked.

"Okay, I confess!" I lowered my voice so nobody could hear. "I am the Princess of Gossip."

I flinched and waited for them to get upset. Freak out. Arrest me.

"Honey," Deborah said. "If your boss isn't here and you're covering for her, it's an admirable attempt. But I must demand to speak to the real Princess of Gossip."

"You don't understand!" I said. "I *am* Princess of Gossip! It's me!"

"Honey, Princess of Gossip is a music industry insider," Deborah said. "She's a professional, not a teenage high school girl nobody."

"But she is!" I said. "I'm not a music industry insider! I am a teenage high school girl nobody! *I'm Princess of Gossip!*"

They gaped at me. There was dead silence. And then I heard a whirring noise.

"I knew it!"

William was behind me, motioning to Cam to keep filming.

"I knew something was shady!" William said. "I said, who is this Avery to be getting all of this swag and attention. Your parents own a business making balloons and toothbrushes! And all your relatives are nobodies in Ohio! You have no connections! I knew it! And now I have my big reveal!"

"William," I said, horrified. "You can't tell anyone."

"Yeah, right, okay," William said. "This is my breakout moment as a paparazzo. I have the picture of the exact moment Princess of Gossip was outed. Can you please tilt your head a little to the left for me."

"William," I said, not tilting anything. "You can't share that."

"You're a gossip blogger," William said. "You know that it's all part of the business. Get the big get. I thought Beckett Howard kissing three girls tonight was a big break. But this is the moment I make it big!"

He ran over to where Griffin was at the DJ table.

"I have to go stop him!" I said.

"You can't run off that quickly, young lady," the hotel manager said, blocking me. "We need to speak with you."

But before he could say anything else, the music had stopped and someone else was speaking.

"Hey, everyone, I'm William Shaw and I wanted to thank our hostess tonight!"

People cheered for me. And, like it happened in slow motion, I heard William drop the bomb.

"Thank you, Avery, who also is known as Princess of Gossip!" William held his camera up and took pictures of the crowd. "Yes, that's right, she is the gossip blogger Princess of Gossip! The gossip blogger who claims she's a music industry insider but is really a high school nobody! You heard it here first, from William Shaw! Cam, is the tape rolling for my big moment?"

Griffin took William's arm.

"Dude," I heard him say. "Give it up."

"No, she is! Ask her! Avery, are you the Princess of Gossip?"

Everyone turned around and looked at me. I wasn't sure what they were thinking. I backed up, trying to think of a way out of this. And in the process bumped into somebody.

"Avery? What are you doing here?"

I spun around. And saw my parents standing and gaping at me.

"Mom? Dad? What are *you* doing here?" I asked them.

"We got this invitation," my mom said, confused. She held out the printout of my evite. I grabbed it and looked at the email address.

To: AJOHNSON

Oh my Gawd, somehow I had sent my father an evite by accident. I must have accidentally plugged in his AJohnson account instead of mine somewhere in the process. And they had actually shown up.

"I thought maybe I'd see Jen Stephanie," my dad said, looking around. "What a coincidence we're all at the same party. So, are there any good celebrity sightings?"

My dad looked around, and instead of celebrity sightings he saw the hotel manager and sponsors surrounding him and my mom, with grim expressions on their faces, looking for an explanation. I was doomed.

35

"You are obviously grounded," my mother said to me as we sat in the hotel lobby after the management had kicked everyone out of the suite. "And we are taking away your computer, except for schoolwork."

"I know," I said. Honestly, at this moment that was a relief. I didn't even want to know what was going to be said about me on the Internet.

Best-case scenario, it would all just fade away. My great hope was that Princess of Gossip fans would just wonder for a few days why I wasn't updating, and then they'd move on to the newest site. And my Team Marisa fans would think I had the flu or something, and someone who was more worthy would start a new site for her.

And we would, say, move back to Ohio, where I wouldn't have to face any of these people again.

"What were you thinking, Avery?" my dad said for the billionth time since they'd gotten the surface story of Princess of Gossip. "No, obviously you weren't thinking. Pretending to be a gossip columnist? Sneaking off to parties without our permission? Throwing parties without our permission? Deceiving and misrepresenting yourself?"

I cringed. Everything he said was painfully accurate.

"You are returning everything you were given when you were masquerading as Princess of Gossip," my mom said.

"I wasn't exactly masquerading as Princess of Gossip," I tried. "I really was her."

"You're a music industry insider?" my mother said. "Inside what? Your bedroom?"

Good-bye, dresses. Good-bye, necklace. Good-bye, oh no, my phone.

"I ate the Godiva chocolate," I said.

"She can't return the chocolate," my dad agreed.

"Albert, this is serious," my mother said. "These people sent her the, what do you call it, swig? To her because they thought she was someone else."

"You're right," I said miserably. "And it's called swag, as in swag bags. Oh no! I forgot about the swag bags!"

"Do you mean the fifty-two bags of CDs and chocolates that the hotel cleaning staff found in the closet?" my mother said. "They've been collected."

I couldn't believe all this had happened in a half hour. William's announcement and my parents' arrival within minutes of each other, combined with the music stoppage and the hotel guy kicking every-one out . . . well, that's how the party ended.

Yeah. I didn't get to talk to anyone to say good-bye, or thanks, or sorry. I did catch people's looks of pity, derision, and annoyance as they got the full story.

"Honey, you didn't commit a horrible crime, but you certainly did deceive people. But your father and I take some responsibility for it."

"We do?" my dad said. "What did we do?"

"We moved Avery away from Ohio," my mother said. "We ripped

her away from her friends and the only life she's ever known. Then we abandoned her with our work hours to the cutthroat world that is Los Angeles."

My dad and I looked at each other, not sure what to do with this dramatic confession.

"Um, Mom," I said. "You're kind of right. But it's not your fault. I wanted to move here. I like it here."

"We don't want you to become a shallow, superficial celebutante," my dad said. "Maybe we—I've—been too focused on celebrities. I won't go chasing Jen Stefani anymore."

"That's a relief, Albert," my mom said. "But back to Avery, I know Hollywood is enticing, but there is a lot of phoniness here. I thought you realized that. You weren't like this back home. In Ohio, you could focus on your real friends without all of the fake Hollywood to seduce you."

"Mom, trust me, my friends weren't that great in Ohio," I said. "They suggested I get fake breasts so I could fit in around here."

"Oh my," my mom said.

"I have some great friends here, actually," I said. "I just let things get out of hand."

"Well, things will be different from now on," my mom said. "We took the day off today and we're going to be around more for you. If you feel overwhelmed, we'll be here for you, honey."

"Starting now!" my father said. "It's time for some old-fashioned family bonding. We're going to spend the whole day together tomorrow. A good old-fashioned game of Wii *American Idol*!"

Oh Gawd. Now that's a punishment.

"Albert, I'm not sure that's a good idea," my mother said.

Thank you, Mother, voice of reason.

"Remember, dear," my mother continued. "How last time you

got so upset when Simon said he was thinking of quitting the business after you tried that song by James Blunt?"

Or not. I was doomed.

"Look, there was no way that was worse than your Beyoncé," my father shot back.

"Maybe we should play something else with emotions running so high as it is, dear," my mother said. "Something to cool us all off, maybe the Wii skiing game."

"I knew it! You're threatened by my karaoke," my dad said. "I'm putting in the AI and you're going down tomorrow!"

I knew there was no way of getting out of this situation. But there was one thing I had to do.

"I know I'm grounded from my phone," I said. "But there's one person I really, really need to call before it gets too late. I need to apologize or it won't be right."

My parents glanced at each other.

"One call," they both said.

"Thanks," I said, getting up and taking my cell from my father. I went to the other side of the lobby and hoped that Jenna would take my call. In case she was going to hang up on me, I texted her to please take my call. And then I dialed her.

"I'm sorry," I said when Jenna picked up the phone.

"I know, you said that," Jenna said. "Thanks for apologizing. I have to go."

"Wait!" I said. "Do you forgive me? I just got caught up in everything. I'm really sorry."

"I know," Jenna said. "It's just that I haven't known you for that long. It was stupid of me to trust you so quickly. I mean, it didn't take long for your inner diva to come out. I guess I didn't know the real you."

"Yes you do!" I assured her. "I'm your friend!"

"I've been burned by that in the past by people who say they're my friends, as you know," Jenna said.

"Well, if it makes you feel any better, I'm being punished. I'm officially grounded from the phone and computer and have to give all of the swag back."

"Well, it doesn't really make me feel better," Jenna said. "It all just makes me feel sad."

And she hung up.

I really had screwed it up. It was just like in *Mean Girls*, when Lindsay drops her friends at her new school for Rachel McAdams. It was so cliché it was embarrassing. I'd really screwed this up.

"Everyone makes mistakes," my dad came over to me. "Don't worry. I understand how tempting it is to become famous. We'll just have to do it together—virtually! Wii *Idol* tomorrow!"

I sighed. I guess this was the kind of fame I deserved.

36

MySpace Comments:

Sunday, 10:00 p.m.

Princess of Gossip exposed!
Who IS the Princess of Gossip? Come check out pictures and the real inside story at www.princessofgossipexposed.com.

```
Princess of Gossip Exposed!

By William "Big Willie" Shaw

Overnight, Princess of Gossip became
a sensation on the Internet. It was
the first site to break the news
of Haley Lane and Kevin Webber's
twosome—the fauxmance she called
Hevin.

    Princess of Gossip, according to
```

her own headline, is a "music industry insider."

Well, princessofgossipexposed has
the shocking true story of the real
identity of Princess of Gossip.

To set the record straight: she is
a fifteen-year-old nobody!

She's Avery Johnson, a fifteen-
year-old high school student with no
connections to the industry. She
just moved here from Ohio!

"She's not even an insider at her
own high school," scoffed school It
Girl Cecilia Singer. "She moved here
from Ohio and thought she could lie
her way to Hollywood. Obviously it
didn't work."

What's so shocking is that Princess of Gossip has tricked her fan
page viewers with false gossip.
Avery Johnson had no knowledge of
celebrity gossip and used the page
to further her lies. Her false story
about Shade from University of Hard
cheating was born out of jealousy of
Shade's girlfriend, whose sister at-
tends Avery's school.

"I can't believe someone would
print such lies," said Delilah

Singer, the ex-girlfriend. "We'd broken up as friends."

Avery's scam was exposed by the investigative work of yours truly at a party that was sponsored by Princess of Gossip's unknowing corporate sponsors. (Photos credited to William "Big Willie" Shaw below.)

"We were under the impression Princess of Gossip would use our generous gifts to host a celebrity-filled function," one of the sponsors said at the party. "Instead, the party was high school kids."

And to top it off, Avery's scam apparently was so complete that she was able to trick celebrity Beckett Howard into being her date to the party. However, like her friends, Beckett dropped her by the end of the party.

"Avery thought she could be like a Cory Kennedy and come out of nowhere and be famous," Cecilia said. "It's a sad cautionary tale to losers everywhere."

Check out our new YouTube channel featuring pics and video of the moment Princess of Gossip got outed, exclusively by William Shaw.

PRINCESS OF GOSSIP

And check out the next Tila Tequila!

    See exclusive videos of Cecilia
Singer—our prediction for the next
big Internet Star!

Comments:
Good thing she got caught before she
spread more lies!
What a loser! Saying mean things
about Shade! I heart University of
Hard!
Princess of Gossip is a FAKE!
Avery Johnson sounds like a lost,
beautiful girl. She found love on
www.matchmakersonline.com and you
can, too!

37

It had been a long, long morning already. My parents had given me permission to do my homework on the computer, and I couldn't help but Google William's exposé. Turned out the press had picked up on it.

It was all over.

"GOSSIP QUEEN DATED BECKETT HOWARD FOR ATTENTION!" IT'S JUST A FAUXMANCE, SAYS NEW GIRLFRIEND DELILAH.

HIGH SCHOOL STUDENT MASQUERADES AS INDUSTRY GOSSIP BLOGGER!

And not just on gossip sites. CNN had a story on it, too.

TEEN GOSSIP QUEEN—WHAT IS WRONG WITH THE INTERNET AND OUR TEENS TODAY?

Ouch. I decided my parents' ban on the Internet except for school might end up being a good thing, after all. I had to ignore people's whispers and stares all day. I was wishing I could travel back in time to a few weeks ago when I was totally invisible. In English class, I kept my head down and ignored Cecilia's pointed stares, laughs, and eye rolls in my direction. And then, Miss Schmitt made her announcement.

"Please join your previous partners and quiz each other on vocabulary."

Oh, no.

Cecilia raised her hand.

"Miss Schmitt," she said sweetly. "I'm finding it difficult to work in a group of three."

"I'll work with Cecilia!" William called out.

"I meant, may just Griffin and I work together," Cecilia said.

"Denied," Miss Schmitt said. "Based on your lackluster performance on the last quiz, Cecilia, you need all the help you can get. Move to your groups."

I almost smiled at the look on Cecilia's face, until I realized it meant we were stuck together, so no glory there. I nervously pulled my chair up to Griffin's desk, keeping as much distance as I possibly could from him and Cecilia.

Unfortunately, I snagged my chair on Cecilia's ginormous Chanel bag and my chair tipped onto the desk with a bang.

People turned around to look at me.

"Oh, the things you do to get attention," Cecilia said, shaking her head and kicking her bag back next to her chair.

"And you don't?" I muttered.

"It just comes naturally. We can't all be Cecilia Singer," Cecilia said. She reached down into her bag and pulled out a black nail file. She leaned back and started to file her nails.

"Miss Singer!" Miss Schmitt called out. "Are you studying your vocabulary words or giving yourself a manicure?"

"Um." Cecilia looked up in a rare moment of speechlessness.

"If you can't work with your group, I will give you a more effective partner," Schmitt said. "Me. Please bring your flash cards up and I will quiz you."

Cecilia opened her mouth.

"*Now*, Miss Singer," Schmitt said.

"You guys, I have my sister's flash cards she bought off that guy," Cecilia whispered frantically. "She's going to know I didn't make them. What if she recognizes them? Griffin, Avery, one of you give me yours."

We all looked up and froze. Miss Schmitt was standing right behind Cecilia.

"Miss Singer!" Schmitt said. "Bring me *your* flash cards. We seem to be in need of a little chat, don't we? And also, do you have your pig's-head project with you? It's overdue."

Cecilia looked panicky as she went to follow Miss Schmitt.

"Busted," Griffin said mildly.

We sat there in silence. I took a deep breath and said what I'd been planning to say to Griffin.

"Obviously she's not the only one whose been busted lately. Well, I guess this is my chance to apologize to you," I said. "I'm sorry about everything."

"There are people who need the apology more than me," Griffin said. "I know it's easy to get sucked into the fame game."

"Well, thanks for DJ'ing the party," I said. "And sorry it ended so badly."

"You had good stuff on that iPod. I did have fun before it all went down," Griffin said. "You have excellent taste in music."

"Thanks," I said. "That's the nicest thing anyone's said to me all day. It's practically the only thing anyone's said to me all day. This whole thing sucks. I guess Cecilia's right. I just wanted attention."

"Well, I don't think you needed to do all that to get attention," Griffin said.

"I know, I know, my parents gave me that lecture. I was a better person before I got sucked into all of this. Shallow. Superficial. Mean. Fake."

I laid my head down on the desk.

"Yeah, I liked you better when you first got here. I guess that was before all this. You were more real," Griffin said.

"Oh, please, nobody liked real," I said. "I mean, even you. You're in love with some girl who has so much silicone in her she looks like the opposite of real."

"What?" Griffin asked.

"Delilah," I said. "You're in love with Delilah. Proving my point. When it comes down to it, even you would choose the perfect blonde with big, you know."

"Do you seriously believe I'm in love with Delilah?" Griffin said.

"Everyone knows it," I said. "So both our hearts were pretty much squashed the other night, I guess. Seeing Beckett and Delilah making out was not one of my shining moments of happiness."

"Yeah, that wasn't good," Griffin agreed. "I didn't trust that guy anyway. I knew something was up with him. Anyway, you're too nice for him."

"Thanks for the compliments," I said. "Thanks for just talking to me. I was thinking about your song, you know, the one about lighting your way. How you wrote, '*I want to shatter the myth/That is you/And find the girl/That's true.*' Well, I feel like I need to find the girl that's true, like who I am," I said. "Like who is the real me when I'm not trying to be Hollywood?"

"This place can be kind of overwhelming," Griffin said. "Since you liked that song, here's another one I wrote a couple days ago."

He flipped through his notebook and ripped out a page. He folded it in half and handed it to me.

I didn't get a chance to look at it before Miss Schmitt's voice cut across the room.

"Mr. King and Miss Johnson! I have not seen one flash card out. Haven't you learned from your partner, Miss Singer? Mr. King, please join me and we shall work together."

"Ohmygosh, I'm so sorry," I said.

"It's not your fault," he said. "But I know whose fault it is."

Cecilia slid back into her seat, and Griffin gave her a look.

"You don't think I pointed out to Schmitt that you two weren't studying?" Cecilia said innocently. "Okay, I did. Your turn to suffer."

Griffin sighed and went to the front of the room.

I sat and glared at Cecilia.

"What?" Cecilia said. "Oh, come on, like you wouldn't have taken that opportunity. First I have to have Schmitt as a partner, and then I have to look at you two."

"What?" I said.

"Griffin. You." Cecilia rolled her eyes. "The steam, the sparks. You two need to just get a room."

"Hello? What the heck are you talking about? Griffin's been in love with your sister forever," I said.

"Oh, please, not since fifth grade," Cecilia said. "Which makes no sense because now she's all hot and has those big bazoongas."

"But he turns bright red every time you talk about her," I said.

"For someone who's supposedly the Princess of Gossip you're

pretty out of it," Cecilia said. "He turns red because he has the hots for *you*."

"He does not!" I said. "What are you talking about."

"Oh, please, it was so obvious from like the first time we were all together," Cecilia said. "During the car ride to school he was all Avery likes this music and Avery told me about this Internet thing that was so cool. Avery's so *real*."

He was?

"Do you like Griffin or something?" I asked.

"Oh, puh-lease. He's a high school boy. I aim way higher," Cecilia said.

I had a sudden flashback to what Jenna had said about Cecilia wanting every guy to want her, even if she didn't want them.

"Who *are* you aiming for?" I asked suddenly.

"I was aiming for Beckett Howard," Cecilia said grumpily, leaning down to put her flash cards back in her bag. "But noooo, my sister had to go as usual and steal him from me. It's not enough she gets Shade. Or anyone she wants. Every time I like a guy, Delilah just flashes cleavage and gives them that smile and they're all hers. I'm sick of—"

Cecilia looked up, stunned, and suddenly seemed to realize she'd just spewed that out.

"Um, whoa," I said. "That sounds like it kind of stinks."

"Whatever," she muttered. "Anyway, don't think you're all that because Griffin liked you. I'm sure he doesn't like you anymore, Princess of Gossip," Cecilia said. "Griffin's into honesty. And hello? Why am I even talking to you? Everyone is ostracizing the Princess of Gossip."

"Ooh, ostracizing," I said. "Your vocabulary session with Schmitt must have worked if you're using big-syllable words."

"Here's two syllables," Cecilia muttered. "Shut and up."

I laughed. I had to admit, Cecilia kind of cracked me up.

"You're kind of funny," I said. "You should think about going into comedy."

"Tell that to my lame-o agent," Cecilia said. "My last two auditions have been for corpses in the *CSI* series. And I didn't even get hired."

I laughed again.

"Well, this is interesting." Griffin came back and sat down at his desk. "Avery's laughing and Cecilia's almost smiling. Should I ask what I missed?"

I looked up at Griffin.

And I felt my face turn red.

38

Schmitt made us go back to our desks for the rest of the class period and do silent reading of the first chapter of our next book. I was happy to learn that our next read would be *Macbeth*. I'd read that last year at my old school, so this was going to help give me a huge breather. I had a lot of catch-up to do with my schoolwork, and I actually meant schoolwork for a change. I had big plans to pull up my grades and get focused. I had to admit, leading a double life as Princess of Gossip had taken its toll on my grades and it was kind of a relief that I could actually study. Javier had said he'd tutor me in chemistry, and I'd gotten extra credit projects in some of my classes, so I thought I was back on track.

I rifled through my tote bag to get out my notebook so I could take notes on the homework I needed to do, and I noticed a half-folded piece of paper. It said "AVERY" on the outside. Oh, it was the lyrics of the song Griffin had written and given to me.

The sun always shines
In L.A.
Life is always fine
That's what they say

But what I see
Are wannabes
Celebrities
Paparazzi

And that's not me
It's just not me

The heat is on
The sun beats down and I look up and say
We need a snow day in L.A.
One day to get away
Not to hide
Just to stay inside
While the blizzard rages in the air
But it's all out there

Inside the only thing
I'll let in
Is you, girl

I suddenly felt all of my feelings just tumble through me. Griffin's song hit home hard. I'd been on such an emotional roller coaster and now it was sinking in that I'd completely let down everyone. And not just Jenna—my parents, Griffin, my fans. I'd let down myself.

I thought back to something Marisa had said in an interview that DMB had sent me, yet another sneak preview I'd gotten. I'd admired her for thinking it and staying true to herself in a world of celebrity. She had said:

The weirdest thing about becoming famous is when you're at the great parties or you're filming on camera or in meetings, and someone calls you a star. For me, it's weird to think about myself as a celebrity, like Jennifer Aniston or JLo. Singing, for me, is what I do. It's my job. Don't get me wrong, I love doing it, but now going to events and doing press is part of my job, like filing papers and running numbers is part of someone else's. It's strange that people think of me as something special because my songs are getting out there. I'm always shocked that people recognize me, but of course it makes me feel special.

But also, it makes me feel pressured. In reality you're faced with things that you may not have expected: not knowing who to trust. Being dissected by tabloids and gossip blogs, which can build you up only to gleefully tear you down. It's easy to forget what's real.

I thought about Griffin's song lyrics and could relate to that feeling of needing a snow day from L.A. I was so deep in thought I was startled when the bell rang. I pretended to pack my tote bag very slowly, until everyone left, including Cecilia and Griffin. This day was getting very confusing, and like in Griffin's song, I needed a break. Unfortunately I was getting one, but not the one I wanted, because now it was lunch period. And yes, I was going to lunch. I was pretty sure I wasn't going to be welcome in the computer lab. I'd even packed a lunch in my tote bag. I planned to sit on the wall and risk getting run over by the skateboard guys.

I started walking down the hall when I saw William duck behind a trophy case. To add to my trauma, he'd been sneaking around and following me around all day, with Cam close behind. I was sure they weren't Cecilia-style pictures. The pictures he'd chosen to post of me on his "exposé" were not flattering.

"William!" I whirled around as he ducked behind a locker. "I see you."

"Busted," William said. "Oh, well. How do you feel now that your secret and embarrassing identity have been revealed? Did you hear that Beckett is dating Delilah and they might get engaged? What do you think about—"

"This is ridiculous. Haven't you tortured me enough with your new website?" I cut him off.

"It's pretty good, isn't it?" he said. "I know I don't have your experience, but—"

"What do you mean my experience?" I said. "Your whole site was about how I had no experience. You outed me and then wrote terrible things about me. Can't you just leave me alone?"

"Jeez, Avery, chill out," William said. "You of all peeps know where I'm coming from. We're celebrity gossipers. I have to use my material when I've got it, and right now you're the story. So just like your victims, now it's your turn."

"Great," I sighed.

"Come on, all buzz is good buzz!" William said. "Just think of all the publicity you're getting for Princess of Gossip from this. I'm only helping stir up some drama."

"Not all buzz is good buzz and I don't want any more publicity," I said. "In fact, my original goal was to be anonymous. Like Cam. See, Cam is smart, he stays in the background, and everyone just ignores him. He doesn't even speak, which is something I probably should have emulated. Right, Cam?"

"Actually." Cam cleared his throat. I'd never heard him speak. "My name's not Cam. It's Troy."

"Troy?" I said. "I thought it was Cam."

"Nah, that's what William calls me because I'm his camera guy," he said. "So everyone just assumes I'm Cam."

"Well, I'll call you Troy," I said. "I'm sure you're more than William's camera guy."

"Thanks," Troy said. "And I'm sorry I had to tape the stuff William did to you. If it makes you feel better, I deleted a bunch of unflattering stuff. You seem like a nice person. And so does your friend, Jenna. She looks really pretty on camera, by the way."

"Okay, cut," William said. "Stop rolling! You deleted tape? I'm the paparazzo, I tell you what to delete. Just shut up and run the camera and do as you're told. You're just the camera guy!"

I watched Troy's eyes narrow.

"*Just* a camera guy?" Troy said, evenly but forcefully. "You'll regret saying those words when I'm the next Steven Spielberg and you're chasing Spencer and Heidi around town. I don't need this to prepare for my film career. You're on your own, Willie. Avery, hang in there."

He slung his camcorder around his neck and walked away down the hall.

"Bye, Troy," I called after him.

"Great, now I have to find a new camera guy," William said in disgust. "Where the heck am I going to find another free silent cameraman at this stage of my career. Avery, I'm starting to think you kind of suck at the whole gossip thing. You're never going to be famous the way you're going."

"My goal was never to become famous," I said. "Actually, my original goal was to just have a fan space for Marisa. Just a nice, supportive MySpace where I could help her find stardom. I'd heard 'The Girl Who' and just wanted to cheer her on. And then came M World, where we could do good things in the name of ce-lebrities."

And that's when I thought of something. I turned around and walked away from the outdoor cafeteria area. I *was* going to com-puter lab, after all. I had an idea.

"Where are you going?" William asked. "You have lunch this period! It's this way! I'm planning a vignette of people's faces when they see you walk into the cafeteria. Horror, shock, disgust, pity—it's going to be a range of human emotions as they see that the once famous Princess of Gossip is just you. A nobody."

I kept walking toward the computer lab, ignoring him. The bell rang, so I walked more quickly. I had just made it to the computer lab door when I heard a voice behind me.

"Excuse me! Students!" A teacher hurried up behind us.

"Class period has started. Do you have a hall pass?"

"Uh . . ." William stammered. And then he pointed at me and shouted, "No! But she doesn't either!"

That kid was a serious narc.

And then Sebastian stuck his head out to see what the commo-tion was.

"She's fine. She's in this classroom with me," Sebastian said. "That guy, though, he's not supposed to be here."

"I'm writing you up for a detention, young man." The teacher turned on William and I slipped inside the computer room.

"Detention?" I heard William say. "I can't today! I have interviews set up for an Internet exposé tell-all! You can't—"

I walked farther into the computer room and took a deep breath, preparing for yet another apology.

"Thanks," I said to Sebastian. "Since I'm here, can I talk to you for a second? In the office?"

Sebastian shrugged and followed me through the computer lab. I looked over at Jenna, who was at one of the stations. I was pretty sure she might have seen me, because she flinched. But she didn't turn my way, and even though I expected it, it still hurt to have her completely shut me out. I walked into the office and Sebastian closed the door behind me.

"I'm sorry for everything," I said. "I apologized to Jenna, too. The party obviously didn't go as planned."

"I pretty much figured that out," Sebastian said.

"Is everything cool with Lee and you?" I asked him.

"Yeah." He smiled a little. "We're cool."

"I'm glad. Now, um, I have a favor to ask you," I said. "I know I don't deserve another one, but it's something to redeem myself and hopefully help others. So I have to ask."

"Well, I owe you one," Sebastian said. "I got an email from Caltech this morning. I've been accepted early with a scholarship. The admissions rep added a note about how cool he thought M World was, and that they were looking forward to the thought of Caltech World."

"No way!" I said, spontaneously giving him a hug. "I'm so happy for you!"

"Here, read the bottom of this," Sebastian said. He handed me a piece of paper off the desk and I read the email.

P.S. I must say that several of us
in the office have greatly enjoyed
visiting M World. My boss is a big
Brad Pitt fan and watching her getting excited while her avatar rode
on the back of his virtual motor-

cycle on the ceiling was a highlight of our admissions season.

"That is the best news I've had all day," I said.

"Yeah, I can imagine," Sebastian said. "Jenna showed me the 'I Hate Princess of Gossip' site or whatever it was that William did. Man, that kid would sell out his mother. At least M World didn't get dragged through the mud."

"I know," I said. "And that leads me to my favor to ask you."

39

Bulletin

Join us for another
M World event

Hosted by Marisa's #1 fan, Princess of Gossip
aka Avery

In 15 minutes!!!

Yes, we were going to do another M World, although with a different purpose this time. It was going to be my chance to apologize to everyone and try to make things at least a little right. I was hoping people would show up, if for no other reason than because they were curious.

I was grounded from the computer for everything except homework, but I asked my parents if I could use it for one more thing. I'd given them the drift, and they'd agreed. I had blitzed a bulletin out from computer lab to all of my former Princess of Gossip "friends." I emailed all my sponsors and everyone on my evite list at the party (including my parents). Sebastian even hacked into the school computer list and blitzed it to all the students.

Then I had two days to wait. And it was a long wait. I spent a lot of it just catching up with Team Marisa. I couldn't bring myself to go to Princess of Gossip.

A lot of my readers weren't too happy with me, either.

> *I mean I know gossip bloggers can be anybody. But a fifteen-year-old nobody? Princess of Gossip sux!*

People felt betrayed, and I could see why. They'd trusted a "music industry insider," and it turned out to be me. But now it was time for one final M World.

I sat at Sebastian's extra desk in the study suite next to his room and shifted around in my chair to make myself comfortable. Sebastian had given me a ride home from school so we could get cracking on M World.

Jenna had found out he was driving me and had taken the bus instead. When I'd walked in, she was talking with her mother in the spa room while her mother got a Botox injection. Then she announced, for my benefit, that she had a lot of homework and was staying in her room. She hadn't come out since.

"You guys getting ready?" Sebastian said from his station across the room. Lee was cross-legged on the floor, with her own lime-green laptop propped on it.

"I'm picking my avatar," Lee said. "You know, I didn't thank you yet, Avery. But I really appreciate what you did. Or more to the point, what you didn't do."

"Um, what didn't I do?" I said.

"You had gossip and pictures of me, but you never posted them on Princess of Gossip," Lee said. "I really appreciate that."

"Well, you said you didn't want publicity." I shrugged. "I wouldn't do that."

"Good thing you're giving up gossip blogging. You're too nice." Lee laughed. "I always say, Hollywood can make you a celebrity but it doesn't mean you're a star. The way people can treat each other in this town is pretty twisted. They build you up to tear you down."

"Yeah, I noticed," I said.

"On to a happier subject, you're really good with these avatars," Lee said.

"Jenna gets credit for those," I said. "She probably won't want to hear it from me, but can you tell her that? Jenna did so much for M World."

I got a little choked up for a minute. I'd invited Jenna, but I hadn't heard anything from her. Sebastian had told me that she'd pretty much shut down. As I thought about the fun we'd had planning M World and doing these things together, I realized that out of everything that had happened, losing Jenna's friendship was the worst part of it.

"Hey, can I be Princess Leia?" Lee said.

"Excellent choice," Sebastian told her.

I remembered when Jenna had made the Princess Leia avatar, because Sebastian was obsessed with her. I looked at Sebastian and Lee together. A random couple, Lee the soap opera star and Sebastian the slightly antisocial nonfamous guy. But it worked.

Unlike Beckett Howard the star and nonfamous me. I still felt completely betrayed, but also it was pretty obvious he wasn't going to be the great love of my life. At first, I would have been happy just to stare at him, I mean please, the guy was crazy hot. And I obviously liked being with the guy who was the center of attention.

But he didn't really like me for being me. I wanted someone to connect with, someone I could be myself with. A nice guy, someone I could be goofy with and real with, and who didn't make me feel like I had to be something more than me.

Whew, okay, then. I shook my head to clear those thoughts and looked at Lee's avatar appearing and disappearing on-screen. I thought about the last time we were here doing this. I wished that Jenna was in the next room, calling out to me about the crazy celebrity avatars she was making. Instead, she was in her room with the door shut and music blasting.

"Hey, Sebastian, give me two minutes," I said.

I took a deep breath and went down the hallway. I knocked on Jenna's door and stuck my head in. She was at her desk, on her computer.

"It's Avery," I said. "I just wanted to tell you some gossip I read about on one of the websites."

"Jeez, Avery. Haven't we had enough gossip?" Jenna asked, without turning around.

"Not the good kind," I said. "This website said that twin soap stars Aliceandra and Anntoinette Sanders renewed their contracts and will survive the flesh-eating plague."

"Yeah," Jenna said. "I know. They emailed me out of the blue. That *is* good gossip."

"So. Um. Can I come in?" I asked her.

"No, I'm really busy right now," she answered.

I wasn't going to push it. I started to walk away when I heard her continue.

"I'm getting ready for some event on M World," Jenna said. "It's starting soon, so I have to get there early to get the best avatar."

I broke into a little smile and went back to Sebastian's room.

As I walked in, I heard my cell phone ring. I checked the number. My parents still had me on groundedness, so I could only use the phone when they called. Not that anyone else was calling me, anyway.

"Hi," I said.

"I got an evite to AJohnson from Princess of Gossip," my dad said. "Was that intentional or another error? It's for a virtual party, but I don't want to show up and have to face hotel management throwing me out again and threatening to sue me."

"I sent it on purpose," I told him. "Albert Johnson plus guest, especially for you. And I assumed you would bring Mom."

"I figured I'd check, since last time it didn't work out so well," my dad said, with a little laugh.

"Just click on the link and it will take you right there," I said. "You'll recognize me."

"Hold on," Dad said. "Oh, your mother wants to know if you think she should be a robot or Wonder Woman. Oh, I can answer that—definitely Wonder Woman. Ooh-la-la."

"Alrighty, I think I'll be going now," I said. "Thank her for letting me go online. I'm hoping you guys can trust me now."

I signed into M World, for what was probably going to be the last time.

    Would you like to enter M WORLD?

Yes.

A big, burly avatar with SECURITY on his T-shirt popped on the screen.

Choose your avatar.

I selected my new avatar. It was a short girl with red hair, wearing an emerald-green T-shirt, jeans, and awkward-looking sneakers. Sebastian had done a really good job making it look like me. It would have been better if Jenna had designed me a better outfit, but I couldn't let my thoughts go there right now.

Let me see if you are cool enough
for this party. Okay, you're in.

And the screen went black. And then . . .

M WORLD!

Suddenly, my avatar was standing inside a small club. It looked like the kind of small, intimate club where I imagined Marisa would want to sing for her fans. Not a lot of hype. Just a cool place to hang out with friends.

"It looks tight," I told Sebastian.

"Welcome to M World!" my avatar walked around saying to people as they came in.

The regulars, like the alien and the cheetah, were there, and lots of new people. It was so weird, because I didn't know who was who. However, when Gwen Stefani came in, dressed in a Team Marisa T-shirt, a black and leopard-print skirt, a L.A.M.B. purse, and spiky boots, I grinned.

"Hey baby hey baby hey," she said. "It's me, Jenna."

"Hi," my avatar responded. "I'm glad you came. Your out-fit rox."

"Yeah, I know!" Jenna yelled from her room down the hall. "But your outfit stinks. I need to dress you next time, okay?"

I grinned. Then I stayed off to the side, watching people walk around. The newbies seemed pretty impressed.

```
woa check out this place
This is cool!
```

Others, not so much.

```
Princess of Gossip sux.
```

"Do you want me to kick out the haters?" Sebastian asked me.

"No, they can stay, if they don't get too offensive," I sighed.

"Good attitude," Lee said. "You have to have a thick skin in the business. Like when I made the Soap Stars Worst-Dressed List two years in a row. I'm glad you didn't have any Worst-Dressed Lists on Princess of Gossip. Imagine seeing yourself on that list after you spent the whole time thinking you looked pretty."

Yet another pressure of being a celebrity.

"Okay, the stage is ready for you, Avery," Sebastian said.

```
Welcome to M World
I'm the Princess of Gossip
```

A couple of avatars said "BOO."

I took a deep breath.

```
You probably know I'm Avery, a high
school nobody with no right to be
Princess of Gossip.
     I wanted to apologize to everyone
I hurt and deceived. I am a normal
person who always was obsessed with
celebrities and the music scene.
When I moved to L.A., I was so ex-
cited, but then I felt really out of
place. I had no friends and I didn't
think I fit in.
     Then I heard a song by a new
singer named Marisa called "The Girl
Who." And the lyrics really meant
something to me.
```

As planned, the lyrics to "The Girl Who" started scrolling along the
ceiling of the club. The background music, without Marisa's voice,
started playing softly.

```
Then I started a MySpace as Marisa's
#1 fan. I thought I could be her
street team. And I started M World.
I'm team captain.
```

Some avatars started saying "??" and "!!"

```
But I got a lot of help from two of
my new friends, Jenna and Sebastian.
     They rock.
```

PRINCESS OF GOSSIP

Some music people thought I was
someone important and sent me tickets to events. That's how I got my
gossip. I posted it as Princess of
Gossip. And it all spiraled out of
control really fast.
    And it made me feel like a Some-
body instead of a Nobody. But I hurt
people along the way. I'm sorry to
everyone.
    Just like Marisa's lyrics say, I'm
the girl who has no place to hide.
    So that's my story. I hope you un-
derstand.

Okay, that was it. I'd apologized for all of my wrongs, and that was the best I could do. And then the weirdest thing happened. The cheetah avatar appeared on the stage next to me.

"Uh, Sebastian?" I called to him. "The cheetah avatar broke through the controlled area and got onstage."

"I know," he called back. "Just wait."

And the cheetah's speech bubble popped up.

Now we invite you to watch a special
message from a Surprise Guest Star!

And a large video screen slowly rose up behind the stage, like it would in a real concert. And suddenly a real video of a fuzzy person came on the screen, kind of like a blurry YouTube.

"Success!" Sebastian said. "My satellite stream worked!"

What the heck was going on? The picture came into focus. And it was Marisa, wearing an emerald-green T-shirt, black jeans, and her trademark emerald-green pendant necklace. She was sitting in what looked like a living room, in a tall chair.

"Hi, everyone," Marisa said in a real voice. "I'm Marisa."

"Aw, yeah!" Sebastian said. "The audio is working. I am a genius!"

"Ohmygosh, ohmygosh!" Jenna practically flew into the room and sat down beside me. "What the heck is going on?"

"I don't know!" I said. "Sebastian made a fake Marisa video or—"

"Avery!" Sebastian said. "It's the real Marisa. It's not fake. She's in real time so pay attention."

"No way you got Marisa to come to M World." I shook my head.

"Marisa and I are both repped by the William Morris agency," Lee said. "So it was easy for my agent to connect me with her and I told her all about you."

"Avery!" Jenna squealed. "Come look! Marisa is talking!"

"When I first heard that a fan had gone to so much trouble to make Team Marisa MySpace and M World, I was really amazed. I originally came on here to thank Avery for all she's done to promote my singing career. And then I got really into M World and had so much fun making new friends and listening to my avatar sing my songs. You may have seen me as the cheetah."

The cheetah avatar danced around the stage.

"The real Marisa is the virtual cheetah?" I was totally stunned. I watched as the real Marisa shifted a little in her chair.

"I have an important announcement to make. Thanks to Avery

and her friends, M World has raised over $14,000 for charity to help Africa and Bono's *REAL* charity. Please consider contributing! I think that overshadows all of this Princess of Gossip business.

"As a special thank-you for Avery and Jenna, I'd like to sing a little song."

The real Marisa pulled out a guitar. And she started to play and sing, a very familiar song.

Jenna and I both screamed. She grabbed me around the neck and we watched like crazy fans sitting front row at a concert.

> *They say I'm this*
> *They say I'm that*
> *I'm nothing special*
> *I just fall flat*
>
> *But I don't care*
> *I just won't share*
> *And give away*
> *What makes me me*
> *And sets me free*
>
> *I'm the girl who*
> *Won't do what they tell me to*
> *The girl who has no place to hide*
> *The girl who won't just go along for the ride*
>
> *Because I'm the girl who*
> *I'm the girl who*
> *You'll wish you knew*

SABRINA BRYAN AND JULIA DeVILLERS

The girl who will make you feel
Nothing you thought was real
Will show you the inside out
I really have no doubt
I'm the girl who you can't do without

I'm the girl who
The girl who
I'm the girl who
You'll wish you knew . . .

The audience went crazy. Speech bubbles said "Clap! Clap! Clap!"

"*Aaah!* M World just had a private concert by Marisa!" Jenna screamed.

I sat there in shock as Marisa kept talking.

"I'm having a meet-and-greet at the signing table. Come say hi. I will be the cheetah wearing a Team Marisa T-shirt."

"Sebastian, Lee, Jenna. I can't believe this happened—" I couldn't say anything else, because I started to choke up. I made my avatar go over and give Jenna's avatar a big hug. And then I went over to give her a real hug.

Then we saw a Superman avatar move over to Jenna's avatar. His speech bubble popped up:

    Jen! Jen Stephanie! Can I have your
    autograph?

"Oh. My. Gawd. "That's my dad," I groaned.

"Your father is Superman?" Jenna said. "I'm glad I found that out before I started flirting with him."

"Of course," Jenna typed back. "Anything for my favorite fan. But I have one favor to ask first. You must forgive your daughter for all of her wrongs. She is just a girl who didn't mean to hollaback."

"Jenna, you are b-a-n-a-n-a-s," I said. "And I mean that in the best possible way."

40

I sat in the computer lab office the next day during lunch period. It felt almost back to normal, as Jenna and I hovered over the computer monitor, catching up on the latest.

"Check out what *US Weekly* said." I pointed to the screen. "Singer Marisa gives special online concert to help fans and raise money for charity. They even give a link to DMB Records. That's great buzz."

"Marisa is the coolest," Jenna said. "I'm excited she gave us those tickets to her show at Troubadour next weekend. VIP, baby!"

"Here's another site." I said. "The headline reads 'Princess of Gossip Turns Around Image by Donating Fourteen Thousand Dollars to Charity, Through One of Her Many Websites.'"

"That's so sweet!" Jenna said. "Your reputation is saved!"

"Uh-oh," I said. "This might not be so sweet. *Access Hollywood* has an interview with Beckett Howard talking about, oh no, the Princess of Gossip."

"Don't watch it," Jenna said.

"No, I have to," I said. I took a deep breath, and we watched. Oh, ugh, Beckett looked extra cute in a dark gray blazer and black T-shirt. Why did he have to look so cute.

Access reporter: Is it true you dated Avery, the Princess of Gossip?

Beckett: It's true. But I didn't know that she was really just a high school student.

Access reporter: You've dated many socialites and half of Young Hollywood. What made you date the Princess of Gossip?

Beckett: I actually met her in my uncle's boutique. My uncle is Christian Palandro and he is known for discovering the next It Girls. He sends them dresses. When I saw Avery was wearing one of his dresses, I knew she must be a somebody. Imagine how horrified I was when I found out she was a nobody!

"Wait, what?!" I yelped. "His uncle is Christian Palandro? He asked me out because of my dress? He told me he asked me out because I was nobody. Idiot!"

"And now he's milking it for publicity," Jenna said. "Creep."

Access reporter: Isn't it also true that you kissed several other girls the night you were on a date with Avery? She was hosting a party, and you blatantly cheated on her?

Beckett: (nervous laughter) No! Of course not!

Access reporter: We have pictures, credited to a William Shaw, that show otherwise.

Some pictures flashed on the screen. Beckett making out with Delilah near the bushes. And Beckett making out with one of the hotel servers in the parking lot!

"Oh my Gawd! You were kissing a worker?"

Delilah Singer suddenly appeared in the video.

Access *reporter: We have special guest and Beckett's new girl-friend Delilah Singer, formerly the girlfriend of Shade from University of Hard.*

"You are such a pig!" Delilah screamed at Beckett, who looked horrified.

Access *reporter: Beckett's new clothing line, BeckHot, will be de-buting in stores in time for the holidays. And that's the scoop, from Access Hollywood!*

Jenna and I looked at each other, then dissolved in laughter.

"Oh my gosh," I said. "He is unbelievable. Poor Delilah. Shade, Beckett. She has terrible taste in men. Then again, apparently so do I. He liked me for his uncle's dress? I can't believe I fell for that."

I got serious for a minute.

"I fell for a lot, didn't I?" I said. "Haley and Kevin, Beckett. Good thing there's Lee to remind me that some celebrities are nice and normal."

"Heck, if Beckett had tried to kiss me, I would have gone for it, too," Jenna said. "I'm still jealous you sat on Javier's lap in car pool. I know he's cheesy but he's so hot . . ."

And then I saw an alert blinking on my screen.

"Wait, I just got a new Google alert," I said. "Yipes! I'm on Perez! Oh, I'm nervous."

I clicked over to Perez Hilton. Yes, there was a story about me. I wasn't so sure about this.

```
I'm joining Team Marisa! You should,
too!
```

> You will love this singer, Marisa.
> The song we've been obsessing over
> is this really pretty ballad of hers
> called "The Girl Who." Such a pretty
> song.
>
> Click on the media player below
> and enjoy: "The Girl Who."
>
> P.S. And I'm going to check out her
> virtual world, too...Think they'll
> make me a Perez avatar?

I looked at Jenna.

"Yes, I'll make him a Perez avatar." Jenna laughed. "I'll give him an extraspecial outfit."

Yeah, M World and Team Marisa were living on. How could they not after all this? I was going to have the next M World party background look like the club where we were going to see Marisa play next weekend. I was going to try to bring people as close to the experience as possible. And after that, I was thinking we could make an M World stadium, so Marisa could sell out a stadium, even if it was virtual. I mean, you never know, it could happen in real life someday, too, right?

"Hey, speaking of outfits," Jenna said. "Do you want to go shopping for an outfit for the concert after school?"

"I'm still grounded from social events until Friday," I said. "But the good news is my parents are going to take me furniture shopping for my room today. You'll have to come over for my very first L.A. sleepover."

I went to check my email and something caught my eye.

```
To: Group email
From: AJohnson@DMBrecords.com
Subject: Marisa publicity

Great news! The buzz on Marisa today
has gone through the roof! As a re-
sult, the attached list of program
directors are putting Marisa on
their main playlists!!!

Allison

P.S. There seems to be a street team
starting called Team Marisa. I'm
going to send the owner of Team
Marisa an autographed Marisa pic-
ture. I will try to track down her
contact information.
```

"Okay, duh," I said. "AJohnson! I'm in your group email list!"
The laughter began again.

"Okay, my cheeks hurt from laughing so hard," I said after a while. "What should I tell Allison? It's not that I don't appreciate an autographed picture of Marisa, but I think I'm a little beyond that," I said. "At least my parents won't make me return that gift."

"Good thing Marisa has you, because I don't think her record label is exactly on top of things," Jenna said.

I looked at the list of program directors who were putting Marisa on their stations. They were the major stations from L.A. to New

York to Miami. This was big-time. I was so excited for Marisa. She totally deserved success.

There was a knock on the office door.

"Hey." Griffin stuck his head in the door. "Miya told me you guys hang here this period. Can I come in?"

41

I looked at Griffin, who was cute today in his brown T-shirt with a button-down thrown over it, and dark jeans.

"Hi, Griffin!" Jenna jumped up. "Bye, Griffin! I just remembered I have to . . . go somewhere else. I'll leave you two alone."

Jenna went out of the office and closed the door.

"She's not exactly subtle," I said.

"I just wanted to return the demos that you left at the party the other night," Griffin said. "There actually were a couple good singers in there."

"Oh, sure," I said. "I loved that one song you played at the party, especially," I said. "It was by a guy and a girl duo."

Griffin shuffled through the CDs.

"Quinn and Jack," he said, holding it up. "A brother-and-sister duo from, how ironic, your home state of Ohio! Just think how you can play a part in new artists' careers. You should give them a little buzz on Princess of Gossip."

"No more Princess of Gossip!" I said. "I'm using my powers for good and not evil from now on. My heart is with Team Marisa and the M World thing, because I'm a true fan."

"You're a good fan to have." He nodded.

"Well," I said. "Um. Speaking of good music, I have a couple extra tickets for the Marisa concert Saturday night. If you want to go and bring a friend, you can have them."

"Thanks," he said. "That'd be great."

"Um," I said. "So. Are you going to bring somebody?"

"Yeah, I will," he said.

"Okay, I'll see you and your date there," I said.

"Well, my date will be Javier," Griffin said. "He's been really stressed out about his PSATs and could use a night out. Why, are *you* bringing somebody?"

"I'm bringing a few people. Jenna, Miya, Sebastian, Lee . . ." I said. "And Troy, the guy we thought was named Cam."

"William's camera guy?" Griffin said.

"Yeah," I said. "He turned out to be a really nice guy. He gave me a lot of the tapes they'd shot so I could destroy them."

"Well, I guess that's cool that you have a date," Griffin said.

"What? No, he's not my date," I said. "Although, swear you won't say anything, I have sort of a devious plan. I was kind of thinking he might get along with Jenna. But shh."

"Jenna and Troy, I won't say a word," Griffin said. I couldn't help but notice that he looked a little relieved, which gave me a boost of confidence.

We were both silent. I thought about how cute he looked and decided to just throw it out there.

"So, um, is it true about what Cecilia said in English class?" I blurted out. "That you used to maybe like me?"

"No," he said.

Oh. Well, I guess that made sense after everything that had happened.

"I still like you," Griffin said.

"You do?" I asked him. "Like, now?"

"You're surprised? Isn't it obvious, after I wrote that song for you?" Griffin said. "I mean, my lyrics said things like, *Inside the only thing/I'll let in/Is you, girl.*"

"You wrote that about me?" I said.

"I called it *Avery,*" he said. "Didn't you notice the title on the paper?"

"I thought you were just writing my name on the paper to give it to me," I said. "I love that song!"

Someone wrote a song for me. Griffin wrote a song for me? I had a little trouble processing this.

"Well, that's good," he said. "I guess since you didn't mention it, not to mention you were into guys like Beckett Howard, I thought you were sending me clear signals you weren't interested."

"You're the one who likes the Delilah Singer type," I said. "I thought you liked her, and there was no way I could compare to that."

"Yeah," Griffin said. "You could."

Griffin leaned in toward me. And then the office door opened.

"Oopsie!" Jenna poked her head in the office. "Didn't mean to interrupt! Didn't know Griffin was still here."

Griffin and I jumped back from each other.

"Anyway, I was just about to ask Avery if you guys wanted a ride to the concert now that I have a car," Griffin asked. "It might be a tight squeeze to fit all of us, though. One of you might have to sit on Javier's lap."

"Ooh!" Jenna squealed. "Pick me! Pick me!"

"Done." Griffin laughed.

"Maybe Avery can sit on *your* lap at the concert," Jenna said mischievously. "I always thought Marisa's newest song would be a good makeout song."

"Jenna!" I said, totally embarrassed. Now I *know* I turned red.

"Oh, give up the charade," Jenna said. "You two are perfect for each other. Just like Javier and I are *not* perfect for each other, but I do want just one opportunity to sit on his lap. He is hot."

"One lap ride will cure you of Javier," I said. "But I have someone else in mind who will be there."

"For me?" Jenna asked. "Who? What's he like?"

"I'm sworn to secrecy," I said. "But this guy has a crush on you. He's a really nice guy. He's kind of dorky, but after Beckett, I'm thinking that nice and dorky can be a good thing."

Jenna + Troy = Joy

Well, that worked.

"Hey," Griffin said. "Not to change the subject, but it's my first day of freedom from being trapped in a car while Cecilia and Miya talk about their diets and future plastic surgery or whatever. Do you guys want a ride home from school?"

"My brother can take me home," Jenna said. "But I think Avery wants a ride."

"Yeah," I said. "I do."

Griffin and I shared a shy smile.

"Well, I better get back to class," Griffin said, holding up the bathroom pass. "They'll start wondering."

He left and bumped right into Sebastian, who was on his way in.

I waited until Griffin was out of sight and then a stupid grin spread over my face.

"Did that just happen?" I asked.

"Yes!!" Jenna said. "And I get to spread this gossip. What hot new redhead from Ohio and cool indie music–type dude are a new couple? Hey, wait! What's your celebrity name going to be?"

Definitely not JoKing.

Griffin + Avery = Gravery?

Erm, no.

Avery + Griffin = Affin

Well. I'd work on it.

"Man! Why is everyone always in my office?" Sebastian stood there with his arms crossed. "This is *my* office. *My* computer."

"Well, may I use it for just a few more minutes?" I asked him sweetly. "Please? I just have to post a quick bulletin."

MySpace BULLETIN

From: Avery [inLA]
Subject: Coming soon!

> The new site:
> Princess of Nossip
> The place for all things nossip! What's "nossip"?
> NotGossip
> Nossip—Not the nasty, negative kind of gossip . . .
> It's all the inside scoop on your favorite stars
> And how you can be their biggest fans!
> Gossip that celebrates celebrities!

Stay tuned for news about M World, the virtual world featuring the hottest stars and introducing the next hot musicians.

Next M World:

World premiere debut of Marisa's next song: "Yes, It's Me."

And introducing up-and-coming music duo Quinn and Jack, with their debut song, "Friends and Family."

It's nossip.

All you've got to do is ADD ME AS A FRIEND & I pinky-swear to give you the *exclusive inside details* every step of the way!